X

LA·ROUE·DE·FORTUNE

THE
LADY OF THE
RIVERS

The Cousins' War

THE
LADY OF THE
RIVERS

PHILIPPA GREGORY

**SIMON &
SCHUSTER**

London · New York · Sydney · Toronto

A CBS COMPANY

First published in Great Britain by Simon & Schuster UK Ltd, 2011
A CBS COMPANY

1 3 5 7 9 10 8 6 4 2

Simon & Schuster UK Ltd
1st Floor
222 Gray's Inn Road
London
WC1X 8HB

www.simonandschuster.co.uk

Simon & Schuster Australia
Sydney

A CIP catalogue record for this book
is available from the British Library.

ISBN HB 978-1-84737-459-2
ISBN TPB 978-1-84737-460-8

Typeset by M Rules
Printed in the UK by CPI Mackays, Chatham ME5 8TD

For Victoria

JACQUETTA'S FAMILY TREE

Note: Dates of birth of Jacquetta's children are approximate

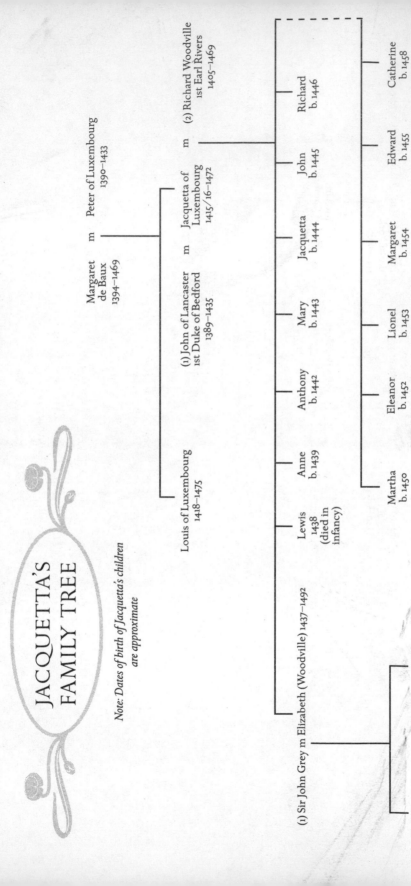

Margaret de Baux 1394–1469 **m** Peter of Luxembourg 1390–1433

Louis of Luxembourg 1418–1475

Jacquetta of Luxembourg 1415/16–1472

(1) John of Lancaster 1st Duke of Bedford 1389–1435 **m**

m (2) Richard Woodville 1st Earl Rivers 1405–1469

(1) Sir John Grey **m** Elizabeth (Woodville) 1437–1492

Lewis 1438 (died in infancy)

Anne b. 1439

Anthony b. 1442

Mary b. 1443

Jacquetta b. 1444

John b. 1445

Richard b. 1446

Martha b. 1450

Eleanor b. 1452

Lionel b. 1453

Margaret b. 1454

Edward b. 1455

Catherine b. 1458

Thomas Grey Marquis of Dorset

Richard Grey

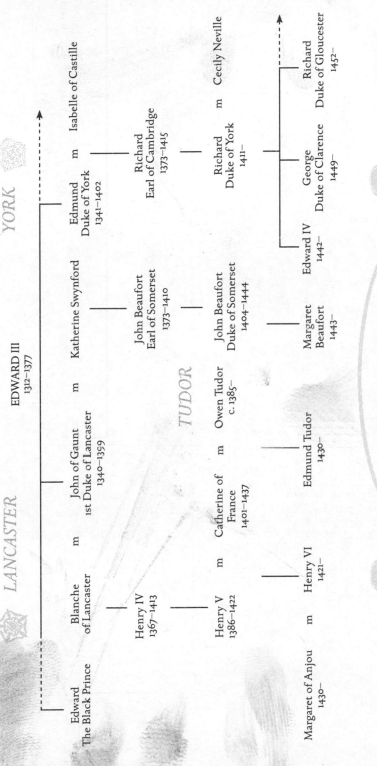

LANCASTER

YORK

EDWARD III
1312–1377

Edward
The Black Prince

John of Gaunt
1st Duke of Lancaster
1340–1399

m

Katherine Swynford

Edmund
Duke of York
1341–1402

m

Isabelle of Castille

Blanche
of Lancaster

John Beaufort
Earl of Somerset
1373–1410

Richard
Earl of Cambridge
1373–1415

Henry IV
1367–1413

John Beaufort
Duke of Somerset
1404–1444

Richard
Duke of York
1411–

m

Cecily Neville

TUDOR

Henry V
1386–1422

m

Catherine of
France
1401–1437

m

Owen Tudor
c.1385–

Margaret
Beaufort
1443–

Edward IV
1442–

George
Duke of Clarence
1449–

Richard
Duke of Gloucester
1452–

Henry VI
1421–

Edmund Tudor
1430–

Margaret of Anjou
1430–

m

THE COUSINS AT WAR
The Houses of York, Lancaster & Tudor
in Summer 1430

CASTLE OF BEAUREVOIR, NEAR ARRAS, FRANCE, SUMMER–WINTER 1430

She sits, this odd trophy of war, as neat as an obedient child, on a small stool in the corner of her cell. At her feet are the remains of her dinner on a pewter platter, laid on the straw. I notice that my uncle has sent good slices of meat, and even the white bread from his own table; but she has eaten little. I find I am staring at her, from her boy's riding boots to the man's bonnet crammed on her brown cropped hair, as if she were some exotic animal, trapped for our amusement, as if someone had sent a lion cub all the way from Ethiopia to entertain the great family of Luxembourg, for us to keep in our collection. A lady behind me crosses herself and whispers, 'Is this a witch?'

I don't know. How does one ever know?

'This is ridiculous,' my great-aunt says boldly. 'Who has ordered the poor girl to be chained? Open the door at once.'

There is a confused muttering of men trying to shift the responsibility, and then someone turns the big key in the cell door and my great-aunt stalks in. The girl – she must be about seventeen or eighteen, only a few years older than me – looks up from under her jagged fringe of hair as my great-aunt stands before her, and then slowly she rises to her feet, doffs her cap, and gives an awkward little bow.

'I am the Lady Jehanne, the Demoiselle of Luxembourg,' my

I

great-aunt says. 'This is the castle of Lord John of Luxembourg.' She gestures to my aunt: 'This is his wife, the lady of the castle, Jehanne of Bethune, and this is my great-niece Jacquetta.'

The girl looks steadily at all of us and gives a nod of her head to each. As she looks at me I feel a little tap-tap for my attention, as palpable as the brush of a fingertip on the nape of my neck, a whisper of magic. I wonder if standing behind her there are indeed two accompanying angels, as she claims, and it is their presence that I sense.

'Can you speak, Maid?' my great-aunt asks, when the girl says nothing.

'Oh yes, my lady,' the girl replies in the hard accent of the Champagne region. I realise that it is true what they say about her: she is no more than a peasant girl, though she has led an army and crowned a king.

'Will you give me your word not to escape if I have these chains taken off your legs?'

She hesitates, as if she were in any position to choose. 'No, I can't.'

My great-aunt smiles. 'Do you understand the offer of parole? I can release you to live with us here in my nephew's castle; but you have to promise not to run away.'

The girl turns her head, frowning. It is almost as if she is listening for advice, then she shakes her head. 'I know this parole. It is when one knight makes a promise to another. They have rules as if they were jousting. I'm not like that. My words are real, not like a troubadour's poem. And this is no game for me.'

'Maid: parole is not a game!' Aunt Jehanne interrupts.

The girl looks at her. 'Oh, but it is, my lady. The noblemen are not serious about these matters. Not serious like me. They play at war and make up rules. They ride out and lay waste to good people's farms and laugh as the thatched roofs burn. Besides, I cannot make promises. I am promised already.'

'To the one who wrongly calls himself the King of France?'

'To the King of Heaven.'

My great-aunt pauses for a moment's thought. 'I will tell them to take the chains off you and guard you so that you do not escape; and then you can come and sit with us in my rooms. I think what you have done for your country and for your prince has been very great, Joan, though mistaken. And I will not see you here, under my roof, a captive in chains.'

'Will you tell your nephew to set me free?'

My great-aunt hesitates. 'I cannot order him; but I will do everything I can to send you back to your home. At any event, I won't let him release you to the English.'

At the very word the girl shudders and makes the sign of the cross, thumping her head and her chest in the most ridiculous way, as a peasant might cross himself at the name of Old Hob. I have to choke back a laugh. This draws the girl's dark gaze to me.

'They are only mortal men,' I explain to her. 'The English have no powers beyond that of mortal men. You need not fear them so. You need not cross yourself at their name.'

'I don't fear them. I am not such a fool as to fear that they have powers. It's not that. It's that they know that _I_ have powers. That's what makes them such a danger. They are mad with fear of me. They fear me so much that they will destroy me the moment I fall into their hands. I am their terror. I am their fear that walks by night.'

'While I live, they won't have you,' my great-aunt assures her; and at once, unmistakably, Joan looks straight at me, a hard dark gaze as if to see that I too have heard, in this sincere assertion, the ring of an utterly empty promise.

My great-aunt believes that if she can bring Joan into our company, talk with her, cool her religious fervour, perhaps educate her, then the girl will be led, in time, to wear the dress of a young woman, and the fighting youth who was dragged off the white horse at Compiègne will be transformed, like Mass reversed, from strong wine into water, and she will become a young woman who can be seated among waiting women, who will answer to a command and not to the ringing church bells, and will then, perhaps, be overlooked by the English, who are demanding that we surrender the hermaphrodite murderous witch to them. If we have nothing to offer them but a remorseful obedient maid in waiting, perhaps they will be satisfied and go on their violent way.

Joan herself is exhausted by recent defeats and by her uneasy sense that the king she has crowned is not worthy of the holy oil, that the enemy she had on the run has recoiled on her, and that the mission given to her by God Himself is falling away from her. Everything that made her the Maid before her adoring troop of soldiers has become uncertain. Under my great-aunt's steady kindness she is becoming once more an awkward country girl: nothing special.

Of course, all the maids in waiting to my great-aunt want to know about the adventure that is ending in this slow creep of defeat, and as Joan spends her days with us, learning to be a girl and not the Maid, they pluck up the courage to ask her.

'How were you so brave?' one demands. 'How did you learn to be so brave? In battle, I mean.'

Joan smiles at the question. There are four of us, seated on a grass bank beside the moat of the castle, as idle as children. The July sun is beating down and the pasture lands around the castle are shimmering in the haze of heat; even the bees are lazy, buzzing and then falling silent as if drunk on flowers. We have chosen to sit in the deep shadow of the highest tower; behind us, in the glassy water of the moat, we can hear the occasional bubble of a carp coming to the surface.

Joan is sprawled like a boy, one hand dabbling in the water, her cap over her eyes. In the basket beside me are half-sewn shirts that we are supposed to hem for the poor children of nearby Cambrai. But the maids avoid work of any sort, Joan has no skill, and I have my great-aunt's precious pack of playing cards in my hands and I am shuffling and cutting them and idly looking at the pictures.

'I knew I was called by God,' Joan said simply. 'And that He would protect me, so I had no fear. Not even in the worst of the battles. He warned me that I would be injured but that I would feel no pain, so I knew I could go on fighting. I even warned my men that I would be injured that day. I knew before we went into battle. I just knew.'

'Do you really hear voices?' I ask.

'Do you?'

The question is so shocking that the girls whip round to stare at me and under their joint gaze I find I am blushing as if for something shameful. 'No! No!'

'Then what?'

'What do you mean?'

'What do you hear?' she asks, as reasonably as if everyone hears something.

'Well, not voices exactly,' I say.

'What do you hear?'

I glance behind me as if the very fish might rise to eavesdrop. 'When someone in my family is going to die, then I hear a noise,' I say. 'A special noise.'

'What sort of noise?' the girl, Elizabeth, asks. 'I didn't know this. Could I hear it?'

'You are not of my house,' I say irritably. 'Of course you wouldn't hear it. You would have to be a descendant of . . . and anyway, you must never speak of this. You shouldn't really be listening. I shouldn't be telling you.'

'What sort of noise?' Joan repeats.

'Like singing,' I say, and see her nod, as if she too has heard singing.

'They say it is the voice of Melusina, the first lady of the House of Luxembourg,' I whisper. 'They say she was a water goddess who came out of the river to marry the first duke but she couldn't be a mortal woman. She comes back to cry for the loss of her children.'

'And when have you heard her?'

5

'The night that my baby sister died. I heard something. And I knew at once that it was Melusina.'

'But how did you know it was her?' the other maid whispers, afraid of being excluded from the conversation.

I shrug, and Joan smiles in recognition of truths that cannot be explained. 'I just knew,' I say. 'It was as if I recognised her voice. As if I had always known it.'

'That's true. You just know,' Joan nods. 'But how do you know that it comes from God and not from the Devil?'

I hesitate. Any spiritual questions should be taken to my confessor, or at the very least to my mother or my great-aunt. But the song of Melusina, and the shiver on my spine, and my occasional sight of the unseen – something half-lost, sometimes vanishing around a corner, lighter grey in a grey twilight, a dream that is too clear to be forgotten, a glimpse of foresight but never anything that I can describe – these things are too thin for speech. How can I ask about them when I cannot even put them into words? How can I bear to have someone clumsily name them or, even worse, try to explain them? I might as well try to hold the greenish water of the moat in my cupped hands.

'I've never asked,' I say. 'Because it is hardly anything. Like when you go into a room and it is quiet – but you know, you can just tell, that someone is there. You can't hear them or see them, but you just know. It's little more than that. I never think of it as a gift coming from God or the Devil. It is just nothing.'

'My voices come from God,' Joan says certainly. 'I know it. If it were not true, I should be utterly lost.'

'So can you tell fortunes?' Elizabeth asks me childishly.

My fingers close over my cards. 'No,' I say. 'And these don't tell fortunes, they are just for playing. They're just playing cards. I don't tell fortunes. My great-aunt would not allow me to do it, even if I could.'

'Oh, do mine!'

'These are just playing cards,' I insist. 'I'm no soothsayer.'

'Oh, draw a card for me and tell me,' Elizabeth says. 'And for

Joan. What's going to become of her? Surely you want to know what's going to happen to Joan?'

'It means nothing,' I say to Joan. 'And I only brought them so we could play.'

'They are beautiful,' she says. 'They taught me to play at court with cards like these. How bright they are.'

I hand them to her. 'Take care with them, they're very precious,' I say jealously as she spreads them in her calloused hands. 'The Demoiselle showed them to me when I was a little girl and told me the names of the pictures. She lets me borrow them because I love to play. But I promised her I would take care of them.'

Joan passes the pack back to me and though she is careful, and my hands are ready for them, one of the thick cards tumbles between us and falls face down, on the grass.

'Oh! Sorry,' Joan exclaims, and quickly picks it up.

I can feel a whisper, like a cool breath down my spine. The meadow before me and the cows flicking their tails in the shade of the tree seem far away, as if we two are enclosed in a glass, butterflies in a bowl, in another world. 'You had better look at it now,' I hear myself say to her.

Joan looks at the brightly painted picture, her eyes widen slightly, and then she shows it to me. 'What does this mean?'

It is a painting of a man dressed in a livery of blue, hanging upside down from one extended foot, the other leg crooked easily, his toe pointed and placed against his straight leg as if he were dancing, inverted in the air. His hands are clasped behind his back as if he were bowing; we both see the happy fall of his blue hair as he hangs, upside down, smiling.

'"*Le Pendu*,"' Elizabeth reads. 'How horrid. What does it mean? Oh, surely it doesn't mean . . .' She breaks off.

'It doesn't mean you will be hanged,' I say quickly to Joan. 'So don't think that. It's just a playing card, it can't mean anything like that.'

'But what does it mean?' the other girl demands though Joan is silent, as if it is not her card, not her fortune that I am refusing to tell.

'His gallows is two growing trees,' I say. I am playing for time under Joan's serious brown gaze. 'This means spring and renewal and life – not death. And there are two trees; the man is balanced between them. He is the very centre of resurrection.'

Joan nods.

'They are bowed down to him, he is happy. And look: he is not hanged by his neck to kill him, but tied by his foot,' I say. 'If he wanted, he could stretch up and untie himself. He could set himself free, if he wanted.'

'But he doesn't set himself free,' the girl observes. 'He is like a tumbler, an acrobat. What does that mean?'

'It means that he is willingly there, willingly waiting, allowing himself to be held by his foot, hanging in the air.'

'To be a living sacrifice?' Joan says slowly, in the words of the Mass.

'He is not crucified,' I point out quickly. It is as if every word I say leads us to another form of death. 'This doesn't mean anything.'

'No,' she says. 'These are just playing cards, and we are just playing a game with them. It is a pretty card, the Hanged Man. He looks happy. He looks happy to be upside down in springtime. Shall I teach you a game with counters that we play in Champagne?'

'Yes,' I say. I hold out my hand for her card and she looks at it for a moment before she hands it back to me.

'Honestly, it means nothing,' I say again to her.

She smiles at me, her clear honest smile. 'I know well enough what it means,' she says.

'Shall we play?' I start to shuffle the cards and one turns over in my hand.

'Now that's a good card,' Joan remarks. '*La Roue de Fortune.*'

I hold it out to show it to her. 'It is the Wheel of Fortune that can throw you up very high, or bring you down very low. Its message is to be indifferent to victory and defeat, as they both come on the turn of the wheel.'

8

'In my country the farmers make a sign for fortune's wheel,' Joan remarks. 'They draw a circle in the air with their forefinger when something very good or something very bad happens. Someone inherits money, or someone loses a prize cow, they do this.' She points her finger in the air and draws a circle. 'And they say something.'

'A spell?'

'Not really a spell.' She smiles mischievously.

'What then?'

She giggles. 'They say "*merde*".'

I am so shocked that I rock back with laughter.

'What? What?' the younger maid demands.

'Nothing, nothing,' I say. Joan is still giggling. 'Joan's country-men say rightly that everything comes to dust, and all that a man can do about it is to learn indifference.'

Joan's future hangs in the balance; she is swinging like the Hanged Man. All of my family, my father, Pierre the Count of St Pol, my uncle, Louis of Luxembourg, and my favourite uncle, John of Luxembourg, are allied with the English. My father writes from our home at the chateau at St Pol to his brother John, and commands him, as the head of our family, to hand over Joan to the English. But my great-aunt the Demoiselle insists we keep her safe; and my uncle John hesitates.

The English demand his prisoner and, since the English command nearly all of France and their ally the Duke of Burgundy commands most of the rest, what they say usually happens. Their common soldiers went down on their knees on the battlefield to give thanks, and wept with joy when the Maid was captured. There is no doubt in their mind that without her the French army, their enemy, will collapse into the frightened rabble that they were before she came to them.

The Duke of Bedford, the English regent who rules the English lands in France, almost all of the north of the country, sends daily letters to my uncle invoking his loyalty to English rule, their long friendship, and promising money. I like to watch for the English messengers who come dressed in the fine livery of the royal duke, on beautiful horses. Everyone says that the duke is a great man and well loved, the greatest man in France, an ill man to cross; but so far, my uncle obeys his aunt, the Demoiselle, and does not hand over our prisoner.

My uncle expects the French court to make a bid for her – they owe their very existence to her after all – but they are oddly silent, even after he writes to them and says that he has the Maid, and that she is ready to return to the court of her king and serve again in his army. With her leading them they could ride out against the English and win. Surely they will send a fortune to get her back?

'They don't want her,' my great-aunt advises him. They are at their private dining table, the great dinner for the whole household has taken place in the hall and the two of them have sat before my uncle's men, tasted the dishes and sent them round the room as a gift to their special favourites. Now they are comfortable, seated at a little table before the fire in my great-aunt's private rooms, her personal servants in attendance. I am to stand during the serving of dinner with another lady in waiting. It is my job to watch the servants, summon them forwards as required, clasp my hands modestly before me, and hear nothing. Of course, I listen all the time.

'Joan made a man out of the boy Prince Charles, he was nothing until she came to him with her vision, then she made that man into a king. She taught him to claim his inheritance. She made an army out of his camp-followers, and made that army victorious. If they had followed her advice as she followed her voices, they would have driven the English out of these lands and back to their foggy islands, and we would be rid of them forever.'

My uncle smiles. 'Oh, my lady aunt! This is a war that has gone on for nearly a century. Do you really think it will end because some girl from who knows where hears voices? She could never drive the English away. They would never have gone; they will never go. These are their lands by right, by true right of inheritance, and by conquest too. All they have to do is to have the courage and the strength to hold them, and John Duke of Bedford will see to that.' He glances at his wineglass and I snap my fingers to the groom of the servery to pour him some more red wine. I step forwards to hold the glass as the man pours, and then I put it carefully on the table. They are using fine glassware; my uncle is wealthy and my great-aunt never has anything but the very best. 'The English king may be little more than a child, but it makes no difference to the safety of his kingdom, for his uncle Bedford is loyal to him here, and his uncle the Duke of Gloucester is loyal to him in England. Bedford has the courage and the allies to hold the English lands here, and I think they will drive the Dauphin further and further south. They will drive him into the sea. The Maid had her season, and it was a remarkable one; but in the end, the English will win the war and hold the lands that are theirs by right, and all of our lords who are sworn against them now will bow the knee and serve them.'

'I don't think so,' my great-aunt says staunchly. 'The English are terrified of her. They say she is unbeatable.'

'Not any more,' my uncle observes. 'For behold! She is a prisoner, and the cell doors don't burst open. They know she is mortal now. They saw her with an arrow in her thigh outside the walls of Paris and her own army marched off and left her. The French themselves taught the English that she could be brought down and abandoned.'

'But you won't give her to the English,' my great-aunt states. 'It would be to dishonour us forever, in the eyes of God and the world.'

My uncle leans forwards to speak confidentially. 'You take it so seriously? You really think she is more than a mountebank? You really think she is something more than a peasant girl spouting nonsense? You know I could find half a dozen such as her?'

'You could find half a dozen who say they are like her,' she says. 'But not one like her. I think she is a special girl. Truly I do, nephew. I have a very strong sense of this.'

He pauses, as if her sense of things, though she is only a woman, is something to be considered. 'You have had a vision of her success? A foretelling?'

For a moment she hesitates, then she quickly shakes her head. 'Nothing so clear. But nonetheless, I must insist that we protect her.'

He pauses, not wanting to contradict her. She is the Demoiselle of Luxembourg, the head of our family. My father will inherit the title when she dies; but she also owns great lands that are all at her own disposition: she can will them to anyone she chooses. My uncle John is her favourite nephew; he has hopes, and he does not want to offend her.

'The French will have to pay a good price for her,' he says. 'I don't intend to lose money on her. She is worth a king's ransom. They know this.'

My great-aunt nods. 'I will write to the Dauphin Charles and he will ransom her,' she tells him. 'Whatever his advisors say, he will still listen to me, though he is blown about like a leaf by his favourites. But I am his godmother. It is a question of honour. He owes all that he is to the Maid.'

'Very well. But do it at once. The English are very pressing and I won't offend the Duke of Bedford. He is a powerful man, and a fair one. He is the best ruler of France that we could hope for. If he were a Frenchman he would be wholly loved.'

My great-aunt laughs. 'Yes, but he is not! He's the English regent, and he should go back to his own damp island and his little nephew, the poor king, and make what they can of their own kingdom and leave us to rule France.'

'Us?' my uncle queries, as if to ask her if she thinks that our family, who already rule half a dozen earldoms and who count kinship to the Holy Roman Emperors, should be French kings as well.

She smiles. 'Us,' she says blandly.

Next day I walk with Joan to the little chapel in the castle and kneel beside her on the chancel steps. She prays fervently, her head bowed for an hour, and then the priest comes and serves the Mass and Joan takes the holy bread and wine. I wait for her at the back of the church. Joan is the only person I know who takes the bread and wine every day, as if it were her breakfast. My own mother, who is more observant than most, takes communion only once a month. We walk back to my great-aunt's rooms together, the strewing herbs swishing around our feet. Joan laughs at me, as I have to duck my head to get my tall conical headdress through the narrow doorways.

'It is very beautiful,' she says. 'But I should not like to wear such a thing.'

I pause and twirl before her in the bright sunlight from the arrowslit. The colours of my gown are brilliant: a skirt of dark blue and an underskirt of sharper turquoise, the skirts flaring from the high belt tied tight on my ribcage. The high henin headdress sits like a cone on my head and sprouts a veil of pale blue from the peak that drops down my back, concealing and enhancing my fair hair. I spread my arms to show the big triangular sleeves, trimmed with the most beautiful embroidery in gold thread, and I lift the hem to show my scarlet slippers with the upturned toes.

'But you cannot work, or ride a horse, or even run in such a gown,' she says.

'It's not for riding or working or running,' I reply reasonably. 'It's for showing off. It is to show the world that I am young and beautiful and ready for marriage. It is to show that my father is so wealthy that I can wear gold thread on my sleeves and silk in my headdress. It shows that I am so nobly born that I can wear velvet and silk; not wool like a poor girl.'

'I couldn't bear to be showed off in such a thing.'

'You wouldn't be allowed to,' I point out disagreeably. 'You have to dress for your position in life; you would have to obey the law and wear browns and greys. Did you really think you were important enough to wear ermine? Or do you want your gold surcoat back? They say you were as fine as any knight in battle. You dressed like a nobleman then. They say that you loved your beautiful standard and your polished armour, and a fine gold surcoat over all. They say you were guilty of the sin of vanity.'

She flushes. 'I had to be seen,' she says defensively. 'At the front of my army.'

'Gold?'

'I had to honour God.'

'Well anyway, you wouldn't get a headdress like this if you put on women's clothes,' I say. 'You would wear something more modest, like the ladies in waiting, nothing so high or so awkward, just a neat hood to cover your hair. And you could wear your boots under your gown, you could still walk about. Won't you try wearing a gown, Joan? It would mean that they couldn't accuse you of wearing men's clothes. It is a sign of heresy for a woman to dress as a man. Why not put on a dress, and then they can say nothing against you? Something plain?'

She shakes her head. 'I am promised,' she says simply. 'Promised to God. And when the king calls for me, I must be ready to ride to arms again. I am a soldier in waiting, not a lady in waiting. I will dress like a soldier. And my king will call for me, any day now.'

I glance behind us. A pageboy carrying a jug of hot water is in earshot. I wait till he has nodded a bow and gone past us. 'Hush,' I say quietly. 'You shouldn't even call him king.'

She laughs, as if she fears nothing. 'I took him to his coronation, I stood under my own standard in Reims cathedral when he was anointed with the oil of Clovis. I saw him presented to his people in his crown. Of course he is King of France: he is crowned and anointed.'

'The English slit the tongues of anyone who says that,' I remind her. 'That's for the first offence. The second time you say it, they brand your forehead so you are scarred for life. The English king, Henry VI, is to be called King of France, the one you call the French king is to be called the Dauphin, never anything but the Dauphin.'

She laughs with genuine amusement. 'He is not even to be called French,' she exclaims. 'Your great Duke Bedford says that he is to be called Armagnac. But the great Duke Bedford was shaking with fear and running around Rouen for recruits when I came up to the walls of Paris with the French army – yes, I will say it! – the French army to claim our own city for our king, a French king; and we nearly took it, too.'

I put my hands over my ears. 'I won't hear you, and you shouldn't speak like this. I shall be whipped if I listen to you.'

At once she takes my hands, she is penitent. 'Ah, Jacquetta, I won't get you into trouble. Look! I will say nothing. But you must see that I have done far worse than use words against the English. I have used arrows and cannon shot and battering rams and guns against them! The English will hardly trouble themselves over the words I have said and the breeches I wear. I have defeated them and shown everyone that they have no right to France. I led an army against them and defeated them over and over again.'

'I hope they never get hold of you, and never question you. Not about words, nor arrows, nor cannon.'

She goes a little pale at the thought of it. 'Please God, I hope so too. Merciful God, I hope so too.'

'My great-aunt is writing to the Dauphin,' I say very low. 'They were speaking of it at dinner last night. She will write to the Dauphin and invite him to ransom you. And my uncle will release you to the Fr . . . to the Armagnacs.'

She bows her head and her lips move in prayer. 'My king will send for me,' she says trustingly. 'Without a doubt he will send for me to come to him, and we can start our battles again.'

It grows even hotter in August, and my great-aunt rests on a daybed in her inner room every afternoon, with the light curtains of silk around the bed soaked in lavender water and the closed shutters throwing barred shadows across the stone floor. She likes me to read to her, as she lies with her eyes closed and her hands folded on the high waistline of her dress, as if she were a sculpted effigy of herself in some shaded tomb. She puts aside the big horned headdress that she always wears and lets her long greying hair spread over the cool embroidered pillows. She gives me books from her own library that tell of great romances and troubadours and ladies in tangled forests, and then one afternoon she puts a book in my hand and says, 'Read this today.'

It is hand-copied in old French and I stumble over the words. It is hard to read: the illustrations in the margins are like briars and flowers threading through the letters, and the clerk who copied each word had an ornate style of writing which I find hard to decipher. But slowly the story emerges. It is the story of a knight riding through a dark forest who has lost his way. He hears the sound of water and goes towards it. In a clearing, in the moonlight, he sees a white basin and a splashing fountain and in the water is a woman of such beauty that her skin is paler than the white marble and her hair is darker than the night skies. He falls in love with her at once, and she with him, and he takes her to the castle and makes her his wife. She has only one condition: that every month he must leave her alone to bathe.

'Do you know this story?' my great-aunt asks me. 'Has your father told you of it?'

'I have heard something like it,' I say cautiously. My great-aunt is notoriously quick-tempered with my father and I don't know if I dare say that I think this is the legend of the founding of our house.

'Well, now you are reading the true story,' she says. She closes her eyes again. 'It is time you knew. Go on.'

The young couple are happier than any in the world, and people come from far and wide to visit them. They have children: beautiful girls and strange wild boys.

'Sons,' my great-aunt whispers to herself. 'If only a woman could have sons by wishing, if only they could be as she wishes.'

The wife never loses her beauty though the years go by, and her husband grows more and more curious. One day, he cannot bear the mystery of her secret bathing any longer and he creeps down to her bath-house and spies on her.

My great-aunt raises her hand. 'Do you know what he sees?' she asks me.

I lift my face from the book, my finger under the illustration of the man peering through the slats of the bath-house. In the foreground is the woman in the bath, her beautiful hair snaked around her white shoulders. And gleaming in the water ... her large scaled tail.

'Is she a fish?' I whisper.

'She is a being not of this world,' my great-aunt says quietly. 'She tried to live like an ordinary woman; but some women cannot live an ordinary life. She tried to walk in the common ways; but some women cannot put their feet to that path. This is a man's world, Jacquetta, and some women cannot march to the beat of a man's drum. Do you understand?'

I don't, of course. I am too young to understand that a man and a woman can love each other so deeply that their hearts beat as if they were one heart, and yet, at the same time, know that they are utterly hopelessly different.

'Anyway, you can read on. It's not long now.'

The husband cannot bear to know that his wife is a strange being. She cannot forgive him for spying on her. She leaves him, taking her beautiful daughters, and he lives alone with the sons, heartbroken. But at his death, as at the death of everyone of our house, his wife Melusina, the beautiful woman who was an undine, a water goddess, comes back to him and he hears her crying around the battlements for the children she has lost, for the husband she still loves, and for the world that has no place for her.

I close the book, and there is such a long silence that I think my great-aunt has fallen asleep.

'Some of the women of our family have the gift of foresight,' my great-aunt remarks quietly. 'Some of them have inherited powers from Melusina, powers of the other world where she lives. Some of us are her daughters, her heirs.'

I hardly dare to breathe, I am so anxious that she should go on speaking to me.

'Jacquetta, do you think you might be one of these women?'

'I might be,' I whisper. 'I hope so.'

'You have to listen,' she says softly. 'Listen to silence, watch for nothing. And be on your guard. Melusina is a shape-shifter, like quicksilver, she can flow from one thing to another. You may see her anywhere, she is like water. Or you may see only your own reflection in the surface of a stream though you are straining your eyes to see into the green depths for her.'

'Will she be my guide?'

'You must be your own guide, but you might hear her when she speaks to you.' She pauses. 'Fetch my jewel box.' She gestures towards the great chest at the foot of her bed. I open the creaking lid and inside, beside the gowns wrapped in powdered silk, is a large wooden box. I take it out. Inside is a series of drawers, each one filled with my great-aunt's fortune of jewels. 'Look in the smallest drawer,' she says.

I find it. Inside is a small black velvet purse. I untie the tasselled threads, open the mouth, and a heavy golden bracelet falls into my hand, laden with about two hundred little charms, each one a different shape. I see a ship, a horse, a star, a spoon, a whip, a hawk, a spur.

'When you want to know something very, very important, you choose two or three of the charms – charms that signify the thing that might be, the choices before you. You tie each one on a string and you put them in a river, the river nearest to your home, the river that you hear at night when everything is silent but the voice of the waters. You leave it until the moon is new. Then you cut all the strings but one, and pull that one out to see your future. The river will give you the answer. The river will tell you what you should do.'

I nod. The bracelet is cold and heavy in my hand, each charm a choice, each charm an opportunity, each charm a mistake in waiting.

'And when you want something: go out and whisper it to the river – like a prayer. When you curse somebody: write it on a piece of paper, and put the paper into the river, float it like a little paper boat. The river is your ally, your friend, your lady – do you understand?'

I nod, though I don't understand.

'When you curse somebody . . . ' She pauses and sighs as if she is very weary. 'Take care with your words, Jacquetta, especially in cursing. Only say the things you mean, make sure you lay your curse on the right man. For be very sure that when you put such words out in the world they can overshoot – like an arrow, a curse can go beyond your target and harm another. A wise woman curses very sparingly.'

I shiver, though the room is hot.

'I will teach you more,' she promises me. 'It is your inheritance, since you are the oldest girl.'

'Do boys not know? My brother Louis?'

Her lazy eyes half open and she smiles at me. 'Men command the world that they know,' she says. 'Everything that men know, they make their own. Everything that they learn, they claim for themselves. They are like the alchemists who look for the laws that govern the world, and then want to own them and keep them secret. Everything they discover, they hug to themselves, they shape knowledge into their own selfish image. What is left to us women, but the realms of the unknown?'

'But can women not take a great place in the world? You do, Great-aunt, and Yolande of Aragon is called the Queen of Four Kingdoms. Shall I not command great lands like you and her?'

'You might. But I warn you that a woman who seeks great power and wealth has to pay a great price. Perhaps you will be a great woman like Melusina, or Yolande, or like me; but you will be like all women: uneasy in the world of men. You will do your best – perhaps you will gain some power if you marry well or inherit well – but you will always find the road is hard beneath your feet. In the other world – well, who knows about the other world? Maybe they will hear you, and perhaps you will hear them.'

'What will I hear?'

She smiles. 'You know. You hear it already.'

'Voices?' I ask, thinking of Joan.

'Perhaps.'

Slowly, the intense heat of the summer starts to fade and it grows cooler in September. The trees of the great forest that surround the lake start to turn colour from tired green to sere yellow, and the swallows swirl around the turrets of the castle every evening, as if to say goodbye for another year. They chase each other round and round in a dizzying train, like a veil being whirled in a dance. The rows on rows of vines grow heavy with fruit and every day the peasant women go out with their sleeves rolled up over their big forearms and pick and pick the fruit into big wicker baskets, which the men swing onto carts and take back to the press. The smell of fruit and fermenting wine is heavy in the village, everyone has blue-stained hems to their gowns and purple feet, and they say it will be a good year this year, rich and lush. When the ladies in waiting and I ride through the village they call us to taste the new wine and it is light and sharp and fizzy in our mouths, and they laugh at our puckered faces.

My great-aunt does not sit straight-backed in her chair, overseeing her women and beyond them the castle and my uncle's lands, as she did at the start of the summer. As the sun loses its heat she too seems to be growing pale and cold. She lies down from the middle of the morning to the early evening, and only rises from her bed to walk into the great hall beside my uncle and nod her head at the rumble of greeting, as the men look up at their lord and lady and hammer on the wooden tables with their daggers.

Joan prays for her, by name, in her daily attendance at church, but I, childlike, just accept the new rhythm of my great-aunt's day, and sit with her to read in the afternoon, and wait for her to talk to me about the prayers floated like paper ships on the waters of rivers that were flowing to the sea before I was born. She tells me to spread out the cards of her pack and teaches me the name and the quality of each one.

'And now read them for me,' she says one day, and then taps a card with her thin finger. 'What is this one?'

I turn it over for her. The dark hooded shape of Death looks back at us, his face hidden in the shadow of his hood, his scythe over his hunched shoulder.

'Ah well,' she says. 'So are you here at last, my friend? Jacquetta, you had better ask your uncle to come to see me.'

I show him into her room and he kneels at the side of her bed. She puts her hand on his head as if in blessing. Then she pushes him gently away.

'I cannot bear this weather,' she says crossly to my uncle, as if the cooling days are his fault. 'How can you bear to live here? It is as cold as England and the winters last forever. I shall go south, I shall go to Provence.'

'Are you sure?' he asks. 'I thought you were feeling tired. Should you not rest here?'

She snaps her fingers irritably. 'I'm too cold,' she says imperiously. 'You can order me a guard and I shall have my litter lined with furs. I shall come back in spring.'

'Surely you would be more comfortable here?' he suggests.

'I have a fancy to see the Rhône once more,' she says. 'Besides, I have business to do.'

Nobody can ever argue against her – she is the Demoiselle – and within days she has her great litter at the door, furs heaped on the bed, a brass hand-warmer filled with hot coals, the floor of the litter packed with oven-heated bricks to keep her warm, the household lined up to say farewell.

She gives her hand to Joan, and then she kisses my aunt Jehanne, and me. My uncle helps her into the litter and she clutches his arm with her thin hand. 'Keep the Maid safe,' she says. 'Keep her from the English, it is my command.'

He ducks his head. 'Come back to us soon.'

His wife, whose life is easier when the great lady has moved on, steps forwards to tuck her in and kiss her pale cool cheeks. But it is me that the Demoiselle of Luxembourg calls towards her with one crook of her skinny finger.

'God bless you, Jacquetta,' she says to me. 'You will remember all that I have taught you. And you will go far.' She smiles at me. 'Farther than you can imagine.'

'But I will see you in spring?'

'I will send you my books,' she says. 'And my bracelet.'

'And you will come to visit my mother and father at St Pol in the spring?'

Her smile tells me that I will not see her again. 'God bless,' she repeats and draws the curtains of her litter against the cold morning air as the cavalcade starts out of the gate.

In November, I am awakened in the darkest of the night, and I sit up in the little bed I share with Elizabeth the maid, and listen. It is as if someone is calling my name in a sweet voice: very high, and very thin. Then I am sure I can hear someone singing. Oddly, the noise is coming from outside our window, though we are high up in the turret of the castle. I pull on my cloak over my nightgown and go to the window and look out through the crack in the wooden shutters. There are no lights showing outside, the fields and the woods around the castle are as black as felted wool, there is nothing but this clear keening noise, not a nightingale but as high and as pure as a nightingale. Not an owl, far too musical and continuous, something like a boy singer in a choir. I turn to the bed and shake Elizabeth awake.

'Can you hear that?'

She does not even wake. 'Nothing,' she says, half-asleep. 'Stop it, Jacquetta. I'm asleep.'

The stone floor is icy beneath my bare feet. I jump back into bed and put my cold feet in the warm space near Elizabeth. She gives a little bad-tempered grunt and rolls away from me, and then – though I think I will lie in the warm and listen to the voices – I fall asleep.

Six days later they tell me that my great-aunt, Jehanne of Luxembourg, died in her sleep, in the darkest hour of the night, in Avignon, beside the great River Rhône. Then I know whose voice it was I heard, singing around the turrets.

As soon as the English Duke of Bedford learns that Joan has lost her greatest protector, he sends the judge Pierre Cauchon, with a troop of men behind him, to negotiate for her ransom. She is summoned by a Church court on charges of heresy. Enormous sums of money change hands: twenty thousand livres for the man who pulled her off her horse, ten thousand francs to be paid to my uncle with the good wishes of the King of England. My uncle does not listen to his wife, who pleads that Joan shall be left with us. I am too unimportant to even have a voice, and so I have to watch in silence as my uncle makes an agreement that Joan shall be released to the Church for questioning. 'I am not handing her over to the English,' he says to his wife. 'As the Demoiselle asked me, and I have not forgotten, I have not handed her over to the English. I have only released her to the Church. This allows her to clear her name of all the charges against her. She will be judged by men of God, if she is innocent they will say so, and she will be released.'

She looks at him as blankly as if he were Death himself, and I wonder if he believes this nonsense, or if he thinks that we, being women, are such fools as to think that a church dependent on the English, with bishops appointed by the English, are going to tell their rulers and paymasters that the girl who raised all of France against them is just an ordinary girl, perhaps a little noisy, perhaps a little naughty, and she should be given three Hail Marys and sent back to her farm, to her mother and her father and her cows.

'My lord, who is going to tell Joan?' is all I dare to ask.

'Oh, she knows already,' he says over his shoulder as he goes out of the hall, to bid farewell to Pierre Cauchon at the great gate. 'I sent a page to tell her to get ready. She is to leave with them now.'

As soon as I hear the words I am filled with a sudden terror, a gale of premonition, and I start running, running as if for my own life. I don't even go to the women's apartments, where the page-boy will have found Joan to tell her that the English are to have her. I don't run towards her old cell, thinking she has gone there to fetch her little knapsack of things: her wooden spoon, her sharp dagger, the prayer-book that my great-aunt gave her. Instead I race up the winding stair to the first floor above the great hall, and then dash across the gallery, through the tiny doorway where the archway knocks my headdress off, tearing at the pins in my hair, and then I hammer up the circular stone stair, my feet pounding on the steps, my breath coming shorter and shorter, my gown clutched in my hands, so that I can burst out onto the flat roof at the very top of the tower and see Joan, poised like a bird ready to fly, balanced on the wall of the turret. As she hears the door bang open she looks over her shoulder at me and hears me scream, 'Joan! No!' and she steps out into the void below her.

The worst thing of all, the very worst thing, is that she does not leap into nothing, like a frightened deer. I was dreading that she would jump, but she does something far worse than that. She dives. She goes headfirst over the battlement, and as I fling myself to the edge I can see that she goes down like a dancer, an acrobat, her hands clasped behind her, one leg extended like a dancer, the other bent, the toe pointed to her knee, and I see that, for that heart-stopping moment as she falls, she is in the pose of *le Pendu*, the Hanged Man, and she is going headfirst to her death with his calm smile on her serene face.

The thud when she hits the ground at the base of the tower is terrible. It echoes in my ears as if it is my own head that has struck the mud. I want to run down to lift her body, Joan, the Maid, crumpled like a bag of old clothes; but I cannot move. My knees have given way beneath me, I am clinging to the stone battlements, they are as cold as my scraped hands. I am not crying for her, though my breath is still coming in gulping sobs; I am frozen with horror, I am felled by horror. Joan was a young woman who tried to walk her own path in the world of men, just as my great-aunt told me. And it led her to this cold tower, this swan dive, this death.

They pick her up lifeless, and for four days she does not move or stir, but then she comes out of her stupor and gets up slowly from her bed, patting herself all over, as if to make sure that she is whole. Amazingly, no bones have been broken in her fall – she has not cracked her skull, nor snapped so much as a finger. It is as if her angels held her up, even when she gave herself into their element. Of course, this will not serve her; they are quick to say that only the Devil could have saved a girl who went head-first like that from such a tall tower. If she had died they would have said God's justice had been done. My uncle, a man of dour common sense, says that the ground is so sodden, after weeks of winter rain, and lapped by the moat, that she was in more danger of drowning than being broken; but now he is determined that she shall leave at once. He doesn't want the responsibility of the Maid in his house, without the Demoiselle to keep everything safe. He sends her first to his house in Arras, the Coeur le Comte, and then we follow, as she is transferred to the English city of Rouen for trial.

We have to attend. A great lord such as my uncle must be there to see justice being done, and his household must stand behind him. My aunt Jehanne takes me to witness the end of the Dauphin's holy guide – the pretend-prophet of the pretend-king. Half of France is trooping to Rouen to see the end of the Maid and we have to be foremost among them.

For someone that they declare is nothing more than a peasant girl run mad, they are taking no chances. She is housed in the Castle Bouvreuil and kept in chains, in a cell with a double-locked door and the window boarded over. They are all in a terror that she will run like a mouse under the door, or fly like a bird through a crack in the window. They ask her to give an undertaking that she will not try to escape and, when she refuses, they chain her to the bed.

'She won't like that,' my aunt Jehanne says sorrowfully.

'No.'

They are waiting for the Duke of Bedford, and in the very last days of December he marches into the town with his guard dressed in the colours of roses, the bright red and white of England. He is a great man on horseback, he wears armour polished so brightly that you would take it for silver and beneath his huge helmet his face is grave and stern, his big beak of a nose making him look like a predatory bird: an eagle. He was brother to the great English king Henry V, and he guards the lands that his brother won in France at the great battle of Agincourt. Now the dead king's young son is the new victor of France, and this is his most loyal uncle: seldom out of his armour or out of the saddle, never at peace.

We are all lined up at the great gate of Bouvreuil as he rides in, and his dark gaze rakes us all, looking from one to another as if to sniff out treason. My aunt and I curtsey low and my uncle John doffs his hat and bows. Our house has been in alliance with the English for years; my other uncle, Louis of Luxembourg, is the duke's chancellor and swears that he is the greatest man ever to rule France.

Heavily, he gets off his horse and stands like a fortress himself, as the men line up to greet him, bowing over his hand, some of them almost going down to their knees. A man comes forwards and, as Bedford acknowledges him with a lordly tip of his head, his glance goes over his vassal's head, and sees me. I am staring at him, of course – he is the greatest spectacle on this cold winter day – but now he is looking back at me, and there is a flash in his eyes which I see and cannot recognise. It is something like a sudden hunger, like a fasting man seeing a banquet. I step back. I am neither afraid nor coquettish, but I am only fourteen years of age and there is something about the power of this man and his energy that I don't want turned in my direction. I slide back a little so I am behind my aunt, and I watch the rest of the greetings masked by her headdress and veil.

A great litter comes up, thick curtains tied tight with gold cord against the cold, and Bedford's wife, the Duchess Anne, is helped out. A small cheer greets her from our men: she is of the House of Burgundy, our liege lords and relations, and we all dip in a little bow to her. She is as plain as all the Burgundy family, poor things, but her smile is merry and kind, and she greets her husband warmly and then stands with her hand comfortably tucked in the crook of his arm and looks about her with a cheerful face. She waves at my aunt and points inside the castle to say that we must come to her later. 'We'll go at dinnertime,' my aunt says to me in a whisper. 'Nobody in the world eats better than the Dukes of Burgundy.'

Bedford takes off his helmet and bows to the crowd in general, raises a gauntleted hand to the people who are leaning from upper windows and balancing on garden walls to see the great man. Then he turns and leads his wife inside and everyone has a sense that we have seen the cast of players and the opening scene of a travelling show. But whether it is a masque, or a party, funeral rites, or the baiting of a wild animal, that has brought so many of the greatest people in France to Rouen: it is about to begin.

ROUEN, FRANCE, SPRING 1431

And then they bodge it. They harass her with erudite questions, query her replies, double back on her answers, write down things she says in moments of weariness and bring them back to her later, define their terms in the most learned ways and ask her what she means, so that she does not understand the question and tells them simply 'pass on' or 'spare me that'. Once or twice she just says, 'I don't know. I am a simple girl with no learning. How would I know?'

My uncle gets an anguished letter from Queen Yolande of Aragon, who says she is certain that the Dauphin will ransom Joan, she just needs another three days, another week to persuade him, can we not delay the trial? Can we not ask for a few days' delay? But the Church has the girl wound tight in the web of inquiry and now they will never let her go.

Everything that highly educated men can do to obscure a simple truth, to make a woman doubt her feelings, to make her own thoughts a muddle, they do to her. They use their learning as a hurdle to herd her one way and then another, and then finally trap her in contradictions of which she can make no sense. Sometimes they accuse her in Latin and she looks at them, baffled by a language that she has only ever heard spoken in church, in the Mass that she loves. How could these very sounds, these familiar beloved tones, so solemn and musical to her, now be the voice of accusation?

Sometimes they bring scandal against her in the words of her own people, old earthy stories from Domrémy of vanity, of false pride. They say she jilted a man before marriage, they say she ran away from good parents, they say she worked in an alehouse, and was free with her favours like any village slut, they say she rode with the soldiers as their doxy, they say she is no Maid but a harlot, and that everyone knew it.

It takes Anne, the kind-hearted little Duchess of Bedford herself, to assert that Joan is a virgin, and to demand that the men who guard her are forbidden from touching or abusing her. They must be ordered that it is not the work of God to assault her. Then, as soon as this order is given, they say that, since she is now so safe, guarded by the word of the duchess, she has no excuse for wearing men's clothes and she must dress in a gown, for now they tell her it is a sin, a mortal sin, to wear breeches.

They turn her head, they puzzle her beyond bearing. They are great men of the Church and Joan is a peasant girl, a devout girl who had always done as the priest ordered until she heard the voices of angels who told her to do more. She cries in the end, she breaks down and cries like a child, she puts on the gown as they order her, and confesses to all the sins that they name to her. I don't know if she even understands the long list. She makes her mark on her confession – she writes her name and then signs a cross beside it as if to deny her signature. She admits that there were no angels and no voices, and that the Dauphin is nothing more than the Dauphin and not the King of France, that his coronation was a sham and her beautiful armour an offence to God and man, and that she is a girl, a silly girl, who tried to lead grown men as if she could know the way better than they. She says she is a vain fool to think that a girl might lead men, she is a woman worse than Eve for giving advice, an assistant to the Devil himself.

'What?' bellows the Duke of Bedford. We are visiting his wife the duchess, seated in her rooms before a good fire, a lute player twanging away in the corner, small glasses of the best wine on every table, everything elegant and beautiful; but we can hear his deplorable English bellow through two closed doors.

We hear the doors bang as the Earl of Warwick flings himself out of the duke's apartments to find out what has gone wrong, and in this revealing burst of rage we see – as if we had ever been in any doubt – that these English never wanted the Church to wrestle with the soul of a mistaken girl and restore her to her senses, bring her to confession, penitence and forgiveness – it has all along been nothing but a witch-hunt determined to find a witch, a bonfire looking for a brand, Death waiting for a maiden. The duchess goes to the door and the servants throw it open before her so we can all hear, disastrously clearly, her husband bellow at Pierre Cauchon the bishop, Cauchon the judge, Cauchon the man, who is there apparently representing – all at the same time – God and justice and the Church, 'For the sake of Christ! I don't want her pleading guilty, I don't want her recanting, I don't want her con-fessed and shriven, I don't bloody well want her imprisoned for life! What safety is there in that for me? I want her as a pile of ashes blowing away in the wind. How much clearer do I have to be? Goddamn! Do I have to burn her myself? You said the Church would do it for me! Do it!'

The duchess steps back rapidly and gestures for the doors to her room to be closed, but we can still hear the regent, swearing and damning his soul at the top of his voice. The duchess shrugs – men will be men, and this is wartime – and my aunt smiles understandingly, the lute player increases his volume as best he can and starts to sing. I go to the window and look out.

In the market square they have a half-built pyre, a strong structure with a big central beam and the wood stacked around it. Joan has confessed and recanted, she has been found guilty of her crimes and sentenced to imprisonment.

But they are not taking the wood away.

My aunt gives me a nod that we are going to leave, and I go to the hall to wait for her as she delays inside the duchess's rooms, saying a few words of farewell. I have my hood pulled up over my head, my hands tucked inside my cape. It is cold for May. I wonder if Joan has blankets in her cell, as the big double doors to the duke's public rooms are thrown open and the duke himself comes quickly out.

I sink down into a curtsey, and I imagine he can barely see me, wrapped in my dark cape in the shadowy doorway. I expect him to brush past; but he pauses. 'Jacquetta? Jacquetta St Pol?'

I sink even lower. 'Yes, Your Grace.'

He puts a firm hand under my elbow and raises me up. His other hand pushes back my hood and turns my face to the light of the open doorway, his hand under my chin as if I am a child, and he is looking to see if my mouth is clean. His men are waiting for him, there must be a dozen people around us, but he acts as if we are quite alone. He stares at me intently, as if he would read me. I look back at him blankly, I don't know what he wants with me and my aunt will be angry if I say the wrong thing to this most important man. I give my lip a little nip and I hear his sudden intake of breath.

'My God, how old are you?'

'I am fifteen this year, Your Grace.'

'And here with your father?'

'With my uncle, Your Grace. My father is Pierre, the new Count of Luxembourg.'

'The new count?' he asks, staring at my mouth.

'On the death of the Demoiselle of Luxembourg,' I mutter. 'My father is now Count of Luxembourg. He was her heir.'

'Of course, of course.'

There seems nothing else to say but still he is staring at me, still he holds me, one hand on my elbow, the other on the edge of my hood.

'Your Grace?' I whisper, hoping he will come to his senses and let me go.

'Jacquetta?' He whispers my name as if he is speaking to himself.

'May I serve you in some way?' I mean to say 'Please let me

go'; but a girl of my age cannot say such a thing to the greatest man in France.

He gives a little choke. 'Indeed, I think you may. Jacquetta, you are going to be a beautiful woman, a beautiful young woman.'

I glance around. His entourage are waiting for him, hardly moving, pretending not to see, not to listen. Nobody here is going to tell him to let me go, and I cannot do so.

'Do you have a sweetheart? Eh? Someone taken your fancy? Some cheeky little pageboy given you a kiss?'

'No, my lord. No, of course not . . . ' I am stammering as if I am in the wrong, as if I have done something as stupid and as vulgar as he suggests. He is chuckling as though to indulge me, but the grip on my elbow is hard as if he is angry. I lean back from his grip, from his avid gaze. 'My father is very strict,' I say feebly. 'The honour of my family . . . I have been staying with my uncle John and his wife Jehanne. They would never allow . . . '

'You don't wish for a husband?' he asks me disbelievingly. 'Don't you think of the man who will marry you, when you are in your bed at night? Do you dream of a young husband who will come for you like a troubadour and speak of love?'

I am trembling now, this is a nightmare. His grip is as hard as ever, but his hawkish face comes closer and closer, and now he is whispering in my ear. I begin to think he has gone mad. He looks at me as if he would eat me, and I have a shuddering sense of a world opening up before me that I don't want to know.

'No, no,' I whisper. But then, as he does not release me, but presses me closer, I have a sudden spurt of anger. I remember in a rush who I am, what I am. 'May it please Your Grace, I am a maid,' I say, the words tumbling. 'A maid of the House of Luxembourg. No man has laid a hand on me, no man would dare. I was in the keeping of the Demoiselle of Luxembourg, a virgin like myself. I am fit to capture a unicorn, and I should not be so questioned . . . '

There is a noise from the duchess's room and the door behind us suddenly opens and at once he drops me, like a boy throwing down a stolen pastry. He turns and stretches out both his hands to his plain little wife. 'My dear! I was just coming to find you.'

Her bright gaze takes me in, my white face, my hood pulled back, and his rosy bonhomie. 'Well, here I am,' she says drily. 'So you need look no more. And I see you found little Jacquetta St Pol instead.'

I curtsey again, as he glances at me as if seeing me for the first time. 'Good day,' he says carelessly, and to his wife he says, confidentially: 'I must go. They are making a muddle of it. I have to go.'

She nods her head to him with an easy smile and he turns and goes out, all his men marching after him with a heavy tread. I dread his wife Anne asking me if her husband spoke to me, what he said, what I was doing with him in the darkness of the hall, why he spoke to me of love and troubadours. For I could not answer such questions. I don't know what he was doing, I don't know why he took hold of me. I feel sick and my knees are trembling to think of his bright eyes on my face and his insinuating whisper. But I know he had no right. And I know that I defended myself, and I know that it is true: I am a virgin so pure that I could capture a unicorn.

But it is worse than this, far worse; she just looks at me steadily, and my sense of outrage slowly drains from me, for she does not ask me what I was doing with her husband, she looks at me as if she knows already. She looks me up and down, as if she knows everything. She gives me a small complicit smile as if she thinks I am some little thief and she has just caught me with my fingers in her purse.

Lord John, the Duke of Bedford, has his way, the great Earl of Warwick has his way, the great men of England have their way. Joan alone, without advisors to keep her safe, changes her mind about her confession, takes off her woman's gown and puts her boy's clothes back on. She cries out that she was wrong to deny her voices, wrong to plead guilty. She is not a heretic, she is not an idolater, she is not a witch or an hermaphrodite or a monster, she will not confess to such things, she cannot force herself to confess to sins she has never committed. She is a girl guided by the angels to seek the Prince of France and call him to greatness. She has heard angels, they told her to see him crowned as king. This is the truth before God, she proclaims – and so the jaws of England snap shut on her with relish.

From my room in the castle I can see the pyre as they build it even higher. They build a stand for the nobility to watch the spectacle as if it were a joust, and barriers to hold back the thousands who will come to see. Finally, my aunt tells me to put on my best gown and my tall hat and come with her.

'I am ill, I cannot come,' I whisper, but for once she is stern. I cannot be excused, I must be there. I must be seen, beside my aunt, beside Anne the Duchess of Bedford. We have to play our part in this scene as witnesses, as women who walk inside the rule of men. I will be there to show how girls should be: virgins who do not hear voices, women who do not think that they know better than men. My aunt and the duchess and I represent women as men would like them to be. Joan is a woman that men cannot tolerate.

We stand in the warm May sunshine as if we were waiting for the starting trumpet of a joust. The crowd is noisy and cheerful all around us. A very few people are silent, some women hold a crucifix, one or two have their hands on a cross at their necks; but most people are enjoying the day out, cracking nuts and swigging from flasks, a merry outing on a sunny day in May and the cheering spectacle of a public burning at the end of it.

Then the door opens, and the men of the guard march out and push back the crowd who whisper and hiss and boo at the opening inner door, craning their necks to be the first to see her.

She does not look like my friend Joan – that is my first thought when they bring her out of the little sallyport of the castle. She is wearing her boy's boots once more, but she is not striding out in her loose-limbed, confident walk. I guess that they have tortured her and perhaps the bones of her feet are broken, her toes crushed on the rack. They half-drag her and she makes little paddling steps, as if she is trying to find her footing on uncertain ground.

She is not wearing her boy's bonnet on her brown cropped hair, for they have shaved her head, and she is as bald as a shamed whore. On her bare cold scalp, stained here and there with dried blood where the razor has nicked her pale skin, they have crammed a tall hat of paper like a bishop's mitre, and on it are written her sins, in clumsy block letters for everyone to see: Heretic. Witch. Traitor. She wears a shapeless white robe, knotted with a cheap piece of cord at her waist. It is too long for her and the hem drags around her stumbling feet. She looks ridiculous, a figure of fun, and the people start to catcall and laugh, and someone throws a handful of mud.

She looks around, as if she is desperate for something, her eyes dart everywhere, and I am terrified that she will see me, and know that I have failed to save her, that even now I am doing nothing, and I will do nothing to save her. I am terrified that she will call my name and everyone will know that this broken clown was my friend and that I will be shamed by her. But she is not looking at the faces crowding around her, alight with excitement, she is asking for something. I can see her urgently pleading; and then a soldier, a common English soldier, thrusts a wooden cross into her hands, and she clutches it as they lift her and push her upwards to the bonfire.

They have built it so high it is hard to get her up. Her feet scrabble on the ladder and her hands cannot grip. But they push her roughly, cheerfully, from behind, hands on her back, her buttocks, her thighs, and then a big soldier goes up the ladder with her and takes a handful of the coarse material of her robe and hauls her up beside him like a sack, turns her round, and puts her back to the stake that runs through the pyre. They throw up a length of chain to him and he loops it around and around her and then fastens it with a bolt behind. He tugs at it, workmanlike, and tucks the wooden cross in the front of her gown, and in the crowd below a friar pushes to the front and holds up a crucifix. She stares at it unblinkingly, and I know, to my shame, that I am glad she has fixed her eyes on the cross so that she will not look at me, in my best gown and my new velvet cap, among the nobility who are talking and laughing all around me.

The priest walks around the bottom of the pyre reading in Latin, the ritual cursing of the heretic; but I can hardly hear him above the yells of encouragement and the rumble of growing excitement from the crowd. The men with the burning torches come from the castle and walk around the pyre, lighting it all the way round the base, and then laying the torches against the wood. Someone has dampened the wood so that it will burn slowly, to give her the greatest pain, and the smoke billows around her.

I can see her lips moving, she is still looking at the upheld cross, I see that she is saying 'Jesus, Jesus', over and over, and for a moment I think that perhaps there will be a miracle, a storm to drown the fire, a lightning raid from the Armagnac forces. But there is nothing. Just the swirling thick smoke, and her white face, and her lips moving.

The fire is slow to catch, the crowd jeer the soldiers for laying a poor bonfire, my toes are cramped in my best shoes. The great bell starts to ring, slowly and solemnly, and though I can hardly see Joan through the thickening cloud of smoke, I recognise the turn of her head under the great paper mitre as she listens and I wonder if she is hearing her angels through the tolling of the bell, and what they are saying to her now.

The wood shifts a little and the flames start to lick. The inside of the pile is drier – they built it weeks ago for her – and now with a crackle and a blaze it is starting to brighten. The light makes the ramshackle buildings of the square jump and loom, the smoke swirls more quickly, the brightness of the fire throws a flickering glow on Joan and I see her look up, clearly I see her form the word 'Jesus', and then like a child going to sleep her head droops and she is quiet.

Childishly, I think for a moment perhaps she has gone to sleep, perhaps this is the miracle sent by God, then there is a sudden blaze as the long white robe catches fire and a tongue of flame flickers up her back and the paper mitre starts to brown and curl. She is still, silent as a little stone angel, and the pyre shifts and the bright sparks fly up.

I grit my teeth, and I find my aunt's hand clutching mine. 'Don't faint,' she hisses. 'You have to stand up.' We stand hand-clasped, our faces quite blank, as if this were not a nightmare that tells me, as clearly as if it were written in letters of fire, what ending a girl may expect if she defies the rules of men and thinks she can make her own destiny. I am here not only to witness what happens to a heretic. I am here to witness what happens to a woman who thinks she knows more than men.

I look through the haze of the fire to our window in the castle, and I see the maid, Elizabeth, looking down. She sees me look up at her and our eyes meet, blank with horror. Slowly, she stretches out her hand and makes the sign that Joan showed us that day by the moat in the hot sunshine. Elizabeth draws a circle in the air with her forefinger, the sign for the wheel of fortune, which can throw a woman so high in the world that she can command a king, or pull her down to this: a dishonoured agonising death.

CASTLE OF ST POL, ARTOIS, SPRING 1433

After a few more months with my uncle John, and then a year-long visit to our Brienne kinsfolk, my mother regards me as sufficiently polished to return home while they plan my marriage, and so I am living at our castle in St Pol when we hear the news that Anne Duchess of Bedford has died and the duke is lost without her. Then a letter comes from my uncle Louis, the duke's chancellor.

'Jacquetta, this concerns you.' My mother summons me to her rooms where I find her seated, my father standing behind her chair. They both look at me sternly and I make a rapid review of my day's doings. I have not completed the many tasks that I am supposed to do, and I skipped attendance at church this morning, my room is untidy and I am behind with my sewing, but surely my father would not come to my mother's apartment to reprimand me for this?

'Yes, Lady Mother?'

My mother hesitates, glances up at my father and then presses on. 'Of course your father and I have been considering a husband for you and we have been looking at who might be suitable – we hoped that ... but it does not matter, for you are lucky, we have had a most advantageous offer. In short, your uncle Louis has suggested you as a wife for the Duke of Bedford.'

I am so surprised that I say nothing.

'A great honour,' my father says shortly. 'A great position for you. You will be an English duchess, the first lady after the king's mother in England, the first lady bar none in France. You should go down on your knees and thank God for this opportunity.'

'What?'

My mother nods, confirming this. They both stare at me, expecting a response.

'But his wife has only just died,' I say weakly.

'Yes indeed, your uncle Louis has done very well for you, to get your name put forwards this early.'

'I would have thought he would have wanted to wait a little while.'

'Didn't the duke see you at Rouen?' my mother asks. 'And then again in Paris?'

'Yes, but he was married,' I say foolishly. 'He saw me ...' I remember that dark predatory look, when I was little more than a girl, and my stepping behind my aunt to hide from it. I remember the shadowy hall and the man who whispered in my ear and then went out to order the burning of the Maid. 'And the duchess was there. I knew her too. We saw her far more than we saw him.'

My father shrugs. 'At any rate, he liked the look of you and your uncle has put your name in his ear and you are to be his wife.'

'He's very old,' I say quietly, directing this at my mother.

'Not very. A little over forty,' she says.

'And I thought you told me he was ill,' I say to my father.

'All the better for you,' my mother says. Clearly she means that an elderly husband may be less demanding than a young one, and if he dies then I shall be a dowager duchess at seventeen, which would be the only thing better than being a duchess at seventeen.

'I had not looked for such an honour,' I say feebly to them both. 'May I be excused? I fear I am not worthy.'

'We are of the greatest family in Christendom,' my father says grandly. 'Kin to the Holy Roman Emperor. How would you not be worthy?'

'You cannot be excused,' my mother says. 'Indeed, you would be a fool to be anything but delighted. Any girl in France and England would give her right hand for such a match.' She pauses and clears her throat. 'He is the greatest man in France and England after the King of England. And if the king were to die . . .'

'Which God forbid,' my father says hastily.

'God forbid indeed; but if the king were to die then the duke would be heir to the throne of England and you would be Queen of England. What d'you think of that?'

'I had not thought of marriage to such a man as the duke.'

'Think now then,' my father says briskly. 'For he is coming here in April, to marry you.'

My uncle Louis, who is Bishop of Therouanne as well as the duke's chancellor, is both host and priest at this wedding of his own making. He entertains us in his episcopal palace and John Duke of Bedford rides in with his guard in the English livery of red and white, as I stand at the doorway of the palace in a gown of palest yellow with a veil of tissue of gold floating from my high headdress.

His page runs forwards to hold his horse's head, and another kneels on the ground alongside and then drops to his hands and knees to form a human mounting block. The duke climbs down heavily, from the stirrup onto the man's back, and then steps down to the ground. Nobody remarks on this. The duke is such a great man that his pages take it as an honour for him to stand on them. His squire takes his helmet and his metalled gauntlets, and steps aside.

'My lord.' My uncle the bishop greets his master with obvious affection and then bows to kiss his hand. The duke claps him on the back and then turns to my father, and my mother. Only when the courtesies with them are complete does he turn to me, and he steps forwards, takes both of my hands, pulls me towards him, and kisses me on the mouth.

His chin is rough with stubble, his breath tainted; it is like being licked by a hound. His face seems very big as it comes down towards me, and very big as he moves away. He does not pause to look at me, or to smile, just that one aggressive kiss, then he turns to my uncle and says, '*Do* you have no wine?' and they laugh for it is a private joke, based on their years of friendship, and my uncle leads the way inside and my mother and father follow them, and I am left for a moment, looking after the older people, with the squire at my side.

'My lady,' he says. He has passed the duke's armour to another, and now he bows to me and doffs his hat. His dark hair is cut straight in a fringe above his brows, his eyes are grey as slate, perhaps blue. He has a funny twist in his smile as if something is amusing him. He is stunningly handsome, I can hear the ladies in waiting behind me give a little murmur. He makes a bow and offers me his arm to take me inside. I put my hand on his and feel the warmth of his hand through the soft leather of his glove. At once, he pulls off the glove so his fingers are holding mine. I feel as if I would like him to take my hand in his, to put his warm palm against mine. I feel I would like him to take hold of my shoulders, to grip me at the waist.

I shake my head to clear my mind of such ridiculous thoughts and I say, abruptly, like an awkward girl: 'I'll go in alone, thank you,' and I drop his hand, and follow them inside.

The three men are seated, wineglasses in their hands, my mother is in a window embrasure, watching the servants bring little cakes and top up their glasses. I go to her side with her ladies in waiting, and my two little sisters who are dressed in their best and trusted to stand with the adults on this most important day. I wish that I was eight years old like Isabelle, and could look at

John, Duke of Bedford, and marvel at his greatness and know that he would say nothing to me, that he would not even see me. But I am not a little girl any more, and as I look across at him, he does see me, he looks at me with a sort of avid curiosity, and this time there is nowhere for me to hide.

My mother comes to my room the night before my wedding. She brings the gown for the next day and lays it carefully in the chest at the foot of my bed. The tall headdress and veil are mounted on a stand, safely out of the way of candles or dust.

My maid is brushing my fair hair before the beaten silver mirror, but as my mother comes in I say, 'You can stop now, Margarethe,' and she twists the long fall into a loose plait, ties it with a ribbon, and goes from the room.

Mother sits awkwardly on the bed. 'I need to speak to you about marriage,' she starts. 'About what your duties will be as a married woman. I suppose you should know.'

I turn on my stool and wait, saying nothing.

'This is a marriage of great advantage to you,' she says. 'We are of Luxembourg, of course, but to gain the position of an English duchess is a great thing.'

I nod. I wonder if she is going to say anything about what happens on the wedding night. I am afraid of the great duke and I am dreading the thought of spending the night with him. The last wedding I went to they put the couple in bed together and in the morning they fetched them out with music and singing and laughing, and then the mother went in and brought out the sheets and they were red with blood. Nobody would tell me what had happened, if there had been some sort of accident. Everyone behaved as if everything was quite wonderful, as if they were pleased at the sight of blood on the linen. Indeed, they were laughing and congratulating the bridegroom. I wonder if my mother is going to explain now.

'But for him, it is not a marriage of advantage,' she says. 'It may cost him very dear.'

'The jointure?' I ask, thinking that it must cost him money to pay me my allowance.

'His allies,' she says. 'He has been in alliance with the Dukes of Burgundy to fight against the Armagnacs. England could not have fought such a war without their support. His wife was Anne of Burgundy – the present duke was her brother – and she made it her business to keep her brother and her husband in good friendship. Now she has died, there is no-one to keep the friendship, no-one to help them resolve their disagreements.'

'Well, I can't,' I say, thinking of the Duke of Burgundy whom I have seen half a dozen times in my whole life, while certainly he has never noticed me at all.

'You will have to try,' my mother says. 'It will be your duty, as an English duchess, to hold Burgundy in alliance with England. Your husband will expect you to entertain his allies and to be charming.'

'Charming?'

'Yes. But there is a difficulty. Because my lord John of Bedford is marrying you so soon after the death of his wife, the Duke of Burgundy is offended at the insult to his dead sister. He has taken it badly.'

'Then why are we marrying so quickly?' I ask. 'If it upsets the Duke of Burgundy? Surely we should leave it a year and not displease him? He is our kinsman, as well as the Duke of Bedford's ally. Surely we should not offend him?'

My mother smiles faintly. 'It makes you a duchess,' she reminds me. 'A greater title even than mine.'

'I could be a duchess next year.' The thought of escaping this marriage, even for a year, fills me with hope. 'We could just be betrothed.'

'Lord John won't wait,' she says flatly. 'So don't hope for that. I just want to warn you that he may lose his ally by marrying you. You must do all that you can to retain the friendship of the

Duke of Burgundy, and remind them both that you are a kinswoman of Burgundy and his vassal. Speak to the Duke of Burgundy privately and promise him that you remember your kinship to the Burgundians. Do all you can to keep the friendship between the two of them, Jacquetta.'

I nod. I really don't know what she thinks I can do, a seventeen-year-old girl, to maintain an alliance of two great men old enough to be my father. But I will have to promise to do my best.

'And the marriage . . .' I begin.

'Yes?'

I take a breath. 'What exactly happens?'

She shrugs, she makes a little face as if talk of it is beneath her, or embarrassing, or even worse – too disagreeable for words. 'Oh, my dear, you just do your duty. He will tell you what he expects. He will tell you what to do. He won't expect you to know anything, he will prefer to be your instructor.'

'Does it hurt?' I ask.

'Yes,' she says unhelpfully. 'But not for very long. Since he is older and practised, he should do his best to see that you are not hurt too badly.' She hesitates. 'But if he does hurt you . . .'

'Yes?'

'Don't complain of it.'

The wedding is to be at midday and I start preparing at eight in the morning when my maid brings me bread and meat and small ale to sustain me through the long day. I giggle when I see the tray heaped with food. 'I'm not going out hunting, you know.'

'No,' she says ominously. 'You are to be hunted,' and the other maids with her all cackle like a pen of hens and that is the last joke I am going to offer all day.

I sit at the table in a sulk, and eat, while they embroider versions of the theme of me being hunted and caught and enjoying the chase, until my mother comes in, and behind her come two serving men, rolling the great wooden barrel of a bath.

They place it before the fire in my bedroom, line it with linen and start to pour in jug after jug of hot water. The maids bustle about bringing drying sheets, and start to lay out my new under-gowns, with much comment about the lace and the ribbons and how fine everything is, and how lucky I am. My mother sees my strained expression and shoos them all from the room except our old nursemaid who is to scrub my back and wash my hair and add jugs of hot water. I feel like a sacrificial lamb being cleaned and brushed before having its throat cut; and it is not a pleasant thought.

But our nursemaid Mary is cheerful and full of her usual clucking approbation of my beautiful hair and my beautiful skin and if she had half my looks she would have run away to Paris – as ever – and when I have bathed and she has dried my hair and plaited it, I cannot help but be encouraged by the linen under-gown with the new ribbons, and by the new shoes and by the beautiful cloth-of-gold gown, and the headdress. The maids come back in to help me dress, and tie the laces of the gown and straighten my headdress and pull the veil over my shoulders and finally pronounce me ready for my wedding and as beautiful as a bride should be.

I turn to the great looking glass that my mother has ordered to be carried into my chamber, and my reflection looks back at me. The maids hold it before me and tip it slightly downwards so that I can first see the hem of my gown, embroidered with little red lions rampant, from the standard of our house, and my red leather slippers with the curling toes. Then they hold the mirror straight, and I can see the cloth-of-gold gown gathered at the high waist and the embroidered heavy belt of gold that is slung low over my slim hips. I gesture and they raise the mirror so I can see the expensive cream lace veiling the low-cut neck of the gown, the gold sleeves falling from my shoulders, with the white linen under-gown revealed tantalisingly through the slashings at the shoulders, and then my face. My fair hair is plaited away and tucked under the tall headdress, and my face looks solemnly at me, enhanced by the silvery reflection of the mirror. My grey eyes are wide in this light, my skin clear and pearly, the mirror makes me look like a statue of a beauty, a marble girl. I gaze at myself as if I would know who I am, and for a moment I think I see Melusina, the founder of our house, looking back at me through moonlit water.

'When you are a duchess you will have a great mirror of your own,' my mother says. 'Everything fine. And you will have all her old clothes.'

'Duchess Anne's clothes?'

'Yes,' she says, as if wearing the wardrobe of a recently dead woman should be a great treat for me. 'Her sables are the best I have ever seen. Now they will be yours.'

'Wonderful,' I say politely. 'Will I get my own clothes as well?'

She laughs. 'You will be the first lady in France, all but the first lady in England. You will be able to have whatever your husband wants to give you. And you will soon learn how to persuade him.'

A woman whispers something behind her hand about how a girl like me might persuade a man as old as he with one hand tied behind her back. Someone says, 'Better with both hands tied,' and a couple of them laugh. I have no idea what they mean.

'He will love you,' my mother promises. 'He is quite mad for you.'

I don't reply. I just look at the young woman in the mirror. The thought of John, Duke of Bedford, running mad for me is not encouraging at all.

The wedding service lasts about an hour. It is all in Latin so half of the vows are incomprehensible to me, anyway. It is not a private plighting of promises, but more a great announcement as the hall of the bishop's palace fills with strangers come to look at me and celebrate my good fortune. When the vows are done and we walk through the crowd, I am escorted by my new husband, my fingertips resting on his sleeve, there is a roar of approbation and everywhere I look I see smiling avid faces.

We sit at the top table, facing the room. There is a bawl of trumpets from the gallery and the first of dozens of plates of food is marched into the room at shoulder height. The servers come to us at the high table first, and put a little from every dish on each golden plate, then the duke points them here and there down the hall, so that his favourites may share our dishes. For everyone else, the great bowls of meat come in and the great platters of white bread. It is a huge feast, my uncle Louis has spared no expense to please his patron and to celebrate my rise to the royalty of England.

They bring in wine in great golden jugs and they pour glass after glass at the high table. The honoured guests, those who sit above the great golden bowl of salt, have as much wine as they can drink, as fast as they can drink it. In the hall the men have tankard after tankard of ale, the best ale: wedding ale specially brewed for today, specially sweetened and spicy.

There is a challenger, who rides his horse right into the hall, and throws down his gauntlet in my name. His horse curves its heavy muscled neck and eyes the tables and the great circular fireplace in the centre of the hall. I have to get up from my place and come round on the raised dais of the high table to give him a golden cup, and then he goes all round the hall at a powerful trot, his rider sitting heavily in the embossed saddle, before cantering out of the double doors. It seems quite ridiculous to me, to ride a horse into dinner, especially such a heavy horse and such a weighty knight. I look up and I meet the gaze of the young squire who is dangerously near to laughter, as I am. Quickly, we both look away from each other's dancing eyes before I betray myself and giggle.

There are twenty courses of meats, and then ten of fish, then everything is taken away and Rhenish wine is served with a voider course of potted fruit, sugared plums and sweetmeats. When everyone has tasted all of these they bring in the final course of marchpane, pastries, sugared fruits and gingerbread decorated with real gold leaf. In comes the Fool who juggles and cracks bawdy jokes about youth and age, male and female, and the heat of the wedding bed, which is the fire to forge a new life. He is followed by dancers and players who perform a masque celebrating the power of England and the beauty of Luxembourg with a beautiful woman, almost naked but for her long green tail of silk, who symbolises Melusina. The best of them all is a costumed lion, the emblem of both our countries, who cavorts and dances with strength and grace, and finally comes, panting a little, to the high table and bows his great head to me. His mane is a mass of golden curls smelling of sacking, his face a mask of painted paper, with a smiling honest look. I have a gold chain to put around his neck and as I stretch towards him and he bows his head to me I recognise the gleam of blue eyes through the mask and know that my hands are on the shoulders of the handsome squire, and that I am standing close enough to embrace him as I put my chain around his neck.

My mother nods to me that we can leave, and the women and the musicians all rise up and dance in a line round the length of the hall and then make an archway with their hands held high and I walk through it, with all the girls wishing me luck and the women calling blessings down on me. I am preceded by my dancing little sisters who scatter rose petals and little golden keys on the floor where I walk. Everyone escorts me up the great flight of stairs to the best chambers and they all seem disposed to crowd into the bedroom with me; but my father stops them at the door, and I go in with just my mother and the ladies of her court.

First they unpin my high headdress and lift it carefully away, and then unpin my hair. My scalp aches as the tightly plaited hair tumbles down and I rub my face. They untie the laces of my gown at my shoulders to take off the sleeves, then they untie the fastenings at the back and drop it to the floor and I carefully step out of it. They take it away to shake it and powder it and store it carefully for the next important event when I will wear it as the Duchess of Bedford, and the red lions on the hem will symbolise the house that once was mine. They untie the laces of my under-gown and strip me naked, then, while I shiver, they throw my nightgown over my head, and put a wrap around my shoulders. They seat me on a stool and bring a bowl of hot scented water and I soak my cold feet and lean back as one of them brushes my hair while the others pull at the embroidered hem of the gown, tidy the fall of the wrap, and put the room to rights. Finally they pat my feet dry, plait my hair, tie a nightcap on my head, and then they throw open the door.

My uncle Louis comes in, dressed in his bishop's cope and mitre, swinging a censer, and he proceeds all round the room, blessing every corner, and wishing me happiness, wealth, and above all fertility, in this great match between England and the county of Luxembourg. 'Amen,' I say, 'amen,' but it seems that he will never stop and then, from the hall below, comes a great rumble of male voices and laughter and the blare of trumpets and the banging of drums and they are bringing my bridegroom, the old duke, to my room.

They carry him shoulder high, shouting 'Hurrah! Hurrah!' and they set him on his feet just outside my door so that he can walk in and they can all tumble in behind him. Hundreds are left in the rooms outside, craning to see, and shouting for others to move up. The Fool capers in, his bladder in his hand, poking at the bed and declaring that it need be soft for the duke will make a heavy landing. There is a roar of laughter at this, which spreads out of the room to the chambers beyond and even down to the hall as the jest is repeated. Then the Fool commands the girls to build up the fire to keep the bed warm, and top up the wed-ding ale for the duke may get a thirst on, and then he may need to get up in the night. 'Up in the night!' he says again, and every-one laughs.

The trumpets blast a summons, deafening in the bedroom,

and my father says, 'Well, we will leave them! God bless and goodnight.' My mother kisses me on the forehead, and all her ladies and half of the guests kiss me too. Then my mother leads me to the bed and helps me climb into it. I sit there, propped on pillows like a hand-carved poppet. On the other side, the duke is throwing off his dressing gown and his squire pulls back the sheets and helps his lord into bed. The squire keeps his eyes down and does not look at me, and I am still, like a stiff little doll, one hand holding the neck of my nightgown tightly under my chin.

We sit bolt upright, side by side, while everyone laughs and cheers and wishes us well, and then my father and my uncle guide and half push the revellers from the room and they close the door on us and we can still hear them, singing their way down the stairs back to the hall and shouting for more drink to toast the health of the happy couple and wet the head of the baby who will be made, God willing, this very night.

'Are you well, Jacquetta?' the duke asks me as the room grows slowly quiet and the candles burn more steadily, now that the doors are closed.

'I am well, my lord,' I say. My heart is beating so loudly that I think he must hear it. More than anything else I am painfully aware that I have no idea what I should do, or what he may ask of me.

'You can go to sleep,' he says heavily. 'For I am dead drunk. I hope you will be happy, Jacquetta. I will be a kind husband to you. But go to sleep now, for I am drunk as a bishop.'

He heaves the bedclothes over his own shoulders, and rolls over on his side, as if there was nothing more to say or do, and within moments he is snoring so loudly that I fear they will hear him in the hall below. I lie still, almost afraid to move, and then, as his breathing deepens and slows, and the snores settle to a steady low roar and grunt, I slip from the bed, take a sip of the wedding ale – since after all it is my wedding day – blow out the candles, and then climb back between the warm sheets beside the unfamiliar bulk of a sleeping man.

I think I will never sleep. I can hear the singing from the hall below and then the noise as people spill out into the courtyard outside and shout for torches and servants to show them to their beds for the night. The steady rumble of my husband's snore is like the roar from a bear pit, pointlessly loud and threatening. I think I will never ever sleep with such a great man in my bed, and amid this buzz of thoughts in my head, and my grumbles to myself about this discomfort, and how unfair it is to me, I slide into sleep.

I wake to find my new husband already awake, pulling on his breeches, his white linen shirt open to his broad waist, his fleshy hairy chest and big belly half-exposed. I sit up in bed and gather my nightgown around me. 'My lord.'

'Good morning, wife!' he says with a smile. 'Did you sleep well?'

'Yes,' I say. 'I think you did?'

'Did I snore?' he asks cheerfully.

'A little.'

'More than a little, I wager. Was it like a thunderstorm?'

'Well, yes.'

He grins. 'You will get used to it. Anne used to say it was like living by the sea. You get used to the noise. It is when there is silence that it wakes you.'

I blink at the opinions of my predecessor.

He comes around to my side of the bed and sits heavily on my feet. 'Ah, excuse me.'

I move out of his way, and he sits again. 'Jacquetta, I am a good deal older than you. I must tell you, I will not be able to give you a son, nor any child at all. I am sorry for that.'

I take a little breath, and wait to see what terrible thing he will say next. I had thought he had married me to get an heir. Why else would a man want a young bride? He answers this at once, before it is even spoken.

'Nor shall I take your virginity,' he says quietly. 'For one thing,

I am unmanned, and so I cannot readily do it; for another, I don't want to do it with you.'

My hand tightens on the nightgown at my throat. My mother will be appalled when she finds out about this. I am going to be in so much trouble with my father. 'My lord, I am very sorry. You don't like me?'

He laughs shortly. 'What man could not? You are the most exquisite girl in France, I chose you for your beauty and for your youth – but for something else too. I have a better task for you than being my bedmate. I could command any girl in France. But you, I trust, are fit to do something more. Do you not know?'

Dumbly, I shake my head.

'The Demoiselle said you had a gift,' he says quietly.

'My great-aunt?'

'Yes. She told your uncle that you had the gift of your family, she said you have the Sight. And he told me.'

I am silent for a moment. 'I don't know.'

'She said she thought you might have. She said she had spoken with you. Your uncle tells me that you studied with her, that she left you her books, her bracelet with charms for foreseeing. That you can hear singing.'

'He told you that?'

'Yes, and I assume that she left her things to you because she thought you would be able to make use of them.'

'My lord . . .'

'This is not a trap, Jacquetta, I am not tricking you into a confession.'

You tricked Joan, I think to myself.

'I am working for my king and for my country, we are near to finding, please God, the elixir that brings a cure for death, and makes the philosopher's stone.'

'The philosopher's stone?'

'Jacquetta, I think we are very close to finding the way to turn iron into gold. We are very close. And then . . .'

I wait.

'Then I will have enough coin to pay my troops to fight for every town in France. Then the rule of England can spread peace over all our lands. Then my nephew can sit firmly on his throne, and the poor people of England can work for their living without being taxed into poverty. It would be a new world, Jacquetta. We would command it. We would pay for everything with gold that we could make in London. We would not have to dig it in Cornwall nor pan for it in Wales. We would have a country richer than any dream. And I am, I think, perhaps only a few months from finding it.'

'And what about me?'

He nods, as I return him to the reality of this wedding-day morning, which is not a real wedding at all. 'Oh yes. You. My alchemists, my astrologers tell me that I need someone with your gifts. Someone who can scry, who can look into a mirror or into water and see the truth, the future. They need an assistant with clean hands and a pure heart. It has to be a woman, a young woman who has never taken a life, never stolen, never known lust. When I first met you they had just told me that they could go no further without a young woman, a virgin, who could see the future. In short, I needed a girl who could capture a unicorn.'

'My Lord Duke . . .'

'You said that. D'you remember? In the hall of the castle at Rouen? You said you were a girl so pure that you could capture a unicorn.'

I nod. I did say it. I wish I had not.

'I understand that you are shy. You will be anxious to tell me you cannot do these things. I understand your reserve. But tell me only this. Have you taken a life?'

'No, of course not.'

'Have you stolen? Even a little fairing? Even a coin from another's pocket?'

'No.'

'Have you lusted for a man?'

'No!' I say emphatically.

'Have you ever foretold the future, in any way at all?'

I hesitate. I think of Joan and the card of *le Pendu*, and the wheel of fortune that bore her down so low. I think of the singing around the turrets on the night that the Demoiselle died. 'I think so. I cannot be sure. Sometimes things come to me, it is not that I call them.'

'Could you capture a unicorn?'

I give a little nervous laugh. 'My lord. It is just a saying, it is just a tapestry-picture. I wouldn't know what one is supposed to do . . .'

'They say that the only way to capture a unicorn is for a virgin to go alone into the forest, that no man can set a hand on it, but that it will come to a virgin and lay its beautiful head in her lap.'

I shake my head. 'I know this is what they say, but I don't know anything about unicorns. My lord, I don't even know if they are real.'

'At any rate, as a virgin you are of great value to me, a very precious thing to me. As a virginal daughter of the House of Melusina, as an heiress of her gifts, you are beyond precious. As a young wife you would be a pleasure to me; but nothing more. I have married you to do far, far more than merely lie on your back and please me. Do you understand now?'

'Not really.'

'Never mind. What I want is a young woman pure in heart, a virgin, who will do my bidding, who is mine, as much as if I had bought a slave from the Turkish galleys. And this is what I have in you. You will learn what I want from you later, you will do what I want. But you won't be hurt or frightened, you have my word.'

He gets to his feet and takes his dagger from the sheath at his belt. 'Now we have to stain the sheets,' he says. 'And if anyone asks you, your mother or your father, you tell them that I got on top of you, that it hurt a little, and that you hope we have made a child. Say nothing about the life we are to have. Let them think you are an ordinary wife and that I have deflowered you.'

He takes his dagger and without another word he makes a quick slice against his left wrist, and the blood wells up quickly from the scratch. He lets it come and then he pulls back the covers of the bed, ignoring me as I tuck my bare feet out of sight, and he holds out his hand and drips a few spots of red blood onto the sheets. I stare at them as the stain spreads, feeling utterly ashamed, thinking that this is my marriage, that starts in my husband's blood, with a lie.

'That'll do,' he says. 'Your mother will come to see this and believe that I have had you. D'you remember what to tell her?'

'That you got on top of me, that it hurt a little, and that I hope we have made a child,' I repeat obediently.

'That I am going to keep you as a virgin is our secret.' He is suddenly serious, almost threatening. 'Don't forget that. As my wife you will know my secrets, and this is the first, and one of the greatest of them. The alchemy, the foreseeing, your virginity, these are all secrets that you must keep, on your honour, and tell no-one. You are of the royal house of England now, which will bring you greatness but also great cost. You have to pay the price as well as enjoy the wealth.'

I nod, my eyes on his dark face.

He rises from the bed, and takes his dagger to the bottom sheet. Without thinking of the cost, he slices a thin strip of linen. Mutely he holds it out to me and I tie it around his wrist over the cut. 'Pretty maid,' he says. 'I shall see you at breakfast,' and then he pulls on his boots and walks from the room.

PARIS, FRANCE, MAY 1433

We travel with a great entourage as befits the ruler of France, especially a ruler who holds his lands by force. Ahead of us go an armed guard, a vanguard under the command of the blue-eyed squire, to make sure that the way is safe. Then, after a little gap to let the dust settle, come my lord duke and I. I ride behind a burly man at arms, seated pillion, my hands on his belt. My lord rides his war horse beside me, as if for company, but he barely says one word.

'I wish I could ride a horse on my own,' I remark.

He glances at me as if he had forgotten I was there at all. 'Not today,' he says. 'It will be hard riding today, and if we meet trouble, we might have to go fast. We can't go at a lady's pace, a girl's pace.'

I say nothing for it is true, I am not much of a rider. Then I try again to make a conversation with him. 'And why is it hard riding today, my lord?'

For a moment he is silent as if considering whether he can be troubled to answer me.

'We're not going to Paris. We're going north to Calais.'

'Excuse me, but I thought we were going to Paris. Why are we going to Calais, my lord?'

He sighs as if two questions are too much for a man to bear.

'There was a mutiny at Calais among the garrison, my soldiers, recruited and commanded by me. Bloody fools. I called in on my way to you. Hanged the ringleaders. Now I'm going back to make sure the rest have learned their lesson.'

'You hanged men on your way to our wedding?'

He turns his dark gaze on me. 'Why not?'

I can't really say why not, it just seems to me rather disagreeable. I make a little face and turn away. He laughs shortly. 'Better for you that the garrison should be strong,' he says. 'Calais is the rock. All of England's lands in northern France are built on our holding Calais.'

We ride on in silence. He says almost nothing when we stop to eat at midday except to ask if I am very tired, and when I say no, he sees that I am fed and then lifts me back to the pillion saddle for the rest of the ride. The squire comes back and sweeps his hat off to me in a low bow and then mutters to my lord in a rapid conference, after which we all fall in and ride on.

It is twilight as we see the great walls of the castle of Calais looming out of the misty sea plain ahead of us. The land all around is intersected with ditches and canals, divided with little gates, each of them swirling with mist. My lord's squire comes riding back when the flag over the top tower of the castle dips in acknowledgement, and the great gates ahead of us swing open. 'Soon be home,' he says cheerfully to me as he wheels his horse round.

'Not my home,' I observe shortly.

'Oh, it will be,' he says. 'This is one of your greatest castles.'

'In the middle of a mutiny?'

He shakes his head. 'That's over now. The garrison hadn't been paid for months and so the soldiers took the wool from the Calais merchants, stole it from their stores. Then the merchants paid to get their goods back, now my lord the duke will repay them.' He grins at my puzzled face. 'It's nothing. If the soldiers had been paid on time it would never have happened.'

'Then why did my lord execute someone?'

His smile dims. 'So that they remember that next time their wages are late, they have to wait on his pleasure.'

I glance at my silently listening husband on my other side. 'And what happens now?'

We are approaching the walls, the soldiers are mustering into a guard of honour, running down the steep hill from the castle which sits at the centre of the town, guarding the port to the north and the marshy land to the south.

'Now I dismiss the men who stole the goods, dismiss their commander, and appoint a new Captain of Calais,' my husband says shortly. He looks across me at the squire. 'You.'

'I, my lord?'

'Yes.'

'I'm honoured, but ...'

'Are you arguing with me?'

'No, my lord, of course not.'

My husband smiles at the silenced young man. 'That's good.' To me he says, 'This young man, my squire, my friend, Richard Woodville, has fought in almost every campaign here in France and was knighted on the battlefield by the late king, my brother. His father served us too. He's not yet thirty years old but I know of no-one more loyal or trustworthy. He can command this garrison and while he is here I can be sure that there will be no mutinies, and no complaints, and no petty thieving. And there will be no arguing about my orders. Is that right, Woodville?'

'Quite right, sir,' he says.

And then the three of us go through the dark echoing doorway and up the cobbled streets, past the hanged mutineers swinging silently on the gallows, through the bowing citizens to the castle of Calais.

'Am I to stay here now?' Woodville asks, as if it is a mere matter of a bed for the night.

'Not yet,' my husband says. 'I have need of you by me.'

We stay only three nights, long enough for my husband to dismiss half of the soldiers of the garrison and send to England for their replacements, long enough to warn their commander that he will be replaced by the squire Sir Richard Woodville, and then we rattle down the cobbled street and out of the gateway and go south down the road to Paris, the squire Woodville at the head of the troop once more, me on the lumbering horse of the man at arms, and my husband in grim silence.

It is a two-day ride before we see the Grange Batelière standing over the desolate countryside outside the city. Beyond it are worked fields and little dairy farms which gradually give way to small market gardens that surround the city walls. We enter through the north-west gate, close to the Louvre, and see at once my Paris home, the Hôtel de Bourbon, one of the greatest houses in the city, as befits the ruler of France. It stands beside the king's palace of the Louvre, looking south over the river, like a building in marchpane, all turrets and roofs and towers and balconies. I should have known that it would be a great house, having seen my lord's castle at Rouen; but when we ride up to the great gates I feel like a princess in a story being taken into a giant's fortress. A fortified wall runs all around, and there is a guard house at every gate, which reminds me, if I were in any danger of forgetting, that my husband may be the ruler but not everyone recognises him as the representative of the God-given king. The one that many prefer to call the King of France is not far away, at Chinon, eyeing our lands and stirring up trouble. The one that we call the King of France and England is safe in London, too poor to send my husband the money and troops he needs to keep these faithless lands in subjection, too weak to command his lords to come to fight under our standard.

My lord gives me several days of freedom to find my way around my new home, to discover the former duchess's jewel box, and her dressing room of furs and fine gowns, and then he comes to my room after Matins and says, 'Come, Jacquetta, I have work for you today.'

I follow him, trotting like a puppy at his heels, as he leads me through the gallery where tapestries of gods look down on us, to a double door at the end, two men at arms on either side, and his squire, Woodville, lounging on the windowsill. He jumps up when he sees us and gives me a low bow.

The men at arms swing open the doors and we go inside. I don't know what I am expecting; certainly not this. First there is a room as big as a great hall but looking like a library in a monastery. There are shelves of dark wood and on them are scrolls and books, locked away behind brass grilles. There are tall tables and high stools so that you can sit up at a desk and unfurl a scroll and read it at your leisure. There are tables made ready for study with pots of ink and sharpened quills and pages of paper ready for taking notes. I have never seen anything like it outside of an abbey, and I look up at my husband with new respect. He has spent a fortune here: each one of these books will have cost as much as the duchess's jewels.

'I have the finest collection of books and manuscripts outside the Church in Europe,' he says. 'And my own copyists.' He gestures to two young men, either side of a stand, one of whom is intoning strange words, reading from a scroll, while the other, painstakingly, writes. 'Translating from the Arabic,' my husband says. 'Arabic to Latin and from there to French or English. The Moors are the source of great knowledge, of all mathematics, all science. I buy the scrolls and I have them translated myself. This is how I have put us ahead in the search for knowledge. Because I have tapped the source.' He smiles, suddenly pleased with me. 'Just as I have with you. I have gone to the very source of the mysteries.'

In the centre of the room is a great table, painted and sculpted. I exclaim in delight, and step closer to examine it. It is enchanting, like a little country, if one could view it from above, flying high over it like an eagle. It is the country of France; I can see the outer wall of the city of Paris, and the Seine flowing through, painted bright blue. I can see the Ile de Paris, a little maze of buildings shaped like a boat itself, set in the river. Then I can see how the land is divided: the top half of France is painted white and red in the colours of England and the bottom half is left blank, and Armagnac flag shows Charles, the pretend king, in his lands at Chinon. A series of scratches shows where the little flags were stabbed, furiously, rapidly, in the plan marking the triumphant march of Joan of Arc, halfway across France, victorious all the way, and then up to the very walls of Paris, only two years ago.

'The whole of France is ours by right,' my husband says, looking jealously at the green lands that lead down to the Mediterranean sea. 'And we will have it. We will have it. I shall win it for God and King Harry.'

He leans forwards. 'Look, we are advancing,' he says, showing me the little flags of St George for England spreading over the east of France. 'And if the Duke of Burgundy will remain true, and a good ally, we can win back our lands in Maine. If the Dauphin is fool enough to attack the duke – and I think that he is – and if I can persuade the duke that we both fight at once ...' He breaks off as he sees I am looking upwards. 'Oh, those are my planets,' he says, as if he owns the night skies quite as much as he does France.

Suspended from criss-crossing wooden beams is a series of beautiful silver spheres, some of them ringed with silver haloes, some with other tiny balls floating nearby. It is such a pretty sight that I forget all about the map and the flags of campaigns and clasp my hands together. 'Oh, how pretty! What is this?'

Woodville the squire gives a little choke of laughter.

'It is not for amusement,' my husband says dourly. Then he nods at one of the clerks. 'Oh well – show the duchess the skies at her birth.'

The young man steps forwards. 'Excuse me, Your Grace, when were you born?'

I flush. Like almost all girls I don't know the date of my birth: my parents did not trouble to record the day and the time. I only know the year and the season, and I only know the season because my mother had a great desire for asparagus when she was carrying me and swears that she ate it too green and her belly-ache brought on my birth. 'Spring 1416,' I say. 'Perhaps May?'

He pulls out a scroll from the library and spreads it across the tall desk. He looks at it carefully, then reaches out and pulls one of the levers, then another, then another. To my absolute delight the balls, with their haloes, and the little balls spinning, descend from the rafters, and move gently around until they are positioned, swaying slightly, in the places in heaven that they held at the moment of my birth. There is a sweet tinkling noise, and I see that the spheres have tiny silver bells attached to the strings that move them, so they play as they take their places.

'I can predict where the planets will be before I start a battle,' my husband says. 'I only launch a campaign when they tell me the stars are propitious. But it takes hours to calculate on paper, and it is easy to make a mistake. Here we have built a mechanism as beautiful and as regular as God made when He put the stars in the sky and set them in motion. I have made a machine like the workings of God Himself.'

'Can you foretell with them? Can you know what will happen?'

He shakes his head. 'Not as I hope that you will do for us. I can tell when the time is ripe, but not the nature of the fruit. I can tell that our star is in the ascendant, but not the outcome of a particular battle. And we had no warning at all of the witch of Arc.'

The clerk tilts his head sadly. 'Satan hid her from us,' he says simply. 'There was no darkness, there was no comet, there was nothing to show her rising, and nothing marked her death, praise to God.'

My husband nods and puts his hand under my arm and leads me away from the table and past the clerk. 'My brother was a man of Mars,' he says. 'Heat and fire, heat and dryness: a man born to fight and win battles. His son is wet and cold, a man young in years but like a child in his heart, damp like a wet baby drinking milk and pissing in his clout. I have to wait for the stars to put some fire into his cause, I have to study for weapons to put into his hand. He is my nephew, I must guide him. I am his uncle, and he is my king; I have to make him victorious. It is my duty; it is my destiny. You will help me in this, too.'

Woodville waits for a moment, then, as my lord seems to have fallen into deep thought, he opens the door to the next room, pushes it wide, and stands back so we can go through. I step into the stone-floored room and my nose prickles at the strange scents. There is a tang like the smell of a forge – hot metal, but also something acidic and sharp. The air is acrid with a smoke that stings my eyes. In the centre of the room are four men, dressed in leather aprons, charcoal fires glowing before them in little braziers set into stone benches, vessels of bronze bubbling like sauce pots. Beyond them, through the open door that leads to an inner yard, I can see a lad stripped to the waist working the bellows of a furnace, heating a great chamber like a bread oven. I look across at Woodville. He gives me a reassuring nod as if to say, 'Don't be afraid.' But the smell of the room is sulphurous, and the furnace outside glows like the entrance to hell. I shrink back and my husband laughs at my pale face.

'Nothing to fear, I told you there would be nothing to fear. This is where they work on the recipes, this is where they try one elixir and then another. Out there we forge the metals and bring them in to be tested. This is where we are going to make silver, gold, to make life itself.'

'It's so hot,' I say weakly.

'These are the fires that make water turn to wine,' he explains. 'That make iron turn to gold, that make earth turn to life. Everything in this world is growing to a state of purity, of perfection. This is where we speed it up, this is where we make the changes to metals and to waters that the world itself does in its deep bowels, over centuries, with heat like hatching an egg into a chicken. We make it hotter, we make it faster. This is where we can test what we know, and see what we learn. This is the heart of my life's work.'

Outside in the yard someone pulls a red-hot bar of metal from the coals of the furnace, and starts to hammer it flat.

'Just think if I could make gold,' he says longingly. 'If I could take iron and purify it so that the common traces were burned from it, washed away, so that we had gold coin. I could hire soldiers, I could reinforce defences, I could feed Paris. If I had my own mint and my own gold mine I could take all of France for my nephew and keep it forever.'

'Is it possible?'

'We know it can be done,' he says. 'Indeed, it has been done, many, many times though always in secret. All metal is of the same nature, everything is made of the same thing: "first matter", they call it in the books, "dark matter". This is the stuff that the world is made of. We have to remake it, make it again. So we take dark matter, and we refine it, and refine it again. We make it transform into its purest and best nature.' He pauses, looking at my puzzled face. 'You know that they make wine with the juice that comes from grapes?'

I nod.

'Any French peasant can do that. First he takes the grapes, then he crushes them for their juice. He takes a fruit – a solid thing, growing on a vine – and makes it into a liquid. That's alchemy itself, making that change. Then he stores it and lets the life within it change that juice into wine. Another liquid but one with quite different properties from the juice. Now I can go further. I have done another change, right here. I can make an essence from wine that is a hundred times stronger than wine, which burns at the sight of a flame, which cures a man of melancholy and watery humours. It is a liquid but it is hot and dry. We call it aqua vitae – the water of life. All this I can do already, I can change juice to aqua vitae – the gold is just the next step, gold from iron.'

'And what am I to do?' I ask nervously.

'Nothing today,' he says. 'But perhaps tomorrow, or the next day, they will need you to come and pour some liquid from a flask, or stir a bowl, or sieve some dust. Nothing more than that, you could have done as much in your mother's dairy.'

I look at him blankly.

'It is your touch I want,' he says. 'The pure touch.'

One of the men, who has been watching a flask bubble and then overflow through a tube into a cooled dish set in a bath of ice, puts it to one side and comes towards us, wiping his hands on his apron and bowing to my husband.

'The Maid,' my husband says, gesturing to me as if I am as much an object as the fluid in the flask or the iron in the furnace. I flinch at being given Joan's name. 'As I promised. I have her. Melusina's daughter and a virgin untouched by any man.'

I put out my hand in greeting but the man recoils from me. He laughs at himself and says, smiling to my husband, 'I hardly dare to touch her. Indeed, I can not!'

Instead, he puts his hand behind his back and bows very low and says directly to me, 'You are welcome, Lady Bedford. Your presence here has been needed for a long time. We have waited for you. We have hoped that you would come. You will bring a harmony with you, you will bring the power of the moon and water with you, and your touch will make all things pure.'

I step awkwardly from one foot to the other, and glance at my husband. He is looking at me with a sort of hot approbation. 'I found her, and I recognised at once what she could be,' he says. 'What she could do. I knew that she could be Luna for us. She has water in her veins and her heart is pure. Who knows what she might not be able to do?'

'Can she scry?' the man asks eagerly.

'She says she has never tried, but she has already foreseen the future,' my husband replies. 'Shall we try her?'

'In the library.' The man leads the way back through the door. My husband snaps his fingers and the two scholars take themselves off into a side room, as the alchemist and Woodville the squire pull a cloth off the biggest looking glass I have ever seen, framed in a case, completely round, shining silver, like a full moon.

'Close the shutters,' my husband says. 'And light the candles.'

He is breathless, I can hear the excitement in his voice, and it makes me fearful. They ring me with candles so that I am encircled in fire and they put me before the big mirror. It is so bright I can hardly see for the winking bobbing flames around me.

'You ask her,' my husband says to the alchemist. 'Before God, I am so excited, I can't speak. But don't tax her overmuch, let's just see if she has a gift.'

'Look in the mirror,' the man commands me quietly. 'Let yourself look in the mirror and let yourself dream. Now, Maid, what can you see?'

I look at the mirror. Surely it is obvious what I can see? Myself, in a velvet gown cut in the very latest fashion with a horned headdress on my head, my golden hair captured in a thick net on each side of my face, and the most wonderful shoes of blue leather. I have never before seen a mirror that could show me myself, all of me, full size. I lift my gown a little so I can admire my shoes, and the alchemist makes a little dry cough as if to remind me to beware vanity. 'What can you see when you look deeply, Duchess?'

Behind me and to the side of me is a dazzle of candles so bright that they drain the colour from the gown, even from the blue shoes, even from the shelves and the books behind me that, as I look, grow darker and more misty.

'Look deep into the mirror and say what you can see,' the man urges again, his voice low. 'Tell us what you can see, Lady Bedford. What can you see?'

The light is overwhelming, it is too bright to see anything, I cannot even see my own face, dazzled by the hundreds of candles. And then I see her, as clearly as the day when we lazed by the moat, as brightly as when she was alive and laughing, before the moment when she drew the card of *le Pendu* in his suit as blue as my shoes.

'Joan,' I say quietly with deep sorrow. 'Oh, Joan. The Maid.'

I struggle to come back to wakefulness through the noise of the alchemist flapping at the candles to put them out. Some must have fallen over when I went down in a faint. Woodville the squire has me in his arms, holding up my head, and my husband is sprinkling cold water in my face.

'What did you see?' my lord demands as soon as my eyelids flutter open.

'I don't know.' For some reason, a sudden pang of fear warns me. I don't want to tell him. I don't want to say Joan's name to the man who had her burned alive.

'What did she say?' He glares at the squire and at the alchemist. 'As she went down? She said something. I heard something. What did she say?'

'Did she say "the Maid"?' the alchemist asks. 'I think she did.'

They both look at Woodville.

'She said "it's made",' he lies easily.

'What could she mean?' The duke looks at me. 'What did you mean? What d'you mean, Jacquetta?'

'Would it be Your Grace's university at Caen?' Woodville asks. 'I think she said "Caen", and then she said "it's made".'

'I saw Your Grace's planned university at Caen,' I say, taking up the prompt. 'Completed. Beautiful. That's what I said: "it's made".'

He smiles, he is pleased. 'Well, that's a good vision,' he says, encouraged. 'That's a good glimpse of a safe and happy future. That's good news. And best of all, we see she can do it.'

He puts out his arm and helps me to my feet. 'So,' he says with a triumphant smile to the alchemist, 'I will bring her back tomorrow, after Mass, after she has broken her fast. Get a chair for her to sit on next time, and make the room ready for her. We will see what she can tell us. But she can do it, can't she?'

'Without a doubt,' agrees the alchemist. 'And I will have everything ready.'

He bows and goes back into the inner room, and Woodville picks up the rest of the candles and blows them out, and my lord straightens the mirror. I lean for a moment against an archway between one set of shelves and another, and my husband glances up and sees me.

'Stand there.' He gestures me to the centre of the arch, and watches as I obey him. I stand still, framed in the arch, wondering what he wants now. He is staring at me as if I were a picture or a tapestry myself, as if he sees me as an object, a new thing to be framed or translated or shelved. He narrows his eyes as if considering me as a vista, or a statue that he might have bought. 'I am so glad that I married you,' he says, and there is no affection in his voice at all but the satisfied tone of a man who has added something to his beautiful collection – and that at a good price. 'Whatever it costs me, with Burgundy, with whoever, I am so glad that I married you. You are my treasure.'

I glance nervously at Richard Woodville who has heard this speech of acquisition; but he is busy throwing the cloth over the looking glass, and quite deaf.

Every morning my lord escorts me to the library and they seat me before the mirror and light the candles all around me, and ask me to look into the brightness and tell them what I see. I find I go into a sort of daze, not quite asleep but almost dreaming, and sometimes I see extraordinary visions on the swimming silver surface of the mirror. I see a baby in a cradle, I see a ring shaped like a golden crown dangling from a dripping thread, and one morning I turn from the mirror crying out, for I see a battle, and behind it another battle, a long lane of battles and men dying, dying in mist, dying in snow, dying in a churchyard.

'Did you see the standards?' my husband demands as they press a glass of small ale into my hand. 'Drink. Did you see the standards? You said nothing clearly. Did you see where the battles were taking place? Could you tell the armies one from another?'

I shake my head.

'Could you see what town? Was it anywhere you recognise? Come and see if you can point out the town on the map. Do you think it is happening right now, or is it a vision from the future that will come?'

He drags me to the table where the little world of France is laid before me and I look, dazed, at the patchwork of ownership and roll of the hills. 'I don't know,' I say. 'There was a mist and an army forcing their way uphill. There was snow and it was red with blood. There was a queen with her horse at a forge and they were putting the horseshoes on backwards.'

He looks at me as if he would like to shake some sense out of me. 'This is no good to me, girl,' he says, his voice very low. 'I can get cursed in any Saturday market. I need to know what is going to happen this year. I need to know what is going to happen in France. I need names of towns and the numbers of rebels. I need to know in detail.'

Dumbly, I look back at him. His face is suffused with darkness in his frustration with me. 'I am saving a kingdom here,' he says. 'I need more than mist and snow. I did not marry you for you to tell me about queens with their horseshoes on back to front. What next? Mermaids in the bath?'

I shake my head. Truly, I know nothing.

'Jacquetta, I swear, you will be sorry if you defy me,' he says with quiet menace. 'This is too important for you to play the fool.'

'Perhaps we should not overtax her?' Woodville suggests, addressing the bookshelves. 'Perhaps every day is too much for her. She is only young and new to the work. Perhaps we should train her up to it, like a little eyas, a young falcon. Perhaps we should release her to ride and walk in the mornings, and only have her scry perhaps once a week?'

'Not if she has a warning!' the duke breaks out. 'Not if it is now! She cannot rest if we are in danger. If this battle in mist and this battle in snow is going to be fought this winter in France, we need to know now.'

'You know that the Dauphin has not the arms or the allies for it to be now.' Woodville turns to him. 'It cannot be a warning of now, it will be a fearful dream of the future. Her head is filled with fears of war, and we ourselves have frightened her. We have put the visions in her mind. But we need to clear her head, we need to give her some peace so that she can be a clean stream for us. You bought her' – he stumbles and corrects himself – 'You found her unspoiled. We must take care not to muddy the waters.'

'Once a month!' the alchemist suddenly remarks. 'As I said at the start, my lord, she should be speaking when her element is on the rise. On the eve of the new moon. She is a being of the moon and of water, she will see most clearly and speak most clearly when the moon is in the ascendant. She should work on those days, under a rising moon.'

'She could come in the evening, by moonlight.' My husband thinks aloud. 'That might help.' He looks critically at me, as I lean back in the chair, my hand on my throbbing forehead. 'You're right,' he says to Woodville. 'We have asked too much of her, too soon. Take her out riding, take her down by the river. And we set off for England next week, we can go by easy stages. She's pale, she needs to rest. Take her out this morning.' He smiles at me. 'I am not a hard task-master, Jacquetta, though there is much to be done and I am in a hurry to do it. You can have some time at your leisure. Go to the stables, you will see I have left a surprise for you there.'

I am so relieved to be out of the room that I don't remember to say 'thank you', and only when the door is closed behind us do I start to be curious.

'What does my lord have for me in the stables?' I ask Woodville as he follows, half a step behind me, down the circular stair from the gallery to the inner courtyard, and as we walk across the cobbles, past the armoury to the stable yard. Menservants carrying vegetables to the kitchens and butchers with great haunches of beef slung over their shoulders fall back before me and bow. The milkmaids coming in from the fields with buckets swinging from their yokes drop down in a curtsey so low that their pails clatter on the cobbles. I don't acknowledge them; now I hardly see them. I have been a duchess for only a few weeks and already I am accustomed to the exaggerated bows that precede me wherever I go, and the reverent murmur of my name as I walk past.

'What would be your greatest wish?' Woodville asks me. He at any rate does not serve me in awestruck silence. He has the confidence born of being at my husband's right hand since he was a boy. His father served the English King Henry V, and then my husband the duke, and now Woodville, raised in the duke's service, is the most trusted and most beloved of all the squires, commander of Calais, trusted with the keys to France.

'A new litter?' I ask. 'One with golden curtains and furs?'

'Perhaps. Would you really want that more than anything else?'

I pause. 'Does he have a horse for me? A new horse of my very own?'

He looks thoughtful. 'What colour horse would you like best?'

'A grey!' I say longingly. 'A beautiful dappled grey horse with a mane like white silk, and dark interesting eyes.'

'Interesting?' He chokes on his laughter. 'Interesting eyes?'

'You know what I mean, eyes that look as if the horse can understand you, as if she is thinking.'

He nods. 'I do know what you mean, actually.'

He gives me his arm to guide me round a cart laden with pikes; we are passing the armoury, and the weapons master is counting in a new delivery with a tally stick. Hundreds, thousands of pikes are being unloaded, the campaign season is starting again. No wonder my husband sits me before the scrying mirror every day to ask me where is the best place to mount our attack. We are at war, constantly at war, and none of us has ever lived in a country at peace.

We go through the archway to the stables and Woodville steps back to see my face as I scan the yard. Each of the horses of the household has a stall facing south so the mellow stone is warmed through the day. I see my husband's four great war horses, their heads nodding over the door. I see Woodville's strong horse for jousting and his other horses for hunting and riding messages, and then I see, smaller than any of them, with bright ears that flick one way and another, the perfectly shaped head of a grey horse, so bright in colour that she is almost like silver in the sunshine of the yard.

'Is that mine?' I whisper to Woodville. 'Is that for me?'

'That is yours,' he says almost reverently. 'As beautiful and as high-bred as her mistress.'

'A mare?'

'Of course.'

I go towards her, and her ears point to listen to my footsteps and my cooing voice as I come close. Woodville puts a crust of bread into my hand and I step up to her and take in the dark liquid eyes, the beautifully straight face, the silvery mane of the horse that I described, here before me, as if I had performed magic and wished her into being. I stretch out my hand and she sniffs, her nostrils wide, and then she lips the treat from my hand. I can smell her warm coat, her oaty breath, the comfortable scent of the barn behind her.

Woodville opens the stable door for me and without hesitation I step inside. She shifts a little to make room for me, and turns her head and sniffs at me, the pockets of my gown, my belt, my trailing sleeves, and then my shoulders, my neck and my face. And as she sniffs me, I turn to her, as if we are two animals coming together. Then slowly, gently, I reach out my hand and she droops her head for my caress.

Her neck is warm, her coat silky, the skin behind her ears is tender and soft, she allows me gently to pull the mane on her poll, to stroke her face, and then she raises her head and I touch her flared nostrils, the soft delicate skin of her muzzle, her warm muscled lips, and hold, in my cupped hand, the fat curve of her chin.

'Is it love?' Woodville asks quietly from the doorway. 'For it looks like love from here.'

'It is love,' I breathe.

'Your first love,' he confirms.

'My only love,' I whisper to her.

He laughs like an indulgent brother. 'Then you must compose a poem and come and sing to her like a woman troubadour, a trobairitz. But what is your fair lady's name?'

I look thoughtfully at her, as she moves quietly away from me and takes a mouthful of hay. The scent of the meadow comes from the crushed grasses. 'Mercury,' I say. 'I think I'll call her Mercury.'

He looks a little oddly at me. 'That's not such a good name. The alchemists are always talking of Mercury,' he says. 'A shape-shifter, a messenger from the gods, one of the three great ingredients of their work. Sometimes Mercury is helpful, sometimes not, a partner to Melusina, the water goddess who also changes her form. A messenger that you have to employ in the absence of any other; but not always reliable.'

I shrug my shoulders. 'I don't want more alchemy,' I insist. 'Not in the stable yard as well as everywhere else. I shall call her Merry but she and I will know her true name.'

'I will know too,' he says; but I have already turned my back on him to pull out wisps of hay to give to her.

'You don't matter,' I observe.

I ride my horse every morning, with an armed escort of ten men ahead of me and ten behind, and Woodville at my side. We go through the streets of Paris, looking away from the beggars starving in the gutters, and we ignore the people who stretch out imploring hands. There is terrible poverty in the city and the countryside is all but waste, the farmers cannot get their produce to market, and the crops are constantly trampled by one or other of the armies. The men run away from their villages and hide in the forests for fear of being recruited or hanged as traitors, so there is no-one but women to work the fields. The price of bread in the city is more than a man can earn, and besides, there is no work but soldiering and the English are late with their wages again. Woodville gives orders that we must ride at a hand-gallop through the streets, not just for fear of beggars but also for fear of disease. My predecessor, the Duchess Anne, died of a fever after visiting the hospital. Now my lord swears that I shall not so much as speak to a poor person, and Woodville rushes me through the streets and I don't draw breath until we are out of the city gates and going through what once were busy gardens, the fertile tilled land that lies between the city walls and the river. Only then does Woodville order the armed men to halt and dismount, and wait for us, while the two of us ride down to the river and take the tow path and listen to the water as if we were a couple riding in a countryside at peace.

We go companionably, side by side, and talk of nothing of any importance. He helps me with my riding, I have never ridden so fine a horse as Merry, and he shows me how to straighten up in the saddle, and gather her up so she curves her neck and stretches out her stride. He shows me how he rides a cavalry charge, bent low over the horse's neck, going ahead of me down the track and thundering back towards us, pulling up at the last moment so Merry sidles and dances on the spot. He teaches me how to jump, getting off his horse to drag little branches of wood across the deserted track, building them higher and higher as my confidence increases. He teaches me the exercises his father taught him in the lanes of England, riding exercises to improve balance and courage: sitting sideways like a girl riding pillion, lying backwards across the horse, with the saddle in the small of my back, while the horse jogs along, sitting up tall and stretching one arm then another up to the sky, crouching down low to touch my stirrups, anything which accustoms the horse to the idea that it must go on steadily and safely, whatever the rider does, whatever happens around it.

'More than once my horse has taken me to safety when I was hurt and didn't have a clue where we were going,' Richard says. 'And my father held the standard before Henry V of England, and so he rode at a gallop all the time, with only one hand on the reins. You will never ride in battle, but we might run into trouble here or in England, and it is good to know that Merry will carry you through anything.'

He dismounts and takes my stirrups and crosses them out of the way, in front of me. 'We'll do a mile at trot, without stirrups. To improve your balance.'

'How should we ride into trouble?' I ask as he gets back on his own horse.

He shrugs. 'There was a plan to ambush the duke only a few years ago as they came back to Paris and he and the Duchess Anne had to take to the forest tracks and ride round the enemy camp. And I hear that the roads in England are now as unsafe as those in France. There are robbers and highwaymen on every English road, and near the coast there are pirates who land and take captives and sell them into slavery.'

We start off at a walk. I seat myself more firmly in the saddle and Merry's ears go forwards. 'Why does the King of England not guard his coasts?'

'He's still a child and the country is ruled by his other uncle, Humphrey, the Duke of Gloucester. My lord and the Duke of Gloucester are the royal uncles, each regents of France and England, until the king takes his power.'

'When will he do that?'

'He should have done it by now, really,' Woodville says. 'He is twelve years old; a boy still, but old enough to rule with good advisors. And he has been crowned at Notre Dame in Paris, and in England, and he has a parliament and a council which have promised to obey him. But he is guided by his uncle the Duke of Gloucester, and all of his friends; and then his mind is changed by his other kinsman, Cardinal Beaufort, a very powerful and persuasive man. Between the two of them he is blown about one way to another, and he never sees our lord the Duke of Bedford, who can do no more than write to him and try to keep him to one path. They say that he does the bidding of the person who spoke to him last.

'But anyway, even if he were older, or firmer, there would be no money to pay for defences from the sea, and the English lords don't make the rule of law run through their lands as they should. Now we shall trot.'

He waits for me to squeeze my legs on Merry and she goes forwards into a trot with me sitting heavily, like a fat cavalry knight, deep in the saddle.

'That's good,' he says. 'Now go forwards to canter.'

'You said trot!'

'You're doing so well,' he says with a grin. I urge Merry on and she goes into her quick-paced canter. I am a little afraid without the stirrups to use as balance but he is right, I can sit in the saddle and grip with my legs as we go cantering down the tow path until he gives the hand-signal to slow, then pull up.

'Why do I have to learn this?' I ask breathlessly as he dismounts again to restore my stirrups.

'In case you lose your stirrups, or one breaks, or if we have to ride away some time, when we can get hold of horses but no saddles. It's good to be prepared for anything. Tomorrow we will practise riding bareback. I shall make you into a horsewoman. Already you could be trusted on a long ride.'

He swings back into his own saddle and we turn the horses' heads for home.

'And why don't the English lords make the rule of law run through the country?' I ask, returning to our conversation. 'In France there are two rules of law, two kings. But at least the lords are obedient to the king who rules in their part.'

'In England, they each make their own little lordship,' he says. 'They use the troubled times as a screen to serve themselves, to gain their own land, to make war on their neighbours. When the young king does decide to take his power, he will find he has to challenge the very people who should be his friends and advisors. He will need my lord duke at his side then.'

'Will we have to go to England and live there? Will I have to live in England?' I ask anxiously.

'It is home,' he says simply. 'And even at its worst, one acre of England is worth ten square miles of France.'

I look at him blankly. 'All you Englishmen are the same,' I tell him. 'You all think that you are divinely blessed by God for no better reason than you had the longbow at Agincourt.'

He laughs. 'We are,' he says. 'We think rightly. We are divinely blessed. And perhaps when we go to England there will be time for me to show you my home. And perhaps you will agree with me.'

I have a little thrill of pleasure, as if something wonderful were going to happen to me. 'Where is your home?' I ask.

'Grafton, Northamptonshire,' he says, and I can hear the love in his voice. 'Probably the most beautiful countryside, in what is the best country in all the world.'

We have one more attempt at scrying at the mirror before it is packed up to travel with us as we start on our journey to England. My lord is anxious for me to predict if it is safe for him to leave France. The Armagnac pretender has no money and no army and is badly advised by his court of favourites, but still my lord John is afraid that if he goes to England there will be no-one who can hold France against this man who claims he is king. I completely fail in my wifely duty to advise him, I see nothing. They sit me on a chair and I stare into the bright reflected candlelight until I am dizzy and – far from fainting – am in danger of falling asleep. For two hours my lord stands behind me and shakes my shoulder when he sees my head nod, until the alchemist says quietly, 'I don't think it is coming to her today, my lord,' and the duke turns and stalks out of the room without a word to me.

The alchemist helps me from the chair and Woodville blows out the candles and opens the shutters to let the smell of smoke out of the room. The small sickle of a new moon looks in on me and I dip a curtsey and turn over the coins in my little pocket and make a wish. The alchemist exchanges a look with Woodville as if they have spent all the evening with a peasant girl who curtseys to a new moon and wishes for a lover, but has no learning and has no vision and is a waste of everyone's time.

'Never mind,' Woodville says cheerfully, offering me his arm. 'We leave for England in the morning and they won't ask you to do this for another month.'

'Are they bringing the mirror with us?' I ask apprehensively.

'The mirror and some of the books; but the vessels and the oven and the forge stay here of course, they will continue with their work while we are away.'

'And do they discover anything?'

He nods. 'Oh yes, my lord has refined silver and gold to a purer level than any man has ever done before. He is working on new metals, new combinations for greater strength or greater suppleness. And of course, if he could make the stone itself . . .'

'The stone?'

'They call it the philosopher's stone, that turns metal to gold, water to the elixir vitae, that gives the owner eternal life.'

'Is there such a thing?' I ask.

He shrugs. 'There have been many reports of it, it is well-known in the old manuscripts that he has had translated here. Throughout Christendom and in the East there will be hundreds, perhaps thousands of men working on it right now. But my lord duke is in the vanguard. If he could find it, if you could help him to find it, we could bring peace to France and to England.'

The noise of the castle packing up and readying for a great journey wakes me at dawn and I go to the chapel to hear Matins as the sun is rising. The priest finishes the service and starts to pack up the sacred pictures and the crucifix and the monstrance. We are taking almost everything with us.

In my own rooms my ladies in waiting are folding my gowns into great travelling chests and calling the pages to cord them up, and the grooms of the household to seal them. The jewel boxes they will carry themselves, my furs will be guarded by the grooms of the household. Nobody knows how long we will stay in England. Woodville becomes very cautious when I ask him. Clearly, my husband is not being adequately supported by his nephew the king, nor financed as he should be by the English parliament that has to raise taxes for the war in France. The purpose of the trip is to make them see that English coins buy French support; and they must pay. But nobody knows how long it will take to make the English understand that they cannot have an army for free.

I am quite at a loss in all the bustle. I have put my books that the Demoiselle left to me for safe-keeping with my husband's library, and they will be guarded by the scholars while we are away. I have put her beautiful cards with my jewels for safety. Her gold bracelet with the charms I carry in a purse slung around my neck. I don't want anyone else touching them. I have dressed for the journey and eaten my breakfast, served in my rooms, by maids in a hurry. I wait about, I don't know what to do to be helpful, and I am too important for anyone to give me a task. The head of my ladies in waiting commands everything in my rooms so I just have to wait for everything to be ready for us to leave, and in the meantime there is nothing for me to do but watch the servants and the ladies running from one task to another.

By midday we are ready to leave, though the grooms of the hall, the stable and the armoury are all still packing things up. My lord takes my hand and leads me down the stairs and through the great hall where the servants are lined up to bow and wish us God speed on our journey. Then we go out into the stable yard, where I blink at the cavalcade preparing to depart. It is like a small town on the move. There is the armed guard: we are travelling with hundreds of soldiers, some in armour but most in livery, and they are waiting beside their horses, taking a last drink of ale, flirting with the maids. There are nearly fifty wooden wagons waiting in order, the ones carrying the valuables at the head of the line, with a guard at the front and back, the boxes chained to the sides of the wagon, sealed with the great Bedford seal. The grooms of the household will ride with these and each has responsibility for his own load. We are taking all our clothes, jewels, and personal goods. We are taking all our household linen, cutlery, glassware, knives, spoons, salt-cellars, spice pots. The household furniture is being shipped too, my lord's groom of the bedchamber has ordered the careful dismantling of my lord's great bed with its covers, curtains and tester, and the grooms of my chambers are bringing my bed, my tables, my beautiful Turkey carpets, and there are two whole wagons just for shipping the household tapestries.

The kitchen servants have loaded their essentials onto a line of wagons; we are bringing food as well as hens, ducks, geese, sheep and a couple of cows that will walk behind the wagons to give us fresh milk every day. The hawks from the mews are loaded on their own specially made carriage, where they can perch, blinded by their hoods; and the leather curtains are already tied down to shelter them, so they are not frightened by the noise of the road. My lord's deerhounds will run alongside the procession, his foxhounds whipped in at the rear. The master of horse has all the work-horses harnessed to the wagons, and all the spare riding horses are bridled and in the care of a groom who rides one horse and leads one on either side. And this is only half the procession.

The wagons, carrying the essential goods to make us comfortable tonight when we stop at Senlis, have already gone; they left at dawn. And amid all this noise and chaos Richard Woodville comes smiling up the stairs, bows to my lord and to me and says, as if hell were not boiling over in the yard, 'I think we are ready, my lord, and what they have forgotten, they can always send on.'

'My horse?' the duke asks. Woodville snaps his fingers and a waiting groom brings my lord's great war horse forwards.

'And my lady is going in her litter?'

'Her Grace said she wanted to ride.'

My lord duke turns to me. 'It is a long way, Jacquetta, we will go north out of Paris and sleep tonight at Senlis. You will be in the saddle for the whole day.'

'I can do that,' I say, and I glance at Woodville.

'She's a strong horse, you chose well,' he says to my husband. 'And the duchess is a good rider, she will be able to keep up. It would probably be more pleasant for her than jolting around in her litter, though I will have it follow behind us, so if she gets tired she can change.'

'Very well then,' the duke agrees. He smiles at me. 'I shall enjoy your company. What d'you call your mare?'

'I call her Merry,' I say.

'God send that we are all merry,' he says, stepping on the mounting block to haul himself into the saddle. Woodville takes me by the waist and lifts me up into my saddle, and then stands back while my lady in waiting bustles forwards and pulls the long skirts of my gown so they fall down either side, hiding my leather riding boots.

'All right?' Woodville asks me quietly, standing close to the horse as he checks the tightness of the girth.

'Yes.'

'I'll be just behind you, if you want anything. If you get tired, or need to stop, just raise your hand. I'll be watching. We will ride for a couple of hours and then stop to eat.'

My husband stands up in his stirrups. He bellows '*À* Bedford!' and the whole stable yard shouts back '*À* Bedford!'. They swing the great gates open and my lord leads the way, out through the crowded streets of Paris, where people stare as we go by and cry out for alms or favours, and then through the great north gate, and out into the country towards the narrow seas and England, the unknown shore that I am supposed to call home.

My lord duke and I ride at the head of the procession so we are not troubled with dust, and once we are away from Paris my husband judges that we are safe enough to go before the armed guard so it is just him and me, Woodville and my lady in waiting riding out in the sunshine as if for pleasure. The road winds ahead of us, well travelled by English merchants and soldiers going through the English lands from the English capital of Paris to the English castle of Calais. We stop to dine at the edge of the forest of Chantilly where they have set up pretty tents and have cooked a haunch of venison. I am glad to rest for an hour in the shade of a tree; but I am happy to go on when Woodville orders the guard into the saddle again. When my husband asks me if I would like to complete the journey sitting in my litter drawn by the mules, I tell him no. The afternoon is sunny and warm, and when we enter the green shade of the forest of Chantilly we put our horses into a canter and my mare pulls a little and is eager to gallop. My husband laughs and says, 'Don't let her run off with you, Jacquetta.'

I laugh too as his big horse lengthens its great pace to draw neck and neck with Merry, and we go a little faster, and then suddenly, there is a crashing noise and a tree plunges down, all its branches breaking together like a scream, over the road in front of us, and Merry rears in terror and I hear my husband bellow like a trumpet, '*À* Bedford! 'Ware ambush!' but I am clinging to the mane and nearly out of the saddle, slipping backwards, as

Merry plunges to the side, terrified by the noise, and bolts, madly bolts. I haul myself into the saddle, cling to her neck, and bend low as she dashes among the trees, flinging herself to right and left, fleeing where her own frightened senses prompt her. I cannot steer her, I have dropped the reins, I certainly cannot stop her, I can barely cling on, until finally she slows to a trot, and then a walk, and then blows out and stops.

Shakily, I slip from the saddle and collapse to the ground. My jacket has been torn by low-hanging branches, my bonnet knocked from my head and is flapping on its cord, my hair is falling down, tangled with twigs. I give a little sob of fear and shock, and Merry turns to one side and nibbles at a shrub, pulling at it nervously, her ears flicking in all directions.

I take hold of her reins so she cannot dash away again, and I look around me. The forest is cool and dark, absolutely silent but for birdsong from high in the upper branches, and the buzz of insects. There is no noise of marching men, creaking wagons; nothing. I cannot even tell where I have come from, nor how far I am from the road. Merry's headlong flight seemed to last for a lifetime, but even if they were close at hand I would not know in which direction. Certainly, she didn't go straight, we twisted and turned through the trees and there is no path for me to retrace.

'Goddamn,' I say quietly to myself like an Englishman. 'Merry, we are completely lost.'

I know that Woodville will ride out to find me, and perhaps he can follow Merry's little hoof prints. But if the falling tree was an ambush then perhaps he and my husband are fighting for their lives, and nobody yet has had time to think about me. Even worse, if the fight is going against them, then perhaps they will be captured or killed and there will be no-one to search for me at all, and then I am in danger indeed: alone and lost in a hostile country. Either way, I had better save myself if I can.

I know that we were travelling north to Calais, and I can remember enough of the great plan in my husband's library to know that if I can get myself onto the north road again there will be many villages, churches, and religious houses where I can find hospitality and help. It is a road well travelled and I am certain to meet a party of English people and my title will command their assistance. But only if I can find the road. I look on the ground around us to see if I can trace Merry's hoof prints and follow them back the way we came, and there is one hoof print in the mud, and then another, a little gap where the leaves cover the ground, but beyond it, the trail picks up again. I take the reins over her head and hold them in my right hand, and say in a voice I try to make sound confident, 'Well, silly girl, we have to find our way home now,' and I walk back the way we came with her following behind me, her head bent, as if she is sorry for the trouble she has caused.

We walk for what seems like hours. The tracks give out after a little while, for the floor of the forest is so thick with leaves and twigs that there are no prints to follow. I guess at the way, and we go steadily, but I am more and more afraid that we are wandering lost, perhaps even going round in circles like enchanted knights in a fairy-tale forest. Thinking this, I am hardly surprised when I hear the sound of water and turn towards it and we come to a little stream and a pool. It is almost a fountain, so round and banked with green moss. I have a moment when I think perhaps Melusina will rise from the magical pool to help me, her daughter; but nothing happens so I tie Merry to a tree and wash my face and drink the water, and then I bring her to the stream and she drops her white head and sucks up the water quietly, and drinks deep.

The trees have made a little glade around the stream and a beam of sunlight comes through the thick canopy of leaves. Still holding Merry's reins, I sit down in the sunshine to rest for a few minutes. In a moment, I think, I will get up and we will put the sun on our left and walk steadily; that will take us north and must take us, surely, to the Paris road where they will, surely, be looking for me. I am so tired, and the sun is so warm, that I lean back against a tree trunk, and close my eyes. In minutes I am fast asleep.

The knight left his horse behind with his comrades, and followed her tracks on foot through the forest, a burning torch held before him, calling her name; calling her name over and over. The forest was unearthly at night; once he caught a glimpse of bright dark eyes and stepped back with an oath and then saw the pale rump of a deer slide away into the shadows. As the moon came up he thought he would see better without the torch, doused it on the ground in the thick leaf mould, and went on, straining his eyes in the silvery half-light. Bushes and trees loomed up at him, darker in the gloom, and without the yellow torchlight he felt he did not want to shout out loudly for her, but instead walked in silence, looking around him all the time, a fear gripping at his heart that he had failed to teach her how to ride, that he had failed to train the horse, that he had failed to tell her what to do in just these circumstances, that he had failed to predict that such a thing might happen: that he had utterly and comprehensively failed her.

At this thought, so awful to him since he had sworn privately that he would serve and protect her to death, he stopped still and put his hand to a tree trunk to support himself, and bowed his head in shame. She was his lady, he was her knight, and at this, the very first test, he had failed; and now she was somewhere lost in the darkness and he could not find her.

He raised his head, and what he saw made him blink his eyes, what he saw made him rub his eyes, to see without a doubt, without a shadow of a doubt, the glimmering white light of an enchantment, a chimera, and at the heart of it, gleaming, a little white horse, alone in the forest. But as it turned its head and he could see its profile, he saw the silvery horn of a unicorn. The white beast looked at him with its dark gaze, and then slowly walked away, glancing over its shoulder, walking slowly enough for him to follow. Entranced, he stepped quietly behind it, guided by the flickering silvery light, and seeing the little hoof prints that shone in the dead leaves with a white fire, and then faded as he walked by.

He had a sense that he should not try to catch the unicorn; he remembered that all the legends warned that it would turn on him, and attack him if he came too close. Only one being in this world can catch a unicorn, and he had seen the capture in half a dozen tapestries and in a dozen woodcuts in story books, since his youngest boyhood.

The little animal turned off the path and now he could hear the splashing sound of water as they came upon a clearing. He bit his tongue on an exclamation as he saw her, asleep like a nymph, as if she were growing in the wood herself, at the foot of the tree as if she were a bank of flowers, her green velvet dress outspread, her brown bonnet like a pillow under her golden hair, her face as peaceful in sleep as a blossom. He stood waiting, uncertain what he should do, and as he watched, the unicorn went forwards, lay down beside her and placed its long head with the silver horn gently in the lap of the sleeping maid, just as all the legends had always said that it would.

The sound of a footstep wakes me. I know at once that I am lost in the wood in danger and that I have foolishly slept. I wake in a panic, in darkness, and I jump up, and Merry, who has been sleeping, head bowed beside me, wheels around to stare, ears pricked, as the two of us see the figure of a man, a dark outline in the shifting twilight. 'Who's there?' I say, my hand clenching on my whip. 'Beware! I have a sword!'

'It's me: Woodville,' the squire says and steps closer so I can see him. He looks pale, as if he is as afraid as me. 'Are you all right, my lady?'

'My God, my God, Woodville! I am so pleased to see you!' I run forwards with my hands outstretched and he falls to his knees, takes my hands, and kisses them passionately.

'My lady,' he whispers. 'My lady. Thank God I find you safe! Are you unhurt?'

'Yes, yes, I was just resting, I fell asleep, I had been walking for so long, trying to find my way back to the road, but then I was so foolish – I sat down and I fell asleep . . . '

He stumbles to his feet. 'It's not far, I have been looking for you all evening, but it's not far.'

'Is it late now?'

'No more than eleven. We're all looking for you. The duke is mad with worry. I was trying to follow your tracks . . . but I would never have found you but for . . . '

'And is my lord duke safe? Was it an ambush?'

He shakes his head. 'Some fool of a peasant felling a tree brought down another across the road. No-one hurt; just bad luck that we were there at the time. We were all only afraid for you. Did you fall?'

'No, she ran off with me, but she didn't throw me. She's a good horse, she only ran because she was afraid and then she stopped.'

He hesitates. 'She led me to you,' he says. 'It is quite a miracle. I saw her in the woods and she brought me to you.'

I hold up the reins I had tied to my wrist. 'I didn't let her go.'

'You had her tethered?'

He gazes around the little clearing, at the silver moonlight on the water, at the shadowy darkness of the trees, as if he is looking for something.

'Yes, of course. But I took her saddle off as you showed me.'

'I saw her,' he says flatly. 'She was loose in the woods.'

'She has been here all the time. I held her reins.'

He shakes his head as if to clear his bewilderment. 'That was well done. I will put her saddle on her, and I can lead you to the road.' He picks up the beautifully worked saddle and slides it on Merry's back. He tightens the girth then he turns to lift me up. For a moment he hesitates, with his hands on my waist. It is as if our bodies have come together, almost without our volition: my head to his shoulder, his hands on my waist. It is as if we are drawn, one to another, like the planets on their wires in my lord's library. Slowly, I realise that I am filled with an emotion I have never felt before, slowly I realise that this is a longing. I turn my face up towards him, and his darkened eyes look down at me, his hands warm, his face almost puzzled as he feels the desire which is slowly pulsing in me. We stand like that together, for a long time. Then, without a word, he lifts me up into the saddle, brushes down my gown, hands me my hat, and leads Merry through the wood towards the road.

CASTLE OF CALAIS, FRANCE, JUNE 1433

We are housed once more in the great castle of the garrison town of Calais, Woodville is greeted as its captain but my lord says he cannot spare him from his side yet to take up residence. I am standing on the battlement at the top of the castle, looking anxiously up at the standard on the tower above my head, which cracks and ripples in the strengthening wind.

'Is it going to be rough?' I ask my husband.

He glances at me. 'You are not afraid? But water is your element.'

I bite my lip on a retort. Personally, I don't think that having a water goddess for an ancestress is a guarantee of freedom against sea-sickness, nor, come to that, shipwreck. 'I am a little afraid. The waves look very high, are they always that big? Do they always break so high on the harbour wall? I don't remember them being like that before.'

He glances out to sea as if to measure them for the first time. 'It's a little rough, perhaps. But we will leave on the next tide. It is too important for us to delay. I have to get to England. I am going to address the parliament, they have to realise that there must be funds released to pay for the campaign season in France. And I have to find some way to get my brother Humphrey to work with our uncle, Cardinal Beaufort. The young king . . .' He breaks off. 'Ah well, at any rate, we have to go and I don't think the journey will be too uncomfortable for you, and there should be no danger. Can you not calm the waters? It's Midsummer Eve; surely you should be able to do a little magic on this of all evenings?'

I try to smile at the weak joke. 'No, I wish that I could.'

He turns and goes into the inner rooms. I hear him shouting for his clerks, and to tell the captain that he must complete loading, for we will leave on the next tide, whatever the weather. Woodville comes up with a warm cape and puts it around my shoulders. 'My lord is worried by events in England. His brother Humphrey, Duke of Gloucester, does not give good advice, his nephew the king is young and inexperienced, and his uncle, Cardinal Beaufort, has his own plans for the kingdom. The two of them, the Duke of Gloucester and the cardinal, try to turn the young king each to their own way of thinking and he is torn between them.'

'Is it safe to sail?'

'Oh yes. It may be a little rough, but I shall see you are comfortable in your cabin, my lady. And Merry safe in her stall. We will sail through the night and in the morning you will wake up in your new country. And my lord will take you to see his new house.'

'Spenhurst?' I ask, trying the odd name in my mouth.

'Penshurst,' he corrects me. 'You will like it, I promise you, it is a most beautiful house in one of the loveliest parts of England, in Kent, which is famous for its apple orchards and fruit gardens. Near to London, but far enough distant that you will not be troubled by too many people. A jewel of a house for a diamond of a duchess.'

'And will we stay there all the time?' I let Woodville lead me from the roof of the tower into the warmth inside the castle. A fire burns in the centre of the round room and he sets a chair for me before it.

'I don't think my lord will be able to rest in the country,' he says. 'He will have to meet with the king and persuade him to give him men and arms to continue the campaigns in France. He will have to explain the campaign to parliament to get their support. He will have to deal with his brother, Duke Humphrey, and their uncle, Cardinal Beaufort. He has much to do.'

'And the king, Henry, will I see him? What is he like?'

He smiles. 'A very young man still, almost a boy, he is only twelve years old. You will have a state entry into London. The duke is a very great man in England as in France, and the young king will greet you.' He smiles again. 'I should think you will like him, he is a charming boy, and he ...' He gives a little laugh, almost as if he is embarrassed. 'I should think he will adore you. He will never have seen anyone quite like you. You will be the most beautiful woman in England as well as the greatest.'

WESTMINSTER PALACE, LONDON, SUMMER 1433

The young king is a disappointment to me. I have no experience of kings since my own county of Luxembourg is not a royal one, my father is a count, our overlords are the Dukes of Burgundy (though they are richer and more powerful than anyone in France) and the last French king, who was said to be most tragically mad, died when I was only a little girl, before I could see him. So I am counting on much from the English boy-king. I hope to see a youth who is the small mirror of his heroic father. After all, my husband's life is devoted to making this king safe in his lands in France. We are both sworn to his service. I am expecting a great being: something halfway between a boy and a god.

Not so. I first see him on our entry into London when we go through the City gates to the sound of singing choirs, and the cheering of the citizens. My husband is an old friend to the people of London, and I am a novelty they delight to see. The men bellow approval of my youth and looks and the women blow me kisses. The London merchants depend upon trade with the English lands in France and my husband is well known for holding the lands in the keeping of England. The merchants and their wives and their households turn out to greet us and show our standards from their overhanging windows. The Mayor of

London has prepared poems and pageants to greet us; in one tableau there is a beautiful mermaid who promises good health, fertility, and ever-flowing waters of happiness. My lord duke holds my hand and bows to the crowd and looks proud of me as they call my name and shout blessings on me.

'The Londoners love a pretty girl,' he says to me. 'I will have their favour forever while you keep your looks.'

The king's servants greet us at the gate of the palace at Westminster and lead us through a maze of courts and gardens, rooms with inner rooms, galleries and courtyards, until finally we come to the king's private rooms. One pair of double doors is flung open, another pair beyond them, then there is a room filled with people in the most beautiful clothes, and finally, like a tiny jack popping from a series of boxes, there is the young king, rising from his throne and coming forwards to greet his uncle.

He is slight and short – that is my first impression – and he is pale, pale like a scholar, though I know that they make him take exercise, ride daily, and even joust with a safety cushion on the top of his opponent's lance. I wonder if he is ill, for there is something about the transparency of his skin and the slow pace of his walk towards us that gives me a feeling of his weariness, and suddenly, I see to my horror that in this light, for a moment, he looks to me like a being made of glass, so thin and translucent that he looks as if he might break if he were to topple on a stone floor.

I give a little gasp and my husband glances down at me, distracted for a moment, and turns to the king his nephew and bows and embraces him in one movement. 'Oh! Take care!' I whisper as if he might crush him, and then Woodville steps smartly across and takes my right hand on his arm, as if he is bringing me forwards to be presented.

'What is it?' he demands urgently in a low whisper. 'Are you ill, my lady?'

My husband has both hands on the boy's shoulders, he is looking into the pale face, into the light-grey eyes. I can almost feel the weight of his grip, I feel that it is too much. 'He's so frail,' I whisper, then I find the true word: 'He is fragile, like a prince of ice, of glass.'

'Not now!' Woodville commands, and pinches my hand hard. I am so surprised at his tone and the sudden sharp pain that I flinch and look at him, and am returned to myself to see that the men and women of the court are all around us, staring at me and my lord and the king, and that Woodville is marching me forwards to make my curtsey, with such determined briskness that I know I must not say another word.

I sink down into a deep curtsey and the king raises me up with a light touch on my arms. He is respectful since I am his aunt, for all that I am only seventeen years old to his twelve: we are both young innocents in this court of hard-faced adults. He bids me welcome to England in a thin little voice that has not yet broken into a man's tone. He kisses my cheeks right and left; the touch of his lips is cold, like the brittle ice that I imagined when I first saw him, and his hands holding mine are thin, I can almost feel the bones of his fingers, like little icicles.

He bids us come in to dinner and turns and leads me in, at the head of all the court. A beautifully dressed woman steps back with a heavy tread, as if to make way for me, begrudgingly. I glance at the young king.

'My other aunt, Eleanor, Duchess of Gloucester,' he flutes in his little-boy treble. 'Wife of my much beloved uncle, Humphrey, Duke of Gloucester.'

I curtsey to her and she to me, and behind her I see the handsome face of my husband's brother the Duke of Gloucester. He and my husband embrace, arms on each other's shoulders, a great hug, but when my husband turns to his sister-in-law Eleanor I see that he looks sternly at her.

'I hope we shall all live merrily together,' the king says in his tentative piping voice. 'I think a family should be as one. A royal family should always be as one, don't you think? We should all love one another and live in harmony.'

'Of course,' I say, though if ever I saw rivalry and envy in a woman, I am seeing it now on the beautiful spoiled face of the Duchess of Gloucester. She is wearing a towering headdress that makes her seem like a giantess, the tallest woman in the court. She is wearing a gown of deep blue trimmed with ermine: the most prestigious fur in the world. Around her neck are blue sapphires and her eyes are bluer than they are. She smiles at me and her white teeth are bared but there is no warmth in her face.

The king seats me on his right-hand side and my lord duke to his left. Next to me comes the Duke of Gloucester, my husband's brother, and his wife goes the other side of my husband. We face the great dining room as if we were their tapestry, their entertainment: bright with the colours of our gowns and capes, sparkling with jewels. They gaze up at us as if we were a masque for their education. We look down at them as the gods might look down on mortals, and as the dishes go round the room we send out the best plates to our favourites as if to remind them that they eat at our behest.

After dinner there is dancing and the Duke of Gloucester is quick to lead me out into a dance. We take our part and then stand as the other couples dance their steps. 'You are so charming,' the duke says to me. 'They told me that John had married a heart-stealer, but I didn't believe it. How is it that I have served my country in France over and over and yet never saw you?'

I smile and say nothing. The true answer would be that while my husband was engaged in endless warfare to keep the English lands safe in France, this worthless brother of his ran away with the Countess of Hainault, Jacqueline, and took on a war all of his own to try to win her lands for himself. He wasted his fortune and might have lost his life there, if his vagrant fancy had not wandered to her lady in waiting, this Eleanor, and then he ran away with her. In short a man driven by his desires and not by duty. A man so unlike my husband that I can hardly believe they are both sons of King Henry IV of England.

'If I had seen you, I would never have come home to England,' he whispers as a turn in the dance puts us together.

I don't know what to reply to this, and I don't like how he looks at me.

'If I had seen you, I would never have left your side,' he says.

I glance over to my husband, but he is talking to the king and not looking at me.

'And would you have smiled on me?' my brother-in-law asks me. 'Would you smile on me now? Or are you afraid of stealing my heart from me even now?'

I don't smile, I look very grave and wonder that he should speak like this to me, his sister-in-law, with such assurance, as if he believes that I will not be able to resist him. There is something repellent and fascinating about the way that he takes me by the waist, which is part of the movement of the dance, and presses me close to him, his hand warm on my back, his thigh brushing against me, which is not.

'And does my brother please you as a husband?' he whispers, his breath warm on my bare neck. I lean slightly away but he tightens his grip and holds me close. 'Does he touch you as a young girl loves to be touched – gently, but quickly?' He laughs. 'Am I right, Jacquetta? Is that how you love to be touched? Gently, but quickly?'

I pull away from him, and there is a swirl of colour and music and Richard Woodville has my hand and has pulled me into the centre of the dancers and has me turning one way and then another. 'Forgive me!' he calls over his shoulder to the duke. 'I am quite mistaken, I have been too long in France; I thought this was the moment that we changed partners.'

'No, you are too soon, but no matter,' the duke says, taking Woodville's abruptly abandoned partner by her hand and forming the chain of the dance as Woodville and I take the little steps in the centre of the circle and then form an arch so everyone dances through, all the partners change again, and I move away, in the movement of the dance, away from the Duke Humphrey.

'What did you think of the king?' my husband asks me, coming to my bedroom that night. The sheets have been turned down for him, the pillows piled high. He gets in with a sigh of exhaustion, and I notice his lined face is grey with fatigue.

'Very young.'

He laughs shortly. 'You are yourself such an old married lady.'

'Young even for his age,' I say. 'And somehow, a little frail?' I don't tell my husband of the sense I had of a boy as fragile as glass, as cold as thin ice.

He frowns. 'I believe he is strong enough, though I agree, he is slight for his age. His father ...' He breaks off. 'Well, it means nothing now what his father was, or how he was as a boy. But God knows my brother Henry was a strong powerful boy. At any rate, this is no time for regrets, this boy will have to follow him. He will just have to grow into greatness. What did you make of my brother?'

I bite my tongue on my first response. 'I don't think I have ever met anyone like him in my life before,' I say honestly.

He laughs shortly. 'I hope he didn't speak to you in a way you did not like?'

'No, he was perfectly courteous.'

'He thinks he can have any woman in the world. He nearly ruined us in France when he courted Jacqueline of Hainault. It was the saving of my life when he seduced her lady in waiting, and ran off to England with her.'

'Was that the Duchess Eleanor?'

'It was. Dear God, what a scandal! Everyone said she had seduced him with love potions and witchcraft! And Jacqueline left all alone, declaring they were married, abandoned in Hainault! Typical of Humphrey, but thank God he left her, and came back to England where he can do no damage, or at any rate less damage.'

'And Eleanor?' I ask. 'His wife now?'

'She was his wife's lady in waiting, then his whore, now she is his wife, so who knows what she is in her heart?' my husband remarks. 'But she is no friend of mine. I am the oldest brother and so I am heir to the throne. If anything happens to King Henry (which God forbid) then I inherit the crowns of England and France. Humphrey comes after me, second to me. She looks at me sometimes as if she would wish me away. She will be praying that you don't have a son who would put her another step from the throne. Can you see with the Sight and tell me, does she cast spells? Is she skilled? Would she ill-wish me?'

I think of the woman with the dazzling sapphires and the dazzling smile and the hard eyes. 'I can see nothing for sure but pride and vanity and ambition.'

'That's bad enough,' my lord says cheerfully. 'She can always hire someone to do the actual spells. Should I have her watched, d'you think?'

I consider the brilliant woman and her handsome whispering husband. 'Yes,' I say, thinking that this is a court very far from my girlhood in the sunny castles of France. 'Yes, I think if I were you, I would have her watched. I would have them both watched.'

All the summer my lord speaks with one great man and then another, then when the seasonal fear of the plague recedes and the parliament returns to London, he meets with the men of the shires and the counties and begs them for funds to wage the war in France. He invokes the support of his uncle the cardinal, he prevails upon his brother to advise the young king. Slowly they realise the service he has done for his country and they tell him that they are so grateful that he can leave his office, retire from his work, abandon his regency in France and return to England, where we can live in his new beautiful house.

'He won't come,' Woodville predicts to me. We are riding in the green lanes around the fields of Penshurst, in Kent. We have been waiting for my lord to leave London and come to his new home for days. 'He won't come now, and he won't stay in England, even though they say he has earned his rest.'

'Is he so very tired? I have not seen him for weeks.'

He shakes his head in despair. 'I would say he was working himself to death. But he won't stop.'

'Why not? If they say that he can?'

'Because he would not leave men like your uncle Louis without his leadership in Paris. He would not leave France without its regent. He would not allow the Armagnacs to come to the peace meetings and make their demands without him there to answer them. A peace has to come; Burgundy is ready for it and probably talking with the Armagnacs behind our backs. The Armagnacs are exhausted and out of men and funds, and you see how my lord struggles to raise an army in England. We are all of us ready for peace, and my lord will see the peace talks through. He will get peace in France before he leaves his post.'

'So we will have to go back to Paris?' I am reluctant to go. I have been using this time in England like a clerk at his lessons. I have been studying English, I have been reading the books in my lord's library, I have employed a scholar to read the alchemy texts with me and explain them. I have been looking for a herbalist to teach me the skills. I don't want to leave all this and go back to the grand palace in the starving city.

'We will. But if you were free to choose, would you rather stay?'

I take a moment to answer; there is something in his voice that warns me that this is an important question. I look from the hedgerows where the red pebbles of the hips gleam among the fading leaves, to the distant hills of the downs, where the beech trees are turning bronze. 'It is a beautiful country,' I say. 'And, actually, I prefer London to Paris.'

He beams with pride. 'I knew you would,' he says triumphantly. 'I knew you would. You are an English duchess, you were born to be an Englishwoman. You should live in England.'

'It does feel very like home,' I concede. 'Even more than France, even more than Luxembourg. The countryside is so pretty and the hills so green. And Paris is so poor and the people so angry, I can't help but like it better here.'

'I said to my father that you were an Englishwoman in your heart.'

I smile. 'And what did your father say?'

'He said that so pretty a duchess should be kept in England where she can flourish.'

'Where does your father live?'

'He has a small manor at Grafton; our family has been there

for many years. He served the duke your husband, and the king before him. I think he will go to war again, and muster his own troop to support us when we go back to France.'

'Is Grafton like here?'

'Just as beautiful,' he says proudly. 'You know, I wish I could take you to Grafton. I so want to take you there. I wish you could see my home.'

Slowly, I glance sideways at him. 'I wish it too,' I say, and then we are both silent.

My lord stays in London and summons Richard to attend him; but every week or so the wagon comes with tapestries, furniture or books that he has bought for the new house. Waiting in the stable yard as they unpack one of these treasure wagons, I am surprised by a dainty woman, wearing the gown of a townswoman and a modest white cap, who is handed down from the back of the wagon and makes her curtsey to me.

'I am Mrs Jourdemayne,' she says. 'His Grace sent me to you with these as a gift.'

She nods her head and a lad jumps out of the wagon behind her with a wooden tray of tiny clay pots, each one holding a nodding head of a green plant. He sets the tray down at my feet and jumps back into the wagon to fetch another and another until I am surrounded by a little lawn of green and Mrs Jourdemayne laughs at my delighted face. 'He said you would be glad,' she observes. 'I am a gardener and a herbalist. He said that I should bring you these and he has paid me for a week's work. I am to stay with you and help you plant a garden of herbs, if you wish it.'

'I do wish it!' I say. 'There is a herb garden here by the kitchen but it is very overgrown, and I don't know what half the things are.'

'Tell the lad where to take the seedling trays and we will start whenever you want,' she says briskly.

I call my pageboy and he leads the way for the two of them while I go inside to fetch a broad hat to shield my face, and gloves for my first lesson as a gardener.

She is an odd gardener. She orders the Penshurst senior man to make twelve beds in the old kitchen garden, and while he is digging over the soil she lifts the little herbs, shows me their leaves and their flowers and tells me of their properties. Each new bed is to be named for a house of the planets.

'This was the comfrey bed,' Ralph says stubbornly. 'Where are we going to put the comfrey now?'

'In the Aquarius bed,' she says smoothly. 'Comfrey is a plant that flourishes under the water sign. And this bed here is going to be the place we grow the plants under the sign of Taurus.'

He puzzles over this all night, and in the morning he has a joke ready. 'What will you plant there? In the Taurus bed? Bull rushes? Bull rushes?' he asks, and doubles up at his own humour. That jest keeps him laughing all day, but Mrs Jourdemayne is not disturbed. She picks out seedlings from her tray of plants and puts them before me. 'Taurus is an earth sign,' she says. 'When the moon is in Taurus, it favours the growth of crops that live below the soil. Root crops like white and purple carrots, onions, and turnips. It favours the herbs of Taurus, like mint and primrose, tansy, wormwood and yarrow. We'll plant these in our Taurus bed.'

I am enchanted. 'You have all these?'

She smiles. 'We can plant some of them now, some of them will have to wait until the moon is in a different phase. But I have brought them all, in the green or in seed. Your lord commanded that you should have all the herbs of England in your garden. He said that you have a gift. Do you?'

I dip my head. 'I don't know. Sometimes I think I know things, sometimes I know nothing. I am studying his books and I shall be glad to learn how to grow herbs and how to use them. But I have no certainty; all that I learn just teaches me that I know nothing.'

She smiles. 'That is the very path of learning,' she says.

All afternoon we spend in the garden on our knees like peasant women, planting the herbs in the beds that she has prepared for them, and as the evening grows cool and the sun starts to set I get to my feet and look around the garden that we have made. Twelve regular beds fan out from the circular seat at the heart of the garden. All of them are dug over and weeded, some of them are already planted. Mrs Jourdemayne has labelled the seedlings with their name and their properties. 'Tomorrow I shall show you how to make tinctures and dry herbs,' she says. 'I will give you my recipes.'

I am so tired from our work that I sleep well; but in the night, as if the rising moon is calling to me as well as to the rising sap of the plants, I wake and see the cool light lying along my bedroom floor. My maid is heavily asleep in the bed beside me. I turn back the covers and go to the window. I can hear something, like the chiming of a bell, and I put a gown around my shoulders and push open my bedroom door, and then go out into the gallery.

In the shadows I can just see the outline of a woman: Mrs Jourdemayne. For a moment I step back, fearful of what she is doing in the darkness. She is standing beside one of the windows and she has thrown it open, the singing is louder as if the clear sweet noise is pouring into the gallery with the moonlight. As she hears my footstep she glances around, her face alert, as if she expects anyone, anything; but she fears nothing.

'Oh, it's you,' she says, though she should curtsey. 'Can you hear it?'

I nod. 'I hear it.'

'I've never heard such a thing before, I thought it was the music of the spheres.'

'I know it,' I say sadly. I reach forwards and I close the window, at once the music is muffled, and then I draw the heavy curtain to shut out both music and moonlight.

She puts out her hand to stop me. 'What is it?' she asks. 'Why do you shut it out? What does it mean?'

'It's nothing to do with you,' I say. 'It is for me. Let me close it out.'

'Why, what is it?'

'I have heard it twice in my life before,' I say, thinking of my little sister who died almost as she drew her first breath, and then the sighing choir that whispered goodbye to my great-aunt. 'I am afraid it is the death of one of my family,' I say quietly. 'It is the singing of Melusina,' and I turn from her and go down the darkened gallery to my bedroom.

In the morning she shows me how to dry herbs, how to make a tisane, how to make a tincture, and how to draw the essence from flowers using a bed of wax. We are alone in the still room, the pleasant smell of crushed leaves around us, the coolness of the stone floor beneath our feet, the marble sink filled with cold water.

'And does the singing tell you of a death?' she asks simply.

'Yes,' I say. 'I pray that my mother and father are well. This seems to be the only gift I have: foreknowledge of loss.'

'Hard,' she says shortly, and passes me a pestle and mortar with some seeds for crushing.

We work together in silence for a while, then she speaks. 'There are herbs especially for a young woman, newly married,' she observes as if to the leaves that she is washing in the sink. 'Herbs that can prevent a baby, herbs that can cause one. They are in my recipe book.'

'You can prevent a baby?' I ask.

'I can even stop one coming when a woman is already with child,' she says with a nasty little smile. 'Pennyroyal, mugwort, and parsley will do it. I have planted the herbs in your garden for you to use when you need. If you ever need.' She glances at the flatness of my belly. 'And if you want to make a baby you have those herbs too, to your hand. Raspberry leaves from your orchard, and weeds, easy enough to find: nettle leaves, and clover flowers from the field.'

I dust off my hands and pick up my slate and chalk. 'Tell me how to prepare them,' I say.

Margery stays for more than the week that she has promised and when she leaves, my herb garden is planted with everything but those plants which need to wait for the descending moon, and the still room already has a few jars of herbs in wine, and a few bunches of herbs hung up to dry. She will go back to London in one of my lord's wagons, her servant-boy with her, and I go to the stable yard to say goodbye. As I watch her clamber nimbly into the cart, a guard of half a dozen, with a messenger in my lord's livery of red and white, clatter into the yard and Richard Woodville swings down from his horse.

'My lady, I bring a message from my lord,' he says. 'He has marked it for you, only.'

I put out my hand, though I can feel my face is trembling and my eyes are filling with tears. I take the letter and break the seal but I cannot see what he has written for my sight is blurred. 'You read it,' I say, handing it to him. 'You tell me.'

'I am sure there is no cause for you to be distressed . . .' he starts, then he reads the few lines and looks at me aghast. 'I am sorry, Your Grace. I am so sorry. My lord writes to tell you that your father has died. There is plague in Luxembourg, but your mother is well. She sent the news to my lord.' He hesitates; he looks at me. 'You knew already?'

I nod. 'Well, I thought it was so. Though I closed the curtain on the moonlight and I tried not to hear the music.'

Mrs Jourdemayne, seated beside the wagoner, looks down at me with shrewd sympathy in her face. 'Sometimes you cannot help what you hear, you cannot help what you see,' she says. 'May the Lord who gave you the gift give you the courage to bear it.'

PARIS, FRANCE, DECEMBER 1434– JANUARY 1435

Woodville does not get his wish that I should see Grafton, though we stay in England for a year, and my lord never gets his wish for an adequate army to serve in France, nor – though he takes power and rules England – can he bring the king's council or parliament into proper order. We cannot stay in England for the city of Paris sends for my lord duke and says that the people there are besieged by robbers, mutinous soldiers and beggars, and starving for lack of supplies.

'He won't refuse them,' Woodville warns me. 'We will have to go back to Paris.'

The seas are rough for the crossing and when we arrive in Calais the garrison is so dispirited that my lord commands Woodville to stay there, raise their spirits, and prepare the soldiers for an attack on the French as soon as the weather allows. Then my lord and I prepare to press on down the muddy roads for Paris.

Woodville stands in the archway of the great gate to bid us farewell. He comes beside me and, without thinking, checks the tightness of the girth on my horse, as he always does. 'How shall I manage without you?' I ask.

His face is grim. 'I shall think of you,' he says. His voice is low and he does not meet my eyes. 'God knows, I shall think of you every day.'

He turns from me and goes to my lord duke. They clasp hands and then my lord leans down from his horse and hugs his squire. 'God bless, lad, hold this for me and come when I send for you.'

'Always,' Woodville says briefly, and then my lord raises his hand and we clatter out over the drawbridge and I realise I don't know when I will see him again, and that I have not said goodbye, nor thanked him for his care of me, nor told him – nor told him . . . I shake my head. There is nothing that the Duchess of Bedford should tell her husband's squire, and there is no reason for me to have tears blurring my sight of the flat road in the flat lands ahead.

This time we ride in the centre of the guard. The countryside is lawless and no-one knows whether a French troop might be riding through, destroying everything they find. We ride at a steady canter, my lord grim-faced, exhausted by the journey, bracing himself for trouble.

It is miserable in the city. We try to keep Christmas in the Hôtel de Bourbon but the cooks are in despair of getting good meat and vegetables. Every day messengers come in from the English lands in France reporting uprisings in distant villages where the people have sworn that they will not endure the rule of the English for another moment. It is little comfort that we hear also that the Armagnac king is also troubled with rebellions. In truth the whole land of France is sick of war and soldiers and is crying a plague on both our houses.

In the new year my lord duke tells me shortly that we are leaving Paris, and I know him well enough now not to question his plans when he looks so angry and so weary at the same time.

'Can you tell me if our luck will turn?' he asks sourly. 'Just that?'

I shake my head. In truth, I think he has bad luck at his heels and sorrow at his shoulder.

'You look like a widow,' he says sharply. 'Smile, Jacquetta.'

I smile at him and I don't say that sometimes I feel like a widow, too.

GISORS, FRANCE, FEBRUARY 1435

My lord sends for Woodville to escort us from Paris to Rouen. He tells me nothing, but I fear that he thinks that the city of Paris would not hold if we were to come under attack, and that we can only be safe in Rouen. He hopes to get there and negotiate for peace with the French court from the heartland of the English-held lands. Woodville comes with extra guards, his face grave, musters the guard in the stable yard, commands the order for greater safety, and helps my lord into the saddle for the first day of riding.

It is a cold damp ride and we break the journey at the well-fortified castle of Gisors, when I wake in the night hearing a terribly rasping noise. It is my husband, flailing in bed as if someone has him by the throat, choking and gasping for breath. I jump up and light a candle from the fire, he is tearing at his nightgown, he cannot breathe. I fling open the bedroom door and call for my maid and send her running for Woodville and for my lord's groom of the stool.

In moments my room is filled with men, and they have lifted my husband up in bed, and flung open the window to give him air. His physician comes with one of the tinctures from the alchemists, and my lord sips, catches his breath, and sips again.

'I am well, I am well,' he croaks, waving his hand at the household who are in the room, or gathered at the door. 'Go, go, all of you, to your beds, there is nothing wrong.' I see the doctor glance at Woodville as if they two know this is a reassuring lie, but Woodville ushers everyone from the room, telling only one man to wait at the door in case of need. Finally the doctor, my lord, Woodville and I are alone.

'I shall send for the physician from Paris,' Woodville says to my husband. 'Fear not, I will send for him now.'

'Yes,' he says heavily. 'There is a weight in my chest, a weight like lead. I can't breathe.'

'Do you think you could sleep?'

'If you raised me up in the bed; but I can't lie flat. I'm tired, Richard, I am as tired as a beaten dog.'

'I will sleep outside your door,' Woodville says. 'The duchess can call me if you wake.'

'She had better go to another room,' my husband says. 'This is no place for her.'

They all look at me as if I am a child who should be spared any distress. 'I shall stay with you,' I say. 'And in the morning I will get some lemon and parsley, and make you a drink that will restore your breath.'

My lord looks at me. 'You are my greatest treasure,' he says again. 'But go to your lady's room for this night. I don't want to wake you again.'

I wrap my night cloak around me and put some slippers on my feet. 'Call me if my lord is taken ill again,' I say to Woodville.

He bows. 'I will, my lady. And I will sleep on the pallet bed on the floor beside him, so I can watch over his sleep.'

I move to the door but my lord delays me with his hand raised. 'Stand there,' he says.

I stand as he bids me, before the open window, and the frosty air comes into the room. 'Put out the lights,' my lord says. The men snuff the candles and the moonlight shines a clear white light into the room, falling on my head and shoulders and illuminating the white of my nightgown. I see Woodville steal a glance at me, a longing glance, and then he quickly looks away.

'Melusina and the moon,' my lord says quietly.

'Jacquetta,' I remind him. 'I am Jacquetta.'

He closes his eyes, he is asleep.

Two days later he is a little better. They bring him news of the Calais garrison and he opens the letter and reads it in silence while we are seated at breakfast in the great hall. He looks around for Woodville.

'Trouble at Calais,' he says. 'You had better get back there, lick the men into order, then come back to me.'

'Are they under attack?' Sir Richard asks coolly, as if he were not being ordered to ride into unknown dangers.

'Their wages haven't been paid again,' my lord says. 'I'll give you a draft on my own treasury. Try to satisfy them. I will write to England for funds.'

Woodville does not look at me at all. 'Will you be able to continue on to Rouen?' he asks.

'I'll manage,' my lord says.

'I will help him,' I say. It is as if I have not spoken. Neither man pays me any attention.

'Go then,' my lord says shortly.

Woodville grips my lord's hand as if he would hold him, and then turns to me for the briefest of moments. I notice once more how very blue his eyes are, and then he has bowed and gone away. He hardly said goodbye.

We go on by gentle stages to Rouen. My lord is not well enough to ride, he travels in a litter and his big war horse is led beside it. It goes uneasily, unhappy with an empty saddle, its head drooping as if it fears the loss of its master. My lord lies in the grand litter that he commissioned for me, drawn by white mules, but he can get no rest in the jolting of the long journey. It is like watching a great plough horse coming wearily to the end of a field, at the end of a long day. My lord is drained of energy and, looking at him, I can almost feel his deathly fatigue in my own young bones.

ROUEN, FRANCE, SEPTEMBER 1435

All through the long summer at Rouen my lord summons his lawyer, and the councillors who have served him, and helped him to rule France for the thirteen hard years of his regency. Each day the envoys come and go from the peace conference that they are holding at Arras, each day my lord has them come to him and tell him of the progress they have made. He offers the young King of England in marriage to a French princess to resolve the conflict over the crown of France, he offers to leave the whole of the south of France under the rule of the Armagnacs; he cannot yield more. But they demand that the English leave all of France, deny our right to the throne – as if we have not spent nearly a hundred years fighting for it! Each day my lord suggests new concessions, or a new way of writing the treaty, and each day his messengers take the high road to Arras as he watches the sunset through the windows of the castle at Rouen. Then one evening I see the messenger gallop from our stable yard and take the road to Calais. My lord has sent for Richard Woodville, and then he sends for me.

His lawyer brings his will to him, and he commands that they make alterations. His entailed property will go to his male heir, his nephew, the young King of England. He smiles ruefully. 'I don't doubt he needs it badly,' he says. 'There is not a penny left in the royal treasury. And I don't doubt he will waste it. He will give it away too readily, he is a generous boy. But it is his by rights, and his council will advise him. God help him between the advice of my brother and my uncle.' To me he leaves my dower share: a third of his fortune.

'My lord . . .' I stammer.

'It is yours, you have been my wife, you have served me as a good wife, you deserve no less. Everything will be yours, while you carry my name.'

'I did not expect . . .'

'No, nor I. Truly, I did not expect to be making my will so soon. But it is your right and my wish that you should have your share. But more than this, I will leave you my books, Jacquetta, my beautiful books. They will be yours now.'

These are treasures indeed. I kneel at his bedside, and put my cheek to his cold hand. 'Thank you. You know I will study them and keep them safe.'

He nods. 'In the books, Jacquetta, in one of them, somewhere is the answer that all men seek. The recipe for eternal life, for the pure water, for the gold that comes from soot, from dark matter. Perhaps you will read and find it when I am long gone.'

There are tears in my eyes. 'Don't say it, my lord.'

'Go away now, child, I need to sign this and then sleep.'

I curtsey and slip from the room, and leave him with the lawyers.

He does not allow me to come to him till the afternoon of the next day and even in that short time I see that he has lost a little more ground. His dark eyes are duller, the great beak of his nose seems bigger in his thinner face; I can see he is failing.

He sits in his great chair, a chair as big as a throne, facing the window so that he can see the road to Arras, where the peace talks are still bickering on. The evening sunlight shines in the window making everything glow. I think this may be his last evening; that he may be setting with the sun.

'This is where I first saw you, in this very castle, d'you remember?' he asks, watching the sun go down into clouds of gold, and a pale ghost of a moon rise in the sky. 'We were in this castle, in the entry-hall of this very castle, for the trial of the Maid?'

'I remember.' I remember only too well, but I have never reproached him with the death of Joan, though I do reproach myself for not speaking out for her.

'Odd that I should be here to burn one Maid, and then find another,' he says. 'I burned her as a witch, but I wanted you for your skills. Odd, that. I wanted you the moment I saw you. Not as a wife, for I was married to Anne then. I wanted you as a treasure. I believed you had the Sight, I knew you were descended from Melusina, I thought you might bring the Stone to me.'

'I am sorry,' I say. 'I am sorry I was not more skilled . . .'

'Oh . . .' He makes a dismissive gesture with his hand. 'It was not to be. Perhaps if we had more time . . . but you did see a crown, didn't you? And a battle? And a queen with horseshoes on backwards? The victory of my house, and the inheritance of my nephew and his line going on forever?'

'Yes,' I say to reassure him, though none of this was ever clear to me. 'I saw your nephew on the throne, and I am sure that he will hold France. It won't be him who loses Calais.'

'You are sure of that?'

At least I can promise him this. 'I am sure it won't be him who loses Calais.'

He nods, and sits in silence for a moment. Then he says very quietly, 'Jacquetta, would you take off your gown?'

I am so surprised that I flinch a little and step back. 'My gown?'

'Yes, and your linen, everything.'

I feel myself glow with embarrassment. 'You want to see me naked?'

He nods.

'Now?'

'Yes.'

'I mean in this daylight?'

'In the sunset, yes.'

I have no choice. 'If you command it, my lord.' I rise up from my chair and I untie the lacing on my top gown and let it drop to my feet. I step out of it, and shyly put it to one side. I take off my ornate headdress and shake the plaits out of my hair. My hair falls over my face as a sort of veil to shield me, and then I slip off my linen petticoats and the fine under-petticoat of silk, and I stand before him, naked.

'Raise your hands,' he commands. His voice is calm, he is looking at me without desire but with a sort of thoughtful pleasure. I realise that I have seen him look at pictures, at tapestries, at statues like this. I am, at this moment, what I have always been to him: an object of beauty. He has never loved me as a woman.

Obediently, I raise my hands over my head, like a swimmer about to dive into deep water. The tears in my eyes are now running down my cheeks at the thought that I have been his wife and his bedfellow, his companion and his duchess, and even now, though he is near to death, still he does not love me. He has never loved me. He never will love me. He gestures that I should turn a little to one side so the last rays of golden sunlight shall fall on my bare skin, turning my flanks and belly and breasts to gold too.

'A girl of flame,' he says quietly. 'A golden maid. I am glad to have seen such a thing before I died.'

I stand obediently still, though I can feel sobs shaking my slight body. At this moment of his death he sees me as an object transmuted into gold; he does not see me, he does not love me, he does not even want me for myself. His eyes go over every inch of me, thoughtfully, dreamily; but he does not notice my tears, and when I get dressed again, I wipe them away in silence.

'I'll rest now,' he says. 'I am glad to have seen such a thing. Tell them to get me into bed, and I will sleep.'

His servants come in, they make him comfortable in his bed, and then I kiss his forehead and leave him for the night. As it happens, that is the last time I see him, for he dies in his sleep that night, and so that was the last he saw of me: not a loving wife but a statue gilded by the setting sun.

They call me at about seven in the morning and I go to his room and see him, almost as I left him. He seems peacefully asleep, only the slow low tolling of the single bell in the tower of Rouen cathedral tells the household and the city that the great Lord John is dead. Then the women come to wash and lay out his body, and the master of the household starts to make the plans for his lying-in at the cathedral, the joiner orders wood and starts to make his coffin, and only Richard Woodville thinks to draw me aside, stunned and silent as I am, from all the bustle and work, and takes me back to my own rooms.

He orders breakfast for me, and hands me over to the ladies of my chamber, telling them to see that I eat, and then rest. The sempstress and the tailors will come at once to measure us up for our mourning clothes, the shoemaker will come to make black slippers for me. The glovemaker will produce dozens of pairs of black gloves for me to distribute to my household. They will order black cloth to swathe the way to the cathedral, and black capes for the one hundred poor men who will be hired to follow the coffin. My lord will be buried in Rouen cathedral and there will be a procession of lords and a great service to bid him farewell, and everything must be done exactly as he would have wished it, with dignity, in the English style.

I spend the day writing to everyone to announce the death of my husband. I write to my mother to tell her that I am a widow like her: my lord has died. I write to the King of England, to the Duke of Burgundy, to the Holy Roman Emperor, to the other kings, to Yolande of Aragon. The rest of the time I pray; I attend every service of the day in our private chapel, and in the meantime the monks at the Rouen cathedral will watch and pray all the hours of the day and night over my husband's body, which is guarded with four knights at every point of the compass: a vigil which will only end with his funeral.

I wait in case God has some guidance for me, I wait on my knees in case I can come to some understanding that my husband has been called to his reward, that at last he has come to lands that he does not have to defend. But I hear and see nothing. Not even Melusina whispers a lament for him. I wonder if I have lost my Sight and that the brief glimpses I had in the mirror were the last views of another world that I will not see again.

In the evening, about the hour of sunset, Richard Woodville comes to my rooms and asks me will I dine in the great hall of the castle among the men and women of our household, or will I be served alone, in my rooms?

I hesitate.

'If you feel you can come to the hall it would cheer them to see you,' he says. 'There are many in deep grief for my lord, and they would like to see you among them, and of course your household will have to be broken up, and they would like to see you before they have to leave.'

'The household broken up?' I ask foolishly.

He nods. 'Of course, my lady. A new regent for France will be appointed by the English court, and you will be sent to the court at England, for them to arrange a new marriage for you.'

I look at him quite aghast. 'I cannot think of marrying again.'

I am not likely to find another husband who asks me for nothing more than that he can see me naked. Another husband is likely to be far more demanding, another husband will force himself on me, and another husband is almost certain to be wealthy and powerful and old. But the next old man will not let me study, he will not let me alone, he is certain to want a son and heir from me. He will buy me like a heifer to be put to the bull. I can squeal like a heifer in the meadow but he will mount me. 'Truly, I cannot bear to be married again!'

His smile is bitter. 'Both you and I will have to learn to serve a new master,' he says. 'Alas for us.'

I am silent, and then I say, 'I will go to the hall for dinner if you think everyone would like it?'

'They would,' he says. 'Can you walk in on your own?'

I nod. My ladies arrange themselves behind me and Richard walks before me to the double doors of the great hall. The noisy chatter behind the doors is quieter than usual: this is a house of mourning. The guards throw the doors open and I go in. At once, all the talk stops, and there is a sudden hush, then there is a rumble and a clatter as every man rises to his feet, pushing back benches and stools, and every man pulls off his hat and stands bareheaded as I go by, the hundreds and hundreds of them, showing respect to me as the duke's young widow, showing their love to him who has gone, and their sorrow at their loss and mine. I walk through them and I hear them whispering 'God bless you, my lady' in a low mutter as I go by, all the way to the dais at the top of the hall, and I stand behind the high table, alone.

'I thank you for your kind wishes,' I say to them, my voice ringing like a flute in the big-raftered hall. 'My lord duke is dead and we all feel the loss of him. You will all be paid your wages for another month and I will recommend you to the new regent of France as good and trustworthy servants. God bless my lord the duke, and God save the king.'

'God bless my lord the duke, and God save the king!'

'That was well done,' Woodville says to me as we walk back to my private rooms. 'Especially the wages. And you will be able to pay them. My lord was a good master, there is enough in the treasury to pay the wages and even some pensions for the older men. You yourself will be a very wealthy woman.'

I pause in a little window bay and look out over the darkened town. An oval three-quarter moon is rising, warm yellow in colour in the deep indigo sky. I should be planting herbs that need a waxing moon at Penshurst; but then I realise that I will never see Penshurst again. 'And what will happen to you?' I ask.

He shrugs. 'I will go back to Calais and then, when the new captain is appointed, I will go home to England. I will find a master that I can respect, offer him my service. Perhaps I will come back to France in an expedition, or if the king does make peace with the Armagnacs, then perhaps I will serve the king at the English court. Perhaps I will go to the Holy Land and become a crusader.'

'But I won't see you,' I say, as the thought suddenly strikes me. 'You won't be in my household. I don't even know where I will live, and you could go anywhere. We won't be together any more.' I look at him as the thought comes home to me. 'We won't see each other any more.'

'No,' he says. 'This will be where we part. Perhaps we will never see each other again.'

I gasp. The thought that I will never see him again is so momentous that I cannot grasp it. I give a shaky laugh. 'It doesn't seem possible. I see you every day, I am so accustomed . . . You are always here, I have walked with you, or ridden with you, or been with you, every day for – what – more than two years? – ever since my wedding day. I am used to you . . . ' I break off for fear of sounding weak. 'What I am really thinking is: who will look after Merry? Who will keep her safe?'

'Your new husband?' he suggests.

'I don't know, I can't imagine that. I can't imagine you not being here. And Merry . . . '

'What about Merry?'

'She doesn't like strange men,' I say foolishly. 'She only likes you.'

'My lady . . . '

I fall silent at the intensity of his tone. 'Yes?'

He takes my hand and tucks it under his elbow and walks me down the gallery. To any of my ladies, seated at the far end by the fire, it looks as if we are walking together, planning the next few days, as we have always walked together, as we have always talked together, constant companions: the duchess and her faithful knight. But this time he keeps his hand on mine and his fingers are burning as if he has a fever. This time his head is turned so close to me that if I looked up at him our lips would brush. I walk with my head averted. I must not look up at him so that our lips brush.

'I cannot know what the future will bring us,' he says in a rapid undertone. 'I cannot know where you will be given in marriage, nor what life might hold for me. But I can't let you go without telling you – without telling you at least once – that I love you.'

I snatch a breath at the words. 'Woodville . . .'

'I can offer you nothing, I am next to nothing, and you are the greatest lady in France. But I wanted you to know, I love you and I want you, and I have done since the day I first saw you.'

'I should . . .'

'I have to tell you, you have to know: I have loved you hon-ourably as a knight should do his lady, and I have loved you passionately as a man might a woman; and now, before I leave you, I want to tell you that I love you, I love you . . .' He breaks off and looks at me desperately. 'I had to tell you,' he repeats.

I feel as if I am becoming as golden and as warm as alchemy could make me. I can feel myself smiling, glowing at these words. At once I know that he is telling the truth, that he is in love with me, and at once I recognise the truth: that I am in love with him. And he has told me, he has said the words, I have captured his heart, he loves me, he loves me, dear God, he loves me. And God knows – though Richard does not – that I love him.

Without another word we turn into a little room at the end of the gallery and he closes the door behind us and takes me in his arms in one swift irresistible movement. I raise my head to him and he kisses me. My hands stroke from his cropped handsome head to his broad shoulders and I hold him to me, closer and still closer. I feel the muscle of his shoulders under his jerkin, the prickle of his short hair at the back of his neck.

'I want you,' he says in my ear. 'Not as a duchess, and not as a scryer. I want you just as a woman, as my woman.'

He drops his head and kisses my shoulder where the neck of

the gown leaves my shoulder bare for his touch. He kisses my collar bone, my neck, up to my jaw line. I bury my face in his hair, in the crook of his neck, and he gives a little groan of desire, and thrusts his fingers in my headdress, pulling the gold net off so that my hair comes tumbling down and he rubs his face in it.

'I want you as a woman, an ordinary woman,' he repeats breathlessly, pulling at the laces of my gown. 'I don't want the Sight, I don't want your ancestry. I don't know anything about alchemy or the mysteries or the water goddess. I am a man of the earth, of ordinary things, an Englishman. I don't want mysteries, I just want you, as an ordinary woman. I have to have you.'

'You would bring me down to earth,' I say slowly, raising my head.

He hesitates, looks down into my face. 'Not to diminish you,' he says. 'Never that. I want you to be whatever you are. But this is who I am. I don't know about the other world and I don't care about it. I don't care about saints or spirits or goddesses or the Stone. All I want is to lie with you, Jacquetta' – we both register this, his first ever use of my name – 'Jacquetta, I just desire you, as if you were an ordinary woman and I an ordinary man.'

'Yes,' I say. I can feel a sudden pulse of desire. 'Yes. I don't care about anything else.'

His mouth is on mine again, his hands are pulling at the neck of my gown, unfastening my belt. 'Lock the door,' I say as he shrugs out of his jerkin, and draws me towards him. The moment when he enters me I feel a searing pain which melts into a pleasure that I have never felt before, and so I don't care about the pain. But I do know, even as we move towards ecstasy, that it is a woman's pain and that I have become a woman of earth and fire, and I am no longer a girl of water and air.

'We have to prevent a child,' Woodville says to me. We have had a week of secret meetings and we are dizzy with desire and delight in each other. My lord's funeral has come and gone and I am waiting to hear from my mother as to what she will command me to do. We are beginning, only slowly, to see beyond the blindness of desire, and to wonder what the future will hold for us.

'I take herbs,' I say. 'After that first night I took some herbs. There will be no child. I have made sure of it.'

'I wish you could foresee what will become of us,' he says. 'For I really cannot let you go.'

'Hush,' I caution him. My women are nearby, sewing and talking among themselves, but they are accustomed to Richard Woodville coming to my rooms every day. There has been much to plan and arrange and Richard has always been in constant attendance.

'It's true,' he says, his voice lower. 'It is true, Jacquetta. I cannot let you go.'

'Then you will have to hold me,' I reply, smiling down at my work.

'The king will command that you go to England,' he says. 'I can't just kidnap you.'

I steal a quick glance at his frowning face. 'Really, you should just kidnap me,' I prompt.

'I'll think of something,' he swears.

That night I take the bracelet that my great-aunt gave me, the charm bracelet for foretelling the future. I take a charm shaped like a little ring, a wedding ring, and I take a charm shaped like a ship to represent my voyage to England, and I take a charm in the shape of the castle of St Pol, in case I am summoned back home. I think that I will tie each of them to a thread, put them in the deepest water of the River Seine, and see which thread comes to my hand after the moon has changed. I am about to start tying the threads on the little charms when I stop and laugh at myself. I am not going to do this. There is no need for me to do this.

I am a woman of earth now; not a girl of water. I am not a maid, I am a lover. I am not interested in foreseeing; I will make my own future, not predict it. I don't need a charm to tell me what I hope will happen. I throw the gold charm, which is like a wedding ring, up in the air and I catch it before it falls. This is my choice. I don't need magic to reveal my desire. The enchantment is already done, I am in love, I am sworn to a man of earth, I am not going to give this man up. All I have to do is consider how we can stay together.

I put the bracelet aside and draw a piece of paper to me and start to write to the King of England.

> *From the Dowager Duchess of Bedford to His Grace the King of England and France:*
>
> *Your Grace and dear nephew, I greet you well. As you know, my late lord has left me dower lands and funds in England and with your permission I will come home and set my affairs in order. My lord's master of horse, Sir Richard Woodville, will accompany me and my household. I await your royal permission.*

I put the charm bracelet away in the purse and return it to my jewel case. I don't need a spell to foresee the future; I am going to make it happen.

ENGLAND, SUMMER 1436

The English court is at its summer pursuit of hunting, travelling and flirtation. The young King of England starts and ends his day in prayer but rides out like a carefree boy for the rest of his day. Richard and I attend the young king as companions and friends, we hunt, dance, play at the summer sports, and join with the court. Nobody knows that every night Richard comes secretly to my room and the best part of the day, the only part of the day when we are alone together, begins.

My dower lands are transferred into my name, the bulk of my lord's great fortune has been paid to his nephew the king. Our house in Paris is gone, lost to the Armagnac king whose star has risen since the death of my lord. My lord's beloved house of Penshurst has gone to his brother Humphrey, Duke of Gloucester; and Eleanor Cobham, the lady in waiting who betrayed the trust of her mistress, now walks down the beautiful allées and admires the roses in the garden as if she were worthy. She will cut the herbs that I planted, she will hang them to dry in my still room, she will take my place in the hall. I resent the loss of nothing from my married life but this.

The two of them, the handsome duke and his beautiful wife, are burning up with pride, and this is their summer of glory. Now that my husband is dead the two of them are next in line to the throne, and every time the young king coughs at dinner, or mounts a horse that looks too strong for him, I see the duchess's head come up, like a hound hearing the horn. Their desire for the throne locks them in conflict with their uncle, Cardinal Beaufort, and the whole court mourns the loss of my husband who was the only man who could hold these rivals together. The young king is advised by the duke in the morning and by the cardinal in the afternoon, and by evening has no idea what he thinks about anything.

I am lulled like a fool by my happiness. I observe Eleanor Cobham but I bear her no malice. I include her in the dazed pity I feel for everyone who is not me, who is not loved by Richard Woodville. She does not sleep next to a man she loves, she does not know his touch as the early summer dawn turns the windows to pearl, she does not know the whisper in the cool morning, 'Oh, stay. Stay. Just once more.' I think nobody in the whole world knows what it is to be in love, to be so beloved. The summer days go by in a haze of desire. But the summer must come to an end. When September comes I will have been widowed for a year and the king's advisors will be considering a new marriage for me. They will want to employ me to bind a difficult English lord more closely to the throne, they will want to put my dower lands into the pocket of a favourite. Perhaps they will find a foreign prince who would take me as a wife to enforce an alliance. They will put me where it suits them and unless we awake and rise up from our enchantment then I predict that I will be married off by Christmas.

Richard is well aware of this danger, but he cannot think how we can prevent it. Richard says that he will go to the king and his council and tell them that he loves me and wants to marry me; but he cannot bring himself to do it, the disgrace would fall on me and I would be no longer a duchess but a commoner's wife, no longer the first lady in the kingdom but a woman of earth indeed. At best, the fortune that my husband left me would be confiscated, and we would be left with nothing. At the worst they could arrest Richard for assaulting one of the royal family, send me to a convent and then marry me off to a man commanded to control me, warning him that his wife is a whore and had better be taught submission.

As each dreamy warm summer day goes by, we know that we are closer to the moment when we will have to part, or face the danger of confessing. Richard torments himself with his fear that he will be the ruin of me; I am only afraid that he will leave me in a fit of self-sacrifice. He says I will be ruined if he declares his love, and he will be destroyed if he does not.

The wise woman, Margery Jourdemayne, visits the court, selling love potions, and telling fortunes, scrying and divining for lost things. Half of what she does is nonsense, but I have faith in her skills as a herbalist. I summon her to my rooms and she comes discreetly late, one evening, a hood drawn over her head, a scarf over her mouth. 'And what does the beautiful duchess want?' she asks me.

I can't help but giggle at the emphasis. 'What d'you call the other duchess?' I ask.

'I call her the royal duchess,' she says. 'And so I please you both. She prefers the thought of the crown to anything. All I can do for her is put her closer to the throne; but what can I do for you?'

I shake my head. I don't want to speculate about the succession, it is treason even to suggest that the young king is not strong and healthy; and he is both. 'I'll tell you what I want,' I say. 'I want a herbal drink to make a baby.'

She slides a sideways look at me. 'You want a baby though you have no husband?'

'It's not for me,' I lie quickly. 'It's for a friend.'

'And is the friend the same age and build as you?' she asks impertinently. 'I have to know, for the herbs.'

'You can make it as if you were making it for me, and give me the recipe.'

She nods. 'It will be ready tomorrow. You – your friend – should drink it every evening.'

I nod. 'Thank you. That will be all.'

She hesitates at the doorway. 'Any woman who dares to make her own destiny will always put herself in danger,' she remarks, almost at random. 'And you, of all people, might foresee this.'

I smile at her warning, and then on impulse I put out my hand to her and make the gesture, the circle drawn in the air with the forefinger: fortune's wheel. She understands, she smiles in reply and goes.

I wait a month, two months, then quietly, at midnight, at the end of summer, Richard lets himself into my room and I slip into his arms.

'I have news for you,' I say. I pour him a glass of the best wine from Gascony. There is a bubble of laughter inside me at the words. I could laugh aloud at my sudden sense of daring, at my joy, at the intensity of my happiness.

'Good news?' he asks.

'Good news,' I say. 'My love, I have to tell you; but now I come to it, I hardly know how to tell you – I am with child.'

The glass falls from his hands and cracks on the stone floor. He does not even turn his head to see the damage, he is deaf to the noise and oblivious to the cost. 'What?'

'I am with child,' I say steadily. 'A good month into my time.'

'What?'

'Actually, I think she will be a girl,' I say. 'I think she will be born early next summer.'

'What?' he says again.

The giggle in my heart threatens to burst out, his appalled expression does not frighten me. 'Beloved,' I say patiently. 'Be happy. I am carrying your child. Nothing in the world could make me more happy than I am tonight. This is the start of everything for me. I am a woman of earth at last, and I am fertile ground, and a seed is growing inside me.'

He drops his head into his hands. 'I have been your ruin,' he says. 'God forgive me. I will never forgive myself. I love you more than anything in the world and I have been the road to your ruin.'

'No,' I say. 'Don't speak of ruin. This is wonderful. This is the solution to everything. We will get married.'

'We will have to get married!' he exclaims. 'Or you will be shamed. But if we marry you are disgraced. God, what a trap I have put myself in, and what a trap I have put you in!'

'This is the way out of the trap,' I say. 'For nobody will make us deny our marriage if we have exchanged our vows and have a child on the way. The council, my mother, the king, everyone will have to accept it. And though they won't like it – they will come to bear it. They say that the king's own mother married Owen Tudor without permission . . .'

'And was disgraced! She slept with the keeper of her wardrobe and never came back to court. Her own son changed the law of the land to prevent a royal widow ever doing such a thing again! That law applies to you!'

'She survived,' I say steadily. 'And she has two handsome boys, half-brothers to the king. Richard, I cannot live without you. I cannot marry another man. We were driven by desire to become lovers, and now we are driven on to marry.'

'I don't want to be your ruin,' he says. 'God forgive me, though I desire you, I won't desire that. I despised Owen Tudor for conceiving a child on the queen he should have served, a man who ruined a woman he should have laid down his life to protect – and now I have been as selfish as him! I should leave right now. I should go on crusade. I should be hanged for treason.'

I take a long pause and then I raise my eyes and give him a look as limpid as a forest pool. 'Oh, have I been mistaken in you? Have I been long mistaken? Do you not love me? Don't you want to marry me? Shall you cast me aside?'

He drops to his knees. 'Before God, I love you and cherish you more than anything in the world. Of course I want to marry you. I love you heart and soul.'

'Then I accept,' I say gleefully. 'I shall be happy to be your wife.'

He shakes his head. 'I should be honoured to marry you, my love, you are far, far above my deserts – but I so fear for you.' The thought strikes him. 'And for our child!' Gently he puts his hand on my belly. 'My God, a child. I shall have to keep the two of you safe. I shall have two to care for now.'

'I shall be Jacquetta Woodville,' I say dreamily, turning the name over. 'Jacquetta Woodville. And she will be Elizabeth Woodville.'

'Elizabeth? You are sure it is a girl?'

'I am sure. She will be Elizabeth, the first of many children.'

'If they don't behead me for treason.'

'They won't behead you. I shall speak to the king, and I shall speak to Queen Catherine, his mother, if I have to. And we will be happy.'

When he leaves me that night, he is still torn between delight that we are to marry, and remorse that he has led me into trouble. I sit up at my window, my hand on my belly, and I look at the moon. Tonight there is a new moon, in the first quarter, a good moon for new beginnings, new hopes, and for the start of a new life. On a whim, I take out the cards that my great-aunt gave me, and I spread them out face down before me. My hand hovers over one card and then another, before I choose one. It is my favourite card of all: the Queen of Cups, the queen of water and of love, Melusina's own card, a card of insight and tenderness. A girl whose card this is will be a queen herself, a beloved queen.

'I shall marry your father,' I say to the little spark of life inside me. 'And I shall bring you into the world. I know you will be beautiful for your father is the most handsome man in

England, but I wonder what you will do with your life, and how far you will go when it all becomes clear to you – when you too see the man that you love, and know the life that you want.'

GRAFTON, NORTHAMPTONSHIRE, AUTUMN 1436

We wait till the court is on its slow way back to London, staying overnight at Northampton. Early one morning, before my ladies are stirring, I slip out of my rooms and meet Richard at the stables. He has Merry saddled and bridled, and his own war horse ready to go, and we ride down the little road to his home village of Grafton. A priest lives here alone, in his retreat, and there is a little chapel near to the manor house. Richard's father is waiting there, his face stern and anxious, and he has brought three witnesses. Richard goes to find the priest as his father steps forwards.

'I hope you know what you are doing, Your Grace,' he says bluntly, as he helps me down from my horse.

'I am marrying the finest man I have ever known.'

'It will cost you dear,' he warns.

'It would be worse to lose him.'

He nods as if he is not so sure, but he offers me his arm and he walks me into the chapel. At the eastern end there is a little stone altar, a cross and a candle burning. Before it stands the priest in the brown gown of the Franciscan order, and beside him, Richard, turning and smiling shyly at me as if we were before a crowd of hundreds and wearing cloth of gold.

I walk to the altar and just as I start to respond to the priest's gentle prompting of our vows the sun comes out, and shines through the circular stained-glass window above the altar. For a moment, I forget what I am to say. There is a veil of colours at our feet on the stone floor of the chapel and I think dizzily that I am here now, marrying the man that I love, and that one day I will stand here when my daughter marries the man of her choice, rainbows beneath her feet, and a crown before her. The sudden vision makes me hesitate, and Richard looks at me. 'If you have any doubts, a moment's doubt, we need not marry,' he says quickly. 'I will think of something, I will make you safe, my love.'

I smile up at him, the tears in my eyes making a rainbow around him too. 'I have no doubts.' I turn to the priest. 'Go on.'

He leads us through our vows and then declares us man and wife. Richard's father kisses my cheeks and gives his son a powerful hug. Richard turns and pays the three clerks he has hired as witnesses, and tells them that if he calls on them they must remember the day and the time and that we were truly married in the sight of God, and he puts his family ring on my finger, and gives me a purse of gold before them all, to prove that I am his wife, that he trusts me with his honour and his fortune.

'What now?' his father asks grimly as we come out of the chapel into the sunshine.

'Back to court,' Richard says. 'And when the moment serves us, we will have to tell the king.'

'He will forgive you,' his father predicts. 'He is a young man quick to forgive anything. It is his advisors that will cause your difficulties. They will call you a mountebank, my son. They will say you are pretending to a lady too far above you.'

Richard shrugs. 'They can say what they like as long as they leave her with her fortune and her reputation,' he says.

His father shakes his head as if he is not sure of that either, and then helps me onto my horse. 'Send for me if you need me,' he says gruffly. 'I am yours to command, Your Grace, and your honour is in my keeping too.'

'You can call me Jacquetta,' I say.

He pauses. 'I was your late husband's chamberlain,' he says. 'It is not right that I should call you by your given name.'

'You were his chamberlain, and I was his duchess, but now, God bless him, he has gone from us and the world is different, and I am your daughter-in-law,' I say. 'And at first they will say that Richard has leapt up, but then they will see that we are going to rise together.'

'How high?' he asks drily. 'The higher you rise, the greater the fall.'

'I don't know how high we will rise,' I say stoutly. 'And I have no fear of falling.'

He looks at me. 'You are ambitious to rise?'

'We are all on fortune's wheel,' I say. 'Without a doubt we will rise. We may fall. But still I have no fear of it.'

WESTMINSTER PALACE, LONDON, AUTUMN 1436

The baby is not yet showing through the graceful sweep of my gowns, though I know that she is growing. My breasts are bigger and tender to the touch, and more than anything else I have a sense of being in company, everywhere I go, even when I am asleep. I decide to take the news of the baby and the marriage to the king's council before the anniversary of my husband's death, before anyone proposes another marriage for me, and so forces me to defy them. I try to choose a good time, but the council is torn between Cardinal Beaufort and his ally the Earl of Suffolk William de la Pole, and their great rival Humphrey, Duke of Gloucester and his court. There is never a time when they are not fretting about safety in the country, and empty chests in the treasury. There is never a moment when they can agree what should be done. I wait for a week after our wedding and then I visit the great favourite William de la Pole in his rooms in Westminster Palace, in the quiet hour before dinner.

'I am honoured,' he says, putting a chair before his table for me. 'And what can I do for you, Your Grace?'

'I have to ask for your help in a matter of some delicacy,' I say. This is not easy, but I press on. 'A personal matter.'

'A personal matter for a beautiful duchess?' he says. 'I take it this is a matter of the heart?'

He makes it sound like a girl's folly. I retain my smile. 'Indeed,' I say. 'To be blunt, sir, I have married without permission and I am hoping that you will take the news to the king, and speak for me.'

There is a painful silence. Then he says, 'Married?'

'Yes.'

His gaze is sharp. 'And who have you married?'

'A gentleman . . .'

'Not a nobleman?'

'No. A gentleman.'

'And he is?'

'Richard Woodville, of my household.'

His gleam of amusement is instantly hidden as he drops his eyes to the papers on the table before him. I know he will be thinking how he can take advantage of my folly. 'And this is a love match, I take it?'

'Yes.'

'You were not prevailed upon nor forced? It was done legally with your consent? There are no grounds for an annulment or a denial? If he seduced you or even persuaded you, then he can be arrested and hanged.'

'There are no grounds for denial, and I want no grounds. This is the husband of my choice, this is a marriage I desired.'

'Desire?' he asks coldly, as if he has never felt it.

He forces me to be shameless. 'Desire,' I confirm.

'The gentleman is to be congratulated; there are many men who would have been glad of your desire. Any man would be glad of your consent. Indeed, the council has been considering your next husband. Several names were proposed.'

I hide a smile at this. There is almost no council but him, Cardinal Beaufort and the Duke of Gloucester. If names were proposed then it will be this man who was proposing them.

'The matter is already settled,' I say stoutly. 'And we are wedded and bedded, there is nothing that can be done. Whoever they have chosen for me is proposed too late. I am married to a good man. He has been very kind to me since the death of my lord John.'

'And I see you have been very kind to him,' he says with a little snigger. 'Exceptionally kind. Well, I will tell His Grace, the king, and you can ask him for forgiveness.'

I nod. It would help me if William de la Pole would recommend this to the king. The king is always given to the opinion of the last man who spoke to him, and the three councillors compete to be the last out of the door. 'Do you think he will be very angry?' The king is a boy of fifteen. It is ridiculous that I should fear his anger.

'No. But I am sure that his council will advise that you must be exiled from court, and they will fine you.'

I nod. 'But you could persuade them to be kind.'

'They will fine you heavily,' he warns. 'The king's treasury is short of money and they all know you have the Bedford fortune. And it is a serious offence to marry without the king's permission. They will say that you don't deserve the money.'

'I have only my dower,' I say. 'Most of the fortune has already gone to the king, and he has given it to his favourites.' I don't say, 'You among them,' but we know that is what I mean. 'My lord's brother, the Duke Humphrey, had the rest, I didn't keep Penshurst.'

'You have the dower of a royal duchess, but you have chosen to be the woman of a squire. I think you will find they will want your dower. You may find you have to live as the wife of a squire. I only hope that in a few years' time you still think you have made a good bargain.'

'I hope you will help me,' I say. 'I am counting on you.'

He just sighs.

He is right. One thousand pounds in gold they demand from us, and they order Richard to return to his post at Calais.

Richard is aghast. 'My God! A fortune! We will never raise it! It is the price of a house and an estate, it is greater than my father's entire fortune. Greater than any inheritance I could hope for. Greater than anything I could win. They mean to ruin us. They are forcing us to part.'

I nod. 'They are punishing us.'

'They are destroying us!'

'We can find the money,' I say. 'And we are banished from court, but we don't care, do we? We can go together to Calais?'

He shakes his head. 'I'm not taking you there. I'm not taking you into danger. The Earl of Suffolk has offered me a property where you can live. He has taken most of your wealth as a fine, and he is prepared to take the rest as a rent. He has said he will lease his manor at Grafton to us. It's not much of a favour since we cannot afford to pay him. But he knows I want it. It is near my home, I have had my eye on it since I was a boy.'

'I will sell my jewels,' I say. 'And books if we have to. I have lands that we can borrow on, some things that we can sell to raise the rent. This is the price of our life together.'

'I have reduced you to the position of a squire's wife with a nobleman's debt,' he says furiously. 'You should hate me. I have betrayed you.'

'How much do you love me?' I counter. I take his hands in mine and I hold them to my heart. I can feel him catch his breath at my touch. He pauses and looks at me.

'More than life itself, you know that.'

'If you had to put a price on it?'

'A king's ransom. A fortune.'

'Then consider, husband mine, that we have a bargain, for our marriage has cost us only a thousand pounds.'

His face lightens. 'Jacquetta, you are my joy. You are worth tens of thousands.'

'Then pack your things for we can leave court this afternoon,' I say.

'This afternoon? Do you want us to flee from disgrace?'

'I want us to be at your home tonight.'

He hesitates for a moment and then his smile breaks out, as he realises what I am saying. 'We will spend our first night together as a married couple? We will go to our bedroom as husband and wife? And tomorrow we will go to breakfast together openly? Ah, Jacquetta, this is the start of everything.' He bows his head and kisses my hands. 'I love you,' he says again. 'And please God, you will always think that you have a good bargain for our thousand pounds.'

I do think it a good bargain. We raise the money for the fine by borrowing against my dower lands, and then we borrow more to buy the manor house at Grafton from the Earl of Suffolk. For all his sly smiles he does not refuse to sell to the disgraced duchess and her squire. He wants our friendship so that we can be his allies in the country as he gains power at court. Richard goes to Calais and prepares the garrison for a siege as my kinsman, the faithless Duke of Burgundy, marches against his former allies. The great lords of England, the Earl of Mortmain and the Duke of York, turn out for their country and Richard holds Calais for them. Finally Humphrey, the Duke of Gloucester, sets sail for Calais and earns much credit for the saving of the town, though, as my husband points out, the siege was already defeated before the king's uncle came in with his standard flying.

I don't care. Richard's courage has been demonstrated to all of England and nobody can doubt his honour. He has come through a siege and several raids without a scratch and returns to England a hero. My first child, the daughter that I had foretold, is born without difficulty when the hedge is bobbing white with May and the blackbirds are singing in the dusk, that first spring in the country. The next year comes our son and heir.

We call him Lewis, and I find I am entranced to have a boy of my making. He has very fair hair, almost silvery, but his eyes are as dark as the sky at night. The midwife who helps me for this, my second time, tells me that all babies' eyes are blue and that both his hair colour and his eyes may change; but he seems to me a boy who is half-fairy with this angelic colouring. His little sister is still sleeping in the Woodville cherrywood crib and so at night I put them in together, side by side on their swaddling boards like pretty little dolls.

Richard says with satisfaction that I am a woman who has forgotten all about being a wife and a lover and that he is a miserably neglected man. He is joking though, and he revels in the beauty of our little daughter and in the growth and strength of our son. The next year I give birth to his sister, my Anne, and while I am confined with her, my father-in-law takes a fever and dies. It was a comfort to him that he lived long enough to learn that we had been forgiven by the king, and summoned back to court. Only with a daughter of just two, a boy of one year old and a new baby in the carved cradle, I am not very eager to go.

'We will never earn enough to pay our debts, living in the country,' my husband advises me. 'I have the fattest cows in Northamptonshire, and the best sheep, but I do swear, Jacquetta, we will live and die in debt. You have married a poor man and should be glad that I don't make you beg in your petticoat.'

I brandish the letter at him with the royal seal. 'No, for see, we are commanded to court for the Easter feast, and I have another letter here from the king's groom of the household asking if we have enough rooms for the king to stay with us on his summer progress.'

Richard all but blenches. 'Good God, no, we cannot house the court. And we certainly cannot feed the court. Is the groom of the household run mad? What sort of house do they think we have?'

'I will write and tell them we have nothing but a modest house, and when we go to court at Easter we must make sure they know it.'

'But won't you be glad to go to London?' he asks me. 'You can buy new clothes and shoes and all sorts of pretty things. Have you not missed the court and all of that world?'

I come around the table to stand behind his chair, lean over and put my cheek to his. 'I shall be glad to be at court again, for the king is the source of all wealth and all patronage and I have two pretty daughters who will one day need to marry well. You are too good a knight to spend your time raising cattle, the king could have no more loyal advisor and I know they will want you to go to Calais again. But no, I have been happy here with you, and we will only go for a little while and come home again, won't we? We won't be courtiers, spending all our time there?'

'We are the squire and his lady of Grafton,' my husband declares. 'Ruined by lust, up to our eyes in debt, and living in the country. This is where we belong, among rutting animals with no money. They are our peers. This is where we should be.'

LONDON, SUMMER 1441

I told the truth when I said that I was happy at Grafton but my
heart leaps with the most frivolous joy when the king sends the
royal barge to take us down the river, and I see the high towers
of Greenwich Castle and the new Bella Court that the Duke of
Gloucester has built. It is so pretty and so rich, I cannot help but
delight in coming to it as a favourite of the court and one of the
greatest ladies in the land once more. The barge sweeps along as
the drummers keep the oarsmen in time and then they shoulder
their oars and the liveried boatmen on the pier catch the ropes
and draw the barge alongside.

I am stepping down the drawbridge when I look up and see
that the royal party has been walking beside the river and is now
strolling to greet us. In front of them all is the king, a boy-king no
longer; he is a young man of nearly twenty, and he comes confidently forwards and kisses me, as a kinsman, on both cheeks, and
gives his hand to my husband. I see the company behind him
surprised at the warmth of his welcome, and then they have to
come forwards too. First the Duke Humphrey of Gloucester, my
former brother-in-law, whom my first husband said would bear
watching, and behind him comes the Duchess Eleanor. She
walks slowly towards the pier, a woman exulting in her own
beauty, and at first I see only the dazzle of vanity, but then I look
again. At her heels is a big black dog, a huge creature, a mastiff

or some sort of fighting dog. The moment I see it I could almost hiss, like a cat will hiss, setting its fur on end, and darkening its eyes. I am so distracted by the ugly dog that I let the duke take my hand and kiss my cheek and whisper in my ear, without hearing a word he says. As his lady, the Duchess Eleanor, comes close I find I am staring at her, and when she steps forwards to kiss me, I flinch from her touch as if she smells of the spittle of an old fighting dog. I have to force myself to step into her cold embrace, and smile as she smiles, without affection. Only when she releases me and I step back do I see that there is no black dog at her heels, and never was. I have had a flicker of a vision from the other world, and I know, with a hidden shudder, that one day there will be a black dog that runs up stone stairs in a cold castle and howls at her door.

As the months go on, I see that I am right to fear the duchess. She is everywhere at court, she is the first lady of the land, the queen in all but name. When the court is at Westminster Palace she lives in the queen's apartments and wears the royal jewels. In procession she is hard on the heels of the king. She treats him with a treacly intimacy, forever laying her hand on his arm and whispering in his ear. Only his radiant innocence saves them from the appearance of conspiracy, or worse. Inevitably, as a dowager duchess of England, I am constantly in her company, and I know she does not like it when people compare us. When we go into dinner I walk behind her, during the day I sit with her ladies, and she treats me with effortless disdain, for she believes I am a woman who wasted the currency of her youth and beauty by throwing it away for love.

'Can you imagine being a royal duchess and lowering yourself to marry a squire of your household?' I catch the hiss of her whisper to one of her ladies as I sew in her rooms. 'What woman would do such a thing?'

I look up. 'A woman who saw the finest of men, Your Grace,' I reply. 'And I have no regrets, and I have no doubts about my husband who returns love with love and loyalty with faithfulness.'

This is a hit at her, for as a mistress turned wife she is always fearfully on the lookout for another mistress who might try to repeat the trick she played on the countess who was her friend.

'It's not a choice I would make,' she says more mildly. 'Not a choice that a noblewoman, thinking of the good of her family, would ever make.'

I bow my head. 'I know it,' I remark. 'But I was not thinking of my family at the time. I was thinking of myself.'

On Midsummer Eve she makes an entry into London, accompanied by the lords and nobles of her special favour, as grand as if she were a visiting princess. As a lady of the court I follow in her train and so hear, as the procession winds through the streets, the less flattering remarks from the citizens of London. I have loved the Londoners since my own state entry into the City and I know them to be people easily charmed by a smile, and easily offended by any sign of vanity. The duchess's great train makes them laugh at her, though they doff their caps as she goes by and then hide their smiling faces with them. But once she has gone by, they raise a cheer for me. They like the fact that I married an Englishman for love, the women at the windows blow kisses at my husband who is famous for his good looks, and the men at the crossroads call out bawdy remarks to me, the pretty duchess, and say that if I like an Englishman so much I might try a Londoner if I fancy a change.

The citizens of London are not the only people to dislike Duchess Eleanor. Cardinal Beaufort is no great friend; and he is a dangerous man to have as an enemy. She does not care that she offends him; she is married to the heir to the throne and he can do nothing to change that. Indeed, I think she is courting trouble with him, wanting to force a challenge to decide once and for all who rules the king. The kingdom is dividing into those who favour the duke and those who favour the cardinal; matters are going to come to a head. In this triumphal progress into London the duchess is staking her claim.

The cardinal's reply comes swiftly. That very next night, when Richard and I are dining at her table in the King's Head in Cheap, her chamberlain comes in and whispers in her ear. I see her go pale, she looks at me as if she would say something, and then she waves away her dinner, rises to her feet without a word to anyone, and goes out. The rest of us look from one to another, her lady in waiting stands up to follow her and then hesitates. Richard, seated among the gentlemen, nods at me to stay seated, and quietly leaves the room. He is gone only a few moments and the shocked silence has turned into a buzz of speculation by the time he comes back in, smiles at each of my neighbours as if to excuse us, takes my hand and leads me from the room.

Outside he throws his cloak over my shoulders. 'We're going back to Westminster,' he says. 'We don't want to be seen with the duchess any more.'

'What's happened?' I ask, clutching at the laces of the cloak as he hurries me down the streets. We jump over the foul ditch in the centre of the lane and he helps me down the slippery stairs to the river. A waiting wherry boat comes to his whistle, and he helps me into the prow. 'Cast off,' he says over his shoulder. 'Westminster Stairs.'

'What is happening?' I whisper.

He leans towards me so that not even the boatman, pulling on his oars, can hear. 'The duchess's clerk and her chaplain have been arrested.'

'What for?'

'Conjuring, or astronomy, divining or something. I could only get a rumour, enough to tell me that I want you right out of this.'

'Me?'

'She's a reader of alchemy books, her husband employs physicians, she's said to have seduced him with love potions, she mixes with men of learning, scholarship and magic, and she's a royal duchess. Does this sound like anyone you know?'

'Me?' I shiver as the oars dip quietly in the cold waters and the boatman pulls towards the stairs.

'You,' Richard says quietly. 'Have you ever met Roger Bolingbroke, a scholar of Oxford? Serves in her household.'

I think for a moment. 'My lord knew him, didn't he? Didn't he come to Penshurst one time? Didn't he bring a shield chart and show my lord the art of geomancy?'

The boat nudges against the Westminster Palace stairs and my husband takes my hand and helps me up the wooden steps to the pier. A servant comes forwards with a torch and lights our way through the gardens to the river entrance.

'He's been arrested,' Richard says.

'What for?'

'I don't know. I'll leave you in our rooms, and then I'll go and see what I can find out.'

I pause under the archway of the entrance and I take his cold hands in mine. 'What do you fear?'

'Nothing yet,' he says unconvincingly, then he takes my arm and guides me into the palace.

Richard comes in at night and tells me that nobody seems to know what is happening. Three of the duchess's household have been arrested: men that I know, men that I greet daily. The scholar Roger Bolingbroke, who came to visit us at Penshurst, and the duchess's chaplain who has served the Mass before me a dozen times, and one of the canons at St Stephen's chapel in this very palace. They are accused of drawing up a horoscope chart for Eleanor. The chart has been found, and they say that it foretells the death of the young king and her inheritance of the throne.

'Ever seen a chart for the king?' my husband asks me tersely. 'He has left the palace for Sheen with nobody but the closest men of his council. We are ordered to stay here. We are all under suspicion, he hates this sort of thing, it terrifies him. His council will come here and there will be questions. They might call on us. My lord Bedford never showed you a chart for the king, did he?'

'You know he drew up charts for everyone,' I say quietly. 'You remember the machine that hung above the plan of France which showed the positions of stars? He used it to show the stars at someone's birth. He drew up a chart for me. He drew up his own. Probably one for you. Certainly, he will have drawn up a chart for the king.'

'And where are all the charts?' my husband asks tightly. 'Where are they now?'

'I gave them to the Duke of Gloucester.' Quietly the horror of this dawns on me. 'Oh, Richard! All the charts and the maps I gave to Duke Humphrey. He said he had an interest. I only kept the books, the ones we have at home. My lord left the books to me, the equipment and the machines I gave to the duke.' I can taste blood in my mouth and I realise that I have peeled the skin from my lip. I put my finger to where the raw skin is stinging. 'Are you thinking that the duchess might have taken the king's chart? Might she have used it? Will they link me to the charges since I gave her husband the king's chart?'

'Perhaps,' is all he says.

We wait. The summer sun burns down on the city and there are reports of plague in the poor areas, near the stinking river. It is unbearably hot. I want to go home to Grafton and my children, but the king has commanded that everyone must stay at court. No-one can leave London, it is like bringing a stewpot to the boil. As the hot air presses on the city like a lid on a cauldron, the king waits, trembling with distress, for his council to unravel the plot against him. He is a young man who cannot tolerate opposition, it strikes at his very sense of himself. He has been brought up by courtiers and flatterers, he cannot bear the thought that someone does not love him. To think that someone might use the dark arts against him fills him with a terror that he cannot admit. The people around him are afraid for him, and for themselves. Nobody knows what a scholar like Roger Bolingbroke could do if he was minded to cause harm. And if the duchess has put him in league with other skilled men, they may have forged a conspiracy against the king to do him deadly harm. What if even now some secret horror is working its way through his veins? What if he shatters like a glass or melts like wax?

The duchess appears at the high table in the Palace of Westminster, seated alone, her face bright and smiling, her air of confidence unshaken. In the airless hall, where the smell of the meat from the kitchens wafts in like a hot breath, she is cool and untroubled. Her husband is at the king's side in Sheen, trying to reassure the young man, trying to counter anything that his uncle the cardinal says, swearing that the young king is beloved, beloved of everyone, vowing on his life that he has never seen a horoscope for the king, his interest in alchemy is merely in the king's service, the herb bed at Penshurst was already planted under the signs of the stars when they got there. He does not know who planted it, perhaps the former owner? I sit with the ladies in the duchess's rooms, and sew shirts for the poor, and say nothing, not even when the duchess suddenly laughs at random and declares that she does not know why the king delays so long at Sheen Palace, surely he should come to London, and then we could all go on progress to the country, and get out of this heat.

'I believe he is coming tonight,' I volunteer.

She glances out of the window. 'He should have come earlier,' she says. 'Now he'll be caught in the rain. There's going to be such a storm!'

A scud of sudden rain makes the women cry out, the sky is black as a crow over London and there is a rumble of thunder. The window rattles in the rising wind and then it is flung open by a gust of icy wind. Someone screams as the frame bangs, and I rise up and go to the window, catch the flying latch and draw it shut. I flinch back from the crack of lightning over the city. A storm is rumbling in, over the king's route, and within moments there is the rattle of hail against the window, like someone flinging pebbles, and a woman turns her pale face to the duchess and cries, 'A storm over the king! You said that there would be a storm over the king.'

The duchess is hardly listening, she is watching me fighting with the wind at the window, and then the words – the accusation – sinks into her awareness and she looks at the woman – Elizabeth Flyte – and says, 'Oh, don't be so ridiculous. I was looking at the sky. Anyone could see there was going to be a storm.'

Elizabeth gets up from her stool, dips a curtsey and says, 'Excuse me, my lady . . .'

'Where are you going?'

'Excuse me, my lady . . .'

'You can't leave without permission,' the duchess says harshly. But the woman has tipped over her stool in her hurry to get to the door. Two other women rise too, uncertain whether to run or stay.

'Sit down! Sit down!' the duchess shrieks. 'I order it!'

Elizabeth tears open the door and flings herself out of the room, while the other women sink to their stools, and one quickly crosses herself. A flash of lightning suddenly makes the scene look bleak and cold. Eleanor the duchess turns to me, her face haggard and white. 'For God's sake, I just looked at the sky and saw that there was going to be a storm. There is no need for all this. I just saw the rain coming, that's all.'

'I know,' I say. 'I know that's all.'

Within half an hour the palace is barring its doors and windows and calling it a witch's wind that blows death down with rain.

Within a day the young king has announced that his aunt the duchess may not come into his presence. The Oxford scholar, the friend of my first husband who came to visit us at Penshurst, is questioned by the council and confesses to heresy and magic. They put him on show, like a bear to be baited. Poor Roger Bolingbroke, a scholar for all his life, a man of learning with a great love for the mysteries of the world and the stars, is put on a stage, like a scaffold, at St Paul's Cross in London, while a sermon is preached against him and against all witches and warlocks, necromancers and heretics who threaten the king's life and his peace, who crowd into his festering city, who seek to enter his ports, who hide themselves in the country villages and do acts of malice, small and great. It is declared that there are thousands of evil men and women, conjuring with black arts to harm the king: herbalists, wise women, liars, heretics, murderers. The king knows they are out there, plotting against him in their malevolent thousands. Now he believes he has found a plot at the heart of his court, at the heart of his dangerously ambitious family.

We all parade around Bolingbroke, circling him and staring at his shame as if he were an animal brought back from the coast of Africa, some new sort of beast. He keeps his eyes down so that he cannot see the avid faces, and need not recognise his former friends. The man who has spent his life in study, thinking about the harmonious nature of the world, sits on a painted chair wearing a paper crown, surrounded by his equipment and his books as if he were a Fool. They have his geomancy board laid on the ground before his feet, and a set of candles specially carved. They have some charts showing the positions of the planets, and the horoscope that they say he drew up for the duchess, at her request. They have a little model of the earth and the planets moving around it. They have brass moulds for casting figures, they have a still for making liquids, and the wax trays used for drawing the perfume of flowers. Worst of all, at his feet is a horrible little creature of wax, like a miscarried rabbit.

I shrink back when I see it, and Richard puts a strong arm around my waist. 'Don't look at it,' he advises me.

I look away. 'What was it?'

'It was a wax image of the king. It is supposed to have a little crown on its head and that golden thread is the sceptre and the little bead is the orb.'

The face is distorted, the feet are formless. I can see the outline of the cape and the dots to show the markings of ermine, but the head is almost melted away. 'What have they done to it?'

'They heated it before a fire so that it would melt and run away. It would make the king's strength flow from him too. They meant to destroy him as the image melted away.'

I shudder. 'Can't we go now?'

'No,' he says. 'We have to be here to show our revulsion at these crimes.'

'I am revolted. I am so revolted I want to go.'

'Keep your head up. Keep walking. You, of all people, have to be seen to be an enemy of this sort of work.'

'Me of all people?' I fire up. 'This is so disgusting it makes me sick.'

'They are saying that the Duchess Eleanor got her husband the duke to marry her with a love potion, so that he could not resist her. They are saying you did the same when you were a girl and my lord duke was a man broken-hearted at the loss of his wife Anne.'

I shudder, averting my eyes from the melted wax poppet. 'Richard . . .'

'I shall keep you safe,' he swears. 'You are my lady and my love. I shall keep you safe, Jacquetta. You will never look for me, and find me gone.'

We come back from the shaming of Bolingbroke to find the duchess's rooms are empty, the door thrown open to her privy chamber, her clothes chests overturned, her cupboards ransacked, her jewellery boxes missing, and the woman vanished.

'Where is the duchess?' my husband demands of her maid in waiting.

She shakes her head, she is crying unstoppably. 'Gone.'

'Gone where?'

'Gone,' is all she can say.

'God save us, the child is an idiot,' Richard snaps. 'You ask her.'

I take her by the shoulders. 'Ellie, tell me, did they arrest Her Grace?'

She dips a curtsey. 'She ran, Your Grace. She's run into sanctuary. She says they will kill her to punish her husband, she says they will destroy him through her. She says it is a wicked plot against him that is going to be the ruin of her. She says Cardinal Beaufort will tear them both down.'

I turn to my husband. 'Sanctuary?'

His face is grim. 'Yes, but she is mistaken. That won't save her.'

'They can't say she is a witch, if she is hiding on holy ground and claiming the safety of the Church.'

'Then they'll accuse her of being a heretic,' he says. 'A heretic can't be protected by the Church. So if she's claimed sanctuary they'll charge her with heresy; it's the only way to get her out. Before this they might have charged her with forecasting. Now they'll accuse her of heresy. And heresy is a worse crime than forecasting. She's put herself in a worse place.'

'The law of men always puts women in a bad place!' I flare up in anger.

Richard says nothing.

'Should we go away?' I ask him very quietly. 'Can we go home to Grafton?' I look around the wreckage of the room. 'I don't feel safe here. Can we go?'

He grimaces. 'We can't go now. It looks like guilt if we go, just as she looks as if she admits guilt by hiding in sanctuary. I think we are better off staying here. At least we can get a ship to Flanders from here, if we need to.'

'I can't leave the children!'

He pays no attention. 'I wish to God your father was still alive, you could have gone on a visit to him.' He squeezes my hand. 'You stay here. I shall go and see William de la Pole the Earl of Suffolk. He'll tell me what's going on in the council.'

'And what shall I do?'

'Wait here,' he says grimly. 'Open these rooms and treat them like your own. Behave as if nothing were wrong. You are the first lady of the kingdom now, the only royal duchess left. Order the ladies to tidy the place up and then have them sew with you, and get someone to read from the Bible. Go to chapel this evening. Parade your innocence.'

'But I am innocent,' I say.

His face is dark. 'I don't doubt that she will say the same.'

She does not say the same. They bring Roger Bolingbroke before her with the horoscope that she commanded he cast for her, with the magical instruments that were the tools of his trade as an explorer of the unknown realms, with the misshapen wax that they say is a melted image of the king, and she confesses to witchcraft and offences against the church. She admits that she has 'long used witchcraft with the Witch of Eye' and then they tell her that the Witch of Eye has been under arrest since the night of the witch's wind.

'Who is the Witch of Eye?' I ask Richard in a hushed whisper, late at night with the curtains of the bed drawn around us.

'Margery Jourdemayne,' he says, his brow knitted with worry. 'Some practising witch, who was taken up for her crimes once before now. Comes from the village of Eye. She is known to the Church as a witch, known to everyone as a witch.'

I gasp in horror.

He looks at me. 'For the love of God, tell me that you don't know her.'

'Not as a witch.'

He closes his eyes briefly in horror. 'What do you know of her?'

'I never did anything with her but study the use of herbs, as my lord commanded, I swear to you, and I would swear to the court. I never did anything with her but study the use of herbs, and she did nothing at Penshurst but plan the herb garden with me, and tell me when the herbs should be cut and when they should be sown. I didn't know she was a witch.'

'Did my lord command you to see her?'

'Yes, yes.'

'Do you have that under his seal? Did he write the order?'

I shake my head. 'He just sent her to me. And you saw her. That time in the stable yard when you came with the message from Luxembourg, and she was leaving with the wagon.'

Richard clenches his hands into fists. 'I can swear that my lord commanded that she serve you ... but this isn't good, it's not good. But perhaps we can glide over this. Perhaps nobody will bring it up, if it was just making a herb bed. At least you never consulted her. You have never ordered her to attend you ... .'

I glance away.

He groans. 'No. Oh no. Tell me, Jacquetta.'

'I took a tincture to prevent a child. You knew about that.'

'The herbs? That was her recipe?'

I nod.

'You told nobody?'

'No-one but you.'

'Then nobody will know. Anything else she made for you?'

'Later ... a drink to get a child.'

He checks as he realises that this was the conception of our daughter, Elizabeth, the baby that forced him into marriage. 'Good God, Jacquetta ...' He throws back the covers and gets out of bed, pulls back the curtain and strides to the fireside. It is the first time he has ever been angry with me. He thumps the bedpost with his fist as if he wishes he could fight the world. I sit up, gather the covers to my shoulders and feel my heart hammer with dread at his rage.

'I wanted a child and I wanted you,' I say unsteadily. 'I loved you, and I wanted us to be married. But I would not have cast a spell for it. I used herbs; not witchcraft.'

He rubs his head, making his hair stand on end, as if these distinctions are beyond him. 'You made our child with a witch's potion? Our daughter Elizabeth?'

'Herbs,' I say steadily. 'Herbs from a herbalist. Why not?'

He casts a furious look at me. 'Because I don't want a child brought to life by a handful of herbs from some old witch!'

'She is not some old witch, she is a good woman, and we have a beautiful child. You are as bad as this witch-hunt with your fears. I took herbs to help me to be fertile. We made a beautiful child. Don't you ill-wish us now!'

'For God's sake.' He raises his voice. 'I am afraid of nothing but you being mixed up with the most notorious witch in England, who has been trying to kill our king!'

'She is not! She would not!' I shout back at him. 'She would not!'

'She is accused.'

'Not by me!'

'By the Lord Chief Justice! And if they look for her associates they will find you, another royal duchess, another woman who dabbles in the unknown, another woman who can call up a storm or capture a unicorn.'

'I am not! I am not!' I burst into tears. 'You know I am not. You know I do nothing. Don't say such things, Richard. Don't you accuse me. You of all people!'

He loses his anger at my tears, and comes quickly across the room, sits beside me and gathers me against his shoulder. 'I don't accuse you, my love. I know. I know you would never do anything to harm anyone. Hush, I am sorry. And you are not to blame.'

'I can't help it that I foresee.'

'I know you can't help it.'

'And you of all people know that my lord put me before the scrying mirror day after day and all I could see was a battle in snow and a queen . . . a queen . . . with horseshoes reversed. He said it was useless. He said I could not foresee for him. I failed him. I failed him.'

'I know. I know you don't conjure. Be still, my love.'

'I did take herbs to get Elizabeth, but that was all. I would never conjure a child. Never.'

'I know, my love. Be still.'

I am silent and as I dry my eyes on the sheet he asks me, 'Jacquetta, does anyone know of this recipe that she gave you but you and her? Did anyone see her with you at Penshurst? Any of the court know that she was there?'

'No. Just servants, and her boy.'

'Then we will have to pray that she keeps her mouth shut about you, even if they take her to the stake.'

'The stake?' I say stupidly.

He nods in silence and then gets back into bed beside me. Together we watch the fire burning down in the grate. 'They will burn her for a witch,' he says flatly. 'And the duchess too.'

The duchess and the witch come before the court charged together with both witchcraft and treason. The duchess claims that she only visited Mrs Jourdemayne for herbs for fertility, and the herbalist gave her a drink, and said that it would make her conceive a child. I sit at the back of the room behind the avid spectators and know that I did exactly the same.

Margery has been charged with witchcraft before, and so they ask her why she continued to practise her arts: the herbs, the incantations, the foreseeing. She looks at the Archbishop of Canterbury, Henry Chichele, as if he might understand her. 'If you have eyes, you can't help but see,' she says. 'The herbs grow for me, the veil sometimes parts for me. It is a gift, I thought it was given by God.'

He gestures at the wax doll that sits before him on the desk. 'This is a most unholy curse, an attempted murder of an anointed king. How could it come from God?'

'It was a poppet to make a child,' she says wearily. 'It was a poppet in the shape of a great lord. See his ermine and his sword. It was a little doll to make a beautiful and talented child who would be an ornament to his country and a treasure to his family.'

Without thinking, my hand steals to my belly where a new

baby is being made who I hope will be an ornament and a treasure.

Mrs Jourdemayne looks at the archbishop. 'You are frightening yourselves with a poppet,' she says rudely. 'Do you great men have nothing better to do?'

The archbishop shakes his head. 'Silence,' he orders.

They have all decided already that this was an image of the king, made for melting. They have all decided that she is a witch, a brand for the burning. Once more, I am watching the most powerful men in the kingdom bring their power to bear on a woman who has done nothing worse than live to the beat of her own heart, see with her own eyes; but this is not their tempo nor their vision and they cannot tolerate any other.

They kill her for it. They take her to Smithfield, the meat market where the innocent cattle of the counties around London walk in to be butchered, and like an obedient lamb, trustingly herded into the bloodstained pen, she goes speechless to the stake and they light the fire beneath her bare feet and she dies in agony. Roger Bolingbroke, who confessed and recanted, finds no mercy either. They hang him on the public gallows, and as he is kicking in the air, whooping for breath, the executioner catches his feet and cuts the rope, restoring him to croaking life, lays him on a hurdle to revive him; but then slices open his belly, pulls out his entrails so that he can see his pulsing heart, his quivering stomach spilling out with his blood, and then they hack him into quarters, his legs from his spine, his arms from his chest, and they send his head with its horrified glare to be set on a spike on London Bridge for the ravens to peck out his weeping eyes. Thomas Southwell, my one-time confessor, the canon of St Stephen's Church, dies of sorrow in the Tower of London. Richard says that his friends smuggled poison to him, to spare him the agony that Bolingbroke endured. The duchess's clerk,

John Home, is sent to prison, awaiting pardon. And the proud duchess is forced to do public penance.

The woman who paraded into London in cloth of gold with the nobility of the kingdom in her train is stripped to her linen shift and sent out shoeless with a lighted taper to walk around Westminster as the people jeer and point at her as someone who was the first lady of the kingdom and is now humbled to dirt. I watch from the steps of the great gate of Westminster Palace as she walks by, her gaze fixed on the cold stones beneath her flinching bare feet. She does not look up to see me, or the women who once scrambled to serve her, but are now laughing and pointing; she does not raise her head, and her beautiful dark hair tumbles over her face like a veil to hide her shame. The most powerful men of the kingdom have dragged a duchess down, and sent her out to be a marvel to the common people of London. They are so deeply afraid of her that they took the risk to dishonour their own. They are so anxious to save themselves that they thought they should throw her aside. Her husband, who is now generally known as the 'good' Duke Humphrey, declares that he was seduced into marriage by her witchcraft; the marriage is instantly declared void. She, a royal duchess, the wife of the heir to the throne, is now a convicted witch in her petticoat; no man will give her his name, and they will keep her in prison for the rest of her life.

I think of the illusion that I saw as we came off the barge at Greenwich, that she was followed by a black dog, a fighting dog, a black mastiff, and the smell that lingered around her despite the perfume and the perfectly washed linen, and I think that the black dog will follow her and will run up and down the stairs of Peel Castle on the Isle of Man, as she waits, long, long years, for her release into death.

GRAFTON, NORTHAMPTONSHIRE, WINTER 1441–1444

As soon as we can be excused from court, Richard and I go back home, to Grafton. The terror of the court is only stoked by the death of the witch, the disgrace of the duchess and the mood of witch-taking. Apprehension of the unknown and fear of the hours of darkness infect all of London. Everyone who has been studying the stars for years, reading books, or testing metal finds a reason to leave for the country and Richard thinks it is safer for us if I – with my perilous ancestry – am far away from court.

At Grafton there is much work to do. The death of Richard's father means that Richard inherits the land and the responsibilities of being the lord of the small village and the keeper of the peace. I too have work to do. The cradle is polished again and the swaddling bands laundered and aired. 'I think this will be another son,' I say to my husband.

'I don't mind,' he says. 'As long as the baby is well and strong and you rise up from childbed as joyfully as you lie down in it.'

'I shall rise up with a son,' I say certainly. 'And he will be an ornament to his country and a treasure to his family.'

He smiles and taps me on the nose. 'You are a funny little thing. What d'you mean?'

'And we shall call him Anthony,' I continue.

'For the saint?' my husband asks. 'Why him?'

'Oh, because he went to the river to preach,' I say. 'I like the thought of honouring a saint who preached to the fishes and they put their little heads out of the water to hear him, and the mermaids said "Amen".'

The next year after Anthony comes another girl, whom we name Mary, and after her, another girl. 'Jacquetta,' my husband declares. 'She's to be named Jacquetta, the most beautiful name for the most beautiful woman.' We are hanging over the little wooden cradle while the baby sleeps, her face turned to one side, her perfect eyelashes closed on her rosy cheek. Her eyelids flicker, she is dreaming. I wonder what a baby dreams? Do they know that they are to come to the parents that we are? Are they prepared for the world we are making? Richard slides his arm around my waist. 'And though we love her, we have to leave her for just a little while.'

'Hmm?' I am absorbed in the clenching of her tiny fist.

'We have to leave her, for only a little while.'

Now he has my attention, I turn towards him in his grip. 'How so?'

'We are to go to France with a great party to fetch home the king's bride.'

'It has been decided?' The marriage of Henry has been a long time coming. My own first husband, Lord John, was picking out French princesses for him, when I was a new bride. 'At last?'

'You have missed all the gossip while you were in confinement, but yes, it is decided at last. And she is a kinswoman to you.'

'Margaret!' I guess at once. 'Margaret of Anjou.'

He kisses me as a reward. 'Very clever, and since your sister is married to her uncle, you and I are to go and fetch her from France.'

At once I look towards my sleeping baby.

'I know you don't want to leave her,' he says tenderly. 'But we will do our duty for Henry, fetch the bride, bring her home and then we will come back here. I am summoned by the king to serve him. I have to go.'

'You are asking me to leave a nursery with six babies,' I say. 'How can I go?'

'I know,' he says gently. 'But you have to do your duty too. You are an English duchess and my wife, and the head of our house is asking you to fetch his bride. When they marry it will bring peace to England and France – the one thing my lord wanted when he died. We have to go, my love. You know that. It is a service to the king and to him, your first husband and my good lord, it is a service to him too.'

NANCY, FRANCE, SPRING 1445

I am not the only unenthusiastic member of the marriage party. Our leader, William de la Pole the Earl of Suffolk, is said to be so mistrustful of the French and so unimpressed with the fortune that Margaret of Anjou brings that, before he left England to start the negotiations last year, he had the king swear that nobody should ever blame him for bringing the French princess to England. Cardinal Beaufort, who now rules everything, may see this as the way to lasting peace; but Duke Humphrey of Gloucester swears that the Valois king will just buy time with this marriage and come against our lands in France. I know my late husband would have feared above everything else that this is a new ruse by the French to make us hand over Anjou and Maine to René of Anjou: the new queen's father. Almost everyone left behind in England, while we spend a fortune on a progress to France, regards the deal that we are making as utterly uncertain to bring peace, costly to make, and most likely to be to our disadvantage.

The bride is brought by her mother from Anjou, and they say that she too is far from enthusiastic for a marriage which will put her in the bed of the king who has been an enemy of France ever since she was a baby.

'You're to go and see her first, before everyone,' my husband tells me. I am standing by the window of the castle, looking down into the stable yard. The horses of the Anjou party, a sorry herd of hacks, are being brushed down and watered, and led into their stables.

'Me? Why me?'

'Her mother knows your mother, they think that you can be her friend. You made much the same journey that she faces, from a Luxembourg castle to the royalty of England. They want you to meet her ahead of the rest of us so that you can introduce her to her new court.'

'I don't know that I'll be any help,' I say, turning to follow him.

'You'll speak the same language and that will be something,' he says. 'She's even younger than you were when the duke married you. She's only fifteen. She'll need a friend at court.'

He takes me to the double doors of the best apartment and steps to one side. The guards swing open the doors and bellow, 'The Dowager Duchess of Bedford!' as I go in.

The first thing that strikes me is that she is tiny, like a pretty doll. Her hair is a real bronze, a red-gold, and her eyes are grey-blue. She wears a gown of slate blue and a headdress perched far back on her head to show her exquisitely pretty face and her perfectly pale complexion. Her gown is scattered with embroidered marguerites – the daisies that are her emblem. The pout of her mouth suggests a spoiled child, but as she hears my name she turns quickly, and the brightness of her smile is endearing.

'Ah! Madame la duchesse!' she exclaims in French and runs forwards and kisses me as if we are old friends. 'I am so glad you have come to see me.'

I curtsey. 'I am glad to meet you, Your Grace.'

'And this is my mama. I was so happy when they told me you would come with the Earl of Suffolk to fetch me, for I thought you would tell me how I am to behave and everything. For you were married to the duke when you were only a little older than I am now? And fifteen is very young to marry, is it not?'

I smile at this nervous ripple of talk.

'Hush,' her mother says. 'The duchess will think you are a chatterbox.'

'It is just that there are so many English people come to see me, and I find it so hard to remember names. And their names are so hard to say!'

I laugh. 'I could not even say the name of my house at first,' I said. 'It is a hard language to learn. But I am sure you will learn it. And everyone speaks French, and everyone is eager to meet you and to be your friend. We all want you to be happy.'

Her lower lip quivers, but she speaks bravely enough. 'Oh, I have started already, and I can say the Earl of Suffolk, and Cardinal Bouffé.'

'Bouffé?' I query.

'Is that not right?'

'Beaufort!' I identify. 'They say it Bow-futt.'

She laughs and spreads out her hands. 'You see! You will teach me how to say these words, and you will teach me how the English ladies dress. Will I have to wear great boots all the time?'

'Boots, Your Grace?'

'For the mud?'

I laugh. 'Ah, they have been teasing you. England does get very muddy, especially in the winter, but the weather is no worse than – say – Paris. I prefer London to Paris and I am very happy in England now.'

She slips her hand in mine. 'And you will stand by me and tell me everyone's name, won't you? And how to say everything?'

'I will,' I promise her, and I feel the grip of her little hand tighten as she turns to her mother and says, 'You had better tell them they can come in. I had better meet them all now.'

She is a delightful little princess, perfect in every detail except that her father, though called a king, cannot conquer his many kingdoms, and never will. She has no dowry, and though she says she brings us the islands of Minorca and Majorca, we all know she will inherit nothing. Everything she requires for the wedding and the journey has been paid for by the treasury of England – and there is nothing left in the treasury of England. She is exquisitely beautiful; but so are many girls of fifteen. She is dearly loved by the French court, the declared favourite of her uncle, the Valois king Charles VII; yet she is not a princess of the House of Valois but only of Anjou. He is not offering one of his own daughters in marriage to the English, but only a niece. In short, most of the English who are sent to fetch her think that we have been cheated: in the peace treaty, in the dower, and in the little princess herself. This is not a good start to a marriage.

She is to be married in the chapel of St George in the palace at Tours, where the Earl of Suffolk will represent the king and stand beside her before the altar, and take her little hand from her father and the French king. Her sister Yolande is to be married at the same time. I know she is nervous but I am surprised to be summoned to her rooms two hours before the wedding and find myself shown alone into her bedroom; no other attendants are present. She is dressed in her wedding gown of white satin embroidered with marguerite daisies of silver and gold thread, but her hair is still plaited, and she is barefoot.

'My mother says you have a gift,' she says, speaking rapidly in French without any preamble. 'She says all the ladies of your house have the gift of foresight.'

I curtsey, but I am apprehensive. 'They say so, Your Grace, but I take all my hopes and fears to my priest and to God. I don't believe it is given to mortal men to know the future and certainly not to women.'

She makes a quick exclamation and jumps onto the bed, careless of the priceless gown. 'I want you to draw my cards for me, I want to know what the future holds.' She pats the bed beside her, inviting me to sit.

I do not respond to the invitation. 'Surely your mother did not suggest this?'

'No, she knows nothing of it, it is quite my own idea. Come, sit beside me.'

'I cannot,' I say, not moving. 'The court of England does not like prophesying or casting horoscopes. They certainly won't like the cards.'

'The court of England will never know,' she says. 'It will be just you and me.'

I shake my head. 'I dare not.'

She looks stubborn. 'If I command it, you will have to. You are my lady in waiting, you have to do what I say.'

I hesitate. If William de la Pole, the Earl of Suffolk, hears that I have upset the princess, there will be serious trouble. 'Of course, my only wish is to obey you, Your Grace. But what if you ask me to do something that your husband, our king, would not like? You must see that puts me in a difficult position. What am I to do then?'

'Oh, then you must do as I ask,' she says simply. 'Because the king will never know, nobody will ever know. But I will have my way in this. I can insist. I do insist.'

I kneel and bow my head, privately cursing her for a spoiled child. 'Your Grace, excuse me, I cannot.'

She pauses. 'All right, then I won't get married,' she declares. 'You can go out and tell them that you have refused to prepare me for my wedding, and so I will not marry. The wedding is off.'

I look up smiling, but she is perfectly serious.

'I mean it,' she says. 'You show me the cards, or I won't marry the king. I insist on seeing my future, I have to know that this is the right thing to do. I won't go ahead without seeing what the future holds for me.'

'I don't have any cards,' I say.

With a smile she lifts her pillow and puts a pack of beautifully coloured cards in my hand. 'Do it,' she says simply. 'It is my order.'

I shuffle the pictures gently. I wonder what will happen if she draws a bad card. Is she such a stubborn fool as to call off the wedding? I run through the arcana in my mind and wonder if I can hide those that show bad prospects. 'What if the cards are not good?' I ask. 'What happens then?'

She puts her hand on mine. 'The wedding will go ahead, and I will never tell anyone that you drew the cards for me,' she promises. 'But I will know in advance that I am going into danger, and what sort of danger it is. I will know to be on my guard. I want to know what is ahead of me. If I am going to die in childbirth within the year, I want to know. If my father and my husband are going to go to war against each other, I want to know. If the English lords who seem to agree on nothing are going to tear each other apart: I want to know.'

'All right,' I say. I can see no way of getting out of it. 'But I am not doing a full spread.' This at least cuts down the possibility of a series of pessimistic prophecies. 'I will do just one card. You take the cards, and shuffle them.'

Her little hands stretch around the thick cards; she interleaves them, and then puts them down.

'And cut.'

She cuts them and then puts the deck together. I spread them out before her in a fan, their faces down, their beautifully painted backs gleaming on the woollen covers of the bed. 'Choose one,' I say. 'One will tell you enough.'

Margaret's red-gold hair falls forwards and she leans across, her pretty face grave, trailing her finger along the pack, and then takes a card and holds it, without looking at it, to her heart.

'Now what?'

I sweep the untouched cards into a pile and then say to Margaret, 'Show it.'

She puts it face up.

It could have been an awful lot worse.

It is the card Joan the Maid saw in my hands, all those years ago: the Wheel of Fortune.

"*La Roue de Fortune*," she reads. 'Is that good? Is that very good?'

The card shows a wheel with two beasts balanced on either side of it, one climbing up, the other tumbling down as the wheel turns. The handle for the wheel is extended beyond the card, so one cannot see who is turning it; perhaps it is spinning at random. Seated at the very top of the card is a funny little blue animal, crowned and holding a sword. My great-aunt told me this little animal shows that it is possible to watch the wheel turn, and feel neither pride nor regret. One can stand above it, and see one's own life both rise and fall with the real indifference that comes from true greatness of spirit. One can look at one's own ambition as if it were all a masque of vanities, a dance for fools. It could not be a more unlikely card for Margaret: she is not at all a girl of indifference.

'It's good and bad,' I say. 'It's a kind of warning that you can rise very high and fall very low. It says that fortune's wheel can take you, by no merit of your own, by no grace of yours, very high indeed. And then it can throw you down very low.'

'So how do I rise again?' she asks me, as if I am some old hedgerow witch who tells fortunes for a groat.

'The whole point is that you can't,' I say impatiently. 'The whole point is that you can't make it happen. The whole point is that you cannot make your own fate. You are on fortune's wheel just like this poor monkey animal in the smart livery who is going to fall down; he can't help himself. You can't help yourself.'

She makes a sulky little face. 'That's not much of a foretelling,' she says. 'And anyway, doesn't the other animal rise up? This little cat thing? Maybe I am the cat thing and I am going to rise and rise.'

'Maybe,' I say. 'But then you go over the top of the wheel and are falling down again. You are supposed to learn to bear it, whichever happens, as if they were both the same.'

She looks blank. 'But they are not the same. Victory and defeat are not the same. I only want victory.'

I think of Joan and the sign she made with her forefinger, the circle in the air that meant that everything was dust. I make the sign to Margaret. 'The Wheel of Fortune,' I say. 'It is your card: you drew it. You insisted on a reading, and this is the card that you got. It tells us that we all only want victory. We all want to triumph. But we all have to learn to endure what comes. We have to learn to treat misfortune and great fortune with indifference. That is wisdom.' I look at her pretty, downcast face and see she has little interest in wisdom. 'But perhaps you will be lucky.'

TITCHFIELD ABBEY, HAMPSHIRE, SUMMER 1445

At first she is lucky. She meets the king and they like each other on sight – why would they not? He is a handsome boyish man of twenty-three, still somehow fragile, with a delicacy inherited from his French mother, and she is a strong-willed beauty eight years his junior. The Earl of Suffolk, William de la Pole, escorting her to her new country and enchanted with her, predicts that they will make a good match: her fire and passion will be softened by his sweetness; he will learn determination and courage from her.

They are married at the abbey at Titchfield in a service that reflects the young king's quiet seriousness. I suspect that Margaret would have preferred something more showy and more grand but there is no money for a great wedding, and anyway, the king said that the wedding should be between him, his bride, and God.

Disastrously, his fool of a confessor, Bishop Ayscough, performs the wedding and warns the serious young king that he should not succumb to lust. He warns him that he should only go to the bride's bed for the purpose of getting heirs to the throne, and not for their pleasure. The boy, who has been cautiously raised by men anxious to protect his innocence, takes the advice like a novice monk and stays away from her bed for a full week.

Margaret is not a young woman to deal patiently with such a husband. She summons me to her room the morning after her wedding and drags me into a window bay. 'He does not like me,' she whispers urgently. 'He got up from my bed as soon as everyone had left the room and spent half the night in prayer, and then he crept in beside me like a mouse and slept all the night without so much as touching me. I am as much a maid as ever I was, the wedding was for nothing.'

I take her hands. 'It will happen,' I say. 'You must be patient.'

'How is the marriage to be binding if it is not consummated?' she demands.

'It will be consummated, he will do the act, Your Grace, and we should be glad that he is not forceful.'

'Is he even a man?' she hisses scornfully, not glad at all.

'He is a man, he is your husband, and he is your king,' I say. 'It will happen. He will do it within the week.' As long as it is not a saint's day, or a holy day, I think to myself, if he can confess straight after the deed. Not in the morning before Mass, never in daylight. He is indeed extremely pious. 'And, Your Grace, when he approaches you, you must accept him without comment, without complaint.'

She tosses her head. 'But I want to be loved. I have always been loved. I want my husband to love me with passion, like in a troubadour tale, like a knight.'

'He does love you, he will love you. But he is not a lustful man.'

The anger goes from her as quickly as it came and the face she turns to me is puzzled. 'Why would he not desire me on the first night, on our wedding night?'

I shrug. 'Your Grace, he is a thoughtful young man, and very spiritual. He will come to you when he thinks the time is right, and then you must be kind to him.'

'But who will be kind to me?' she asks pitifully.

I smile and pat her cheek as if she were my younger sister and not my queen. 'We will all be kind to you,' I promise. 'And you will be happy.'

LONDON, SUMMER 1445–1448

Margaret is lucky in that she is young and beautiful and the Londoners take to her on sight and cheer her coronation. She is lucky in that she is endearing – I am not the only one who comes to love her and watch for her safety. Around her little court she gathers a collection of people who adore her. Me, she keeps close, her dearest friend and confidante. She loves Alice, William de la Pole's wife, too, and the three of us are inseperable in these early years of her marriage except for when I go to Grafton for my confinements, a new baby, John, and one who comes early and is especially small and precious on that account: Richard.

But she makes some mistakes and they are grave ones. Her liking for William de la Pole leads her to insist that he be consulted in the king's councils, and he – already a great man – rises to even higher importance through her favour. The two of them speak against the king's uncle, Duke Humphrey of Gloucester, and they whip up suspicion against him so powerfully that he is accused of trying for the throne on his own account, treason against his own nephew. The shock is too great for the duke and he dies before they can bring him to trial. At once there is a storm of gossip which declares that the good duke was murdered, and people point the finger of blame at William de la Pole. After the loss of this, his last uncle, the king leans yet more on his other advisors, and consults the opinion of his young wife. This is a terrible choice. She is little more than a girl, she knows nothing about England, in truth she knows nothing about anything.

The king's other favourite is Edmund Beaufort, the Duke of Somerset, and Margaret is dazzled by the dashing penniless duke who calls her cousin and kisses her on the mouth in greeting. He is the most handsome man at court, always beautifully dressed in velvet studded with jewels, always riding a big black horse, though they say he has not a penny in the world and is sworn up and down from his handsome dark head to his best leather soles to the moneylenders of London and Antwerp. He brings the queen little gifts, fairings that he picks up in the market, and they delight her, as he pins a little brooch to the hem of her dress, or offers her a piece of candied peel, popping it in her mouth as if she were a child. He speaks to her in rapid intimate French, and tucks a blossom behind her ear. He teases her as if she were a pretty maid and not a queen, he brings musicians in, and dancers; the court is always merry when Edmund Beaufort is in attendance and the king and queen command him to stay at court all the time.

Perhaps it would have been better if they had not done so. But the handsome young duke is ambitious and he asks and gets the command of the English forces in Normandy, as if they were toy soldiers for his amusement. The young king and queen can refuse him nothing. They load all their favourites with offices and money, and the court becomes a hen-house of strutting jealousy.

We all do well out of this. They are prodigal with titles and posts, they give away their own lands, the places at court for free, the opportunities for trade and bribery, licences to import, licences to export. Crown lands, which are supposed to pay for the king's living throughout his reign, get thrust into greedy hands, in a helter-skelter of generosity. William de la Pole finds himself ennobled beyond his dreams, made into a duke, the first man without royal blood ever to take such a title. Edmund

Beaufort gets a dukedom too, it is a hiring fair of honours. The king and queen take it into their heads that Edmund Beaufort should be given a fortune to match his title, he should be given a fortune to match the famously wealthy Richard Duke of York, a royal kinsman. No – better still – he should overmatch the great Duke of York, and the young king and queen say they will give him whatever it takes to do so.

Even Richard and I are swept along on this torrent of gifts. They give us a great London house, and then my husband comes to me and says, smiling, 'Tell me, my darling, what name d'you think I should have?'

'Name?' I ask, and then I realise what he is saying. 'Oh! Richard! Is the king to give you a title as well?'

'I think it is more the favour of the queen to you,' he says. 'But at any rate I am to be a baron. I am to be awarded an order of nobility for great service to my country – or at least, because the queen likes my wife. What d'you think of that?'

I gasp. 'Oh, I am so pleased. I am so very pleased for you. And for our children too! We will be so very grand.' I pause uncertainly. 'Can the king just make up titles like this?'

'The two of them think they can and, what is more dangerous: they do. Never was a young couple with so little power and money in more of a hurry to give it all away. And they will drive the rest of the court mad. Anyone that she likes, or that he trusts, gets loaded with favours; but good men are excluded. Richard, Duke of York, gets nothing, not even a civil hearing. They say they won't have him in the council now; though he is known as a good man and the best advisor they could have. But he is ignored and worse men than he are praised to the skies. I shall be made a baron for no better reason than you keep her company.'

'And what name shall we have, my lord? You will be Sir Richard Woodville, Baron – what?'

He pauses for a moment. 'Baron Grafton?' he asks.

'Baron Grafton,' I repeat, listening to the sounds. Even after all these years in England I still have a strong accent. 'I really can't say it.'

'But I wondered if you would like a title which came from your family. One of your family names?'

I think for a moment. 'I don't really want to remind everyone that I am a daughter of Luxembourg, that I am French,' I say cautiously. 'The mood is more and more against the French. I was telling the queen, only the other day, that she should speak English in public. I am an English dowager duchess and I am a good Englishwoman now. Give me an English name and let our children have English titles.'

'Water!' he exclaims. 'For your ancestor.'

I laugh. 'You can't be Baron Water. But what about Baron Rivers?'

'Rivers . . .' He rolls the word over in his mouth. 'That's fine. Rivers. It's a good English name, and yet it is a tribute to your family. Baron Rivers I shall be and, please God, one day I shall be an earl.'

'No, really, would they ever make you an earl? Would they give away so much?'

'My dear, I am afraid they would give away the kingdom itself. They are not careful monarchs and they are advised by rogues.'

I mention my husband's anxiety about their extravagance as tactfully as I can to the queen but she tosses her head. 'We have to keep our friends satisfied,' she says to me. 'We cannot rule the country without William de la Pole: he is the greatest man in the land. And Edmund Beaufort is in such debt! We have to help him.'

'Richard Duke of York?' I suggest as a man they should reward.

'We cannot hold France without Edmund Beaufort. He is the only man we could trust to hold our French lands, and to restore those lands that we should return to their true owner.'

'Your Grace?' I am dumbfounded at the suggestion that we should restore our lands to the French, and she flushes, as guilty as a child. 'To hold our lands,' she corrects herself. 'Edmund Beaufort is the only man we can trust.'

'I think that Richard, Duke of York, is the only man to succes-fully hold French lands since my first husband, the Duke of Bedford,' I observe.

She throws her hands in the air. 'Perhaps, perhaps, but I can trust no-one but Edmund Beaufort and William de la Pole. The king himself can neither take decisions nor lead an army. These men are everything to me. They are the father and' – she breaks off and blushes – 'friend that I need. They both deserve the high-est of honours, and we will give honours where they are due.'

WESTMINSTER PALACE, LONDON, SUMMER 1449

I can tell at once that something terrible has happened. Richard comes into our private rooms and takes my hands, his face grim. 'Jacquetta, you must be brave.'

'Is it the children?' My first thought is always for them, and my hand goes to my belly where another life is growing.

'No, thank God. It is my lord's legacy, the lands of Normandy.'

I don't really have to ask him, I guess at once. 'Have they been lost?'

He grimaces. 'All but. Edmund Beaufort has offered the French almost all of Normandy including Rouen, in return for his safety in Caen.'

'Rouen,' I say quietly. My first husband John, Duke of Bedford's grave is there. I have property there.

'This is a bitter blow,' Richard says. 'And all of us who fought to keep the English lands in France, nearly a hundred years of long warfare, and so many lives lost – good comrades and brothers –' He breaks off. 'Well, we will find it hard to forgive the loss.'

WESTMINSTER PALACE, LONDON, SPRING 1450

Richard was right. Nobody can forgive the loss. The parliament turns on William de la Pole, and his new titles and his new honours cannot save him from the rage of the English as the men who had farmed and the soldiers who had fought in Normandy come home defeated and homeless, and complain bitterly, bitterly, at every market cross and crossroads, that they have been betrayed by their commanders who should have stood by them, as they had stood to arms for more than a hundred years.

In the streets the London traders call out to me as I ride by, 'What would Lord John have thought of it, eh? What would your lord have said?' and I can do nothing more but shake my head. I feel with them – what did we fight for, what did we die for, if the lands we won are to be handed back as part of a treaty, as part of a marriage, on the whim of a king who never fought for them as we fought for them?

They blame it all on William de la Pole, since it is treason to speak against the king. And they call him to parliament and accuse him of treason, extortion, and murder. They say that he has been planning to seize the throne and set up his little son John and his ward Margaret Beaufort as king and queen, claiming the throne in her right.

'What is going to happen?' I ask the queen, who is striding

back and forth in her rooms, the long train of her gown swishing like the tail of an angry cat.

'I will not allow him to face the charges. He will not be demeaned by such charges. His Grace the king has saved him. He has ruled that he, the king, shall be judge and jury of his friend William.'

I hesitate. After all this is not my country, but I really don't think the king can just step in like this. 'Your Grace, I think he cannot. A nobleman has to be tried by his peers. The House of Lords will have to examine him. The king may not intervene.'

'I say that no good friend of mine will be questioned in public like that. It is an insult to him, it is an insult to me. I have demanded that we protect our friends and the king agrees with me. William will not go before parliament. He is coming to my rooms tonight, in secret.'

'Your Grace, this is not the English way. You should not meet any man alone, and certainly not in secret.'

'You will be there,' she says. 'So they can say nothing vile about our meeting. Though, God knows, they say enough vile things already. But we have to meet in secret. The parliament has become mad with jealousy, and now they are calling for his death. I cannot rule this kingdom without William de la Pole. I have to see him and decide what we should do.'

'The king . . . '

'The king cannot rule without him. The king cannot choose a course and hold to it on his own. You know what the king is like. I have to have William de la Pole at the side of the king; he cannot be steady without William to hold him to a course. We have to have William at our side. We have to have his advice.'

At midnight, the queen orders me to let William de la Pole in through the little door that connects the two royal apartments. The duke strides through, ducking his head under the stone lintel, and then, to my amazement, the king comes in quietly behind him, like his pageboy. 'Your Grace,' I whisper and sink down.

He does not even see me, he is shaking with distress. 'I am forced! I am abused!' he says at once to Margaret. 'They dare to insult me. They want to rule me! William – tell her!'

She looks at once to de la Pole as if only he can explain. 'The lords are refusing to accept that the king can examine me alone, as you wanted,' he explains. 'They are demanding that I am tried by my peers for treason. They deny the king's right to judge on his own. I am accused of betraying our interests in France. Of course, I have only ever done what you commanded. And the peace treaty demanded the return of Maine and Anjou. This is an attack on you, Your Grace, on you, and on me, and on the king's authority.'

'You will never stand trial,' she promises him. 'I swear it. They shall withdraw.'

'Your Grace ...' I whisper, taking hold of her sleeve,'you cannot promise this.'

'I have found him innocent of all charges,' the king says. 'But still they are calling for him to be tried and executed. They have to obey me! They must be made to listen to me!'

'If they want you, they will have to come and get you!' she swears passionately to William de la Pole. 'They will have to get past me if they want to get you. They will have to take you from my chambers, if they dare!'

I slide my hand into hers and give her a little tug. But the king looks at her with admiration, he is fired up by her anger. 'We will defy them! I will be king. I will rule how I choose: with you as my wife and William as my advisor. Does anyone dare say I cannot do this? Am I king or not?'

Of the three of them, only the newly minted duke does not bluster. 'Yes, but we can't resist them,' he says quietly. 'What if they come for me? What if the lords turn out their forces? Despite all you have said? You have allowed every lord in London to keep his own small army. Every enemy of mine can command hundreds of men. What if their armies come for me?'

'Could you go to France?' I ask him very softly. 'To Flanders? You have friends there. Till it all blows over?'

The king looks up, suddenly flushed. 'Yes, yes, go now!' he commands. 'While they are planning their next move. Go now. They will come for you and find the bird flown! I will give you gold.'

'My jewels!' the queen commands me. 'Fetch them for him.'

I go as she orders, and pick out a few of her smallest pieces, marguerites made of pearls, some inferior emeralds. I put them in a purse and when I come back to the shadowy room the queen is weeping in the duke's arms and he has the king's own cloak around his shoulders and is slipping a fat purse into his pocket. Begrudgingly, I give him the queen's pearls and he takes them without a word of thanks.

'I will write to you,' he says to them both. 'I will not be far, just Flanders. And I will come home as soon as my name is cleared. We will not be parted for long.'

'We will visit you,' she promises. 'This is not goodbye. And we will send for you, and write. You shall send messages with your advice. And you will come home soon.'

He kisses her hand and pulls his hood over his head. He bows to the king and nods to me and slides through the little door and is gone. We hear his footsteps going quietly down the stair, and then the muffled closing of the outer door as the king's chief advisor goes out into the night like a thief.

The king and queen are cock-a-hoop like children who have defied a stern governor. They do not go to bed at all that night, but stay up by the fireside in her rooms whispering and giggling, celebrating their victory over the parliament of their own country, praising themselves for defending a man named as a traitor. At dawn the king goes to Mass and orders the priest to say a prayer of thankfulness for danger passed. While he is on his knees, praising the mercy of Jesus and exulting in his own cleverness, the City of London wakes to the astounding news that the man it blamed for the loss of France and the arrival of a penni-less French princess, for rewarding himself from the royal treasury, for the destruction of the peace of England, has been released by the king and is sailing away, merrily away, for a brief exile, gold in his pocket, the queen's jewels in his hat, and will return as soon as he can be certain that his head is safe on his shoulders.

The queen cannot hide her delight, nor her contempt for those who say that she is utterly misguided. She will heed no warning, neither from my husband nor the other men who serve the king, who say the people are whispering that the king has forgotten his loyalty to his own lords and commons, that a friend of a traitor is a traitor himself – and what can be done with a treacherous king? She remains stubbornly delighted, thrilled with their defiance of parliament, and nothing I can say warns her to take care, not to blazon her triumph in the face of people who were, after all, only calling for good government of a country which is flung about like a toy of spoiled children.

I think that nothing will dampen their joyous high spirits. The news comes that William de la Pole has had to flee from the mob out of London, that he is hiding for as long as he dares at his own house in the country, and then finally that he has set sail. All over the country there are uprisings against men who are blamed for giving the king bad advice, who are blamed for associating with William de la Pole. Then, a few days later, one of the queen's maids in waiting comes running to find me and says I must go at once! at once! to the queen who is gravely ill. I do not even stop to find Richard, I run to the royal apartments, bustling past the guards on the door, shooing pages out of my way, and find the rooms in an uproar, and the queen nowhere to be seen.

'Where is she?' I demand, and someone points to the bed-room door.

'She swore we could not go in.'

'Why?' I ask. They shake their heads.

'Is she alone?'

'The Duchess of Suffolk, William de la Pole's wife, is in with her.'

At that name, my heart sinks. What has he done now? Slowly, I go to the door, tap on the panel, and then try the handle. It opens, and I step inside.

At once I remember what a young woman she is, just twenty years old. She looks very small in the big royal bed, lying hunched up as if wounded in the belly, her back to the room, her face to the wall. Alice de la Pole is seated on a stool by the fire, her face buried in her hands.

'C'est moi,' I whisper. 'It's me. What's wrong?'

The little queen shakes her head. Her headdress has fallen off, her hair is tumbled all around her, her shoulders are shaking with silent sobs. 'He's dead,' is all she says, as if her world has ended. 'Dead. What will I do?'

I stagger and put my hand out to steady myself. 'My God, the king?'

Violently, she bangs her head into her pillow. 'No! No!'

'Your father?'

'William. William . . . my God, William.'

I look at Alice, his widow. 'I am sorry for your loss, my lady.'

She nods.

'But how?

Margaret raises herself on her elbow and looks over her shoulder at me. Her hair is a mass of gold, her eyes red. 'Murdered,' she spits.

At once, I glance at the door behind me, as if a killer might come in for us. 'By whom, Your Grace?'

'I don't know. That wicked Duke of York? Other lords? Anyone who is cowardly and vile and wants to pull us down and destroy us. Anyone who denies our right to govern as we wish, with the help of whoever we choose. Anyone who sails in secret and attacks an innocent man.'

'They caught him at sea?'

'They took him on board their ship and beheaded him on the deck,' she says, her voice nearly muffled by sobs. 'God damn them to hell for cowards. They left his body on the beach at Dover. Jacquetta!' Blindly, she reaches out to me and clings to me as she wails. 'They put his head on a pole. They left his head like a traitor's head. How shall I bear this? How shall Alice bear this?'

I hardly dare to glance over to William de la Pole's widow, who sits in silence while William de la Pole's queen is breaking her heart over him.

'Do we know who?' I repeat. My first fear is, if someone dares to attack the king's favourite advisor, who will they come for next? The queen? Me?

She is crying so hard she cannot speak, her slender body is shaking in my arms. 'I must go to the king,' she says finally, pulling herself up and wiping her eyes. 'This will have broken his heart. How will we manage without him? Who will advise us?'

Dumbly, I shake my head. I don't know how they will manage without William de la Pole, nor what sort of world is opening before us when a noble lord in his own ship can be kidnapped and beheaded with a rusty sword on a rocking boat and his head left on a pike on the beach.

GRAFTON, NORTHAMPTONSHIRE, SUMMER 1450

As the warmer months come the king and queen agree to travel north. They give out that they want to be away from London during the hot weather when plague often comes to the city, they say that they want to see the good people of Leicester. But those of us who live in the palace know that the guards have been doubled at the gates, and that they are employing tasters for their food. They are afraid of the people of London, they are afraid of the men of Kent, they are afraid that whoever murdered William de la Pole blames them for the loss of France, for the continual stream of defeated soldiers and settlers who come every day into every English port. There is no money to pay the London suppliers, the queen mistrusts the people of the city. The court is going to Leicester; in truth it is running away to hide in Leicester.

Richard and I are granted leave to go and see our children at Grafton, as the court goes north, and we ride quickly out of London, which has become a surly city of secretive people whispering on street corners. There is a rumour that the king and queen will take a great revenge on the county of Kent. They blame the very seashore where William de la Pole's dishonoured body was dumped. Lord Say of Knole and his heavy-handed son-in-law who is Sheriff of Kent say that together they will hunt down the guilty men and execute them and every one of their family; they say they will empty Kent of people, they will make it a wasteland.

Once we are out of the city, away from city walls, Richard and I ride side by side, holding hands like young lovers, while our small armed guard falls back and rides behind us. The roads are clear and dry, the grass verges dotted with flowers, the birds singing in the greening hedgerows, ducklings on the village ponds and roses in blossom.

'What if we never went back to court?' I ask him. 'What if we were just to be the squire of Grafton and his lady?'

'And our nursery of children?' he smiles.

'Many, many children,' I say. 'I am not satisfied with eight, and one on the way, I am hoping for a round dozen.'

He smiles at me. 'I should still be summoned,' he says. 'Even if I were the smallest quietest squire of Grafton, with the largest family in England, I should still be mustered and sent to war.'

'But you would come home again.' I pursue the thought. 'And we could make a living from our fields and farms.'

He smiles. 'Not much of a living, my lady. Not the sort of living you want. And your children would marry tenant farmers and their children would run wild. Do you want a dirty-faced little peasant for a grandchild?'

I make a face at him. He knows how much I prize our books and our musical instruments, and how determined I am that all my children shall read and write in three languages, and master all the courtly skills.

'My children have to take their place in the world.'

'You are ambitious,' he says.

'I am not! I was the first lady in France. I have been as high as any woman could dream. And I gave it up for love.'

'You're ambitious for your family and for your children. And you're ambitious for me – you like me being a baron.'

'Oh well, a baron,' I say, laughing. 'Anyone would want their husband to be a baron. I don't count that as being ambitious. That is just ... understandable.'

'And I understand it,' he says agreeably. 'But would you really want to live always in the country and not go back to court?'

I think for a moment of the nervous king and the young queen. 'We couldn't leave them, could we?' I ask wistfully.

He shakes his head. 'It is our duty to serve the House of Lancaster, and – something else – I don't know how they would manage without us. I don't think we could just walk away and leave them. What would they do?'

We stay at Grafton for a week. It is the best time of the year, the orchards are rose-pink with the bobbing blossoms, and the cows are calving. The lambs are with their mothers in the higher meadows, running and frisking with their tails like woolly ribbons dancing behind them. The hay in the meadows is growing tall and starting to ripple in the wind and the crops are green and rich, ankle-deep. My older children, Elizabeth, Lewis, Anne and Anthony, have been staying with our cousins, to learn their manners and how to behave in a great household, but they come home to be with us for the summer. The four little ones, Mary, Jacquetta, John, and Richard, are beside themselves with excitement at having their big sisters and brothers home. Mary, the seven-year-old, is the leader of the little battalion, the others her sworn liegemen.

I am weary with this new pregnancy and in the warm afternoons I take the four-year-old, little Diccon, in my arms for his afternoon nap and we lie down together, drowsy in the warmth of the day. When he is asleep and it is very quiet, I sometimes take the painted cards and turn them over, one after another, and look at them. I don't shuffle them or deal them out, I don't attempt to read them. I just look at the familiar pictures and wonder what life will bring me, and these my beloved children.

In the day Richard listens to the unending complaints of the people around us: the moving of a fence line, of cattle being allowed to stray and spoiling a crop. As lord of the manor it is his job to ensure that the rule of law and justice runs throughout our lands, whether or not our neighbours take bribes and order jurors what sentence they should bring in. Richard visits the local gentry to remind them of their duty to turn out for him in case of need, and tries to reassure them that the king is a strong lord, that the court is trustworthy, that the treasury is secure and that we will keep the remaining lands in France.

I work in my still room, Elizabeth my earnest apprentice, steeping herbs in oil, checking the cut and dried herbs, pounding them down into powder and conserving them in jars. I do this by the order of the stars and I consult my lord's books for how it should be done. Now and then I find a book I had overlooked which talks of making the aqua vitae, the water of life itself, or of burning off impurities by the touch of distilled waters; but I remember Eleanor Cobham behind the cold walls of Peel Castle, and I take the book from Elizabeth and put it on a high shelf. I never grow or dry any but the herbs that would be known to a good cook. Knowledge is just another thing to conceal, these days.

I am hoping that we will stay at home for another month; I am tired by this pregnancy and daring to hope that I might spend the whole summer in the country, that the king and queen will prolong their travels and leave us in peace. We have been riding out to visit some neighbours and come home in the sunset to see a royal messenger waiting by the water pump. He gets to his feet when he sees us and hands Richard a letter sealed with the royal crest.

Richard tears it open and scans it. 'I have to go,' he says. 'This is urgent. I shall have to muster a troop as I ride.'

'What has happened?' I ask as I slip down from my saddle.

'There's a rising in Kent, as any fool could have foreseen.

The king commands me to ride at his side and carry the royal standard.'

'The king?' I can hardly believe that our king is going to ride out at the head of his men. His father was a remarkable commander of men at a far younger age; but our king has never worn his armour except for jousting. 'The king is going himself?'

'He was very angry about de la Pole – God rest his soul,' he reminds me. 'He swore vengeance and the queen swore she would see the murderers dead. Now he has his chance.'

'You will be careful.' I take his arm to look up into his face. Between us is the unspoken thought that his commander will be a young man who has never seen any sort of warfare, not even a distant siege. 'You will have to advise him.'

'I'll keep safe,' my husband says wryly. 'And I'll keep him safe too, if I can. They have ordered the Sheriff of Kent to turn the county into a deer park, to drive out every man, woman and child: there will be hell to pay. I have to get back and see if I can advise them into some sense. I have to find a way to persuade them to rule the country with some sort of harmony. They make enemies every time they address parliament. The queen rides through the streets of London as if she hates the very cobbles. We have to serve them, Jacquetta. We have to guide them to follow their best interests, we have to get this royal couple back into the hearts of their people. It is our duty. It is our task. It is what our lord the Duke of Bedford would have wanted us to do.'

I hold him in my arms in bed that night and in the cool morning I find I am filled with unease. 'You will just ride out with the king to show his standard? You won't go into Kent, Richard?'

'I hope that nobody will be going into Kent,' he says grimly.

He finishes his breakfast and I trail out into the stable yard after him, pursuing my fears. 'But if there is some kind of guard put together to punish the people of Kent, you won't join it?'

'Burning thatch? Spit-roasting a poor man's cow?' he asks. 'I have seen it done in France and I never thought it a way to win loyalty. The Duke of Bedford himself said to me that the way to win a man's heart was to treat him fairly and make him safe. That will be my advice, if anyone asks me. But if anyone orders me out in the king's name, I will have to go.'

'I will follow you as soon as you send for me.' I try to sound confident, but my voice is thin and anxious.

'I will be waiting for you,' he vows, suddenly warm, as he realises I am afraid. 'You take care of yourself and the baby that you are carrying. I will be waiting for you. I will always be there waiting for you. Remember I have promised you – you will never look for me in vain.'

I tidy the house and command the servants to prepare them for my departure. I hear gossip that the king and queen have gone back to London and that the king himself has ridden out against the people of Kent. Then a message comes from Richard, written in his own hand.

> *Beloved,*
> *I am sorry to trouble you. The king has been persuaded by the queen not to march into Kent himself, but he has ordered me to pursue the outlaws at the head of his guard and I am doing so. Trust me that I will be safe and come home to you when this is over. Your Richard.*

I put the scrap of paper inside my gown, against my heart, and I go to the stable. 'Saddle up,' I say to the household guard. 'And tell them to get my mare ready for a journey. We are going back to London.'

LONDON, SUMMER 1450

All the way I ride with a heavy heart. I have such a strong sense that Richard is in danger, that he is outnumbered, that the thickly forested county of Kent will hide ambushes, traps, armies of the people who will take him, as they took William de la Pole, and behead him without clergy, with a rusty sword.

We take the London road in silence, but as we pass through the vegetable gardens and little dairy farms, the captain of my guard orders the men to close up, and starts to look around him, as if he fears we are unsafe.

'What is it?' I ask.

He shakes his head. 'I don't know, my lady. Something . . .' He pauses. 'Too quiet,' he says, speaking to himself. 'Hens shut up before sunset, shutters closed on the cottages. Something's not right.'

I don't need to be told twice. Something is wrong. My first husband the duke used to say that if you ride into a town and feel that something is wrong it is usually because something is wrong. 'Close up,' I say. 'We'll get inside the City before the gates close, and we'll go to our London house. Tell your men to be alert and look about them. We'll go on at a canter.'

He beckons the men to close up and we ride towards the City gates. But almost as soon as we are through Moorgate and in the narrow streets I can hear the swell of noise, people cheering, laughing, trumpets tooting and the banging of a drum.

It sounds like a May Day procession, it sounds like joy unleashed, but there must be hundreds of people on the streets. I glance at my men, who draw their horses closer to mine in a defensive square.

'This way,' the captain says, and leads us at a swift trot through the winding streets till we find our way to the great wall that runs around my London house. The torches, which are always kept burning either side of the gateway, are missing from the sconces. The gates themselves, which should be either barred for night or flung hospitably wide, are half-open. The sweep of the cobbles approaching the house is empty; but there is a scattering of litter and the front door is ajar. I glance at George Cutler, the captain, and see my unease in his eyes.

'Your ladyship . . .' he says uncertainly. 'Better that I go in, and see what's amiss here. Something has gone wrong, perhaps . . .'

As he speaks a drunken man, no servant of mine, weaves out through the half-open gates and shambles past us, disappearing down the lane. Cutler and I exchange glances again. I kick my feet out of the stirrups and swing down from my horse, and throw her reins to one of the guard.

'We'll go in,' I say to Cutler. 'Draw your sword and have two men behind us.'

They follow me as I walk across the cobbles to the house, my London home, that I was so proud to receive and so pleased to furnish. One of the front doors is thrown off the hinges, there is the smell of smoke. As I push the other door open and go inside, I can see that a mob of people has run through the rooms, and taken whatever they thought was of value. There are pale squares on the walls where my tapestries, the Duke of Bedford's tapestries, once hung. A huge wooden sideboard, too heavy to carry off, has been stripped of the pewter ware that it held, carved doors left banging. I go to the great hall. All the trenchers and wine jugs and drinking vessels are gone, but, absurdly, the huge beautiful tapestry which was behind the great table is still there, untouched.

'My books,' I say and jump up to the dais and through the door behind the great table and up the short flight of stairs into the upstairs solar. From there it is two steps through a wreckage of precious broken glass, into the gallery, and there I pause, and look around me.

They have taken the brass grilles off the shelves, they have taken the brass chains that fettered the books to the reading desks. They have even taken the quills and the pots of ink. But the books are safe, the books are untouched. They have stolen everything made of metal but damaged nothing of paper. I snatch up a slim volume and hold it to my cheek.

'Get these safe,' I say to Cutler. 'Get your men in to put them in the cellar and board it up and mount a guard. These are worth more than the brass grilles, more than the tapestries. If we can salvage these then I can meet my first husband at the Last Day of Judgement. They were his treasures and he trusted them to me.'

He nods. 'I am sorry about the rest of it . . . ' He gestures at the wrecked house where the wooden staircase is scarred by sword cuts. Someone has hacked off the carved newel post, and taken it away, as if to behead me by proxy. In the painted beams above, there is smoke blackening the ceiling. Someone tried to burn us to the ground. I shudder at the smell of the scorched plaster.

'If the books are safe, and my lord is safe, then I can start again,' I say. 'Board the books up for me, Cutler. And take down the big tapestry too, and anything else you find of value. Thank God we took the best stuff with us to Grafton.'

'What will you do?' he asks. 'My lord will want you to find a safe haven. I should go with you.'

'I'll go to the palace,' I say. 'I'll go to Westminster. Meet me there.'

'Take two men with you,' he advises. 'I will make all safe here. And then we'll follow you.' He hesitates. 'I have seen worse done,' he volunteers. 'It looks as if they came through on a whim and took anything that was of great value. It was not an assault. You need not fear them. It was not directed at you. They are people driven to despair by poverty and fear of the lords. They are not bad people. It's just they cannot bear it any more.'

I look around the smoke-blackened hall, at the spaces where the missing tapestries used to be and the hacked banister. 'No, it was an assault,' I say slowly. 'They did all that they wanted to do. It was not directed at me – but it was directed at the lords, at the wealthy, at the court. They no longer think that they have to wait at the gates, they no longer think they have no choice but to beg. They no longer think that we command them by right. When I was a girl in Paris and married to the Duke of Bedford we were hated by the people of the city, by the people of France. We knew it, and they knew it. But nobody even dreamed that they could breach the gates and come inside and destroy our things. They think this now in London. They no longer obey their masters. Who knows where they will stop?'

I walk out. The guard outside is holding my horse, but already a crowd has gathered and is murmuring against them. 'You two, come with me,' I say. 'You two, go in and set it to rights.'

I snap my fingers and one of the guard helps me into the saddle. 'Go quickly,' I urge him, under my breath. 'Into the saddle and onwards.'

He does as I bid him and we are away from the courtyard and some distance from my house before anyone knows we are gone. I don't look back. But I remember, as I ride down the road, the dark smear of the smoke stain in the hall of my house, and my realisation that the people had come into my house and taken what they wanted, and done just what they wished.

'To Westminster Palace,' I say. I want to be with the court, behind the walls of the palace, guarded by the royal guard. London no longer feels safe for me. I have become like the queen – a woman uneasy in the heart of her own home.

We round a corner and suddenly we are swirled into a mob of people, dancing laughing cheering people, a great joyous May Day crowd. Someone gets hold of my bridle, and I clench my hand on my whip, but the face that turns up towards me is beaming. 'Easy!' I say quickly to the guard at my side who is spurring forwards, his hand on his sword.

'God be praised, we have our champion!' the woman says, sharing her happiness with me. 'He is coming, God bless him! He is coming, and he will petition for our rights and the good times will come again!'

'Hurrah!' shout half a dozen people in earshot, and I smile as if I know what is happening.

'Good woman,' I say. 'I have to get through, let me go, I have to meet my husband. Let me go.'

Someone laughs. 'You'll get nowhere till he has come! The streets are packed with people like pilchards in a barrel. There is no going through nor going round.'

'But won't you come and see him? He is coming over the bridge.'

'Oh, come,' somebody else says. 'You will never see the like of this again, this is the greatest thing to ever happen in our lifetime, in any lifetime.'

I look around for my two men but they cannot keep their place at my side. They are separated from me by a dozen merrymakers, we are totally outnumbered. I wave to one. 'Go your ways,' I call. 'I am safe enough. You know where we will meet.' Clearly, there is no point trying to resist this crowd and our safest way is to join with them. One of my men jumps from his horse and pushes his way through to come alongside me.

'Steady on!' someone says. 'No shoving. Whose livery are you wearing?'

'Leave me,' I whisper. 'Meet me later. You know where. Don't upset them.'

It is the safest way, but I see him struggle to obey the order.

'High and mighty!' someone complains. 'The sort that should be brought down.'

'Are you a king's man?' someone demands. 'Think you should have everything and care nothing for the poor man?'

At last, he takes his cue. 'Not I!' he says cheerfully. 'I am with you all!'

I nod at him, and the movement of the crowd takes him from me, almost at once. I let my horse walk with them. Familiarly, a woman rests her hand on my horse's neck. 'So where are we going?' I ask her.

'To the bridge, to see him come across the bridge!' she says exultantly. 'I see you are a lady but you will not be ashamed of the company he keeps. He has gentry and squires with him, knights and lords. He is a man for all the people, of all degree.'

'And what will he do for us when he comes?'

'You don't know? Where have you been?'

Smiling, I shake my head. 'I have been in the country, all this is a surprise to me.'

'Then you have come back to the City at the very hour of its joy. He will speak for us at last. He will tell the king that we cannot bear the taxation, that the fat lords will ruin us all. He will order the king to ignore the French slut, his wife, and take good advice from the good duke.'

'The good duke?' I query. 'Who do you call the good duke now?'

'Richard Duke of York, of course. He will tell the king to lie with his worthless wife and get us a son and heir, to take our lands in France back again, to send away the wicked men who steal the wealth of the country and do nothing but make their own fortunes and fight among themselves. He will make this king as great as the king before and we will be happy again.'

'Can one man do all this?' I ask.

'He has raised an army and defeated the king's men already,' she says delightedly. 'They chased after him to Sevenoaks and he struck them down. This is our champion. He has defeated the royal army and now he takes the City.'

I can feel a pain hammering in my head. 'He destroyed the king's army?'

'Led them on, turned on them and struck them down,' she says. 'Half of them ran away, half of them joined him. He is our hero!'

'And what of the lords who led the men?'

'Dead! All dead!'

Richard, I think to myself in silence. Surely the two of us did not come so far, and risk so much, for Richard to be ambushed by a hedge-sparrow commander at the head of patchwork rebels, and killed outside Sevenoaks? Surely I would know if he were injured or dead? Surely I would have heard Melusina sing or felt the very spheres dance sorrowfully one with another, to mourn him? Surely the man that I have loved for all my adult life, loved with a passion that I did not even know was possible, could not, cannot be dead in a Kentish ditch, and I not know?

'Are you ill, mistress?' she asks. 'You've gone white as my washing.'

'Who commanded the royal army?' I ask; though I know it was him. Who else would they send but Richard? Who has more experience, who is more reliable? Who is more loyal and honourable than my husband? Who would they choose if not my beloved?

'Ah, now that I don't know,' she says cheerfully. 'All I know is that he is dead now, for sure. Are you taken ill?'

'No, no,' I say. My lips are numb. All I can say is the one word. 'No. No.'

We crowd together through the narrow streets. I cannot get away now; even if I could get the horse out of the crowd I don't think I could ride. I am limp with fear, quite unable to take up the reins, even if the crowd would let me. And then, at last, we are at Bridgegate and the crowd thickens and pushes. My horse becomes anxious at being so crowded, her ears flicker and she shifts from one leg to another; but we are hemmed in so fast that she cannot move and I cannot dismount. I can see the Lord Mayor of the City as he leaps up on a milestone, balancing with a hand on the broad shoulder of one of the City's guard, and shouts to the crowd, 'I take it it is your will that Captain Mortimer and his men enter the City?'

'Yea!' comes the roar. 'Open the gates!'

I can see that one of the aldermen is arguing, and the Lord

Mayor gestures that he shall be roughly taken away. The guards throw open the gate and we look out through the gateway beyond the drawbridge. On the south side, there is a small army waiting, standards furled. As I watch, they see the gate flung open, they hear the encouraging bellow of the crowd, see the red of the mayor's robe, and they unfurl their banners, fall into ranks and march briskly along the road. People are throwing flowers from the upper storeys of the buildings, waving flags and cheering: this is the procession of a hero. The drawbridge is dropped before them and the clang as it goes down is like the clash of cymbals for a conqueror. The captain at the head of the men turns and, using a great sword, slices through the ropes of the bridge, so that it cannot ever be raised against him. Everyone around me is shouting a welcome, the women are blowing kisses and screaming. The captain marches before his army, his helmet under his arm, his golden spurs sparkling at his boots, a beautiful cape of deep blue velvet rippling from his shoulders, his armour shining. Before him comes his squire, holding a great sword before him, as if he is leading a king, entering into his kingdom.

I cannot tell if it is Richard's sword, I don't know if this man is wearing my husband's hard-won spurs. I close my eyes and feel the coldness of the sweat under my hat. Could he be dead without my knowing it? When I get to the palace will the queen herself comfort me, another widow at court, like Alice de la Pole?

The Lord Mayor steps forwards, the keys to the City on a scarlet cushion, and bows his head to the conqueror, and hands him the keys. From all around, crowds of men are spilling out of the City gate to fall in with the soldiers behind the captain and they are greeted by his army with slaps on the back and settled into rough ranks that march past us, waving at the girls and grinning at the cheers, like an army of liberation, come at last.

The crowd follows him. I swear if he marches on Westminster at the head of such a crowd, he can seat himself on the king's marble throne, this is a man with the City in his hand. But he leads the way to Candlewick Street where the London stone stands proudly in the street to mark the very heart of the City. He strikes the stone with his sword and at the ringing sound the crowd bellows in exultation. 'Now is Mortimer the lord of this city!' he shouts, and stands by the stone, holding his shield in one hand and his sword over his head, while the men cheer him.

'To dine!' he declares, and they all move with him to Guildhall, where the Lord Mayor will spread a dinner for him and his offi-cers. As the crowd goes with him, eager for the off-cuts of beef and the broken baskets of bread, I slip from my horse, take hold of her reins, and lead her carefully out of the crowd, hoping to creep away unnoticed.

I edge down a side road, and then into a smaller alley. I am almost lost but I climb on a step and struggle up into the saddle and turn east, letting the slope of the street take me towards the river. I remember when I was a girl on my way to England, I was lost in the forest and Richard found me. I cannot believe that he will not come looking for me again. It does not seem possible that I should have touched him for the last time, kissed him for the last time; and now I cannot remember the last words I said to him. At least we parted lovingly, I know that. I cannot remember the words that we said nor how we looked; but I know that we parted tenderly, because we always parted tenderly. We used to kiss each other goodnight, we would kiss each other at breakfast. He was always loving to me, even when he should not have thought of me as anything but his lady. Even when I trapped him into giving me our child, and insisted on a secret marriage. For fourteen years he has been lover and husband, and now I am afraid that he is lost to me.

I give my horse her head and let her pick her way through the maze of dirty streets. She knows well enough where the West-minster stables are, and I do not care. When I think of Richard dead in a ditch in Kent, I want to lie down in the gutter and die myself. I put my hand on my belly and think of the child who will never know her father. How can it be that I shall not show Richard his new baby?

It is growing dark as we come to one of the many back gates to the rambling palace. I am surprised to find no-one on sentry duty. I would have expected the gates to be closed and manned with a double guard; but it is like the king to be careless, and without my husband who would command the guard?

'Hi!' I shout as I come close. 'Holla! Open the gate!'

Silence. Silence where there are usually scores of people coming and going. Silence where I would have expected a shouted challenge. I rein the horse in, remembering that, when you feel that something is wrong, it is because something is wrong. 'Open the lantern gate!' I shout, readying myself to turn the horse and spur her away if we are attacked. 'Open the lantern gate for the Duchess of Bedford!' Slowly, the small door in the great gate creaks open, and a stable lad peers nervously out.

'The Duchess of Bedford?'

I pull down my hood so he can see my face. 'Myself. Where is everybody?'

His pinched white face looks up at me. 'Run away,' he says. 'Everyone but me and I couldn't go because my dog is sick, and I didn't want to leave him. Had I better come with you?'

'Run where?'

He shrugs. 'Run away from Captain Mortimer and his army. Some of them ran to join him, some of them ran away.'

I shake my head. I cannot understand this. 'Where is the king, and the queen?'

'Run away too,' he says.

'For God's sake! Where are they, boy?'

'Run away to Kenilworth,' he whispers. 'But I was told to tell no-one.'

I grip onto my horse's mane with cold hands as my heart thuds. 'What? They have abandoned the City?'

'They sent out an army to chase Mortimer back to Kent, but Mortimer turned on them and beat them good. The royal commanders were all killed, the army ran back to London except for those that joined Mortimer. Half of them joined Mortimer. I wish I had gone.'

'Who were the commanders that were killed?' I ask quietly. My voice is steady, and I am pleased at that.

He shrugs. 'All the king's lords, I don't know: Lord Northumberland, Baron Rivers . . . '

'They are dead? All of them?'

'They didn't come back, at any rate.'

'The king?'

'The king wouldn't go to war,' he says contemptuously. 'He went out with his standard but he wouldn't go to war. He kept half his army back and sent out the lords with the other half. And when what was left of them came running back and said they had lost, he and the queen ran off to Kenilworth, the Duke of Somerset, Edmund Beaufort, with them, and Lord Scales went to the Tower.'

'Is Scales there now? Has he fortified the Tower?'

He shrugs. 'I dunno. What's going to happen to me?' he asks.

I look at him, my face as blank as his own. 'I don't know. You'd better look out for yourself.'

I turn my horse from the stable gate of Westminster, since there is no safety there for either of us. I think I had better get to the Tower before nightfall. She steps out bravely enough but we are both weary, and on every street corner there is a brazier and someone roasting meat, and men drinking ale and swearing that the good times have come and that Mortimer will advise the king and there will be no more taxation and no more cheating of the poor and the bad advisors will be driven away. They call me to join them, and they curse me when I shake my head. In the end I have to throw a coin and wish them well, and for the last few streets I pull my hood over my face and sit low in the saddle and hope to sidle by, like a thief in my own city.

I get to the gate of the Tower at last. There are sentries on every wall and they shout down at me, as soon as they see me, 'Halt! Who's there? Stand where you are!'

'The Duchess of Bedford!' I call back, showing them my face. 'Let me in.'

'Your husband the baron has been searching for you all evening,' the young guardsman says as he throws open the gate, comes out to take my bridle, and help me down from the horse. 'Your men came in and said they had lost you. He was afraid you had been captured by the mob. He said he would see them swing for treason if so much of a hair of your head was hurt. He told them! I have never heard such language.'

'My husband?' I ask, suddenly dizzy with hope. 'Did you say my husband was looking for me?'

'Like a madman ...' he starts, then he turns to listen, as we both hear the clatter of hooves on the cobbles. He shouts, 'Horses! Close the gate!' and we rush inside as the gates creak behind us and then I hear Richard shout, 'Rivers! Open up!' and they fling open the double gates and his little band of men rides in like thunder, and he sees me in a moment and jumps down from his horse and catches me up in his arms and kisses me as if we were a squire and his lady once more, and could not bear to part.

'Dear God, I have ridden all round London looking for you,' he gasps. 'I was so afraid they had taken you. Cutler at the house said you were going to Westminster, and the boy at Westminster knew nothing.'

I shake my head, tears running down my face, laughing at the sight of him. 'I'm safe! I'm safe! I got caught up in the crowd and separated from our men. Richard, I thought you were dead. I thought you had been killed in an ambush in Kent.'

'Not I. Poor Stafford was killed, and his brother, but not I. Are you safe? Do you feel well? How did you get here?'

'I got swept up in the crowd. I saw him enter London.'

'Jack Cade?'

'The captain? He is John Mortimer.'

'Jack Cade is his name but he's calling himself Mortimer, and John Amend-All, and all sorts of names. The name Mortimer brings out the supporters of Richard of York for him, it's York's family name. Cade is borrowing it or worse, the duke is lending it. Either way it means more trouble. Where did you see him?'

'Crossing the bridge, and getting the keys of the City.'

'Getting the keys?' my husband demands, dumbfounded.

'They greeted him as a hero, all the common people and the mayor and the aldermen too. He was dressed like a nobleman coming to rule.'

He lets out a whistle. 'God save the king. You'd better tell Lord Scales, he's in command here.'

He tucks his hand under my elbow and leads me to the White Tower. 'Are you tired, beloved?'

'A little.'

'And you feel well? The baby?'

'All right, I think. All well.'

'Were you frightened?'

'A little. My love, I thought you were dead.'

'Not I.'

I hesitate. 'You have seen our house?'

'Nothing that we can't repair when this is over.'

I glance at him. 'They walked in through the door and took what they wanted. It will be hard to repair that.'

He nods. 'I know. But we will do it. Now, I'll get you some wine and some meat as soon as we find Scales. He'll need to know where Cade is tonight.'

'Dining with the Lord Mayor, I think.'

Richard pauses and looks at me. 'A man who has brought an army out of Kent and defeated the king's men has the keys to the City of London and is dining with the Lord Mayor?'

I nod. 'They greeted him like he was freeing them from a tyrant. The Lord Mayor and all the aldermen welcomed him to the City like a hero.'

Richard scowls. 'You'd better tell Scales,' is all he says.

Lord Scales is in a state of ill-concealed terror. He is using the Constable of the Tower's house and he has double guards on the front and back doors and at the windows. Clearly, he fears that his king has abandoned him and the City together to the men from Kent. His men may be of the royal guard and have taken the king's shilling but what is to say that they are not Kentishmen, or that they do not have a family making a poor living at Dover? Half of them have come from Normandy and feel betrayed; why should they defend us now, who let them be driven from their own homes? When I tell him that Cade was welcomed as a hero he tells me that I must have been mistaken. 'He is a scoundrel and a villain,' he rules.

'There were many in his train who were gentlemen,' I say. 'I could see they had good horses and good saddles. Cade himself rode like a man accustomed to command. And there was only one alderman in the whole of the City who did not welcome him.'

'He's a villain,' he says rudely.

I raise an eyebrow at Richard. He shrugs as if to say that I have done my best to give this most nervous commander an idea of the enemy, and if he is too afraid to listen then I need do no more. 'I'll take my wife to my rooms and get her something to eat,' he says to Lord Scales. 'Then shall I come back and we can plan an attack? Perhaps tonight when they have wined and dined? While they are celebrating? Or as they march back to Southwark? We could catch them in the narrow streets before the bridge and push them over?'

'Not tonight! Not tonight!' Scales says quickly. 'Besides, I am expecting reinforcements from the king. He will send us men from the Midlands.'

'They can't come for days, if they come at all,' my husband says. 'Surely we should attack them now, before they expect it, while they are drinking.'

'Not tonight,' Scales repeats. 'These are not Frenchmen, Rivers. Our experience is no use here. These are treasonous peasants, they fight around back streets and in hiding. We should wait till we have a great force to overwhelm them. I will send another message to the king and ask for his command.'

I see my husband hesitate, and then he decides not to argue. He throws his cape around my shoulders and takes me to his lodgings. We have our usual rooms near the royal apartments in the Tower, but it feels strange, with the king and queen so far away, and the drawbridge up and the portcullis down and us besieged among the people who are our countrymen.

'It's damnable,' my husband says shortly, snapping his fingers for the serving man to leave the tray of food. 'Damnable. And the very men who should be putting down this unrest are either too half-hearted or too afraid to act. Get you to bed, sweetheart, and I will join you after I have posted a watch. That we should be all but besieged in the Tower of London? At war in England with Englishmen? It beggars belief.'

We live under siege in the Tower, at war in our own country, besieged in our own capital city. Every day my husband sends out men and even the kitchen girls to get news in the market place and at the City gates. They come back saying that Cade's army is camped south of the river with more joining them every day. Richard's great fear is that the uprising will spread and the men of Hampshire and Sussex will join the men of Kent. 'What about our home?' I ask him, thinking of the children in their nursery. 'Should I go back to them?'

'The roads aren't safe,' he says, scowling with worry. 'I'll send you with a guard as soon as I know what is happening. But I don't even know if the king is safely at Kenilworth. We have sent messages but heard nothing back yet. If he's besieged ...' He breaks off.

It feels like the end of the world. If the common people rise against the king, if they are armed with weapons they have won from us, if they are commanded by a man who has been trained by us and embittered by losses in France, then there is no hope that the world we know can continue. Only a heroic king who could capture the love of the people could save us – and we have only King Henry, hiding at Kenilworth, his beautiful armour laid aside after its one and only outing.

A message comes from the rebel army. They want Lord Say, the man who was Lord of Kent, sent out for trial. 'We cannot release him to them,' my husband says to the commander, Lord Scales. 'They will kill him.'

'We are holding him here under arrest for treason,' the lord says reasonably enough. 'He could well have been tried and found guilty and then he would have been executed anyway.'

'The king sent him here for his safety, not to charge him with treason, as we both know, my lord. The king would have released him. You know the king would have forgiven him anything he has done.'

'I shall release him to them, and if he is innocent of all they say, then he can tell them so,' Lord Scales says.

My husband swears under his breath and then speaks clearly. 'My lord, if we send Lord Say out to them, guilty or innocent, they will kill him. This is not a release, it is to push him out of safety to his death. If this doesn't matter to you now, then I ask you what you will do if the rebels ask for me to be sent out to them. What would you like us to do when they ask for you?'

His lordship glowers. 'I wasn't the man who said I would make a deer park out of Kent. I didn't say they were too good for hanging and should be pushed into the sea.'

'You are advisor to the king, as are we all. They could name any one of us and ask for us to be sent out. Are we going to obey the servants? Are they our new masters?'

Lord Scales rises from his seat behind the great dark wooden table and goes to the arrowslit window that looks towards the City. 'Woodville, my old friend, I know you are right; but if they attack us with the numbers they have now, they are likely to take the Tower, and then we will all be at their mercy, your wife as well as us.'

'We can hold out,' my husband says.

'They have a full-size army at Southwark, and every day more men come from Essex and camp out there. There are hundreds now. Who knows how strong they may become? If they come from Essex, what's to stop them coming from Hertfordshire? From Nottinghamshire? What if they can raise the whole country against us?'

'Better strike now then, before they grow any stronger.'

'What if they have the king, and we don't yet know it?'

'Then we will have to fight them.'

'But if we negotiate with them, promise them a pardon, say that their grievances will be resolved, promise them an inquiry, they will go back to their little farms and get the hay in.'

'If we pardon them, we will have taught them that they can take up arms against the King of England,' my husband objects. 'And that is a lesson we may regret one day.'

'I cannot risk the safety of the Tower,' Lord Scales says firmly. 'We cannot attack, we must prepare to defend. At the worst, Lord Say buys us time.'

There is a silence as my husband absorbs the fact that they are going to send one of the peers of England out to face a mob that wants him dead. 'You are the commander,' he says stiffly. 'I am here under your command. But my advice is that we defy them.'

That afternoon they send Lord Say out to Guildhall where those aldermen who have the stomach for it, and the rebels who are eager for it, create a little court for the day. They persuade his lordship to confess, find him a priest and take him to Cheapside for execution. His son-in-law, the Sheriff of Kent, William Crowmer, thinks himself lucky to be released from the Fleet prison, and steps out of the stone doorway cheerfully, thinking a rescue party has come for him, only to find a scaffold waiting for him outside the gates. They don't even bother to try him, but string him up without ceremony.

'God forgive them,' my husband says as we stand on the walls of the Tower, hidden by the parapet, looking down into the streets below. A dancing, singing, chanting mob is weaving its unsteady way through the narrow lanes towards the Tower. My husband interposes his broad shoulder before me, but I peep around his arm and see what is leading the procession. They have the head of Lord Say on a pike, bobbing along at the front of the crowd. Behind on another pike is the stabbed head of William Crowmer, the sheriff who promised to lay waste to his county of Kent. As they come within range of the Tower gates they pause and bawl defiance, and then dance the two heads together. The dead faces bump, the pike-bearers jiggle the pikes so the mouths knock one against another. 'They're kissing! They're kissing!' they howl and roar with laughter at the spectacle. 'Send us out Lord Scales!' they bellow. 'He can have a kiss too!'

Richard draws me back into the shadow of the wall. 'My God,' I say quietly. 'This is the end, isn't it? This is the end of the England we have known. This is the end of everything.'

Next night, at dinner, I see Richard put his head down over his plate and eat steadily, hardly pausing for breath, but drinking no wine at all. Throughout the meal his servants come and whisper brief messages in his ear. After dinner there is never dancing or singing, not even playing at cards, but tonight it is even more hushed and nervous. The remnants of this beleaguered court stand around in groups and exchange fearful whispers. Then Richard stands up on the steps of the dais and raises his voice. 'My lords, gentlemen: a number of the gentlemen and merchants of London tell me that they are weary of Cade and his men running riot through the City. Also, matters are getting worse and no man can be sure that his home and his goods are safe. Cade has lost control of his men and they are looting the City. The London men tell me that they are determined to push the soldiers out of the City, back to their camp at Southwark tonight, and I have agreed that we will join with them to drive the rebels back, raise the drawbridge and close the gate. They are not going to enter London again.'

He raises his hand at the buzz of noise. 'Lord Scales will command,' he says. 'We will muster in the courtyard at nine of the clock, weapons will be distributed now. I expect all able-bodied men to arm and come with me.'

He steps down, and men crowd around him at once. I hear him explaining the plan, and sending men to get their weapons. I stand a little closer and wait for him to turn to me.

'I'll leave a guard on the Tower,' he says. 'Enough to hold it. The king is sending reinforcements from the Midlands, they will be here tomorrow, or the next day. You'll be safe here until I come back.'

He sees the unspoken question in my face. 'If I don't come back, you should put on your plainest clothes and make your way on foot, out of the City,' he says. 'Cutler will go with you or any of our men. Once you are out of the City you can buy or borrow horses to get home. I can't tell what will happen then. But if you can get home to the children, you can live off our lands, and you should be safe there until it all comes right again. Our tenants would stand by you. Jacquetta, I am sorry. I never thought it would come to this. I didn't mean to bring you out of France to danger in England.'

'Because if the rebels take London, then nowhere is safe?' I ask him. 'If you cannot drive them out of the City then they will take England in time?'

'I don't know how this will end,' he says. 'A king who leaves London to the peasants and a half-pay captain? A penniless crowd who say that they own the City? I don't know what might happen next.'

'Come back,' is all I can manage.

'It is my intention,' he says tightly. 'You are the love of my life. I will come back to you if I possibly can. I have sworn it. I am going to be there at the baptism of our new baby, my love. And God willing, make another.'

A vision of the dancing head of Lord Say comes to my mind and I blink to try to rid myself of it. 'Richard, God send you back safely to me,' I whisper.

I watch them muster in the great central yard of the Tower and then leave quietly by the sally-port, into the silent streets. I climb to the walkway at the top of the walls that run around the Tower and stand by a soldier on guard to watch them make their way quietly to the City. Richard has them in squares, four men by four men, all of them with pikes, many with swords, most of them with muffled feet. I see all this, but I am trying to see more. I am trying to see if there is a shadow over them, if they are marching out to their death. Especially, I am looking for the tall figure of my husband, at the head of his division, his sword drawn, his hooded head looking this way and the other, every sense alert, vibrantly alive, angry to have been brought to this.

I glimpse him only briefly before they slip between the crowded buildings but I have no sense of premonition. Richard seems, as he always has been, so passionately alive, so vital, that there could never be a shadow over him. For a moment I think that perhaps this proves that he will come home in the morning in triumph, and then I think that if he were going out to certain death he would still go out to it with his head up, his shoulders squared, and his footstep light.

Then we wait. We can hear some shouting from the street and we have the cannon trained on the raggle-taggle army camped in the marshes below the Tower, and pointed north to the streets, but no-one comes within range. The fighting is going on hand-to-hand, in one street after another as the rebels surge forwards and the apprentices and merchants, well armed and defending their homes, push them back. My husband commanding one wing of our forces and Lord Scales commanding another fight their way through the treacherous streets, always heading for the river. The rebels make a stand before Bridgegate where the lanes grow close and narrow, but the soldiers from the Tower push forwards and push on and gradually they yield, falling back over the bridge, a yard at a time. This time the doors of the houses on the bridge are barred and the shutters are over the windows, the tradesmen and merchants on the bridge are battened inside their homes, sick of the disorder and fearing worse as the slow battle grinds across the river, a yard at a time. The grinning heads of Lord Say and William Crowmer look down from the spikes of the bridge as their murderers are pressed back, one slow pace after another, and the royal army doggedly pushes on.

Forewarned by me, my husband has thick coils of rope and craftsmen in the vanguard of the men, and as soon as they force their way past the anchor points, he has the workmen ringed with a guard as they feverishly replace the ropes that I saw Jack Cade slash with his stolen sword. Desperately the men work, fearing arrows and missiles from the rebel army, as my husband, at the head of his men, fights with his sword in one hand and an axe in another, going forwards and forwards until Cade's army is thrust to the far side of the bridge, then at a shouted command from my husband and a blast of trumpets, loud above the noise, the royal army breaks off, runs back to its own side, and with a rumble and a roar the drawbridge is raised and my husband leans on his bloody sword, grins at Lord Scales and then looks back along the long twenty-span bridge at the English dead who are being rolled carelessly into the river, and the wounded who are groaning and calling for help.

That night he sits in a deep hot bath in our rooms and I soap the nape of his neck and his strong muscled back as if we were a peasant and his doxy taking their annual bath on Shrove Tuesday. 'Good,' he says. 'Pray God the worst of this is over.'

'Will they beg for forgiveness?'

'The king has sent pardons already,' he says, his eyes closed as I pour a jug of hot water over his head. 'Hundreds of them, blank forms of pardons. Hundreds of them, without a thought. And a bishop to fill in the names. They are all to be forgiven and told to go home.'

'Just like that?' I ask.

'Just like that,' he says.

'Do you think they will each take a pardon and go home and forget all about it?'

'No,' he says. 'But the king hopes that they were misled and mistaken and that they have learned their lesson and will accept his rule. He wants to think that it is all the fault of a bad leader and the rest of them were just mistaken.'

'Queen Margaret won't think that,' I predict, knowing the power of her temper and that she learned how to rule over a peasantry who were held down by force and deference.

'No she won't. But the king has decided on pardons, whatever she thinks.'

Jack Cade's army, which was so brave and so filled with hope for a better world, lines up to take the pardons, and seems to be glad to do so. Each man says his name and Bishop William Waynflete's clerk, in the rebel camp with a little writing desk, writes each name down and tells each man to go home, that the king has forgiven his offence. The bishop blesses them, signing the cross over each bowed head, and tells them to go in peace. Jack Cade himself lines up for his piece of paper and is publicly forgiven for leading an army against the king, killing a noble lord and invading London. Some men see this as the king's weakness, but the greatest number of them think themselves lucky to get off scot-free, and they go back to their poor homes where they cannot pay their taxes, where they cannot get justice, where the great lords ride roughshod over them – and hope for better times. They are just as they were before; but more bitter – and still the good times have not come.

But not Cade. I find my husband in the stables, his face dark with temper, ordering our horses in a bellowing voice. It seems that we are going back to Grafton, we are going back to Grafton 'at once!', the roads are safe enough if we take a good guard.

'What's the matter?' I ask. 'Why are we going now? Isn't the king coming? Should we not stay in London?'

'I can't stand to see him, nor her,' he says flatly. 'I want to go home for a while. We'll come back, of course we will, we will come back the moment they send for us; but before God, Jacquetta, I cannot stomach the court a moment longer.'

'Why? What has happened?'

He is tying his travelling cape on the back of his saddle and his back is to me. I go behind him and put my hand on his shoulder. Slowly he turns to face me. 'I see you're angry,' I say. 'But speak to me: tell me what has happened.'

'The pardons,' he says, through his clenched teeth. 'Those damned pardons. Those hundreds of pardons.'

'Yes?'

'Jack Cade took his pardon in the name of John Mortimer. The name he used in battle.'

'So?'

'So they chased after him, despite his pardon, and they have captured him, despite his pardon. He showed them his pardon, signed by the king, blessed by the bishop, written fair in the name of John Mortimer. But they are going to hang him in the name of Jack Cade.'

I pause, struggling to understand. 'The king gave him a pardon, he can't be hanged. He just has to show his pardon, they cannot hang him.'

'The king's pardon is in one name, which they know him by. They will hang him under another.'

I hesitate. 'Richard, he should never have been pardoned in the first place.'

'No. But here we show everyone that his very cause was just. He said that there was no rule of law, but that the lords and the king do as they please. Here we prove it is so. We make a peace on the battlefield while he is in arms, while he is strong and we are weak; when he is near to victory and we are trapped in the

Tower. We give him a pardon, that is our word of honour, but we break it as soon as he is a fugitive. The king's name is on the pardon, the king gave his word. Turns out that means nothing. The pardon is worth no more than the paper, the king's own signature nothing more than ink. There is no agreement, there is no justice, we betray our own cause, we are forsworn.'

'Richard, he is still our king. Right or wrong, he is still the king.'

'I know, and that is why I say that we will come back to court and serve him again. He is our king, we are his people. He gave us our name and our fortune. We will come back to court in the autumn. But I swear to you, Jacquetta, I just can't stomach it this summer.'

GRAFTON, NORTHAMPTONSHIRE, SUMMER 1450

We arrive at our home at the height of the year with the harvest coming in, and the calves weaned from the cows. In the loft the apples arc laid in rows, strict as soldiers, and one of the tasks for Lewis, now twelve, is to go up every day with a basket and bring down eight apples for the children to eat after their dinners. I am feeling weary with this baby and as the evenings are cool and quiet I am happy to sit by the fire in my small chamber and listen while Richard's cousin Louise, who serves as governess to the oldcr ones and nurse to the babies, hears them read from the family Bible. Anthony at eight has a passion for books and will come to me to look at the pictures in the volumes of Latin and old French that I inherited from my husband, and puzzle out the words in the difficult script. I know that this autumn he and his brothers and sisters can no longer be taught by the priest but I must find a scholar to come and teach them. Lewis especially must learn to read and write in Latin and Greek if he is to attend the king's college.

The baby comes in the middle of August and we fetch down the family crib, polish it up, launder the little sheets and I go into my confinement. She is born easily, she comes early without great trouble, and I call her Martha. Within a few weeks Richard has taken her into the small chapel where we were married and she is christened, and soon I am churched and up and about again.

It is her, the new baby, that I think of when I start up out of bed one night, as alert as if I had heard someone suddenly call my name. 'What is it?' I demand into the darkness.

Richard, groggy from sleep, sits up in the bed. 'Beloved?'

'Someone called my name! There is something wrong!'

'Did you have a bad dream?'

'I thought . . . ' Our lovely old house is silent in the darkness; a beam creaks as the old timbers settle. Richard gets out of bed and lights a taper at the dying fire and then lights a candle so that he can see me. 'Jacquetta, you are as white as a ghost.'

'I thought someone woke me.'

'I'll take a look around,' he decides, and pulls on his boots and drags his sword out from under the bed.

'I'll go to the nursery,' I say.

He lights me a candle and the two of us go out together into the dark gallery above the hall. And then I hear it. The strong sweet singing of Melusina, so high and so pure that you would think it was the sound of the stars moving in their spheres. I put my hand on Richard's arm. 'Do you hear that?'

'No, what?'

'Music,' I say. I don't want to say her name. 'I thought I heard music.' It is so clear and so powerful that I cannot believe he cannot hear it, like silver church bells, like the truest choir.

'Who would be playing music at this time of night?' he starts to ask, but already I have turned to run down the corridor to the nursery. I stop at the door and make myself open it quietly. Martha, the new baby, is asleep in her crib, the nursemaid in the truckle bed nearest to the fire. I put my hand on the child's rosy cheek. She is warm but not in fever. Her breath comes slowly and steadily, like a little bird breathing in a safe nest. In the high-sided bed beside her sleeps Diccon, humped up with his face buried into the down mattress. Gently I lift him and turn him on his back so I can see the curve of his sleeping eyelids, and his rosebud mouth. He stirs a little at my touch but he does not wake.

The music grows louder, stronger.

I turn to the next bed. John, the five-year-old, is sprawled out in sleep as if he is too hot, the covers kicked sideways, and at once I fear that he is ill but when I touch his forehead he is cool. Jacquetta, next to him, sleeps quietly, like the neat little six-year-old girl that she is, Mary in bed beside her stirs at the light from my candle but still sleeps. Their eleven-year-old sister Anne is in a truckle bed beside them, fast asleep.

Anthony, eight years old, in the bigger bed, sits up. 'What is it, Mama?'

'Nothing, nothing,' I say. 'Go to sleep.'

'I heard singing,' he says.

'There is no singing,' I say firmly. 'Lie down and close your eyes.'

'Lewis is really hot,' he remarks, but does as he is told.

I go quickly to their bed. The two boys sleep together and as Anthony turns on his side I see that Lewis, my darling son, is flushed and burning up. It is his fever that has made their shared bed so hot. As I see him, and hear the insistent ringing music, I know that it is Lewis, my darling twelve-year-old son, who is dying.

The door behind me opens and Richard my husband says quietly, 'It's all secure in the house. Are the children well?'

'Lewis,' is all I can say. I bend to the bed and I lift him. He is limp in my arms, it is like lifting a dead body. Richard takes him from me, and leads the way to our bedroom.

'What is it?' he asks, laying the boy on our bed. 'What is wrong with him? He was well during the day.'

'A fever, I don't know,' I say helplessly. 'Watch him while I get something for him.'

'I'll sponge him,' he suggests. 'He's burning up. I'll try to cool him down.'

I nod and go quickly to my still room. I have a jar of dried yarrow leaves and a bunch of the white blossom hangs from one of the beams. I set a pot on to boil and make a tea from the blossom and then steep the leaves in a bowl of the boiled water. I am fumbling in my haste and all the time the music is ringing in my head, as if to tell me that there is no time, that this is the song of mourning, that all this brewing of tea that smells of summer harvests is too late for Lewis, all I need for him is rosemary.

I take the drink in a cup and the soaking leaves in the jar and run back up to the bedroom. On the way I tap on the door of my lady in waiting and call, 'Anne, get up, Lewis is sick,' and hear her scramble inside.

Then I go into our bedroom.

Richard has stirred the fire and lit more candles but he has drawn the bed curtains so Lewis's face is shaded from the light. Lewis has turned away, I can see the rapid breaths as his thin little chest rises and falls. I put the mug and the jar on the table and go to the bedside.

'Lewis?' I whisper.

His eyelids flutter open at the sound of my voice.

'I want to go in the water,' he says, quite clearly.

'No, stay with me.' I hardly know what I am saying. I raise him so his head is against my shoulder and Richard presses the mug of yarrow tea into my hand. 'Take a little sip,' I say gently. 'Come along. Take a little sip.'

He turns his head away. 'I want to go in the water,' he repeats.

Richard looks desperately at me. 'What does he mean?'

'It is a vision from the fever,' I say. 'It means nothing.' I am afraid of what it means.

Lewis smiles, and his eyelids flicker open, and he sees his father. He smiles at him. 'I shall swim, Father,' he says firmly. 'I shall swim,' and he turns his head and takes a little breath like someone preparing to dive in deep cool waters, and I feel his body quiver as if with joy, and then go still and quiet, and I realise that my son has gone from me.

'Open the window,' I say to Richard.

Without a word he turns and opens the window as if to let the little soul out and up to heaven. Then he comes back and puts the sign of the cross on Lewis's forehead. He is still warm, he is slowly cooling, I think the sweet waters of his dream are washing him down.

Anne taps on the door, opens it, and sees me lay Lewis gently down on the bed.

'He's gone,' I say to her. 'Lewis has gone from us.'

Hardly knowing what I am doing I step towards Richard and he puts his arm around me and holds me close to him. 'God bless him,' he says quietly.

'Amen,' I say. 'Oh Richard, I could do nothing. I could do nothing!'

'I know,' he says.

'I'll go and see the other children,' Anne says into the silence. 'And then I'll get Mrs Westbury to come and wash the body.'

'I'll wash him,' I say at once. 'And I'll dress him. I don't want anyone else to touch him. I'll put him . . . ' I find that I can't say the word 'coffin'.

'I'll help you,' Richard says quietly. 'And we'll bury him in the churchyard and know that he has just gone ahead of us, Jacquetta, and that one day we will swim in the water too, and find him on the other side.'

We bury my son in the churchyard near to his grandfather and Richard orders a grand stone monument with room for our names too. The rest of the children do not take the fever; even the new baby, Martha, is well and strong. I watch them, filled with a terror, for a week after we bury Lewis, but none of them so much as sneezes.

I think that I will dream of Lewis but I sleep deeply every night and dream of nothing at all. Until one night, a month after his death, I dream of a river, a deep cool river studded with yellow water lilies, flowing over a bed of gold and bronze stones, and golden kingcups growing on the green reedy banks; and I see my boy Lewis on the far side of the river, pulling on his linen shirt and his breeches, and he is smiling at me and waving to show that he is going to run on ahead, just a little way ahead. And in my dream, though I want to hold him back, I wave at him and call to him that I will see him later, that I will see him soon, that I will see him in the morning.

Our retreat to Grafton lasts only for a little while. In September the king's messenger rides down the green lanes and up to our front gates. The wide wooden doors swing open and he comes across the courtyard, the royal standard before him, a guard of six riding with him. I am walking back from chapel in the morning, and I pause as I see the gate admit him and I wait, my back to the door of our house, with a sense of danger coming our way. Behind my back I cross my fingers, as if a childish sign can prevent trouble.

'A message for Baron Rivers,' he says, dismounting and bowing.

'I am the Dowager Duchess, Lady Rivers,' I say, holding out my hand. 'You can give it to me.'

He hesitates. 'My husband is hunting,' I continue. 'He will be back tomorrow. In his absence I rule here. You had better give the message to me.'

'I beg your pardon, Your Grace,' he says and hands it over. The royal seal is shiny and hard. I break it, and look up to nod to him.

'You will find ale and bread and meat for you and your men in the hall,' I tell him. 'And someone will show you where to wash. I will read this and send a reply when you have eaten and rested.'

He bows again and the guards give their horses to the stable boys and go into the house. I wait and then walk slowly to a stone bench let into the wall at the side of the garden and sit in the warm sunshine to read the letter.

It is a letter of appointment, another great honour for us. It is an acknowledgement of Richard's service in the late troubles, it shows that the lords of the Privy Council were watching to see who was quick of mind and brave of heart and ready to serve them – even if the king and queen had run away to Kenilworth and saw nothing. It says that Richard is appointed as Seneschal of Gascony, the rich land around Bordeaux that the English have held for three hundred years and hope to hold forever. Once again, Richard and I are to be an occupying force in France. Reading through the lines I guess that the king, shocked by the loss of English lands in Normandy by Edmund Beaufort, Duke of Somerset, is inspired to fortify the lands in Gascony with a more experienced commander. This appointment is an honour, it will bring with it the danger and difficulty of strengthening the forces around Bordeaux, holding the lands against French incursions, keeping the people loyal to England, and reversing their sense that they are all but abandoned by a homeland which cannot rule itself, let alone maintain lands overseas.

I look up from the letter. It is grief which makes me feel that nothing matters. I know this is a great honour, to rule Gascony is a great command. The Rivers are rising, even if one of us is missing. And there is no point in letting my heart ache for the one who is missing.

I look at the letter again. In the margin, like a monk illustrating a manuscript, the king has written in his own clerkish hand.

Dear Rivers,

Oblige me by going at once to Plymouth and mustering and organising a force to take to Gascony and a fleet to carry them. You should set sail on 21 September, no later.

Below this the queen has written to me: '*Jacquetta – Lucky you! Going back to France!*'

'Lucky' is not how I feel. I look around the yard, at the warm red-brick walls capped with white coping stones that lean against the old chapel, the apple tree bowing low with the weight of the last of the fat fruit, ready for picking, the barn which abuts the granary, filled with hay, and our house set plumb in the middle of it all, warm in the sunshine, peaceful this morning, my children at their lessons. I think that the king is setting my husband a task which will likely be impossible, and that once again I have to go to a new country, a new city, and hope to survive among people who begrudge our very presence.

I try to encourage myself by thinking that Gascony will be beautiful in autumn, that perhaps I will be able to see my brothers and sisters, that winter in Bordeaux will be crisp and bright and clear and that spring will be glorious. But I know that the people of the country will be surly and resentful, the French a constant threat, and we will wait for money from England to pay the soldiers, and end up paying out of our own pocket, while at home there will be endless accusations of failure and even treason. I will have to leave my children behind in England. I don't want to go, and I don't want Richard to go either.

I wait for a long time until the royal messenger comes out into the yard, wiping his mouth on his sleeve, sees me, sketches a bow, and waits. 'You can tell His Grace that my husband and I will leave for Plymouth at once,' I say. 'Tell him that we are honoured to serve.'

He smiles ruefully, as if he knows that the service of this king may be an honour but is only a sinecure for the very few favourites who can get away with doing nothing or even fail outright, like Edmund Beaufort, Duke of Somerset, who is now Constable of all England, as a reward for running to Kenilworth when there was dangerous work to do in Kent. 'God save the king,' he says, and goes off to the stable to find his horses.

'Amen,' I respond, thinking that perhaps we should pray that the king is saved from himself.

PLYMOUTH, AUTUMN 1450–1451

One whole year we live between Grafton, London and Plymouth. One long year while we struggle with the burghers of Plymouth, trying to persuade them to house and equip an invasion fleet. One whole year while my husband assembles a fleet from the privately owned ships of merchants, traders, and the few great lords who keep their own vessels. By mid-winter, months after we were supposed to sail, he has more than eighty boats tied up at the quaysides of Plymouth, Dartmouth, Kingsbridge, and more than three thousand men housed in inns and rooms, cottages and farms, all round Devon and Cornwall: waiting.

That's all we do; from autumn, through winter to spring, we wait. First we wait for the men who have been promised by their lords to march to Plymouth, ready to embark. Richard rides out to meet them and bring them in, finds them quarters, finds them food, promises them wages. Then we wait for the ships that have been requisitioned to come in; Richard rides all around the West Country, buying up little sailing ships in their home ports, demanding that the greater merchants make their contribution. Then we wait for the stores to arrive; Richard rides to Somerset, even into Dorset, to get grain, then we wait for the lords who will sail with the invasion to finish the merry days of Christmas and come to Plymouth, then we wait for the king's command that we should finally set sail, then we wait for the spring northerlies to die down, and always, always, always, we wait for the ship which will bring the money from London so that we can pay the harbourside merchants, the ship owners, the sailors, the men themselves. Always we wait: and the money never comes when it should.

Sometimes it comes late, and Richard and I have to send to Grafton and our friends at court to lend us money so that we can at least feed the army before they march out into the farms around the port, and steal to feed themselves. Sometimes it comes; but in such small amounts that we can only pay the outstanding debts and offer the men just a quarter of their pay. Sometimes it comes as tally sticks that we take to the king's custom houses and they say, regretfully, 'Yes, it's good, my lord; I grant your right to be paid. But I have no money to pay you with. Come again next month.' Sometimes it is promised and never comes at all. I watch Richard, riding to the little towns of Devon, trying to appease the local land-lords who are furious at having this hungry horde quartered upon them. I watch him pursue roving bands of the men who were supposed to be his army and are becoming brigands. I watch Richard begging the ship-masters to keep their vessels ready to sail in case the order for the invasion comes tomorrow, the next day, or the day after. And I watch Richard when the news comes from France that the French king has advanced on Bergerac and Bazas and taken them. In spring we hear his forces are advancing on English lands on either side of the Gironde, he sets siege to Fronsac on the Dordogne, and the townspeople wait behind its great walls, swearing they will not give up, certain that our army is coming to relieve them. Our army is on the quayside, where the ships are bobbing, when we hear that Fronsac has surrendered. The English settlers are appealing for help, they vow that they will fight, that they will resist, that they are Englishmen and count themselves as Englishmen born and bred, they stake their lives on their faith in us, they swear that their countrymen will come to their aid. I watch Richard trying to hold his army together, trying to hold his fleet together, sending message after message to London, pleading with the court to send him the order to sail. Nothing comes.

Richard starts to say that when he gets the order to sail he will leave me behind, he dare not take me to Bordeaux if the place is going to come under siege. I walk along the protective wall of the harbour and look south to the lands of France that my first husband used to command, and wish that we were both safely home in Grafton. I write to the queen myself, I tell her that we are ready to go to the rescue of Gascony but we can do nothing without money to pay the soldiers, and that while they kick their heels in the farms and villages they complain of their treatment by us, their masters and lords, and the working men and women of Devon see how badly the soldiers and sailors are treated and say that this is a kingdom where a man is not rewarded for doing his duty. They mutter that the men of Kent had it right – that this is a king who cannot hold his own lands here or abroad, that he is badly advised. They whisper that Jack Cade called for Richard, Duke of York, to be admitted to the king's councils and that Jack Cade was right, and died for his belief. They even say – though I never tell her this – that she is a French woman squandering the money that should go to the army so that her own country can seize the land of Gascony, and England be left with nothing in France at all. I beg her to tell her husband to send the order for his fleet to set sail.

Nothing comes.

In July we hear that Bordeaux has fallen to the French. In September the first refugees from Bayonne start to arrive in tattered craft and say that the whole of the duchy of Gascony has been captured by the French while the expedition to save them, commanded by my unhappy husband, waited in the dock at Plymouth, eating the stores and waiting for orders.

We have been living in a little house overlooking the harbour for all of this long year. Richard uses the first-floor room as his headquarters. I go up the narrow stairs, to find him at the small-paned window, looking out at the blue sea, where the wind is blowing briskly towards the coast of France, good sailing weather; but all his fleet is tied up at the quayside.

'It's over,' he says bluntly to me as I quietly stand beside him. I put my hand on his shoulder; there is nothing I can say to comfort him in this, his moment of shame and failure. 'It is all over, and I did nothing. I am seneschal of nothing. You have been the wife firstly of John Duke of Bedford, a mighty lord, the regent of all of France, and secondly to the seneschal of nothing.'

'You did all that you were commanded to do,' I say softly. 'You held the fleet and the army together, and you were ready to sail. If they had sent the money and the order you would have gone. If they had sent the order alone, you would have gone without the money to pay them. I know that. Everyone knows that. You would have fought unpaid, and the men would have followed you. I don't doubt that you would have saved Gascony. You had to wait for your orders; that was all. It was not your fault.'

'Oh,' he laughs bitterly. 'But I have my orders now.'

I wait, my heart sinking.

'I am to take a force to defend Calais.'

'Calais?' I stumble. 'But surely the King of France is at Bordeaux?'

'They think that the Duke of Burgundy is massing to attack Calais.'

'My kinsman.'

'I know, I am sorry, Jacquetta.'

'Who will go with you?'

'The king has appointed Edmund Beaufort, Duke of Somerset, as Captain of Calais. I am to go and support him as soon as I have dismissed the ships and sailors and the army from here.'

'Edmund Beaufort, Duke of Somerset?' I repeat, disbelievingly. This is the man who lost us Normandy. Why would he be trusted with Calais, but for the king's unswerving belief in his kinsman and the queen's misplaced affection?

'Please God he has learned how to soldier through defeat,' my husband says grimly.

I lean my cheek against his arm. 'At least you can save Calais for the English,' I say. 'They will call you a hero if you can hold the castle and the town.'

'I will be commanded by the man who gave away Normandy,' he says gloomily. 'I will be in service to a man that Richard, Duke of York has named as a traitor. If they don't send us men and money there either then I don't know that we can hold it.'

GRAFTON, NORTHAMPTONSHIRE, AUTUMN 1451

Richard's mood does not lift as he prepares to leave for Calais. I send for Elizabeth, my oldest girl, to come home to see her father before he leaves. I have placed her at the house of the Grey family at Groby Hall, near Leicester, just fifty miles away. They are a wealthy family, with kinsmen all around the country, ruling thousands of acres. She is supervised by the lady of the house: Lady Elizabeth, heiress to the wealthy Ferrers family. I could not have chosen anyone better to teach my girl how a great woman runs her household. There is a son and heir at home, young John Grey, who rode out against Jack Cade, a handsome young man. He will inherit the estate, which is substantial, and the title, which is noble.

It takes her a day to ride home, and she comes with an armed escort, the roads are so dangerous with wandering bands of men, thrown out of France without a home to go to, or wages. Elizabeth is fourteen now, nearly as tall as me. I watch her, and have to stop myself smiling: she is such a beauty and she has such grace. At her age I was probably her match for looks but she has a calmness and a sweetness that I never had. She has my clear pale skin and my fair hair, she has grey eyes and a perfectly regular face like the sculpted marble face of a beautiful statue. When she laughs she is a child; but sometimes she looks at me and I think, dear God, what a girl this is: she has the Sight from Melusina, she is a woman of my line, and she has a future before her which I can neither imagine nor foresee.

Elizabeth's sister Anne is her little shadow; at just twelve she copies every gesture of Elizabeth's and follows her around like a devoted puppy. Richard laughs at me for my adoration of my children and my favourite of them all is Elizabeth's brother: Anthony. He is nine and a brighter scholar never lost count of the hours in a library. But he is not just a boy for his books, he plays with the village lads and can run as fast and fight as hard as they, with fists or in wrestling. His father is teaching him to joust and he sits on a horse as if he were born in the saddle. You never see him shift to the leap of the horse: they are as one. He plays tennis with his sisters and is kind enough to let them win, he plays chess with me and makes me pause and puzzle over his moves, and sweetest, warmest of all, he goes down on one knee for his mother's blessing night and morning, and when I have put my hand on his head, he jumps up for a hug and will stand at my side, leaning lightly against me, like a foal at foot. Mary is eight this year, growing out of her dresses every season, and devoted to her father. She follows him everywhere, riding all day on her fat little pony so that she can be at his side, learning the names of the fields and the tracks to the villages so she can go out to meet him. He calls her his princess and swears he will make a marriage for her to a king who will have no kingdom but will come and live with us so no-one will ever take her away. Our next child, just a year younger, Jacquetta, is named for me but she could not be less like me. She is Richard's daughter through and through, she has his quiet humour and his calmness. She keeps a distance from her brothers' and sisters' tumblings and quarrels, and she laughs when they appeal to her to serve as judge and jury from the pinnacle of the wisdom of a seven-year-old. In the nursery, unruly as puppies, are my two boys John and Richard, six and five years old, and in the well-polished cradle is the new baby, the sweetest best-tempered baby of them all: Martha.

As Richard assembles the men he will take to Calais and starts to teach them how to use the lances, how to stand against a charge, how to march in an attack, I have to keep telling myself that this is the right thing to do – to send him off with the blessings of all his children; but there is something about gathering them together to say goodbye that fills me with dread.

'Jacquetta, are you fearful for me?' he asks me one evening.

I nod, almost ashamed to say yes.

'Have you seen anything?' he asks.

'Oh no! Thank God! No, it is not that. I don't know anything at all, nothing more than that I fear for you,' I assure him. 'I have not tried to scry or foretell since you told me to put it aside, after the trial of Eleanor Cobham.'

He takes my hands and kisses them, first one and then the other. 'My love, you must not fear for me. Do I not always tell you I will come home to you?'

'Yes.'

'Have I ever failed you?'

'Never.'

'I lost you once and swore I would never lose you again,' he says.

'You found me by moonlight.' I am smiling.

'By luck,' he says, a man of earth as always. 'But I swore then that I would never lose you again. You have nothing to fear.'

'Nothing,' I repeat. 'But I should tell you – I am with child again, and you will have a new baby next summer.'

'Dear God, I can't leave you,' he says at once. 'This changes everything. I can't leave you here, not alone with the children, to face another childbed.'

I had hoped he would be pleased; I am determined to hide my own fears. 'Beloved, I have been brought to bed nine times, I think I know how to do it by now.'

His face is creased with worry. 'The danger is always the same,' he says. 'The danger of childbirth is the same the first time as the last. And you have lost one son, and I thought then your heart would break. Besides, the news from London is bad. The queen is certain to want you at her side, and I will be stuck in Calais with Edmund Beaufort.'

'If you even get there.'

He falls silent and I know he is thinking of the idle ships and the army that wore out their time with a year of waiting, while their countrymen died outside Bordeaux.

'Don't look like that, I should not have said it. I am sure you will get there and then you will hold Calais for us,' I say quickly.

'Yes, but I don't like to leave you here while the king is clinging to Somerset and York is building an affinity of more and more men who think as he does that the king is badly advised.'

I shrug. 'There is no way out, my love. The baby is coming and I had better have her here, rather than come with you to Calais and give birth in a garrison.'

'You think it will be another girl?' he asks.

'The girls will be the making of this family,' I predict. 'You wait and see.'

'Queens militant?'

'One of these girls is going to make a marriage which will make our fortunes,' I say. 'Why else would God make them so beautiful?'

I speak bravely enough to Richard but when he musters his men and marches out of the courtyard and down the road to London where they will take ship to Calais, I am very low. My daughter Elizabeth finds me walking with my thick cape around my shoulders, my hands in a fur muff, beside the river, as the frosty banks and the icy reeds match my mood. She comes forwards and links her arm in mine and matches her steps to mine. I am only a head taller than her now, she keeps pace with me easily.

'Are you missing Father already?' she asks gently.

'Yes,' I say. 'I know I am a soldier's wife and I should be ready to let him go but each time it is hard and I think that it gets harder, not easier.'

'Can you foretell his future?' she asks quietly. 'Can't you see that he will come home safely? I am certain this time he will be safe. I just know it.'

I turn and look at her. 'Elizabeth, can you foresee things at will?'

She gives a little shrug of the shoulders. 'I'm not sure,' she says. 'I don't know.'

For a moment I am back in that hot summer, in the chamber of my great-aunt Jehanne as she showed me the cards and gave me the bracelet of charms, and told me the story of the women of our family.

'It's not something that I would press on you,' I say. 'It is a burden as well as a gift. And these are not the times for it.'

'I don't think you can press it on me,' she replies thoughtfully. 'I don't think it is a gift you can give – is it? I just sometimes have a sense of things. At Groby, there is a corner, a cloister by the chapel, and when I walk there I can see someone, a woman, almost a ghost of a woman; she stands there and she has her head on one side as if she is listening for me, she waits almost as if she is looking for me. But there is no-one there really.'

'You know the stories of our family,' I say.

She gives a gurgle of laughter. 'It is me who tells the story of Melusina every night to the little ones,' she reminds me. 'They love it, and I love it.'

'You know that some of the women of our family have inherited gifts from Melusina. Gifts of the Sight.'

She nods.

'My great-aunt Jehanne taught me some ways to use the gift, and then my lord the Duke of Bedford had me work with his alchemists, and sent a woman to teach me about herbs.'

'What did you do with alchemists?' Like any child she is fascinated by forbidden magic. The skill with herbs is too ordinary for her, she has learned it in my still room. She wants to know about dark arts.

'I read the books with them, sometimes I stirred a mixture or poured it out to cool.' I am remembering the forge in the inner courtyard and the great room like a vast kitchen in the wing of the house where they heated and cooled the liquor and stones. 'And my lord had a great mirror where he wanted me to scry – to see the future. He wanted to see the future of the English lands in France.' I make a little gesture. 'I am glad now that I could not see clearly. It would have broken his heart, I think. I thought I failed him at the time but now I think I served him best by not seeing.'

'But you could see?'

'Sometimes,' I say. 'And sometimes, like with the cards or with the charms, you get a glimpse of what might be. And sometimes you show yourself only your own desires. And sometimes – though very rarely – you can put your heart in your own desires and bring them about. Take the dream and make it come into being.'

'By magic?' she breathes. She is quite entranced at the thought of it.

'I don't know,' I tell her honestly. 'When I knew that your father was in love with me and I was in love with him, I wanted him to marry me and make me his wife and bring me to England but I knew that he would not dare. He thought I was too far above him and he would not be my ruin.'

'Did you make a spell?'

I smile, thinking back to the night when I brought out the charms but realised that I needed nothing but my own determination. 'A spell and a prayer and knowing your desire are all the same thing,' I say. 'When you lose something precious and you go to the chapel and you kneel before the little glass window of St Anthony and you pray to him to find the thing you need, what are you doing but reminding yourself that you have lost something and you want it back? What are you doing but showing yourself that you want it? And what is that but calling it back to you? And so often, when I pray, I remember then where I left it, and go back to find it. Is that an answer to prayer or is it magic? Or is it simply letting myself know what I want and seeking it? The prayer is just the same as a spell, which is just the same as knowing your desire that calls the thing back to your mind, and so back to your hand. Isn't it?'

'A spell would bring it back to you, you wouldn't just find it!'

'I believe that a desire and a prayer and a spell are all the same thing,' I say. 'When you pray you know that you want something, that's always the first step. To let yourself know that you want something, that you yearn for it. Sometimes that's the hardest thing to do. Because you have to have courage to know what you desire. You have to have courage to acknowledge that you are unhappy without it. And sometimes you have to find courage to know that it was your folly or your wrongdoing which lost it; before you make a spell to bring it back, you have to change yourself. That's one of the deepest transformations that can be.'

'How?'

'Say one day, when you are married, you want a baby, a child?' She nods.

'First you have to know the emptiness of your womb, of your arms, of your heart. That can hurt. You have to have the courage to look at yourself and know the loss that you feel. Then you have to change your life to make a space for the child who will not come. You have to open your heart, you have to make a safe place for the baby. And then you have to sit with your longing and your desire and that can be the most painful. You have to sit with your longing and know that you may not get what you want; you have to encounter the danger of longing for something without the expectation of getting your desire.'

'But this never happened to you,' she suggests.

'In my first marriage,' I say quietly, 'I knew that my husband would not have a child. But I had to let myself know that I was different from him. I longed for a baby, and I wanted to be loved.'

'Did you wish for it?' she asks. 'Did you make a spell to make him change?'

'I didn't try to change him, but I had to know the sorrow of what was missing in my life. I had to find the courage to know that I had made the mistake of marrying a man who would not love me for myself, and who would not give me a child, and once I knew that, truly knew that I was an unloved maid – though a married woman – then I could wish that someone loved me.'

'And you wished for Father.'

I smile at her. 'And for you.'

She blushes in pleasure. 'Is this magic?'

'In a way. Magic is the act of making a wish come about. Like praying, like plotting, like herbs, like exerting your will on the world, making something happen.'

'Will you teach me?' she asks.

I look at her consideringly. She is a daughter of our house and perhaps the most beautiful girl we have ever had. She has the inheritance of Melusina and the gift of Sight. One of my children must inherit the cards my great-aunt gave me and the bracelet of charms – I think I always knew that it would be Elizabeth, the child born of desire, of the herbs, and my wish. And as my great-aunt Jehanne said: it should be the oldest girl.

'Yes,' I say. 'These are not the times, and these are forbidden skills; but I will teach you, Elizabeth.'

Over the next few weeks I show her the bracelet of charms and the cards and I teach her about herbs that she will not find in Lady Elizabeth Grey's still room. I take all the older children out on one frosty day and teach them how to find water in underground springs by holding a peeled wand in their hands and feeling it turn in their palms. They laugh with delight as we find a spring in the water meadow, and a dirty old drain from the stable yard.

I show Elizabeth how to open a page of her Bible and then think and pray over the text that comes to her. I give her a freshwater pearl on a little cord and teach her how to watch it swing in answer to a question. And more importantly than anything else I start to teach her how to clear her mind, how to know her desires, how to judge herself; putting aside favour and indulgence. 'The alchemists always say you have to be pure. You are the first ingredient,' I tell her. 'You have to be clean.'

When the time comes for her to go back to Groby Hall she tells me that the young man of the house, John Grey, is a most handsome young man, kind and beautifully mannered, and that she wishes he would see her for herself, and not just as a girl being educated by his mother, one of three or four young women that Lady Grey has in her keeping.

'He does,' I assure her. 'He sees you already. You just have to be patient.'

'I like him so much,' she confesses, her eyes down and her cheeks warm. 'And when he speaks to me I say nothing of any sense. I speak like a fool. He must think me a fool.'

'He doesn't.'

'Shall I use a love potion on him? Dare I?'

'Wait for spring,' I advise her. 'And pick some flowers from an apple tree in his orchard. Choose the prettiest tree ... '

She nods.

'Put the petals in your pocket. And when the tree fruits, take one apple and give him half to eat with honey, and keep the other.'

'Will that make him love me?'

I smile. 'He will love you. And the petals and honeyed apple will give you something to do while you wait.'

She giggles. 'You're not much of a spell-maker, Lady Mother.'

'When a beautiful young woman wants to enchant a man she doesn't need much of a spell,' I assure her. 'A girl like you needs to do nothing much more than stand under an oak tree and wait for him to ride by. But do you remember about wishing?'

'Pure in heart,' she says.

Together we go out to the stable yard. The guard to take her back to Groby is mounted and ready. 'One last thing,' I say and take her hand before she climbs on the mounting block. She turns to listen. 'Don't curse,' I say to her. 'No ill-wishing.'

She shakes her head. 'I wouldn't. Not even Mary Sears. Not even when she smiles at him and curls her hair around her finger, and is so quick to sit beside him.'

'Ill-wishing is a curse on the woman who does it, as well as the one who receives it. When you put such words out in the world they can overshoot – like an arrow – that's what my great-aunt Jehanne told me. A curse can go beyond your target and harm another. A wise woman curses very sparingly. I would hope that you never curse at all.' Even as I speak I feel the shadow of the future on her. 'I pray that you never have cause to curse,' I say.

She kneels for my blessing. I put my hand on the pretty velvet bonnet and her warm fair head. 'Bless you, my daughter, and may you remain pure in heart and get your desires.'

She peeps up at me, her grey eyes bright. 'I think I will!'

'I think you will,' I say.

LONDON, SPRING 1452

With my husband serving as Captain in Calais, I return to court in the cold weather of January and find everyone talking about the treason of Richard, Duke of York, who is said to be preparing a complete rebellion against the king his cousin because of his hatred of the Duke of Somerset.

The queen is determined that the threat shall be faced and defeated. 'If he is against the Duke of Somerset, he is against me,' she says. 'I have no better or more trustworthy friend. And this Richard of York wants him tried for treason! I know who the traitor is! But he shows his hand at last and confesses that he is against the king.'

'He asks only for the great lords to intercede for him with the king,' I remark calmly. 'He wants them to put his case to the king. And in the meantime, he swears his loyalty.'

She throws the manifesto that York has sent around the main towns of the kingdom on the table before me. 'Who do you think this means? York says that the king is surrounded by enemies, adversaries and evil-willers. He is attacking the king's advisors. That's you, he means, and your husband, as well as Somerset and me.'

'Me?'

'Jacquetta, he accuses me of being William de la Pole's lover; do you think he would blink at calling you a witch?'

I feel the room grow very still and cold. I put my hand to my belly as if to shield the new life within. The ladies in waiting in earshot look up at me, their eyes wide, but say nothing.

'He has no cause for such an accusation,' I say quietly, though I can hear my heart hammering. 'You yourself know that I would never play with such toys. I don't use herbs except for my family's health, I don't even consult with wise women. I read nothing but permitted books, I speak to no-one . . .'

'He has no cause to say anything,' she declares. 'What cause does he have to speak against Edmund Beaufort, Duke of Somerset? Against me? But remember that he is my enemy and your enemy too. And that if he can destroy you he will do so, just to hurt me.'

She takes her seat at the fireside, and I read the manifesto more carefully. The Duke of York demands that Edmund Beaufort be charged with treason and arrested. He warns against bad advisors who have gathered around the queen, foreign-born advisors, ill-wishers. In truth, he says nothing against me by name. But I cannot rid myself of the familiar pulse of fear.

The king is inspired to warlike behaviour by the threat to his friend Edmund Beaufort the Duke of Somerset. Nothing else would waken him but a threat to his beloved cousin. Suddenly he is active, courageous, determined. He declares his absolute faith in Edmund Beaufort and his other advisors. He declares that Richard, Duke of York, is a rebel, and he demands forces to be mustered from all the towns, counties and shires. The king's army pours in from all around the kingdom. Nobody wants to support the Duke of York, only the men of his affinity, and those who share his hatred of Edmund Beaufort for their own reasons go to his standard and start to create an army.

Henry calls for his armour once more, again has his war horse saddled up. The lads in the yard tease his standard bearer that he will have another nice ride out for a day, and assure him that they will keep his dinner warm for him, for he will be back before sunset; but the lords of council and the commanders of the army are not laughing.

The queen and the ladies of her court go down to the frosty jousting green at Westminster to see the parade of the lords ride by on their way out to do battle with the Duke of York.

'I wish your husband were here to support him,' she says to me as the king mounts his great grey war horse, his standard before him and his crown on his helmet. He looks much younger than his thirty years, his eyes bright and eager; his smile, as he waves to Margaret, is excited.

'God save him,' I say, thinking of the battle-hardened forty-year-old Duke of York mustering his own men.

The trumpets blow, the drummers sound the pace of the march, the cavalry go out first, their standards bright in the icy sun-light, their armour glinting, their horseshoes thunderous on the cobbles, and then after them come the archers and after them the pikemen. This is only a small part of the royal army; tens of thousands of men are waiting for the king's orders at Blackheath. His councillors have mustered a mighty army for him. From there he will march north to confront the rebel duke.

The march does not happen. Richard, Duke of York, comes into the royal tent and kneels before his king, praying earnestly that the king dismiss the favoured Duke of Somerset and citing old injuries: the loss of the lands in France, the shameful surren-der of Rouen, and finally the likely destruction of the garrison of Calais by his selfish seizing of command, which is certain to fail.

He can do no more, he can say no more.

'We don't care,' Margaret says to me, as I brush her hair before bed that evening. 'We don't care what he thinks of Edmund Beaufort, we don't care what he says about Calais, or about me, or about you. He knew he was defeated when we raised an army three times the size of his. He knew he would have to withdraw everything he said. He knew he would have to beg our pardon. He is a broken man. His rebellion is ended. We have broken him.'

I say nothing. The duke does indeed kneel to the king in public and swear never to assemble his men again. The country sees that the king is beloved and the duke is not. The country sees that Edmund Beaufort is unassailable and the Duke of York is defeated.

'*I don't doubt the duke is outwardly penitent; but I doubt that the duke's complaints are over,*' Richard writes to me from Calais.

The royal couple at any rate are united in their joy. Margaret treats her young husband as if he had returned victorious from a mighty war. 'He rode out,' she justifies herself to me. 'And if there had been fighting I believe he would have led it. He was at the head of his army and he didn't run for Kenilworth.'

The king takes to riding out every day in his beautifully engraved armour, as if to be ready for anything. Edmund Beaufort comes back from Calais and rides beside him, his dark handsome face turned attentively to the king, agreeing with everything he says. The court moves to Windsor, and in an excess of happiness the king offers a pardon to everybody, for anything.

'Why does he not arrest them all and behead them?' Margaret demands. 'Why pardon?'

It seems to be his way. After he has issued pardons to all the rebels his new enthusiasm for warfare spills over into a proposal for an expedition – to go to Calais and use the garrison as a base to reconquer the English lands in France. For the king this would be to step in the footsteps of his more heroic father, for Edmund Beaufort it would be to redeem his reputation. I expected the queen to be thrilled at the thought of Beaufort and the king on campaign but I find her in her room picking over some embroidery, her head down. When she sees me she shifts up in her seat and beckons me beside her. 'I cannot bear for him to take such a risk,' she says to me quietly. 'I cannot bear to think of him in battle.'

I am surprised, and pleased at her emotion. 'Are you so tender to His Grace the king?' I ask hopefully. 'I know I cannot bear it when Richard goes to war.'

She turns her pretty head from me as if I have said something too foolish to answer. 'No. Not him. Edmund, Edmund Beaufort. What would become of us if he were to be hurt?'

I take a breath. 'These are the fortunes of war,' I say. 'Your Grace should perhaps hold a special intercessory Mass for the safety of the king.'

She brightens at the thought of it. 'Yes. We could do that. It would be terrible if anything were to happen to him. He would leave no heir but Richard, Duke of York, and I would rather die myself than see York inherit the throne after all he has said and done. And if I were to be widowed I would never be married again, as everyone will think I am barren.' She looks askance at my broadening body. 'You don't know what it is like,' she says. 'To wait and to hope and to pray but never, never to have a sign of a child coming.'

'There is still no sign?' I ask. I had hoped that she might be with child, that the king militant might have been more of a husband than before.

She shakes her head. 'No. None. And if the king goes to war he will face my uncle the King of France on the battlefield. If Henry withdraws or retreats, then everyone will laugh at us.'

'He will have good commanders in the field,' I say. 'Once he gets to Calais Richard will put a strong standard bearer beside him, to keep him safe.'

'Richard was beside him before, when all he had to face was Jack Cade and a rabble,' she says. 'A half-pay captain and a band of working men with pitchforks. You didn't see the king then, Jacquetta, he was terrified. He was frightened like a girl. I've never seen him ride as fast as when we left London.' She puts her hand over her mouth as if to stop disloyal words. 'If he runs from the French king I will be shamed to the ground,' she says very quietly. 'Everyone will know. All my family will know.'

'He will have his friends beside him,' I say. 'Men who are

accustomed to warfare. My husband, and Edmund Beaufort the Duke of Somerset.'

'Edmund has sworn to save Calais,' she says. 'And he is absolutely a man of his word. He swore to me, he went down on his knees and swore to me that nobody would blame me for the loss of Calais, that he would keep it for England and for me. He said it would be his gift to me, like the little fairings he used to give me. He said he would have a golden key made and I can wear it in my hair. They will sail in April.'

'So soon?'

'The king has told the Calais garrison to send all their ships to ferry him across the narrow seas. He is taking a great army and a thousand sailors to sail his ships. He is going in April without fail, he says.'

I hesitate. 'You know, once he gets the fleet assembled, he must go,' I say carefully. 'It is very hard to keep a force together, waiting.'

The queen has no idea that I am talking of a year of our lives that Richard and I wasted on the quayside at Plymouth, waiting for her husband to do what he had promised. She has no idea of what that cost us.

'Of course,' she says. 'Edmund Beaufort will get the ships without fail, and then the king will go. Edmund will keep him safe, I know it.'

I see that Edmund Beaufort has completely filled the place of William de la Pole in the affections of the young couple. The king has always needed a man to command him, he is afraid without someone at his side. And the queen is lonely. It is as simple as that.

'My lord Beaufort will take the king to Calais; thank God that we can rely on him.'

THE WEST OF ENGLAND, SUMMER 1452

He does not go. Edmund Beaufort, Duke of Somerset, commands my husband to muster a fleet in Calais and sail with it across the narrow seas to escort the king to France to start his campaign. Richard in Calais recruits the fleet and waits for the order to send the ships to bring the English army to Calais; but spring comes and goes and the order never comes.

I enter my confinement in Grafton, glad to know that Richard is not campaigning this year, and, as it happens, I am right about the baby, I am always right about my babies. I hold my wedding ring on a thread over my curved belly and when it swings clockwise it is a boy and if it is a girl, it circles counter-clockwise. This is hedge-magic, superstition and nonsense that the midwives believe, that the physicians deny. I smile and call it nonsense; but it has never been wrong. I call the new little mite Eleanor and put her in the wooden cradle that has now rocked nine of Richard's children, and write to tell him that he has a little girl, that she has his dark curling hair and blue eyes, and that he is to take leave from Calais, come home, and see his new daughter.

He does not come. The garrison is under pressure from the Duke of Burgundy, whose forces are mustered nearby; they fear he may set a siege. Although Richard is just across the narrow seas and Calais is only a day's sail away, it feels as if we have been parted for a long time, and that he is far away.

In the nursery one night, while the wet nurse is having her dinner in the hall below, I sit with my new baby and look at her sleeping in the cradle and I take my great-aunt's cards from the hanging pocket at my belt, and shuffle them, cut them, and take the one card and put it on the little embroidered blanket in the baby's crib. I want to know when I will see Richard again, I want to know what the future holds for me.

It is the Fool, a peasant man with a stick over his shoulder, a gaping bag at the end of it, without a fortune now but with hopes. In his other hand he carries a stick to help him stride out on the road ahead. A dog pulls at his breeches, his lowly nature which draws him back from his destiny; but he goes onwards. He keeps trying. It is a card that tells the reader to set off in hope, that great things can be achieved, that one should walk out filled with courage, even if one is a fool to hope. But what catches my eye is the white rose he wears in his cap. I sit for a long time, the card in my hand, wondering what it means to be an adventurer with a white rose in your cap.

When I return to court I ask the queen if Richard may come home but she and the king are distracted by news of trouble, petty uprisings and discontents in all the counties around London. They are the old complaints, stated all over again. Jack Cade was hunted down to his death, but his questions were never answered, and his demands – for justice, for the law, for fair taxation and an end to the court favourites – go on and on. The men of Kent turn out for another unnamed captain, saying that the king must dismiss his favourites who steal the royal fortune and give him bad advice, the men of Warwickshire take up arms, saying that Jack Cade is still alive and will lead them. The king, deaf to all complaints against him, sets out on a summer progress determined to try men for treason and, wherever he goes, Edmund Beaufort the Duke of Somerset rides alongside, a companion and confidant, and sits beside the king when they go south and west to Exeter. Together they pass the death sentence on men who have done nothing more than complain of the duke's influence.

The men here in the dock are the very ones who complained of having troops quartered on them for a year, the very ones who said that we should go to Gascony and reclaim it, who raged against the waste and the shame of the army on the quayside of Plymouth. They saw, as none of this court will ever see, the spendthrift folly of creating an army and then leaving it with nothing to do. Now they will die for saying that. They said nothing more than Richard and I said to each other when the sailors wore out their patience and the soldiers ate up all the stores. But these men said it aloud when spies were listening and now they will die, for the king's forgiving nature spins on its axis and suddenly turns to reveal its dark side and is sour.

'It is sorry work,' Edmund Beaufort, Duke of Somerset, remarks to me, as he sees me walk slowly back from chapel to the queen's rooms at Exeter. 'But you must not let yourself be saddened by the sins of the country people, my lady.'

I glance at him, he seems genuinely concerned. 'I saw the cost to them of the expedition that never sailed,' I say briefly. 'It was my husband who quartered the soldiers on them. We knew at the time that it was hard. And this is another price that they have to pay.'

He takes my hand and tucks it into his arm. 'And there was a heavy cost to you,' he says sympathetically. 'It was hard on you, I know, and on your husband, Lord Rivers. There is no better commander in England, and no safer man to hold Calais. There was no doubt in my mind he did everything he could to keep the army ready.'

'He did,' I say. 'And he will do everything in Calais, but if the king sends no wages to pay the troops then the garrison will turn against us. Just as Kent turned against us, just as Devon is turning against us now.'

He nods. 'I am trying, my lady,' he says, as if he is answerable to me. 'You can tell your husband that he is never far from my thoughts. I am Constable of Calais, I never forget my duty to your husband and the garrison. There is no money in the treasury and the court eats gold, every time we move it is a small fortune, and the king, God bless him, will have all the money for the colleges he is building to the glory of God, and for his friends who strive for their own glory. But I am trying, I will satisfy the king and I will not see your husband and his comrade Lord Welles left short of funds in Calais.'

'I am glad of it,' I reply quietly. 'I thank you for him.'

'And now we are sending an expedition to Bordeaux, as we promised,' he says brightly.

'Bordeaux?' I say blankly. 'Bordeaux again?'

He nods. 'We have to support the English in France,' he says. 'They are overrun by the French but they swear they will defy them and open the gates of Bordeaux to us if we can only get an army out to them. We can recapture the lands we lost. I am going to send John Talbot Earl of Shrewsbury. You will remember him well, of course.'

John Talbot was one of my first husband's most loyal and trusted commanders, famous for lightning raids and his utter bloody determination to win. But he is old now, and after he was captured and released by the French he made a sacred promise never again to arm against the French king. 'Surely he is too old to go to war,' I say. 'He must be sixty if he is a day.'

'Sixty-five,' the duke smiles. 'And as ready and brave as he ever was.'

'But he was paroled by the French. He promised not to fight again. How can we send him? He is a man of such honour – surely he won't go?'

'His presence alone will put the heart in them,' he predicts. 'He will ride at the head. He will not carry his sword but he will ride before them. It's a glorious thing he does, and I will see him supported with a good army. I am doing my best, Lady Rivers. I am doing my very best.' He raises his arm so that he can kiss my fingers, resting in the crook of his elbow, a graceful unusual gesture. 'It is my pleasure to serve you, Lady Rivers. I would have you think of me as your friend.'

I hesitate. He is a charming man, a handsome man, and there is something about his intimate whisper that would make any woman's heart beat a little faster. I cannot help but return his smile. 'I do,' I say.

We go west, through surly countryside where the people cannot earn enough to pay their taxes and who see the coming of our spendthrift court as an added burden, and we hear that Eleanor Cobham, who was once the Duchess of Gloucester, has died in her prison at Peel Castle on the Isle of Man. She died in silence of heartbreak and loneliness; they would not let her take her own life quickly and cleanly by a plunge from the battlements or a dagger in the veins of her wrist. They would not allow her to live any life at all; but they would not allow her death either. Now they are saying that her spirit haunts the castle in the shape of a big black dog that runs up and down the stairs as if looking for a way out.

I tell the queen that Eleanor Cobham is dead but I do not say that I think Eleanor was a woman like Margaret herself, a woman like me: one who expects to take a great place in the world, who can see the world and wants to make it bend to her will, who cannot walk easily in the small steps of a demure woman, nor bow her head to the authority of men. I do not say that I saw the black dog when I first met the duchess and smelled its fetid breath beneath her perfume. I am sorry for the duchess and the black dog that followed her, and I give a little shudder when I think that they took her into imprisonment for study- ing as I have studied, for seeking the knowledge that I have learned, and for being a woman in her power: just like me.

This summer progress is not a merry tour to celebrate a king joyously passing through his kingdom in the best days of the year; it is a sour visitation into each town when the citizens and the clergy turn out to welcome the king and then find he has come to hold a court in their guildhall, and summon their friends to answer charges. A man can be accused of treason for a word spoken out of turn, an ale-house brawl is defined as rebellion. When accused and in the dock, he is invited to name others and a spiral of spite, gossip and then charges follows. We go into the very heartlands of Richard, Duke of York, the wild beautiful country on the way to Wales, and put his tenants, his liegemen and his vassals on trial. The queen is triumphant at this gauntlet that they are throwing down before the Duke of York. Edmund, Duke of Somerset, is gleeful that though York accused him of treason, the court is now on his very doorstep, arraigning the tenants of York for the exact same crime.

'He will be beside himself!' he declares to the queen, and they laugh together like children who rattle sticks against the cage of a travelling bear to make him growl. 'I have found an old peasant who claims that he heard the duke declare that Cade was only saying what most men think. That's treason. I have an ale-house keeper who says that Edward March, his son and heir, thinks the king is simple. I shall call him into court and the king shall hear what the duke's own boy dares to say against him.'

'I shall forbid the king from staying at York's home, Ludlow Castle,' the queen says. 'I shall refuse to go there. I shall snub Duchess Cecily. And you must support me.'

Edmund Beaufort nods. 'We can stay with the Carmelite Friars,' he says. 'The king always likes staying in a monastery.'

She laughs, throwing back her head so that the lace from her high headdress brushes his cheek. Her face is flushed, her eyes are bright. 'He does love a monastery,' she agrees.

'I do hope they have good singers,' he says. 'I so love plainsong. I could listen to it all day.'

She gives a little scream of laughter and slaps his arm. 'Enough, enough!'

I wait till he has left, though I think he would have stayed longer if someone had not come from the king's rooms and said that the king was asking for him. He leaves then, kissing her hand, lingering over it. 'I shall see you at dinner,' he whispers – though of course he will see us all at dinner – and then he leaves, throwing a smiling wink at me as if we are special friends.

I take a seat beside her and I glance around to see that none of her other ladies are in earshot. We are staying at Caldwell Castle, Kidderminster, and the best rooms are small; half the queen's ladies are sewing in another gallery.

'Your Grace,' I begin carefully. 'The duke is a handsome man, and a good companion, but you should take care that you are not seen to enjoy his company too much.'

Her sideways look is gleeful. 'Do you think he pays much attention to me?'

'I do,' I say.

'I am a queen,' she observes. 'It is natural that men are going to gather round me, hoping for a smile.'

'He doesn't have to hope,' I say bluntly. 'He is getting your smiles.'

'And did you not smile on Sir Richard?' she asks sharply. 'When he was nothing more than a knight in your husband's household?'

'You know I did,' I say. 'But I was a widow then, and I was the widow of a royal duke. I was not a married woman and a queen.'

She gets to her feet so quickly that I am afraid that I have offended her, but she takes me by the hand and pulls me with her, into her bedchamber, closing the door behind her and putting her back to it, so that no-one can come in.

'Jacquetta, you see my life,' she says passionately. 'You see my husband. You hear what they say of him, you know what he is. You see him giving out pardons like the Pope to the duke but trying poor men for treason. You know he didn't come to my bedroom in the first week of our marriage because his confessor said that our marriage had to be holy. You know that he is a man of melancholic humour: cool and moist.'

I nod. It is undeniable.

'And Somerset is a man of fire,' she breathes. 'He rides out with an army, he is a commander of men, he has seen battles, he is a man of passion. He hates his enemies, he loves his friends, and to women . . . ' She gives a little shiver. 'To women he is irresistible, they all say it.'

I put my hands to my mouth. I would rather be putting them over my ears.

'I wouldn't be the first woman in the world to have a handsome admirer,' she says. 'I am queen, half the court is in love with me, it is how the world is. I can have a handsome chevalier.'

'No you cannot,' I contradict her. 'You cannot smile on him. You cannot allow him any favours, nothing at all, not even permission to adore you from a distance, not until you have a son and heir by the king.'

'And when is that going to happen?' she demands. 'And how is it going to happen? I have been married seven years, Jacquetta. When is he going to get me with child? I know my duty as well as any woman. Every night I go to bed and lie in the cold sheets, waiting for him to come. Some nights he does not come at all, some nights he comes and spends the night kneeling in prayer at the foot of the bed. The whole night, Jacquetta! What do you expect me to do?'

'I didn't know it was so bad,' I say. 'I am sorry. I had no idea.'

'You must know,' she says bitterly. 'You are lying. You know, all my ladies know. You come to wake us in the morning and we are lying side by side as if we were dead and made of stone on our tombs. Have you ever caught us wrapped in each other's arms? Have you ever heard us call through the door "Not now! Come back later"? You have only to look at him and you would know. You cannot imagine that he is a lusty passionate man who is going to father a strong son on me? We don't even rumple the sheets.'

'Oh Margaret, I am so sorry,' I say tenderly. 'Of course I didn't think he was lusty. But I did think that he came to your bed, and did his duty.'

She shrugs her shoulders. 'Sometimes he does,' she says bitterly. 'Sometimes he rises up from his prayers, crosses himself, and makes a feeble effort. Can you think how that feels? But he doesn't have his heart in it, it is almost worse than nothing at all – an act of duty. It chills my skin, it makes me shudder. I look at you, Jacquetta, and I see you with a baby in your belly every year, and I see how Richard looks at you, and how you steal away early from dinner to be together, even now, and I know it is not the same for me. It is never going to be the same for me.'

'I'm sorry,' I say.

She turns her face away and rubs her eyes. 'It is not the same for me. It will never be the same for me. I will never be loved like you are loved. And I think I am dying inside, Jacquetta.'

GRAFTON, NORTHAMPTONSHIRE, AUTUMN 1452

I withdraw from court in the autumn to spend some time with my children and to make sure that my lands are in good heart at Grafton Manor, and my tenants paying their rents and not whispering behind their hands against the king and court. I am glad to be away. Without the company of Richard I find I am impatient with the flirtations and excitement of the ladies in waiting, and I cannot like the new vindictiveness that I see developing in the king. The Duke of Somerset says that the king is showing his power, growing into majesty; but I cannot admire it. They are calling his progress a 'harvest of heads' and saying that every summer he will work his way around the counties where men have risen against him, or even spoken against him, and judge like a modern Solomon. He seems to take equal pleasure in tenderly pardoning as in harsh sentencing; and no man can know, when he is called before this king, whether he is going to meet a saint or a tyrant. Some men are paraded before him naked with a halter round their necks and he sees their shame and their weakness and forgives them with tears, letting them kiss his hands and praying with them. Another old lady defies him with a curse, refuses to confess to anything and she is hanged. The king weeps then too, in sorrow for a sinner.

And I am glad to be away from the queen's rooms where I see

that she grows closer and closer to Edmund Beaufort. They are thrown together all the time by the king's need of him, and it means that Margaret, still only a young woman of twenty-two, is in the constant company of the man who commands England, who advises her husband, and counsels her. Of course she admires him, her husband holds him up as the very model of a perfect lord. He is the most handsome man at court, he is regarded as the champion of England, and he is clearly in love with her. He looks after her as she goes by, he whispers in her ear, he takes her hand on the least pretext and he places himself beside her, her partner in games, her companion in walks, his horse rides next to hers. Of course she knows that she may not feel anything for him but respect and cousinly affection. But she is a young and passionate woman, and he is a seductive man. I think that no power in the world could stop her looking for him, smiling when she sees him and simply glowing with joy when he comes to sit beside her and whispers in her ear.

And as for the king – he rests on the duke, as if Edmund is his only comfort and his peace of mind. Ever since the rise of Jack Cade when the king fled from London, he cannot feel safe in his own capital city, nor in any of the counties of the south. He may go through them every summer dispensing his spiteful justice with the gallows; but he knows he is not beloved. He only feels safe in the middle lands of England, at Leicester, Kenilworth and Coventry. He relies on Edmund Beaufort to assure him that – despite all appearances – everything is well. Edmund reports that he is beloved, the people faithful, the court and the men of the household honest, Calais secure and Bordeaux certain to be restored. It is a comforting list and Beaufort is persuasive. His warm honeyed tongue seduces the king and the queen together. The king praises Edmund to the skies as his only reliable advisor, he lauds him as the man whose military skill and courage will save us from rebels great and small. He thinks that Edmund can manage the parliament, that Edmund understands the commons, and all the time the queen smiles and says that Edmund is a very great friend to them both, and she will go riding with him the next morning, while the king prays in his chapel.

She has learned to be cautious – she knows well enough that she is watched all the time and that people judge her harshly. But her pleasure in his company and his hidden desire for her is apparent to me; and this is enough to make me glad to leave a court with this dangerous secret at the very heart of it.

Richard is to come home to me at last, and sends to tell me he is on his way. We are to celebrate the marriage of Elizabeth. She is fifteen, she is ready for marriage, and the boy that I had picked out in my mind and whose name I whispered to the new moon has found the courage to speak to his mother about her.

Lady Grey herself wrote to me with the proposal that her son John might marry our daughter. I knew that if Elizabeth stayed in their house for any length of time John Grey would fall in love with her, and his parents would see the benefit of the match. And she picked the apple blossom and gave him the fruit to eat. She is more than pretty, she has real beauty; and Lady Grey cannot bear to refuse her beloved son anything. Besides, as I foresaw, Lady Grey is a woman of her own mind, a commander of her own acres, a queen in her county, and once she had the training of my daughter she soon believed that no better-mannered girl could exist. She taught her how to keep the still room, she taught her how the linen room should be. She preached to her the value of well-trained maids, she took her into the dairy to watch as they churned the famous Groby butter and skimmed the fat cream. She taught her how to keep the account books and to write a civil letter to the Grey kinsmen all around the country. Together they climbed the little hill that they call Tower Hill, and looked over the Ferrers acres, and Lady Grey remarked that all this had come to her on the death of her father, she had brought it to Sir Edward on their marriage, and now her beloved son John will inherit it all.

Elizabeth, who knew well enough how to run a household, who knew how to prepare herbs for the still room, indeed knows how they should be grown and when harvested, who knows the properties of a hundred plants and how to call the venom out of them – she is my daughter, after all – had the good sense and the good manners never to correct the lady of the house; but simply learned how it was done at Groby. Of course, she already knew how linen should be folded, or cream skimmed, she knew how a county lady should command her maids, actually she knows far more than Lady Grey will ever dream: for she has learned from me how a royal court is run and how things were done in the courts of France and of Luxembourg. But she accepted the orders of the woman who would be her mother-in-law as a polite young woman should, and gave every appearance of a girl eager to learn the right way that things should be done: the Groby way. In short, as she picked and dried the herbs for the Groby still room, prepared the oils, polished the silver and watched the cutting of the strewing rushes, my daughter enchanted the hard-hearted lady of Groby, just as she enchanted the son of the house.

It is a good match for her. I had it in mind for years. She has my name and her father's position in our county; but next to no dowry. Service to this king has not brought us a fortune. It seems to be profitable only for those lords who take their fees and do nothing. Those courtiers who do nothing but sympathise with the king and conspire with his wife can take a great profit, as we see from the rich lands that were given to William de la Pole and the extraordinary wealth that Edmund Beaufort now enjoys. But my husband took sixty lancers and nearly six hundred archers with him to Calais, all trained under his command, all wearing our livery, and all paid by us. The treasury has promised to reimburse us, but they might as well date the tally sticks the day of judgement; for the dead will rise from their graves before we can take the sticks into the treasury and get a full repayment. We have a new name and a beautiful house, we have influence and a reputation, we are trusted by both the king and the queen; but money – no, we never have any money.

With this marriage my Elizabeth will become Lady Grey of

Groby, mistress of a good part of Leicestershire, owner of Groby Hall and the other great properties in the Grey family, kinswoman to all the Greys. It is a good family, with good prospects for her, and they are solidly for the king and fiercely opposed to Richard, Duke of York, so we will never find her on the wrong side if the dispute between the Duke of York and his rival, the Duke of Somerset, grows worse.

Elizabeth is to go to her wedding from our house with her father and me, and all the children except the two babies. But Richard is not yet home.

'Where is Father?' she asks me the day before we are due to leave. 'You said he would be here yesterday.'

'He will come,' I say steadily.

'What if he has been delayed? What if he could not get a ship? What if the seas were too rough to sail? I cannot be married without him to give me away. What if he does not get here?'

I put my hand on my wedding ring, as if to touch his fingers that placed it there. 'He will be here,' I say. 'Elizabeth, in all the years that I have loved him, he has never failed me. He will be here.'

She frets all the day and I send her to bed that night with a tisane of valerian, and when I peep into her room she is fast asleep in her bed, her hair plaited under her nightcap, seeming as young as her sister Anne, who shares the bed with her. Then I hear the noise of horses in the stable yard and look from her window, and there is the Rivers standard, and there is my husband, heaving himself wearily from his horse, and in a moment I am down the stairs and out through the stable door and in his arms.

He holds me so tightly that I can hardly breathe, and then he turns my face up to his and kisses me.

'I daresay I stink,' is the first thing he says when he gets his breath. 'You must forgive me. The tide was against us and so I have ridden hard to get here tonight. You knew I would not fail you, didn't you?'

I smile up at his handsome well-worn well-loved face: the man I have adored for so many years. 'I knew you would not fail me.'

The Greys have a small chapel at their house, opposite the great hall, where the young couple exchange the vows which are solemnly witnessed by both sets of parents and the brothers and sisters. Our family fills up the chapel. I can see Lady Grey look at the ranks of my children and think that her son is marrying fertile stock. After the wedding we walk through the cloister to the hall, and there is a feast and singing and dancing, and then we prepare them for bed.

Elizabeth and I are alone in the bedroom that is going to be hers. It is a beautiful room, looking north over the pleasure grounds, towards the meadows and the river. I am feeling tender-hearted, this is my girl, the first child of mine to marry and leave her home. 'What do you foresee for me, Lady Mother?' she asks.

This is a question I have been dreading. 'You know I don't foresee any more,' I say. 'That was something in my girlhood. They don't like such things in England and I have put it aside. If it comes to me or to you it is without our bidding. Your father does not like it.'

She gives a little giggle. 'Oh, Lady Mother!' she says reproach-fully. 'That you should stoop so low, and on my wedding day.'

I cannot help but smile. 'Stoop so low as to what?'

'As to lie,' she whispers. 'And to me! On my wedding day! I understand now that you foresaw that John would love me, and I him. I picked the apple blossom and I gave him the apple, just as you said. But long before that, the moment I first saw him, I knew exactly what you intended when you sent me here. I was standing before his mother when she was at her table in the rents room, and he came in the door behind her – I had not even known he was at home – and the moment I saw him, I knew why you had sent me to Groby and what you thought would happen.'

'And were you glad? Was I right to send you?'

Her joy shines out of her bright grey eyes. 'Very glad. I thought, if he were to like me, I should be the happiest girl in England.'

'That was not foreseeing, that was nothing more than knowing that you are beautiful and lovable. I could have sent you to any handsome young man's household and he would have fallen in love with you. There was no magic in that but a girl and a boy in springtime.'

She is glowing. 'I am glad. I wasn't sure. I am so glad that he is in love but not enchanted. But surely you have looked to see my future? Did you put the charms in the river? What did you draw from the waters? Did you look for us in the cards? What will my future be?'

'I didn't read the cards.' I lie to her, my little daughter, I lie barefaced like a hard-hearted old witch, denying the truth on her wedding night, and I lie to her with my face completely serene. I am going to tell her a lie that is utterly convincing. I will not have my foresight overshadowing her present happiness. I will deny my gift, deny what it has shown me. 'You are mistaken, my dear, I didn't read the cards and I didn't look in a mirror. I didn't put any charms in the river because I didn't have to. I can predict your happiness without any craft. Just as I knew he would love you. I can tell you that I know you will be happy, and I think there will be children, and the first one quite soon.'

'Girl or boy?'

'You will be able to tell that yourself,' I smile. 'Now you have your own wedding ring.'

'And I will be Lady Grey of Groby,' she says with quiet satisfaction.

I feel a shiver, like a cold hand on the nape of my neck. I know that she will never inherit here. 'Yes,' I say, defying my better knowledge. 'You will be Lady Grey of Groby and the mother of many fine children.' This is what she must hear as she goes into her wedding bed on her wedding night. 'God bless you, my darling, and give you joy.'

The girls tap on the door and come into the room in a flurry, with rose petals for the bed and the jug of wedding ale and a bowl of scented water for her to wash with and her linen gown, and I help her get ready, and when the men come in, boisterous and drunk, she is lying in her bed like a chaste little angel. My husband and Lord Grey help John in beside her and he blushes furiously, like a boy, though he is twenty-one; and I smile as if I am wholly happy; and I wonder what it is that stops my heart in fear for the two of them.

In two days we go back to our own house at Grafton, and I never tell Elizabeth, or anyone, that I did indeed read the cards for her, the very day that Lady Grey wrote to me to ask what dowry Elizabeth might bring to the marriage. I sat at the table looking out over the water meadow and the dairy, certain of her happiness, and took the cards in my hand. I turned over three, chosen at random, and all three were blank.

The card-maker had put three spare cards in the pack when he first painted the pictures, three cards just like the others with brightly coloured backs but nothing on the front, spares for use in another game. And it was the three cards with nothing to say which came to my hand when I went to foresee Elizabeth's future with John Grey. I had hoped to see prosperity and children, grandchildren and a rise in the world, but the cards were empty of anything. There was no future that I could see, for Elizabeth and John Grey: no future for them at all.

PALACE OF PLACENTIA, GREENWICH, LONDON, CHRISTMAS 1452

Richard and I attend the court at Greenwich for Christmas and find the festivities and the hunts and the music and the dancing all under the command of Edmund Beaufort, who is such a centre of the happiness of the court that he is almost a king himself. He makes much of Richard, recommending him to the king as the man certain to hold Calais for us, and often takes him aside to discuss how an English expedition might force its way out of the Calais lands into Normandy once more. Richard follows his usual rule of fealty and loyalty to his commander, and I say nothing about the way that the queen's eyes follow them when they talk together. But I know I have to speak to her again.

I am forced to speak to her, driven to it, by a sense of duty. I almost smile to feel so bound; for I know this is the influence of my first husband, John, Duke of Bedford. He never avoided a difficult duty in his life and I feel as if he has laid on me the obligation to serve England's queen even if it means challenging her behaviour and calling her to account.

I choose a moment when we are preparing for a masque of Edmund Beaufort's planning. He has ordered that the queen should have a gown of white, fastened high at the waist with a plaited gold cord, and that her hair should be loose. She is supposed to represent a goddess; but she looks like a bride. He has designed new sleeves for the white gown, cut so short and so wide that you can see her arms almost to the elbow. 'You will have to wear another set of sleeves,' I say frankly. 'These are quite indecent.'

She strokes the inside of her arm. 'It feels so lovely,' she says. 'My skin feels like silk. It feels so wonderful to be this . . .'

'Naked,' I finish for her; and without another word I find another pair of sleeves in her chest of clothes and start to lace them on. She lets me exchange the sleeves, without a word of complaint, and then sits before her mirror. I wave away her maid and take the hairbrush to stroke out the tangles from the long red-gold ringlets that fall almost to her waist. 'The noble duke Edmund Beaufort pays you much attention,' I say. 'It is noticeable, Your Grace.'

She gleams with pleasure. 'Ah, you said before, Jacquetta. This is an old song. But he looks at me as a good courtier, a chevalier.'

'He looks like a man in love,' I say bluntly, expecting to shock her. But I am horrified to see the colour flame in her cheeks. 'Oh, does he?' she asks. 'Does he really?'

'Your Grace – what is happening? You know you should not be speaking of real love. A little poetry, a little flirtation is one thing. But you cannot think of him with desire.'

'When he speaks to me, I come alive.' She addresses my reflected image in the mirror, and I see her face gleaming and silvery through the looking glass. It is as if we are in another world, the world of the scrying mirror, and such things can be said. 'With the king it is as if I am caring for a child. I have to tell him that he is in the right, that he should ride out like a man, that he should rule like a king. I have to praise him for his wisdom and coax him when he is upset. I am more a mother to him than a lover. But Edmund –' She gives a little shuddering breath, lowers her eyes and then looks up at the mirror and shrugs, as if there is nothing she can do.

'You must stop seeing him,' I say hastily. 'Or only see him when others are present. You must keep your distance.'

She takes the brush from my hand. 'Don't you like him?' she asks. 'He says he likes and admires you. He says he is your friend. And he trusts Richard above all others. He praises him to the king.'

'Nobody could help but like him,' I say. 'He is handsome, charming and one of the greatest men in England. But that doesn't mean that the queen should feel anything for him but cousinly affection.'

'You're too late to tell me,' she says, her voice silky and warm. 'It is too late for me. It's not cousinly affection. It is far beyond that. Jacquetta, for the first time in my life I feel as if I am alive. For the first time in my life I feel as if I am a woman. I feel beautiful. I feel desired. I cannot resist this.'

'I told you before,' I remind her. 'I warned you.'

Again, she lifts her beautiful shoulders. 'Ah, Jacquetta. You know as well as I do what it is to be in love. Would you have stopped if someone had warned you?'

I don't answer her. 'You will have to send him away from court,' I say flatly. 'You will have to avoid him, perhaps for months. This is a disaster.'

'I can't,' she says. 'The king would never allow him to go. He won't let him out of his sight. And I would just die if I did not see him, Jacquetta. You don't know. He is my only companion, he is my chevalier, he is my champion: the queen's champion.'

'This is not Camelot,' I warn her grimly. 'These are not the times of the troubadours. People will think badly of you if they see you so much as smile at him, they will accuse him of being your favourite, or worse. What you are saying here is enough to have you put aside and sent to a nunnery. And if anyone heard you say it: it would be the end of him. Already he is hated and envied for being the favourite of the king. If one word gets out to the people that you favour him, they will say the most terrible things. You are the queen, your reputation is like Venetian glass: precious and fragile and rare. You have to take care. You are not a private lady, you cannot have private feelings.'

'I will take care,' she says breathlessly. 'I swear I will take care.' It is as if she is bartering for the right to be with him, and that she would offer anything for that right. 'If I take care, if I don't smile on him or ride too close to him, or dance with him too often, I can still see him. Can't I? Everyone will think he is with us all the time at the king's command, nobody need know that he makes me so happy, that it makes my life worth living, just to be with him.'

I know I should tell her that she should never be alone with him at all, but her face is too imploring. She is lonely, and she is young, and it is miserable to be a young woman in a great court when nobody really cares for you. I know that. I know what it is like to have a husband who hardly sees you, but that there is one young man who can't take his eyes from you. I know what it is like to burn up in a cold bed.

'Just take care,' I say, though I know I should tell her to send him away. 'You will have to be careful all the time, every day of your life. And you cannot see him alone. You must never be alone with him. This cannot go beyond the chevalier and his honourable love for his lady. It cannot go beyond your secret joy. It has to stop here.'

She shakes her head. 'I have to talk with him,' she says. 'I have to be with him.'

'You cannot. There can be no future for the two of you but shame and disgrace.'

She leaves her mirror and moves to the great bed with the rich golden hangings. She pats it invitingly and slowly I come towards her. 'Will you draw a card for him?' she asks. 'Then we would know the answers. Then we would know what future there might be.'

I shake my head. 'You know that the king doesn't like the cards,' I say. 'It is forbidden.'

'Just one card. Just once. So that we might know what is to come. So that I will take care?'

I hesitate, and in a moment she is at the bedroom door and

calling for a pack of playing cards. One of the ladies offers to bring them through but the queen takes them at the bedroom door and hands them to me. 'Go on!' she says.

Slowly, I take the cards and shuffle them. Of course, we play cards all the time at court; but the feeling of them in my hand as I seek only one, seek to divine the future, is quite different. I hand them to her.

'Shuffle them. Then cut the cards,' I say very quietly. 'And cut them again.'

Her face is entranced. 'We will foretell his future?'

I shake my head. 'We cannot foretell his future, he would have to ask for the card, he would have to choose. We can't do it without him. But we can tell how his life will touch yours. We can see which card shows his feeling for you, and yours for him.'

She nods. 'I want to know that,' she whispers longingly. 'Do you think he loves me, Jacquetta? You have seen him with me. Do you think he loves me?'

'Spread the cards,' I say.

She makes a fan of the cards, their bright faces downwards.

'Now choose.'

Slowly, one finger moving across the painted backs, she muses on her choice, and then she points. 'This one.'

I turn it over. It is the Falling Tower. The tower of a castle, struck perhaps by lightning, a jagged streak of light flaming into the roof of the tower, the walls going one way, the roof the other. Two little figures fall from the tower to the grass below.

'What does it mean?' she whispers. 'Will he take the tower? Does it mean he will take the kingdom?'

For a moment I cannot understand her meaning. 'Take the kingdom?' I repeat in horror. 'Take the kingdom!'

She shakes her head, denying the very thought, hand over her mouth. 'Nothing, nothing. But what does it mean? This card – what does it mean?'

'It means an overturning of all things,' I say. 'Disruption of the times. Perhaps a fall of a castle . . . ' Of course, I think of Richard,

who is sworn to hold the castle of Calais for this very commander. 'A fall from on high, look, here are two people falling
down from the tower, a rising of those who are low, and in the
end, everything different. A new heir takes the throne, the old
order is changed, everything is new.'

Her eyes are shining. 'Everything is new,' she whispers. 'Who
do you think is the king's true heir?'

I look at her in something close to horror. 'Richard, Duke of
York,' I say flatly. 'Like him or not. Richard, Duke of York, is the
king's heir.'

She shakes her head. 'Edmund Beaufort is the king's cousin,'
she whispers. 'He could be the true heir. Perhaps this is what the
card means.'

'It never comes out quite how I think it will be,' I warn her.
'This is not a prediction, it is always more like a warning. D'you
remember the Wheel of Fortune card? The card you drew on
your wedding day that promises what rises will fall, that nothing
is certain?'

Nothing I can say can dull her joy, her face is shining. She
thinks I have foreseen the change of everything and she is longing for something to change. She thinks that the tower shown
in the card is her prison; she wants it broken down. She thinks
the people who are clearly falling are breaking free. She thinks the
lightning shaft that destroys and burns will break down the old
and make new. There is nothing I can say that she will hear as a
warning.

She makes the gesture that I showed her on her wedding day,
the circling forefinger that shows the rise and the fall of life.
'Everything new,' she whispers again.

In bed, that night, I confide my worries to Richard, skirting over
the queen's infatuation for the duke, but telling him only that she
is lonely and that the duke is her closest friend. Richard is sitting

up, beside the warmth of the fire, his gown thrown over his naked shoulders. 'No harm in friendship,' he says stoutly. 'And she is a pretty girl and deserves some companionship.'

'People will talk.'

'People always talk.'

'I am afraid that she may become too fond of the duke.'

He narrows his eyes as if he would scrutinise my thoughts. 'Are you saying she might fall in love with him?'

'I wouldn't be surprised if she did. She is young, he is handsome, she has nobody else in the world who shows any sign of caring for her. The king is kind to her and considerate, but he has no passion in him.'

'Can the king give her a child?' Richard asks bluntly, going to the very core of the matter.

'I think he can,' I say. 'But he does not come often to her room.'

'The man's a fool,' my husband says. 'A woman like Margaret cannot be neglected. D'you think the duke has eyes for her?'

I nod.

Richard scowls. 'I think you could trust him to do nothing which would endanger her or the throne. It would be a selfish villain who would seduce her. She has everything to lose, and it would cost the throne of England as well. He's no fool. They are close, they are bound to be close, they are both in attendance on the king for most of every day. But Edmund Beaufort is running this kingdom through the king, he would not jeopardise his own future – never mind hers. The most important thing is for her to get an heir.'

'She can hardly do it alone,' I say crossly.

He laughs at me. 'No need to defend her to me. But while there is no child then Richard, Duke of York, is the rightful heir, but the king keeps favouring others of his family: Humphrey, Duke of Buckingham, who takes precedence, and Edmund Beaufort. Now I hear he is bringing his half-brothers, the Tudor boys, to court as well. It makes everyone uneasy. Who does he think is his heir? Would he dare to put Richard, Duke of York, aside for one of these favourites?'

'He's young,' I say. 'She's young. They could get a child.'

'Well, he's not likely to die on campaign like his father,' my husband the soldier says cruelly. 'He keeps himself safe enough.'

At the end of the twelve days of Christmas Richard has to go back to his post at Calais. I go down to the river to see him set sail. He is wearing his thick travelling cloak against the cold wintry mist and he wraps it around us both as we stand on the quayside. Inside the warmth, my head against his shoulder, my arms tight around his broad back, I hold him as if I cannot bear to let him go. 'I'll come to Calais,' I promise.

'Sweetheart, there is nothing for you there at all. I will come home again at Easter, or earlier.'

'I can't wait till Easter.'

'Then I will come sooner. Whenever you bid me. You know that. When you want me I will come.'

'Can't you just go and inspect the garrison and come back?'

'Perhaps; if there is no expedition into Normandy this spring. The duke hopes to mount one. Does the queen say anything?'

'She says whatever the duke says.'

'If we don't have an expedition by spring there won't be one this year, and I can come home to you,' he promises.

'You had better come home in the summer,' I warn him. 'Whatever happens. I will have something I will want you to see.'

In the warm shelter of the cloak his hand goes to my belly.

'You are a ruby, my Jacquetta. A wife of noble character worth more than rubies. Are you with child again?'

'Yes, again,' I say.

'A summer baby,' he says with pleasure. 'Another for the House of Rivers. We are making a nation, my love. The Rivers are becoming an estuary, a lake, an inland sea.'

I giggle.

'Will you stay at court with the queen for now?'

'Yes, I will. I'll go down to Grafton for a few days to see the children and then I'll come back to court. At the very least, I can guard her from slander.'

Concealed by his cloak he squeezes me. 'I like the thought of you as a model of respectability, my love.'

'I am a very respectable mother of nine,' I remind him. 'Soon ten, God willing.'

'Good God, that I should feel like this for a mother of ten,' he remarks, taking my hand and holding it against his breeches.

'God forgive me that I should feel like this for a married man and a father of ten,' I say, pressing against him.

There is a shout from the deck of the ship above us. 'I have to go,' he says reluctantly. 'We have to catch the tide. I love you, Jacquetta, and I will come home soon.'

He kisses me hard and quickly, and then he steps back and runs up the gangplank to the ship. Without his cloak, without his warmth, without his smile, I feel very cold and alone. I let him go.

THE TOWER OF LONDON, SPRING 1453

I come back to court after a week at Grafton in time for the great celebration in the Tower of London where the king's half-brothers Edmund and Jasper Tudor are made earls. I stand beside the queen as the two young men kneel before the king for their investiture. They are the sons of Queen Catherine of Valois, the king's mother, who made a second marriage as imprudent as my own. After her husband Henry V died leaving her a widow with a baby, she did not, as everyone hoped, retire to a nunnery and spend the rest of her life in respectable grief. She stooped even lower than I did and fell in love with the keeper of her wardrobe, Owen Tudor, and married him in secret. She left an awkward situation when she died, with Tudor as her surviving widower or abductor – depending on your judgement – and his two sons as half-brothers to the King of England or two bastards to a madly incontinent queen mother – depending on your charity.

King Henry has decided to acknowledge his half-brothers, deny his mother's shame, and count them as royal kinsmen. What this will do to the expectations of the several men who are in line to inherit the throne is beyond understanding. These Tudors will just add to the confusion around the throne. The king honours the Duke of Buckingham, who counts himself as the greatest duke of England, but favours Edmund Beaufort the

Duke of Somerset above anyone else. And all the while his true heir is the only man not here and never welcomed at court: Richard Plantagenet, Duke of York.

I glance at the queen, who must be shamed by her failure to solve all this by producing a son and heir, but she is looking down at her folded hands, her eyelashes veiling her expression. I see Edmund Beaufort look quickly away from her.

'His Grace is generous to the Tudor boys,' I remark.

She gives a little start at my words. 'Oh, yes. Well, you know what he is like. He can forgive anyone anything. And now he is so afraid of the common people and of the York affinity that he wants to gather his family around him. He is giving the boys a fortune in lands and recognising them as his half-brothers.'

'It is good for a man to have his family around him,' I say cheerfully.

'Oh, he can make brothers,' she says, and the unspoken words 'but not a son' remain unsaid.

As the winter nights become lighter and the mornings become golden rather than grey we receive great news from Bordeaux where John Talbot, Earl of Shrewsbury, four times the age of his pageboy, sweeps through the rich cities of Gascony, wins back Bordeaux and looks set to reclaim all the English lands. This sends the court into an ecstasy of confidence. They declare that first we will win back all of Gascony and then we will win back all of Normandy and Calais will be secure and Richard will be able to come home. Margaret and I are on the river walk in the gardens at Westminster, wrapped in our winter furs but feeling the spring sunshine on our faces, and looking at the first daffodils of the season.

'Jacquetta, you are like a lovesick girl,' she says suddenly.

I jump. I had been looking at the river and thinking of Richard, over the sea in Calais; furious – I am sure – that he is not leading the campaign in Bordeaux. 'I am sorry,' I say with a little laugh. 'I do miss him. And the children.'

'He will be home soon,' she assures me. 'Once Talbot has won back our lands in Gascony, we can make peace again.'

She takes my arm and walks beside me. 'It is hard to be parted from people that you love,' she says. 'I missed my mother so much when I first came to England, I feared that I would never see her again, and now she writes to me that she is ill and I wish I could go to her. I wonder if she would have sent me away if she had known what my life would be like, if she had known that she would never see me again, not even for a visit.'

'She knows at least that the king is kind to you, and a gentle husband,' I say. 'When the Greys asked me for Elizabeth my first thought was would he be kind to her. I think every mother would want that for her daughter.'

'I so want to be able to tell her I am with child,' she says. 'That would make her happy, that is the one thing she wants – that everyone wants. But maybe this year. Perhaps one will come for me this year.' Her eyelids sweep down and she smiles, almost to herself.

'Oh, dear Margaret, I hope so.'

'I am more contented,' she says quietly. 'I am even hopeful. You need not fear for me, Jacquetta. It is true that I was very unhappy this summer, and even at Christmas time; but I am more contented now. You were a good friend to warn me to take care. I listened to you, I thought about what you said. I know I must not be indiscreet, I have put the duke at a distance and I think everything is going to be all right.'

There is something going on here – I don't need the Sight to see it. There is a secret here, and a hidden joy. But I cannot complain of her behaviour. She may smile on the duke; but she is always at the side of the king. She does not linger with the duke in the gallery nor let him whisper in her ear any more. He comes to her rooms, as he always has done; but they talk of matters of state and there are always companions with him, and ladies with her. It is when she is alone or quiet among the crowd that I look at her and wonder what she is thinking, when she folds her hands so demurely in her lap and gazes down, her eyes veiled, smiling to herself.

'And how is your little girl?' she asks a touch wistfully. 'Is she well and fat and pretty like all your babies always seem to be?'

'Thank God she is strong and growing well,' I say. 'I called her Eleanor, you know. I sent them all Christmas fairings and we had a couple of days of such fine weather when I was down with them. I took the older ones hunting and the younger ones sledging. I will go back to see them at Easter.'

That night the queen dresses in her new gown of darkest red, a colour no-one has seen before, especially bought for her from the London merchants, and we go into the king's presence chamber with the ladies behind us. She takes her seat beside the king and the little Beaufort heiress, Margaret, comes into the room, dressed far too ornately, paraded by her shameless mother. The child is wearing a gown of angelic white trimmed with red silk roses, as if to remind everyone that she is the daughter of John Beaufort, first Duke of Somerset, a great name but, God forgive him, not a great man. He was Edmund Beaufort's older brother but he made a fool of himself in France and came home and died, so promptly and conveniently – just ahead of a charge of treason – that Richard says it was by his own hand and it was the only good thing he ever did for his family. This scrap of a girl with the great name and greater fortune is his daughter, and the niece of Edmund Beaufort.

I see her staring at me and I smile at her. At once she flushes scarlet and beams. She whispers to her mother, obviously asking who I am, and her mother very rightly gives her a pinch to make her stand straight and silent, as a girl at court should do.

'I am giving your daughter in wardship to my dearly loved half-brothers, Edmund and Jasper Tudor,' the king says to the girl's mother, the dowager duchess. 'She can live with you, until it is time for her to marry.'

Amusingly, the child looks up as if she has an opinion about this. When no-one so much as glances at her she whispers to her mother again. She is a dear little thing and so anxious to be consulted. It seems hard to me that she will be married off to Edmund Tudor and sent away to Wales.

The queen turns to me and I lean forwards. 'What do you think?' Margaret asks.

Margaret Beaufort is of the House of Lancaster, Edmund Tudor is the son of a queen of England. Any child they conceive will have an impressive lineage, English royal blood on one side, French royal blood on the other, both of them kin to the King of England.

'Is the king making his brother over-mighty?' the queen whispers.

'Oh, look at her,' I say gently. 'She is a tiny little thing, and a long way from marriageable age. Her mother will keep her home for another ten years, surely. You will have half a dozen babies in the cradle before Edmund Tudor can wed or bed her.'

We both look down the room at the girl whose little head is still bobbing up and down as if she wishes someone would speak to her. The queen laughs. 'Well, I hope so, surely a little shrimp like that will never make a royal heir.'

The next night I wait for a quiet moment in the hour before dinner when the queen is dressed and the duke and king have not yet come to our rooms. We are seated before the fire, listening to the musicians. I glance at her for her nod of permission, and then draw my stool a little closer.

'If you are waiting for a chance to tell me that you are with child again, you need not choose your time,' she says mischievously. 'I can see it.'

I blush. 'I'm certain it will be a boy, I am eating enough to make a man, God knows. I have had to let my belt out.'

'Have you told Richard?'

'He guessed, before he left.'

'I shall ask the duke to let him come home. You will want him at home with you, won't you?'

I glance at her. Sometimes the almost annual evidence of my reliable fertility makes her wistful; but this time she is smiling, her joy for me is without shadow. 'Yes. I would want him home, if the duke can spare him.'

'I shall command it,' she smiles. 'The duke tells me he will do anything for me. It is a little request for a man who has promised me the moon.'

'I will stay at court until May,' I say. 'And then after my confinement I will join you on the summer progress.'

'Perhaps we won't go very far this year,' she says.

'No?' I am slow to grasp her meaning.

'Perhaps I too will want an easy summer.'

At last I understand her. 'Oh Margaret, is it possible?'

'I thought you had the Sight!' she crows. 'And here I am, sitting before you, and I think . . . I am almost certain . . .'

I clasp her hands. 'I think so too, I see it now. I really do.' There is something about her luminous skin and the curves of her body. 'How long?'

'I have missed two courses, I think,' she says. 'So I haven't told anyone yet. What d'you think?'

'And the king lay with you before Christmas? And gave you pleasure?'

She keeps her eyes down, but her colour deepens. 'Oh, Jacquetta – I did not know it could be like that.'

I smile. 'Sometimes it can.' Something in her smile tells me that she knows, at last, after eight years of marriage, of the joy that a man can give his wife, if he cares to do so, if he loves her enough to want to make her cling to him and yearn for his touch.

'When would I be sure?' she asks.

'Next month,' I say. 'We will get a midwife I know and trust to talk with you and see if you have the signs, and then you can tell His Grace yourself next month.'

She does not want to write to her mother until she is quite certain, and this is a little tragedy, for while she is waiting for the signs that she is with child, a message comes from Anjou to say that Margaret's mother, Isabella of Lorraine, has died. It is eight years since Margaret said goodbye to her mother and came to England for her wedding, and they were never especially close. But it is a blow to the young queen. I see her in the gallery with tears in her eyes and Edmund Beaufort holding both her hands in his own. Her head is turned towards him as if she would put her face to his broad shoulder and weep. When they hear my footsteps they turn to me, still handclasped.

'Her Grace is distressed about the news from Anjou,' the duke says simply. He leads Margaret to me. 'Go with Jacquetta,' he says tenderly. 'Go and let her give you a tisane, something for grief. It is hard for a young woman to lose her mother and such a shame that you never told her –' He breaks off his words and puts the queen's hands in mine.

'You have something you can give her? Don't you? She should not cry and cry.'

'I have some well-known herbs,' I say carefully. 'Will you come and lie down for a little while, Your Grace?'

'Yes,' Margaret says and lets me lead her away from the duke to the seclusion of her rooms.

I make her a tisane of Tipton's weed, and she hesitates before she drinks it. 'It will not hurt a baby?'

'No,' I reply. 'It is very mild. You shall have a draught of it every morning for a week. Grief would be worse for a baby; you have to try to be calm and cheerful.'

She nods.

'And you are sure?' I ask her quietly. 'The midwives told me that they were almost certain?'

'I am certain,' she says. 'I will tell the king next week, when I miss my course again.'

But she does not tell him herself. Oddly, she summons his chamberlain.

'I have a message for you to take to the king,' she says. She is sombre in her dark blue mourning clothes, and I am sorry that the loss of her mother has taken the brightness from her joy. Still, when she tells the king they will both be elated. I assume she is going to invite the king to come to her rooms. But she goes on: 'Pray give my compliments to the king and my good wishes, and inform him that I am with child.'

Richard Tunstall simply goggles at her: he has never been asked to take such a message in his life. No royal chamberlain ever has. He looks at me, as if for advice, but I can do nothing but show, by a little shrug, that he had better take the message that this queen wishes to send to her husband.

He bows and steps backwards out of the room, and the guards close the door quietly behind him.

'I'll change my gown, the king is certain to come to me,' she says.

We hurry to her room and change her from her dark blue gown to one of pale green, a good colour for spring. As her maid holds the dress out for her to step into, I can see that she has a rounded belly where she was once so spare, and her breasts fill the fine linen shift. I smile at the sight of her.

We wait for the king to come bursting in, his face alight with joy, his hands held out to her, we wait for an hour. We hear the watchman giving the time, and then finally we hear the footsteps outside and the guards throw open the doors to the queen's apartments. We all rise to our feet, expecting to see the king rush in, his boyish face beaming. But it is Richard Tunstall again, the king's chamberlain, with a reply to the queen's message.

'His Grace bid me tell you this: that the news is to our most singular consolation and to all true liege people's great joy and comfort,' he says. He gulps and looks at me.

'Is that all?' I ask.

He nods.

The queen looks blankly at him. 'Is he coming to me?'

'I don't think so, Your Grace.' He clears his throat. 'He was so happy that he rewarded me for bringing the news,' he volunteers.

'Is he coming to visit Her Grace before dinner?'

'He has called his jeweller to see him. He is having a special jewel made for the queen,' he says.

'But what is he doing now?' she asks. 'Right now? As you left him?'

Richard Tunstall gives another bow. 'He has gone to give thanks in his private chapel,' he says. 'The king has gone to pray.'

'Good,' she says dismally. 'Oh, good.'

We don't see the king until that evening, when he comes to visit the queen in her rooms before dinner as usual. He kisses her hand before us all and tells her that he is most pleased. I glance round the room and see that all her ladies in waiting are looking, like me, bewildered. This is a couple who have conceived their first child – after nearly eight years of waiting. This child makes their marriage complete and their throne secure. Why do they behave as if they are barely acquainted?

Margaret is queenly, she gives no sign of expecting more warmth or enthusiasm from him. She bows her head and she smiles at the king. 'I am very happy,' she says. 'I pray that we have a son, and if not, a beautiful daughter and a son the next time.'

'A blessing either way,' he says kindly, and gives her his arm and leads her into dinner, seats her most carefully at his side and then tenderly chooses for her the very choicest pieces of meat and the softest pieces of bread. On his other side, Edmund Beaufort, Duke of Somerset, smiles on them both.

After dinner she says that she will retire early. The court rises as we withdraw and when we get to the queen's rooms she leaves her ladies and, beckoning me, goes into her bedroom.

'Take off my headdress,' she says. 'I am so tired and it makes my head ache.'

I untie the ribbons and lay the tall cone to one side. Underneath is the pad which keeps the heavy weight balanced upright on her head. I untie that too and then let down her hair. I take up a brush and gently start to free the tightly braided plaits, and she closes her eyes.

'That's better,' she says. 'Plait it up loosely, Jacquetta, and they can send in a glass of warm ale.' I twist the thick red-gold hair into a plait, and help her take off her surcoat and gown. She pulls on a linen gown for the night and climbs into the big bed, looking like a little child among the rich hangings and thick covers.

'You are bound to feel weary,' I say. 'You can just rest. Everyone will want you to rest.'

'I wonder what it will be,' she says idly. 'Do you think a boy?'

'Shall I get the cards?' I ask, ready to indulge her.

She turns her head away. 'No,' she says, surprising me. 'And don't you think about it, Jacquetta.'

I laugh. 'I am bound to think about it. This is your first baby; if it is a boy, he will be the next King of England. I am honour-bound to think of him, and I would think of him anyway for love of you.'

Gently, she puts a finger over my lips, to silence me. 'Don't think too much then.'

'Too much?'

'Don't think about him with the Sight,' she says. 'I want him to bloom like a flower, unobserved.'

For a moment I think that she is afraid of some old horrible hedge-witchery, casting the evil eye or ill-wishing. 'You cannot think that I would do anything to harm him. Just thinking about him would not harm . . . '

'Oh, no.' She shakes her golden head. 'No, dear Jacquetta, I don't think that. It's just that . . . I don't want you to know everything . . . not everything. Some things are private.' She blushes and turns her face away from me. 'I don't want you to know everything.'

I think I understand. Who knows what she had to do to gain the interest of such a cool husband? Who knows how seductive she must have been to get him off his knees and into her bed? Did she have to try sluts' tricks that left her feeling ashamed of herself? 'Whatever you did to conceive this child, it is worth it,' I say stoutly. 'You had to conceive a child and if you have made a son it is all the better. Don't think badly of yourself, Margaret, and I will think of nothing at all.'

She looks up. 'Do you think that nothing would be a sin that gave England an heir?'

'It was a sin for love,' I say. 'And hurt no-one. Then it's forgivable.'

'I don't need to confess it?'

I think of Bishop Ayscough who told the young king not to bed his wife in the first week for fear that the young couple would experience the sin of lust. 'You needn't confess anything you did to get this child. It had to be done, and it was an act of love, and men don't understand such things. Priests the least of all.'

She gives a little sigh. 'All right. And don't you think about it.'

I wave my hand like a veil over my face. 'I won't think. I have not a thought in my head.'

She laughs. 'I know you can't stop yourself thinking, I know that. And I know you have the Sight sometimes. But don't look for this baby, promise me you will not look for him? And think of him as a wild flower which grows and is a thing of beauty; but nobody knows how it was planted nor how it came to be there.'

'He's the son of Marguerite the Daisy,' I say. 'He can be the flower that we rejoice to see in springtime, whose coming means spring.'

'Yes,' she says. 'A wild flower that comes from who knows where?'

GRAFTON, NORTHAMPTONSHIRE, SUMMER 1453

I keep my word to the queen and don't puzzle over this long-delayed conception, and she keeps her word to me and speaks to Edmund, Duke of Somerset, and he sends my husband home to me, as I go into confinement at Grafton. I have a boy and we call him Lionel. My daughter Elizabeth, a married lady, comes and attends me in my confinement, very serious and very helpful, and I find her hanging over the cradle and cooing to the baby.

'You will have your own soon,' I promise her.

'I hope so. He is so perfect, he is so beautiful.'

'He is,' I say with quiet pride. 'Another son for the House of Rivers.'

As soon as I am strong enough to return to court I get a message from the queen asking me to join them on progress. Richard has to return to the garrison of Calais and it is painfully hard for us to part again.

'Let me come to Calais,' I beg him. 'I can't bear to be without you.'

'All right,' he says. 'Next month. You can come and bring all the younger children; I can't bear to be without you and them either.'

He kisses my mouth, he kisses both of my hands, and then he mounts his horse and rides away.

CLARENDON PALACE, WILTSHIRE, SUMMER 1453

The court itself is merry, travelling around the western counties and seeking out traitors and rabble-rousers. The Duke of Somerset has chosen the route and says that gradually the people are coming to learn that they cannot speak evil of the king, that there is no future in their demands and – more important than anything else – that Richard, Duke of York, will never be a power in the kingdom and so allying with him, or calling on his name, is a waste of time.

Edmund Beaufort is especially attentive to the king this summer, urging him on to be more and more severe in his judgements and rigorous in his sentencing. He strengthens his mind by applauding his decisions, and encourages him to speak out. The duke accompanies the king to chapel and brings him to the queen's rooms before dinner where the three of them sit and talk, and the duke makes them laugh with his account of the day, sometimes mocking the ignorant people who have been before him.

The queen cannot ride in her condition, and Edmund Beaufort has trained a beautiful set of matched mules to carry her litter. He himself rides beside her, keeping his great horse reined back to the slow speed of the mules, watching her for any sign of fatigue. He consults me almost every day to make sure that I am happy with the queen's health, with her diet, with her exercise. Every day I assure him that she is well, that her belly is growing as it should, that I am certain that the baby is strong.

Almost every day he brings her a little gift, a posy of flowers, a poem, a little lad to dance for her, a kitten. The king and queen and the duke travel around the green lanes of Dorset in absolute accord, and whenever the queen steps down from her litter or turns to go up a stair, the duke's hand is out to support her, his arm to hold her steady.

I had seen him before as a charmer, a seducer, a rogue; but now I see something better in him, a man of great tenderness. He treats her as if he would spare her any fatigue, as if he has dedicated his life to her happiness. He serves the king as a most loyal friend and he serves her as a knight of chivalry. More than this, I don't want to see; I won't let myself see.

In August we reach Wiltshire, and stay at the old royal palace at Clarendon, in the lush water meadows near Salisbury. I love this chalk meadowland and the broad watery valleys. The runs after the deer go on for hours through the woodland of the valley floors and then we burst out onto the high downland and gallop across the even cropped grass. When we halt to eat we can see half of England spread before us. The palace is set among flowering meads, flooded into lakes for half the year, but a network of clean streams and pools and rivers in this high summer. The duke takes the queen fishing and swears that they will catch a salmon for her dinner, but they spend most of the day with her resting in the shade while he casts a line and gives her the rod to hold, and then casts the line again as the dragon-flies dance over the kingcups and the swallows fly low over the water, skimming their little beaks into their own darting reflections.

We come home late in the evening as the clouds in the sky are like peach and lemon ribbons, swirled above the horizon. 'It will be another beautiful day tomorrow,' the duke predicts.

'And the next day?' she asks him.

'Why not? Why should you not have a beautiful day every day of your life?'

She laughs. 'You would spoil me.'

'I would,' he says sweetly. 'I would like you to have a beautiful day every day.'

She takes his arm to help her up the stone steps to the great front door of the hunting lodge. 'Where is the king?' he asks one of the gentlemen of the bedchamber.

'In the chapel, Your Grace,' the man replies. 'With his confessor.'

'I'll come to your rooms then,' Edmund Beaufort says to the queen. 'Shall I sit with you before dinner?'

'Yes, come,' she says.

The ladies arrange themselves on stools and the window-seats, the queen and the duke sit in a window embrasure, talking quietly together, their heads close, and then there is a knock and the doors are thrown open for a messenger from France, who comes hastily in, dirty from the road, and with his face grave. Nobody could doubt for a moment that he brings bad news.

The duke leaps swiftly to his feet. 'Not now,' he says sharply. 'Where is the king?'

'He has given orders not to be disturbed,' the man says. 'But my orders are to come at all speed and give my message at once. So I've come to you. It's Lord Talbot, God bless him, and Bordeaux.'

The duke grabs the man by the arm and marches him out of the door, without a word to the queen. She is already on her feet; I go to her side. 'Be calm, Your Grace,' I say quickly. 'You must be calm for the baby.'

'What's the news?' she asks. 'What's the news from France? Edmund!'

'A moment,' he throws over his shoulder, turning his back on her as if she were an ordinary woman. 'Wait a moment.'

There is a little gasp of shock from her ladies at how he speaks to her, but I put my arm around her waist and say, 'Come and lie down, Your Grace. The duke will bring you the news when he has it. Come now.'

'No,' she says, pulling away from me. 'I must know. Edmund! Tell me!'

For a moment he is in rapid conversation with the messenger; but when he turns he looks as if someone has struck him in the heart. 'It's John Talbot,' he says quietly.

I feel the queen stagger as her knees go weak and she drops down in a faint. 'Help me,' I say quickly to one of the ladies in waiting, but it is the duke who brushes past us all and picks the queen up into his arms and carries her through her private rooms into her very bedroom, and lays her on the bed.

'Fetch the physicians,' I snap at one of the ladies and run in after them. He has half laid her on the bed, he is kneeling on the royal bed, his arms are around her, he is bending over her, holding her like a lover, whispering in her ear. 'Margaret,' he says urgently. 'Margaret!'

'No!' I say. 'Your Grace, Lord Edmund, let her go. I'll take care of her, leave her.'

She holds him by his jacket, her two hands grasping him tightly. 'Tell me it all,' she whispers desperately to him. 'Tell me the worst, quickly.'

I slam the bedroom door and put my back to it, before anyone can see that he has his hands either side of her face, that she is holding his wrists, that they are scanning each other's eyes.

'My love, I can hardly bear to tell you. Lord Talbot is dead and his son too. We have lost Castillon that he was defending, we have lost Bordeaux again, we have lost everything.'

She quivers. 'Dear God, the English will never forgive me. We have lost all of Gascony?'

'All,' he says. 'And John Talbot himself, God bless his soul.'

The tears spill over from her eyes and pour down her cheeks, and Edmund Beaufort drops his head and kisses them away, kisses her like a lover trying to comfort his mistress.

'No!' I cry again, utterly horrified. I come to the bed and put my hand on his arm, pulling him away from her; but they are blind and deaf to me, clinging together, her arms around his neck, he is half lying on her, as he covers her face with kisses and whispers promises that he cannot keep, and at that moment, at that terrible, terrible moment, the door behind us opens and Henry, King of England, comes into the room and sees the two of them, wrapped in each other's arms: his pregnant wife and his dearest friend.

For a long moment he takes in the scene. Slowly, the duke lifts his head and, gritting his jaw, gently releases Margaret, laying her back on the bed, pressing her shoulders to make her stay on the pillows, lifting her feet and straightening her gown around her ankles. Slowly, he turns to face her husband. He makes a little gesture with his hands to Henry, but he says nothing. There is nothing he can say. The king looks from his wife, raised on one elbow, white as a ghost on her bed, to the duke standing beside her, and then he looks at me. He looks puzzled, like a hurt child.

I reach out to him, as if he were one of my own children, cruelly struck. 'Don't look,' I say foolishly. 'Don't see.'

He puts his head on one side, like a whipped dog, as if he is trying to hear me.

'Don't look,' I repeat. 'Don't see.'

Strangely, he steps towards me and lowers his pale face to me. Without knowing what I am doing, I lift my hands to him and he takes one and then the other and cups my palms over his eyes, as if to blindfold himself. For a moment we are all quite frozen: my hands over his eyes, the duke waiting to speak, Margaret leaning back on her pillows, her hand over her curving belly. Then the king presses my hands hard against his closed eyelids and repeats my words: 'Don't look. Don't see.'

Then he turns away. Without another word, he turns his back on all three of us, and walks from the room, quietly closing the door behind him.

He does not come to dinner that night. The queen's dinner is served in her privy rooms; a dozen ladies and I sit down to eat with her and send half the courses back untouched. Edmund, Duke of Somerset, takes the head of the table in the great hall and tells the hushed diners that he has bad news for them: we have lost the last of our lands in France, except for the pale, town and garrison of Calais, and that John Talbot the Earl of Shrewsbury has died riding out for a forlorn cause that his gallantry and courage would not allow him to refuse. The town of Castillon begged him to come and relieve the French siege, and John Talbot could not turn a deaf ear when his countrymen asked for help. He held to his vow that he would not put on armour against the French king who had released him on that condition. So he rode out without armour, at the head of our troops, into battle without a weapon or a shield. It was an act of the most perfect chivalry and folly. An act worthy of the great man that he was. An archer felled his horse and an axeman hacked him to death as he was pinned down underneath it. Our hopes of holding our lands in France are over, we have lost Gascony for the second, and almost certainly the last, time. Everything that was won by this king's father has been lost by his son, and we have been humiliated by France that once was our vassal.

The duke bows his head to the silent great hall. 'We will pray for the soul of John Talbot and his noble son, Lord Lisle,' he says. 'He was a most gentle and perfect knight. And we will pray for the king, for England, and St George.'

Nobody cheers. Nobody repeats the prayer. Men say 'Amen, Amen' quietly and pull out their benches and sit down and eat their dinner in silence.

The king goes to bed very early, the gentlemen of his chamber tell me, when I go to enquire. They say he seemed very tired. He did not speak to them. He did not say one word. I tell the queen and she bites her lip and looks at me, white-faced. 'What d'you think?' she asks. She seems as frightened as a little maid.

I shake my head. I don't know what to think.

'What should I do?'

I don't know what she should do.

In the morning, the queen is heavy-eyed from a sleepless night. Again she sends me to the king's rooms to ask how is His Grace, this morning. Again the groom of the bedchamber tells me that the king is weary, this morning he is sleeping late. When they told him that it was time for Lauds he just nodded and went back to sleep. They are surprised because he never misses chapel. They tried to wake him again for Prime but he did not stir. I go back and tell the queen that he has slept through the morning and is still asleep.

She nods and says she will take breakfast in her rooms. In the great hall the Duke of Somerset breaks his fast with the court. Nobody speaks very much, we are all waiting for more news from France. We are all dreading more news from France.

The king sleeps on till midday.

'Is he ill?' I ask the groom of the wardrobe. 'He never sleeps like this usually, does he?'

'He was shocked,' the groom says. 'I know that. He came into his rooms as white as a dove and lay down on the bed without a word to anyone.'

'He said nothing?' I am ashamed of myself for this question.

'Nothing. He said not one word.'

'Send for me as soon as he wakes,' I say. 'The queen is concerned about him.'

The man nods and I go back to the queen's rooms, and tell her that the king lay down to sleep and said nothing to anyone.

'He said nothing?' she repeats, as I did.

'Nothing.'

'He must have seen,' she says.

'He saw,' I say grimly.

'Jacquetta, what do you think he will do?'

I shake my head. I don't know.

All day he sleeps. Every hour I go to the door of the king's rooms and ask if he has woken. Every hour the groom of the chamber comes out, his face more and more worried, and shakes his head: 'Still sleeping.' Then, when the sun is setting and they are lighting the candles for dinner, the queen sends for Edmund Beaufort.

'I'll see him in my presence chamber,' she says. 'So that everyone can see we are not meeting in secret. But you stand before us so we can talk privately.'

He comes in looking grave and handsome and kneels before her till she tells him that he can sit. I stand absent-mindedly between them and the rest of the ladies and his entourage, so that nobody can hear their quiet-voiced conversation above the ripple of the harp.

They exchange three urgent sentences and then she rises to her feet and the court rises too and she grits her teeth and leads the way into dinner, like the queen she is, to the great hall, where the men greet her in silence and the king's chair is empty.

After dinner she calls me to her side.

'They can't wake him,' she says tightly. 'The grooms tried to wake him for dinner but he would not stir. The duke has sent for the physicians to see if he is sick.'

I nod.

'We'll sit in my rooms,' she decides, and leads the way from the hall. As we go out there is a whisper like a breeze, men saying one to another that the king is mortally weary.

We wait for them to report in the queen's presence chamber, half the court gathered around, waiting to hear what is wrong with the king. The door opens and the physicians come in and the queen beckons them to enter her private rooms, with the duke, and me, and half a dozen others.

'The king seems to be in good health, but he is sleeping,' one of the doctors, John Arundel, says.

'Can you wake him up?'

'We judged it best to let him sleep,' Dr Faceby replies, bowing. 'It might be best to let him sleep and wake when he is ready. Grief and a shock will sometimes be healed with a sleep, a long sleep.'

'A shock?' the duke asks sharply. 'What shock has the king had? What did he say?'

'The news from France,' the doctor stumbles. 'I believe the messenger blurted it out.'

'Yes, he did,' I say. 'The queen fainted and I took her into her rooms.'

Margaret nips her lip. 'Does he speak?'

'Not a word, not a word, since last night.'

She nods as if it is of no matter to her whether he speaks or not, she is only concerned for his health. 'Very well. Do you think he will wake in the morning?'

'Oh, almost certainly,' Dr Faceby answers. 'Often someone will sleep deeply after distressing news. It is the body's way to heal itself.'

'And wake remembering nothing?' she asks. The duke looks down at the floor as if indifferent.

'You may have to tell him of the loss of Gascony all over again, when he wakes,' the doctor agrees.

She turns to the duke. 'My lord, please give the king's grooms the order that they should wake him, as usual, in the morning, and prepare his rooms and his clothes as usual.'

He bows. 'Of course, Your Grace.'

The physicians take their leave. One of them will sit in the king's bedroom to watch over his sleep. The duke's entourage and the queen's ladies leave behind the doctors. The couple take one stolen moment when the duke is at her side, and everyone is leaving, and no-one observing them.

'It'll be all right,' he whispers. 'We'll say nothing. Nothing. Trust me. It will be all right.'

Mutely she nods, and he bows and goes out of the room.

The next day they go to wake the king but he does not wake. One of the grooms of the bedchamber comes to the door and tells me that they had to lift the king to the close stool, clean him and change his nightgown which he had soiled. If one of them holds him on the close stool he will pass water, and they can wash his face and hands. They can sit him in a chair though his head lolls and if one of them holds his face up, the other can pour a little warm ale down his throat. He cannot stand, he cannot hear them, he does not respond to a touch. He shows no hunger and he would lie in his filth.

'This isn't sleep,' the groom says bluntly. 'The doctors are fooling themselves. Nobody sleeps like this.'

'D'you think he is dying?' I ask.

The man shakes his head. 'I've never seen anything like it in my life before. It's like he's enchanted. Like he's cursed.'

'Don't say such a thing,' I reply at once. 'Never say such a thing. He's just sleeping.'

'Oh aye,' he repeats. 'Sleeping, as the doctors say.'

I walk slowly back to the queen's rooms, wishing that Richard were with me, wishing that I was at home in Grafton. I have a terrible fear that I have done something very wrong. I am filled with fear, superstitious fear as if I have done something terrible. I wonder if it was my command to the king to see nothing that has blinded him. I wonder if he is the victim of my accidental power. My great-aunt Jehanne cautioned me to always be careful what I wished for, to consider very carefully the words of bless-ings or of curses. And now I have told the King of England, 'Don't look! Don't see!' and he has closed his eyes and neither looks nor sees.

I shake my head, trying to dispel my own fears. Surely I must have said words like this a dozen times and nothing has happened? Why would I have the powers to blind the King of England now? Perhaps he is just very tired? Perhaps he is, as the doctors think, shocked by the news from France? Perhaps he is like one of my mother's aunts who froze up and lay still, lay quite like the king, neither speaking nor moving until she died years later. Perhaps I am frightening myself to think that it was my command that has made him blind.

In her rooms the queen is lying in her bed. I am so afraid of what I may have done that I recoil on the threshold of her darkened room, and whisper, 'Margaret.' She raises her hand, she can move, she is not enchanted. One of her younger ladies is at her side, while the rest of them are in the room outside, whispering about the danger to the baby, and the shock to the queen, and the likelihood of everything going terribly wrong, as women always do when one is near to childbirth.

'Enough,' I say irritably, as I close the door on the queen's chamber so she cannot hear these fearful predictions. 'If you can't say anything cheerful then don't speak at all. And you, Bessie, I don't want to hear another word about your mother's travails in childbed. I have been brought to bed eleven times, raised ten, and never endured one quarter of the pains you report. Indeed no woman could have borne what you describe. The queen may well be as lucky as me.'

I stamp past them to the queen's rooms and send away my little maid with one wave of my hand. She goes in silence and for a moment I think the queen is asleep; but she turns her head and looks at me, her eyes dark and hollowed with fatigue and fear.

'Has the king woken this morning?' Her lips are chapped where she has been biting them, she looks haggard with worry.

'No,' I say. 'Not yet. But they have washed him and he has taken a little breakfast.'

'He is sitting up?'

'No,' I say uncomfortably. 'They had to serve him.'

'Serve him?'

'Feed him.'

She is silent. 'It's a blessing in a way,' she says. 'It means he says nothing rashly, in temper, at first thought. It gives us time to consider. I keep thinking that it is a blessing in a way. It gives us time to . . . prepare.'

'In a way,' I agree.

'What do the doctors say?'

'They say they think he will wake, perhaps tomorrow.'

'And then he will be himself again? And remember everything?'

'Perhaps. I don't believe that they really know.'

'What shall we do?'

'I don't know.'

She sits on the side of the bed, her hand cupped on her belly, and rises to her feet to look out of the window. Below her are the beautiful gardens running down to the river where a punt bobs invitingly at a landing stage, and a heron stands still and quiet in the water. She sighs.

'Do you have any pain?' I ask anxiously.

'No, no, I can just feel the baby moving.'

'It is most important that you remain calm.'

She laughs shortly. 'We have lost Gascony, next the French are certain to attack Calais, the king has gone to sleep and cannot be wakened, and . . .' She breaks off. Neither of us has mentioned the duke taking her into his arms as an accustomed lover, kissing her face, promising to keep her safe. 'And you tell me to remain calm.'

'I do,' I say stoutly. 'For all this is nothing to losing the child. You have to eat and you have to sleep, Margaret. This is your duty to the child. You might be carrying a boy, it might be a prince for England. When all this has been forgotten we will remember that you kept the prince safe.'

She pauses, she nods. 'Yes. Jacquetta, you are right. See? I will sit. I will be calm. You can bring me some bread and some meat and some ale. I will be calm. And fetch the duke.'

'You cannot see him alone,' I specify.

'No. I know that. But I have to see him. Until the king wakes, he and I will have to decide everything together. He is my only advisor and help.'

297

I find the duke in his rooms, gazing blankly out of the window. He whirls around when his men hammer on the door and as they throw it open I see the whiteness of his face and the fear in his eyes.

'Jacquetta,' he says, and then corrects himself. 'Your Grace.'

I wait till they have closed the door behind me. 'The queen commands your presence,' I say shortly.

He takes up his cape and his hat. 'How is she?'

'Anxious.'

He offers me his arm and childishly I pretend not to see the gesture but precede him to the door. He follows me out and we walk down the sunny gallery towards the royal rooms. Outside the leaded windows I can see swallows swooping low over the water meadows, and hear the birds singing.

He strides faster to come alongside me. 'You blame me,' he says shortly.

'I don't know anything.'

'You blame me but, Jacquetta, I assure you, the first move was ...'

'I don't know anything, and if I know nothing then I cannot be questioned, and I cannot confess,' I say, cutting him off. 'All I want to do is to see Her Grace at peace and strong enough to carry her child to full term and bring him into the world. All I pray is that His Grace the king wakes up with a calm mind and we can tell him the sad news from Gascony. And I hope, of course, all the time, ceaselessly, that my husband is safe in Calais. Other than these thoughts, I don't venture, Your Grace.'

He nods his head and we walk in silence.

In the queen's rooms I see that the three ladies in waiting are sitting in the window-seats pretending to sew while craning their necks to eavesdrop. They rise up and curtsey and make a bustle as the duke and I enter and I tell them to sit again, and I nod to a couple of musicians to play. This covers the whispers between the queen and the duke. She allows him to sit on a stool at her side and she beckons me to join them.

'His Grace says that if the king does not waken within a few days we cannot stay here.'

I look at him.

'People will start to wonder and then there will be gossip. We can say that the king is weary and he can ride in a litter back to London.'

'We can draw the curtains of the litter,' I agree. 'But what then?'

'The queen has to go into her confinement at Westminster Palace. That's been planned for months, it can't be changed. I suggest the king stays quietly in his rooms.'

'People will talk.'

'We can say he is praying for her health. We can say he is keeping monastic hours.'

I nod. It is possible that the king's illness can be kept from everyone but a small court circle.

'What about meeting with the lords? What about the king's council?' I ask.

'I can handle them,' the duke says. 'I will take decisions in the name of the king.'

I look sharply at him and then I lower my eyes so he cannot see my shock. This is to make himself all but King of England. The queen will be in confinement, the king asleep, Edmund Beaufort will step up from being Constable of England to King of England.

'Richard, Duke of York, is likely to object,' I remark to the floor beneath my feet.

'I can handle him,' he says dismissively.

'And when the king wakes?'

'When the king wakes we will all go back to normal,' the queen says. Her voice is strained, her hand on her belly. 'And we will have to explain to him that when he was taken so suddenly ill we had to decide what to do without consulting him.'

'He is likely to be confused when he wakes,' the duke says. 'I asked the physicians. They say that he may have troubling dreams, fantasies. He will be surprised at waking. He will not be able to tell what is real and what is a bad dream. Best that it should be in his own bedroom at Westminster, with the country well ruled.'

'He may remember nothing,' the queen says. 'We may have to tell him again all about the loss of Gascony.'

'We must make sure that he hears the news first from us, and that we tell him the truth gently,' the duke supplements.

They look like conspirators, their heads close together, whispering. I glance around at the queen's rooms; no-one else seems to see anything out of the ordinary. I realise that I am the only one who suddenly sees a sickening intimacy.

The queen rises to her feet and gives a little moan at a twinge of pain. I see the duke's hand fly out, and then he checks the gesture: he does not touch her. She pauses and smiles at him. 'I am all right.'

He glances at me like a young husband prompting a nurse. 'Perhaps you should rest, Your Grace,' I respond. 'If we are to travel to London.'

'We will go the day after tomorrow,' the duke rules. 'I will order them to get everything ready at once.'

WESTMINSTER PALACE, LONDON, AUTUMN 1453

The rooms for the royal confinement are prepared, according to the traditions of the royal household. The tapestries are taken down, the windows shuttered tight and hung with thick material to keep out the disturbing light and draughts of air. The fires are banked up: the rooms must be kept warm, every day the fire-boys haul logs up as far as the firmly barred doors. No man, not even the working boys, can come into the queen's rooms.

Fresh rushes are scattered on the floor, especially herbs that are helpful in childbirth: shepherd's purse and motherwort. A low birthing bed is brought into the room and dressed with special sheets. They bring in the royal cradle: an heirloom sent over from Anjou, of beautiful carved wood inlaid with gold. They make it up with the finest linen trimmed with lace. They prepare the swaddling board for the baby, his bands and his cap are all washed and pressed and made ready. An altar is set up in what is usually the privy chamber, and a screen placed between the bedroom and the chamber so the priest can come in and serve the Mass and the queen observe him without being seen. She will make her confession from behind a veiled screen. Not even an ordained priest can come into these rooms for six weeks before the birth and for six weeks after.

In practice, in most households, a loving husband will break the rules and come in to see his wife during her confinement, as soon as the baby is born, washed, swaddled and laid in the cradle. Many husbands will not touch her until she has been churched, believing that she is unclean after the travail of childbed, and might contaminate him with female sin – but a husband like Richard disregards such fears as superstitions. He is always tender and affectionate and loving at these times and brings me fruit and sweetmeats that the older women say are not allowed, and has to be chased from the room by the midwives who protest that he will disturb me, or wake the baby, or make work for them.

No man will come near the poor little queen, of course. No man is allowed in the royal confinement chamber and her husband, the only one who might trespass, is in his own shadowy room washed daily as if he were a big overgrown baby, fed as if he were in his dotage, limp as a new corpse.

We are holding the terrible news of the king's health tightly within the walls of the palace. The grooms of his chamber know; but they are so appalled at the work they have to do, and the collapse of the man they knew, that it has not been hard for Edmund Beaufort to take each one aside, swear him to secrecy and threaten him with the most terrible punishments if he so much as whispers a word outside the walls. The king's household – his companions and his grooms, his pageboys, his master of horse and the grooms in the stable – know only that the king is stricken with an illness that makes him very tired and very weak, incapable of riding, and they wonder what can be wrong with him, but they are not troubled very much. It is not as if he was ever a lusty man who called for four hunters in the morning and would ride one after another, as each foundered. The quiet life of the king's stables remains quiet; and only the men who see him inert in his bed in his peaceful bedroom realise how gravely ill the king has become.

We are helped in our rule of silence by the fact that most of the lords and gentry had left London for the summer and are slow to return. The duke does not summon parliament so the country

gentry have no reason to come into the city, and everything that
has to be decided in the kingdom is done with a handful of men
in the king's council in the name of the king but under the signature of the duke. He tells them that the king is unwell, too
fatigued to come to council and he, Edmund Beaufort, as his
most trusted kinsman will hold the king's seal and use it to ratify
any decision. Almost no-one suspects that the king is quite incapable of coming to the council. Most of them think he is in his
private chapel, praying for the health of the queen, studying in
silence, and that he has given the seal and the authority to
Edmund Beaufort, who has always commanded so much
anyway.

But the rumours start, as they are bound to do. The cooks
remark that they never send good joints of meat into the king's
rooms but only soups, and then some fool of a groom says that
the king cannot chew his food, and then hushes himself and says,
'God save him!' and takes himself off. Of course the physicians
come and go in and out of the king's rooms and anyone seeing
them is bound to notice that there are strange doctors and
physicians, herbalists and practitioners of all sorts coming at the
bidding of the duke and going into the king's rooms. The physicians would not dare to speak; but they are attended by servants
and have messengers bringing them herbs and physic. After
a week of this, the duke invites me to his rooms and asks me
to tell the queen that it is his advice that the king be taken to
Windsor, where they can more easily nurse him without the news
getting out.

'She won't like it,' I tell him frankly. 'She won't like him being
kept there, and her trapped here in confinement.'

'If he stays here then people will start to talk,' he says. 'We
cannot keep it secret. And she will want to avoid gossip more
than anything else.'

I curtsey and go to the door.

'What do you think?' he asks me as my hand is on the latch.
'What do you think, Your Grace? You're a woman of gifts. What

do you think will become of the king? And what of the queen if he never recovers?'

I say nothing. I am too old a hand at court to be led into speculation about the future of a king by the man who is standing in his shoes.

'You must have thoughts,' he says impatiently.

'I may have thoughts; but I have no words,' I say and leave him. But that night I dream of the Fisher King of the legend: a country commanded by a king too frail and too weak to do anything but go fishing, while a young woman has to rule the land alone, and longs for a man who can stand at her side.

The queen finds her confinement tedious, and the daily reports from Windsor Castle only make the days worse. They are torturing the king with one remedy after another. The reports speak of draining him of cool fluids, and heating of his vital parts, and I know that they mean cupping him to draw off his blood and then burning him where he lies, silent as a crucified Christ, waiting to rise again. Some nights I get up from the little bed that I have in the queen's room and pull up the corner of the tapestry over the window; so that I can see the moon, a big warm harvest moon, so near to earth that I can see every wrinkle and pockmark on her face, and I ask her, 'Did I bewitch the king? Did I ill-wish him? In that moment of fright when I bade him see nothing did I, in truth, make him blind? Could such a thing be? Could I be so powerful? And if it was me – how can I take the words back and restore him?'

I feel very alone with this worry. Of course I cannot share it with the queen who has her own guilt and fear. I dare write nothing to Richard; such thoughts should not be in my mind, never on paper. I am sick and tired of being trapped in these shadowy rooms: the queen's confinement is long and anxious for us all. This should be the happiest autumn of her life, with a baby on the way at last; but instead we are all filled with fear about the king, and now some of the ladies are whispering that the baby will be born asleep too.

When I hear this I go down to the river and sit on the pier as the sun is setting and look over the swiftly moving water that flows towards the sea, and I whisper to Melusina that if I ever said a word that wished the king blinded, I take back that word now. If I ever had a thought that he should see nothing, then I deny that thought now, and I wish with all my heart that the baby born to the queen will be well and healthy and live long and happy. I go slowly back to the palace not knowing if the river has heard my wishes, or if the river can do anything anyway, or if the moon can understand how desolate a mere woman can feel, far from her husband and in a world that is filled with danger.

I walk in to a hushed bustle. 'Her waters have broken,' a maid hisses, running past me with some clean linen.

I hurry into the bedroom. The midwives are here already, the rockers are making up the cradle with clean sheets and the soft-est blanket, the mistress of the bedchamber is heating a poker to mull the special birthing ale, and the queen herself is standing at the foot of the best bed, bent over, holding the bedpost, sweat on her white face, gripping her lower lip in her teeth. I go straight to her. 'The pain passes,' I say. 'Moment by moment, it comes and it goes away again. You have to be brave.'

'I am brave,' she says furiously. 'No-one shall ever say otherwise.'

I see the irritability of childbirth and I take a damp cloth soaked in lavender water and gently wipe her face. She sighs as the pain recedes and then braces herself for the next wave. It takes a long time to come. I glance at the midwife. 'Going to take a while,' she says wisely. 'We'd all better have a mug of ale and a sit down.'

It does take a while – all night – but next day, on the day of St Edward, she gives birth to a boy, a precious Lancaster boy, and the safety and the inheritance of England is assured.

I go outside to the presence chamber and there are the lords of England, waiting for news. Edmund Beaufort is among them, not standing forwards, as he usually does, commanding the room, but away from the bedchamber door, a little aside, making himself one of the crowd. For once in his life he is not claiming pride of place and this makes me hesitate, not knowing if I should go directly and tell him. He is the Constable of England, he is the most favoured lord in the land, he commands the Privy Council, they are his nominated men in parliament. He is the favourite of king and queen and we are all accustomed to giving way to him. I would normally speak to him before any other.

Of course, the first man to have the news should be the baby's father: the king. But he, God bless him, is far, far away. There is no protocol for today, and I don't know what I am supposed to do. I hesitate for a moment, and then as all the talk dies down and the men turn to look at me in expectant silence, I say simply, 'My lords, I give you joy. The queen has been brought to bed of a handsome boy and has named him Edward. God save the king.'

A few days later, as the baby thrives and the queen rests, I am coming back to the queen's chambers after a walk in the gardens of the palace when I hesitate. At the closed door of her rooms is a young boy and a couple of guards wearing the white rose of the House of York on their livery. I know at once that this will mean trouble, as I open the door and go inside.

The queen is seated on her chair by the window, the wife of Richard Duke of York standing before her. Margaret has not invited her to sit, and the flush of colour in Cecily Neville's cheeks tells me that she is well aware of the snub. She turns as I come in and says, 'Her Grace, the Dowager Duchess, will confirm all that I say, I am sure.'

I sweep her a small curtsey. 'Good day to you, Your Grace,' I say politely, and I go and stand beside the queen, my hand resting on the back of her chair, so that Cecily can be in no doubt which side I am on, whatever she is here for, whatever she hopes I will confirm.

'Her Grace has come to ask me to make sure that her husband is invited to all meetings of the royal council,' the queen says wearily.

Cecily nods and says, 'As he should be. As his family always has been. As the king promised he would be.'

I wait.

'I have been explaining to Her Grace that since I am in confinement I can play no part in the business of ruling,' the queen says.

'Really, you should not be seeing visitors at all,' I remark.

'I am sorry to come, but how else is my husband's position to be considered?' the duchess says, looking remarkably impenitent. 'The king will see no-one, and is not even attended by a court. And the Duke of Somerset is no friend to my husband.' She turns to the queen again. 'You do the country a great disservice when you do not let my husband serve,' she says. 'He is the greatest magnate in the kingdom and his loyalty to the king is unquestioned. He is the king's closest cousin and his heir. Why is he not invited to attend the king's council? How can business be agreed without considering his opinion? You call on him quickly enough when you want arms and money; he should be there when the decisions are taken.'

The queen shrugs. 'I will send the Duke of Somerset a note,' she offers. 'But I understand that not much is being undertaken. The king has withdrawn into prayer and I am still confined. I imagine the duke is managing day-to-day affairs as best he can with a few advisors.'

'My husband should be one of the advisors,' the duchess insists.

I step forwards and make a little gesture towards the door. 'I am sure the queen is glad that you brought it to her attention,' I say. Unwillingly, the duchess allows herself to be guided away. 'And since Her Grace has said that she will write a note to the duke, I am sure your husband will receive his invitation to the council.'

'And he must be there when they present the baby to the king.'

I freeze at this and exchange a quick aghast look with the queen. 'Forgive me,' I say when Margaret is silent. 'You know I was not brought up in an English court. And this is the first time I have been present at the birth of a prince.' I smile, but she – a

307

born and bred Englishwoman – does not. 'Please tell me. How is the baby presented to the king?'

'He has to be presented by the Privy Council,' Cecily Neville says with just a hint of glee at my discomfort. I think she knows that we had not planned for this. 'In order for the baby to be accepted as the heir to the throne and the prince of the realm he has to be presented by the Privy Council to the king, and the king has to formally accept him as his son and heir. Without that – he is not the heir to the throne. If he is not recognised by his father he cannot be recognised as heir to England. He cannot take his titles. But there can be no difficulty, can there?'

Margaret says nothing, but leans back in the chair as if she is exhausted.

'Can there?' the duchess asks again.

'Of course not,' I say smoothly. 'I am sure the Duke of Somerset has all the arrangements in hand.'

'And you will make sure that my husband is invited to attend,' Cecily insists. 'As is his right.'

'I will take the queen's note to the duke myself,' I assure her.

'And of course we will all be so happy to attend the baptism,' she adds.

'Of course.' I wait to see if she has the gall to ask if she can be godmother but she contents herself with curtseying to the queen and stepping backwards for a few paces before letting me escort her to the door. We go out together. Outside in the presence chamber is the handsome boy that I noticed earlier, who jumps to his feet. It is her oldest boy, Edward, and as he sees me he makes a bow. He is the most bonny child, golden-brown hair, dark grey eyes, a merry smile, and tall, perhaps up to my shoulder, though he is only eleven.

'Ah, you have your boy with you,' I exclaim. 'I saw him as I came in but I did not recognise him.'

'This is my Edward,' she says, her voice warm with pride. 'Edward, you know Lady Rivers, the Dowager Duchess of Bedford.'

I extend my hand and he bows and kisses it.

'What a heartbreaker,' I say to her with a smile. 'He is just the same age as my boy Anthony, isn't he?'

'Only months apart,' she says. 'Is Anthony at Grafton?'

'Staying with his sister at Groby,' I say. 'Learning his manners. I think your boy is taller than mine.'

'They shoot up like weeds,' she says, disguising her pride. 'And the shoes they get through! And the boots! Of course I have two other boys and Richard in the cradle.'

'I have four boys now,' I reply. 'I lost my first, Lewis.'

At once she crosses herself. 'God keep them safe,' she says. 'And Our Lady comfort you.'

This talk of children has united us. She steps closer to me and nods towards the queen's chamber. 'Did it go well? Is she well?'

'Very well,' I say. 'It took all night and she was brave and the baby came out quite perfect.'

'Healthy and strong?'

'Giving suck, giving tongue,' I tell her in the old country saying. 'A bonny boy.'

'And the king? Is he well? Why is he not here? I would have thought he would have come to see his son?'

My smile is guileless. 'He is serving God and his people in the best way that he can,' I say. 'On his knees for the safe delivery of his son and the security of an heir for England.'

'Oh yes,' she says. 'But I had heard he was taken ill at Clarendon Palace, and came home in a litter?'

'He was tired,' I say. 'He had spent most of the summer pursuing and sentencing rebels. Both this year and last he spent all the days of summer making sure that justice runs through the lands. Sometimes your lands, as it happens.'

She flings up her head at the implied rebuke. 'If the king favours one man over his closest kin, his true friends and best advisors, there is always going to be trouble,' she says hotly.

I raise my hand. 'Forgive me,' I say. 'I did not mean to suggest that your tenants are exceptionally unruly, or your father's family, the Nevilles, make exceptionally irritable neighbours in the north of England. I meant only that the king has worked hard to see that his rule runs through all England. When the duke your husband comes to council I am sure he will be able to reassure his peers that there is no hint of rebellion anywhere on his lands, and that his kinsmen, your family, can learn to live in peace with the Percys in the north.'

She folds her lips on an angry reply. 'Of course,' she says. 'We all want only to serve and support the king. And the north cannot be divided.'

I smile at her boy. 'And what do you hope to do when you are grown, Edward?' I ask. 'Will you be a great general like your father? Or is it the Church for you?'

He ducks his head. 'One day I shall be head of the House of York,' he says shyly to his shoes. 'It is my duty to be ready to serve my house and my country however I am needed, when my time comes.'

We have an impressive christening for the royal baby. The queen herself orders a cloth-of-gold train for his gown that is brought from France, and costs more than the gown of his godmother, Anne the Duchess of Buckingham. The other godparents are the Archbishop of Canterbury and Edmund Beaufort the Duke of Somerset.

'Is that wise?' I ask her quietly as she tells her confessor the names of the godparents she has chosen. She is on her knees before the little altar in her privy chamber, I am kneeling beside her, the priest behind the screen. Nobody can hear my urgent murmur.

She does not turn her head from her clasped hands. 'I would have no-one else,' she whispers. 'The duke shall care for him and protect him as if he was his own.'

I shake my head in silence but I can see what she has done. She has surrounded her boy with the court party: people she trusts, people that Somerset has appointed, and Somerset's kin. If the king were to never speak again she would have put a small army around her boy who should protect him.

Anne the Duchess of Buckingham carries the precious child to the font in Westminster chapel. Cecily Neville glares at me from among the ladies as if I am responsible for yet another snub to her husband, Richard, Duke of York, who should have been a godfather. Nobody remarks on the king's absence, for a christening is the business of the godparents, and of course the queen is still in her confinement. But the secret cannot be kept forever, and the king surely cannot be ill forever? Surely he must get better soon?

At the christening feast Edmund Beaufort takes me to one side. 'Tell the queen that I will call the great council, including the Duke of York, and take the baby prince to visit the king at Windsor.'

I hesitate. 'But, Your Grace, what if he does not wake at the sight of his child?'

'Then I will insist that they acknowledge the baby without the king's recognition.'

'Could you do that without them seeing him?' I say. 'They all know that he is ill but if they see him all but lifeless . . .'

He makes a little grimace. 'I can't. Tell the queen I have tried but the council insists that the child is presented to the king. Anything else would look too odd, they would think he is dead and we are concealing it. We have been blessed with a longer time than I dreamed possible. But it has come to an end now. They have to see the king, and the child has to be presented to him. There is nothing we can do to avoid this any longer.' He hesitates. 'There is one thing I had better tell you, and you had better forewarn the queen: they are saying that the child is not the true-born son of the king.'

I stiffen, alert to danger. 'They are?'

He nods. 'I am doing what I can to quash the rumours. These allegations are treason, of course, and I will see anyone who gossips ends up on the gallows. But with the king hidden away from court, people are bound to talk.'

'Do they name another man?' I ask him.

He looks at me, his dark eyes quite without guile. 'I don't know,' he says; though he does know. 'I don't think it matters,' he says; though it does matter. 'And anyway, there is no evidence.' This at least is true. Please God there is no evidence of any wrongdoing. 'But the Duke of York has stirred up the council and so the baby has to be seen and at least held by the king.'

A council of twelve lords comes to the palace to take the baby upriver to be presented to his father, Somerset at their head. I am to go with them, along with the baby's nurses and rockers. Anne the Duchess of Buckingham, his godmother, will come too. It is a cold autumn day but the barge is well curtained and the baby is swaddled on his board and then wrapped in furs. The nurse holds him in her lap at the back of the boat, the baby's rockers seated near her, the wet nurse close by. Two barges follow us: the Duke of Somerset and his friends in one, the Duke of York and his allies in another. It is a fleet of undeclared enmity. I stand in the bow of the boat looking at the water, listening to the soothing swish of the river against the barge and the dip and pull of the oars in the current.

We sent ahead to say that the lords would visit the king but I am shocked when we land at Windsor and go through the quiet castle to the upper ward. When the king and court leave one castle for another then the servants take the chance to clean and shut down the state rooms. When we sent the king to Windsor without the court, they did not open all the bedrooms, nor the kitchens that cook for hundreds, the state rooms, the echoing stables. Instead the king's tiny entourage is camped in his own private rooms and the rest of the castle is empty, quite desolate. The king's beautiful presence chamber, which is usually the heart of the court, has a shabby neglected air; the servants have not cleaned the hearth and the flickering flames show that they have only just lit the fire. It feels cold and deserted. There are no tapestries on the walls and some of the shutters are closed so the room is shadowy and cool. There are old rushes on the floor, musty and dry; and half-burned rushlights in the sconces. I crook my finger to the groom of the household to call him to my side. 'Why was the fire not lit earlier? Where are the king's tapestries? This room is a disgrace.'

He ducks his head. 'Forgive me, Your Grace. But I have so few servants here. They are all at Westminster with the queen and the Duke of Somerset. And the king never comes out here anyway. Would you want me to light the fire for the physicians and their servants? Nobody else visits and our orders are to admit no-one who does not come from the duke.'

'I would want you to light the fire so the king's rooms are bright and clean and cheerful,' I tell him. 'And if you haven't enough servants to keep the rooms clean then you should have told us. His Grace should be better served than this. This is the King of England, he should be served in state.'

He bows at the reproof, but I doubt that he agrees with me. If the king can see nothing, what is the point of tapestries on the walls? If no-one comes then why sweep the state rooms? If there are no visitors then why light a fire in the presence chamber? The Duke of Somerset beckons me to join him at the double doors of the privy chamber. There is only one man on duty. 'No need to announce us,' the duke says. The guard opens the door for us and we slip in.

The room is transformed. Usually it is a pretty chamber with two bay windows overlooking the water meadows and the river, the windows on the other side overlooking the upper ward where there is always the sound of people coming and going, horses clip-clopping on the cobbles, sometimes music. The rooms are always busy with the courtiers and the advisors to the king. Usually, there are tapestries on the walls and tables laid with little objects of gold and silver, little painted boxes and curios. Today the room is empty, horribly bare but for a great table laid with the tools of the physicians' trade: bowls for cupping, lances, a big jar of wriggling leeches, some bandages, some ointments, a box of herbs, a record book with daily entries of painful treatments, and some boxes holding spices and shavings of metals. There is a heavy chair with thick leather straps on the arms and legs where they bind the king to keep him still while they force drinks down his throat, or lance his thin arms. There is no seat to the chair but underneath there is a bowl to catch his urine and faeces. The room is warm enough, there is a fire in the grate, and it is clean; but it is more like one of the best rooms in the Bethlem hospital for the mad than a royal privy chamber. It is like a room for a well-nursed madman; not for a king. The duke exchanges one horrified glance with me. Nobody coming in here is going to imagine that the king has been on retreat from the world, quietly praying.

The king's chief three physicians, solemn in their dark gowns, are standing behind the table; they bow but say nothing.

'Where is His Grace the king?' the duke asks.

'He is being dressed,' Dr Arundel says. 'They will bring him through now.'

The duke takes a step forwards towards the bedchamber and then checks, as if he does not want to see inside. 'Bring him out,' he says shortly.

The doctor goes to the king's bedchamber door and opens it wide. 'Bring him,' he says. From inside we can hear furniture shift, and I find I am clutching my hands together, hidden in my sleeves. I am afraid. I am afraid of what is going to come out. Then a brawny man, dressed in royal livery, comes through the door carrying a heavy chair like a royal throne, set on a base with handles, like a litter. Behind him, holding the rear handles, comes another porter, and on the chair, head lolling, eyes closed, is all that is left of our king.

He is well dressed in a gown of blue with a surcoat of red, and his thin dark hair has been combed to his shoulders. He has been shaved but they have nicked him and there is a drop of blood on his throat. With his head lolling it looks as if they are bringing out a murdered man, his wounds bleeding in the presence of his killers. He is held steady in the chair by a band around his waist and another strap around his chest; but his head sags to one side and when they put the chair down, it falls to his chest and he nods like a doll. Gently, the doctor raises him up and positions his head erect; but he does not stir at the touch. His eyes are closed, his breathing is heavy, like a man in drunken sleep.

'The Fisher King,' I whisper to myself. He looks exactly like a man under an enchantment. This is not an illness of this world: this has to be a curse laid on him. He looks like the wax image of a king that they lay on the coffin at a royal funeral, not a living man. Only the rise and fall of his chest, and the little noise that he makes from time to time, a little snuffling snore, tells us that he is alive. Alive but not a living man. I glance at the duke: he is looking at his king with an expression of horror. 'This is worse than I thought,' he says quietly to me. 'Far worse.'

The doctor steps forwards. 'He is in good health – otherwise,' he says.

I look at him blankly. This state cannot be described as good health. He is like a dead man. 'Does nothing make him stir?'

He shakes his head, he gestures at the table behind. 'We have tried everything,' he says. 'We go on trying. At about noon every day, after he has broken his fast, we spend an hour trying to wake him, and every evening before dinner for another hour. But he seems to hear nothing, and he feels no pain. Every day we tell him that he must wake, sometimes we send for a priest to call on him to do his duty, to reproach him for failing us; but he shows no signs of hearing or understanding.'

'Is he getting any worse?'

'No worse; but no better.' He hesitates. 'I think his sleep is a little deeper than when it first came on him.' He gestures politely to the other doctors. One of them shakes his head. 'Opinions vary.'

'Do you think he might speak when we bring his son in to him?' the duke asks the doctors. 'Does he ever say anything? Does he even dream?'

'He never says anything,' Dr Faceby volunteers. 'But I think he dreams. Sometimes you can see his eyelids moving, sometimes he twitches in his sleep.' He glances at me. 'Once he wept.'

I put my hand to my mouth at the thought of the king weeping in his sleep. I wonder if he is seeing in another world, I wonder what he has been watching. He has been asleep for nearly four months, it is a long dream. What can a four-month dream show a sleeping man?

'Could we prompt him to move at all?' The duke is thinking of the shock to the council, seeing the king like this for the first time. 'Could he hold the baby if we put it in his arms?'

'He is quite limp,' Dr Arundel says. 'I am afraid he would drop the baby. You could not trust him with anything of value. He is, himself, quite incapable.'

There is an appalled silence.

'This has to be done,' the duke decides.

'At least move that terrible chair,' I say, and the two porters lift the chair with the straps and the close stool and carry it out.

The duke looks blankly at me. Neither of us can think of anything that will make this better. 'Fetch them in,' he says to me.

I go out to the waiting lords. 'His Grace the king is in his privy chamber,' I say and stand to one side as they go in, the rockers and the nurse following with the duchess. I am foolishly relieved to see that the baby's dark blue eyes are open, blinking at the ceiling; there would have been something very horrible if the baby had been sleeping like his father.

In the privy chamber the lords have made an embarrassed half-circle around the king. Not a word is spoken, I see one man cross himself. Richard, Duke of York, looks grim at the sight of the sleeping king. One man is shielding his eyes from the sight, one is weeping. They are all deeply shocked. Anne Duchess of Buckingham was forewarned of the state of the king by her kins- man Edmund Beaufort but she is pale. She plays her part in this grotesque tableau, as if she presents a baby to his half-dead father every day of her life. She takes the child and walks towards the motionless king, strapped in his chair.

'Your Grace,' she says quietly. 'This is your son.' She steps for- wards, but the king does not lift his arms to receive the child. He is completely still. Awkwardly, the duchess holds the baby against his chest, but the king does not move. She looks to the Duke of Somerset who takes the baby from her, and lays it in the king's lap. He does not stir.

'Your Grace,' the duke says loudly. 'This is your son. Raise your hand to acknowledge him.'

Nothing.

'Your Grace!' the duke says again, a little louder. 'Just nod your head to acknowledge your son.'

Nothing.

'Just blink, sire. Just blink to say that you know this is your son.'

Now it is as if we are all enchanted. The physicians are still, looking at their patient, hoping for a miracle, the duchess wait- ing, the duke with one hand holding the baby on the king's unmoving knees, the other on the king's shoulder, squeezing him, hard and then harder, so his strong fingers are digging into the king's bony shoulder, pinching him cruelly. I am silent, standing still. For a moment I feel as if the king has a plague of stillness and we are all going to freeze and sleep with him, an enchanted court around a sleeping king. Then the baby lets out a little cry and I step forwards and catch him up as if I fear that he might be infected with sleep.

'This is hopeless,' the Duke of York says abruptly. 'He sees and hears nothing. My God, Somerset: how long has he been like this? He can do nothing. You should have told us.'

'He is still king,' the duke says sharply.

'Nobody is denying that,' Richard, Duke of York, snaps. 'But he has not recognised his son, and he cannot transact the business of the kingdom. He is a king like a babe himself. We should have been told.'

Edmund Beaufort looks round for support, but even the lords who are sworn to his house and hate and fear the Duke of York cannot deny that the king has not recognised his son, does nothing, sees nothing, hears nothing, is far, far from us – who knows where?

'We will return to Westminster,' Edmund Beaufort announces. 'And we will wait for His Grace to recover from this illness.' He throws a furious look at the doctors. 'The good physicians will waken him, I know.'

That night as I start to doze in my bedchamber at Westminster Palace I wonder at a sleep that is unbroken, a sleep like death; except that in this sleep one would dream and stir and then sleep again. What would it be like to stir a little and glimpse the physicians and that terrible room with the chair and the knives and the leeches, and then slide back into sleep, unable to protest? What would it be like to open one's mouth in the silent scream of a dream and fall asleep mute? When I fall asleep I dream again of the Fisher King, of a king who can do nothing as his kingdom falls into chaos and darkness, and leaves a young woman without her husband, alone. The Fisher King is wounded in his groin, he can neither father a child nor hold his lands. The cradle is empty, the fields are bare. I wake in the night and thank God that I have done so, that the enchantment that is lying like a blanket of darkness on the king has not smothered me, and I wonder, I shake my head on my pillow and wonder if it is my fault, if I commanded the king to be blind, if it was my incautious words that blinded him?

When I wake in the dawn light, I am clear-headed and alert at once, as if someone is calling my name, and I get up and go to the jewellery box that my great-aunt Jehanne gave me. There, untouched, is the purse of charms, and this time I choose a crown, to symbolise the king's return. I tie four different thin ribbons to this one charm. I choose a white ribbon to symbolise winter, if he will come back to us in the winter, a green ribbon if he will not come back till spring, a yellow ribbon if he will come back for haymaking, and a red ribbon if he will come back a year from now, when the berries are in the hedges. Then I tie each of these ribbons to four black strings, and take them to the riverside walk where the Thames is flowing high and fast as the tide is coming in.

There is nobody about as I walk down to the little wooden pier where the wherry-boatmen pick up their passengers, and so I tie the four dark threads to one of the stanchions of the pier and I throw the little crown with the coloured ribbons as far out as it will go, out into the river, and then I go back to the queen's confinement room where she waits for her time of cleansing to be over and her release into the light.

I leave the crown in the water for a week, while the queen comes out of her confinement and is churched in a magnificent service where all the duchesses of the kingdom walk behind her, to honour her, as if their husbands are not locked in a struggle to decide how the prince shall be recognised and how the kingdom shall be commanded while the king sees nothing and commands nothing. Now that the queen is returned to the world the duke can come to her rooms and he tells her that the Earl of Salisbury, brother-in-law to the Duke of York, is saying publicly that the baby was not got by the king, and that there are many, dangerously many, who believe him. The queen lets it be known that anyone who listens to such slander need never come again to court, she tells her friends that no-one should even speak to the

Earl of Salisbury or to his spiteful son, the Earl of Warwick. She tells me that Richard, Duke of York, their kinsman, and even his duchess Cecily, are her enemies, her enemies to death, and that I must never speak to any of them ever again. What she does not do is comment on what they are saying, what many people are saying: that the king is not man enough to make a son, and that the baby is not a prince.

The queen and Edmund Beaufort decide that they must redouble the efforts to waken the king, and they hire new physicians and experts. They change the laws against alchemy, and men of learning are allowed to study once again and asked to consider the causes and cures of unknown illnesses of the mind. Everyone reopens their forges, refires their ovens, starts to send for foreign herbs and spices; herbalism, even magic, is permitted if it can cure the king. They command the doctors to treat him more powerfully, but since nobody knows what is wrong with him, nobody knows what should be done. He has always been known to be melancholic so they try to change his humour. They feed him burning-hot drinks and spicy soups to make him hotter, they make him sleep under thick furs heaped up on the bed, with a hot brick at his feet and a warming pan on either side of him until he sweats and weeps in his sleep; but still never wakens. They lance his arms and bleed him to try to drain the watery humours, they poultice his back with paste of mustard seed till it is red and raw, they force boluses down his throat and purge him with enemas so that he vomits and voids in his sleep, burning waste that leaves his skin red and sore.

They try to make him angry by beating his feet, by shouting at him, by threatening him. They think it is their duty to taunt him with cowardice, with being a lesser man than his father. They abuse him terribly, God forgive them, they shout things in his face that would have broken his heart if he had heard them. But he hears nothing. They hurt him when they slap him – they can see his cheeks redden under the blows. But he does not rise up and leave them, he lies inert as they do what they want to him. I fear this is not treatment but torture.

In Westminster I wait for my week and then I know that the morning has come when I wake again at dawn, wake as if I am alert in every part of my body and my mind is clear as the cold water washing round the pier. The four threads are there, safely tied to the leg of the pier, and I hope with all my heart that when I choose a black thread it will pull out the white ribbon on the crown so that I can see that the king will return to us this winter.

The sun is coming up as I put my hand on the threads and I look east towards it, as it rises over the heart of England. There is a dazzle on the water from the rising sun, a wintry sun, a white and gold and silver wintry sun, in a cold blue sky, and as it rises and the mist swirls off the river I see the most extraordinary sight: not one sun but three. I see three suns: one in the sky and two just above the water, reflections of mist and water, but clearly three suns. I blink and then rub my eyes but the three suns blaze at me as I pull on the thread and I find it comes lightly, too lightly, into my hand. I don't have the thread with the white ribbon that would mean the king would come back to us in winter, nor even the green which would mean the king would come back to us in spring. I pull on one thread after another and find all four ribbons empty with no crown; there is no crown at all. The king will never come back to us: instead there will be the rise of a new dawn, and three suns in splendour.

I walk slowly back to the palace, a bunch of wet ribbons in my hand, and I wonder what three suns over England can mean. As I near the queen's rooms I can hear noise, soldiers grounding their weapons, and shouting. I pick up my long gown and hurry forwards. Outside her presence chamber there are men in the livery of Richard, Duke of York, his white rose on their collar. The doors are flung open to reveal the queen's personal guards standing irresolute as the queen shouts at them in French. Her women are screaming and running inwards to the privy chamber, and two or three of the lords of the council are trying to command quiet, as York's guard get hold of Edmund Beaufort, the Duke of Somerset, and march him out of the chamber and past me. He casts one furious look at me, but they take him past too fast for me to say anything, not even to ask where he is going. The queen comes flying out after him and I catch her, and hold her, as she bursts into a flood of tears.

'Traitors! Treason!'

'What? What is happening?'

'The Duke of Somerset has been accused of treason,' one of the lords tells me, as he rapidly withdraws from the queen's chamber. 'They are taking him to the Tower. He will have a fair trial, the queen need not be distressed.'

'Treason!' she screams. 'You are the traitor, you, to stand by as that devil of York takes him!'

I help her back through the presence chamber, through the privy chamber and into her bedroom. She flings herself on her bed and bursts into tears. 'It's Richard, Duke of York,' she says. 'He has turned the council against Edmund. He wants to destroy him, he has always been his enemy. Then he will turn on me. Then he will rule the kingdom. I know it. I know it.'

She raises herself up, her hair spilling from the plaits on either side of her face, her eyes red with tears and temper. 'You hear this, Jacquetta. He is my enemy, he is my enemy and I will destroy him. I will get Edmund out of the Tower and I will put my son on the throne of England. And neither Richard, Duke of York, nor anyone else will stop me.'

Christmas comes and goes. Richard takes a ship from Calais and spends only the twelve days of the festival with me at the quiet court, and then says he has to return. The garrison is on the verge of mutiny and could come under attack at any time. The men do not know who is in command, and they are afraid of the French. Richard has to hold the garrison for Edmund Beaufort, and for England, against enemies within and without. Once again we are on the quayside, once again I am clinging to him. 'I'll come with you,' I say desperately. 'We said I should come with you. I should come now.'

'Beloved, you know I would never take you into a siege, and God alone knows what is going to happen.'

'When will you come home again?'

He gives a resigned little shrug. 'I have to hold my command until someone relieves me of it, and neither the king nor the duke is going to do that. If Richard, Duke of York, seizes power then I will have to hold Calais against him, as well as against the French. I will have to hold it for Edmund Beaufort. He gave me the command, I can only return it to him. I have to go back, beloved. But you know I will return to you.'

'I wish we were just squires at Grafton,' I say miserably.

'I wish it too,' he says. 'Kiss the children for me and tell them

323

to be good. Tell them to do their duty and that I am doing mine.'

'I wish you were not so dutiful,' I say disagreeably.

He kisses me into silence. 'I wish I could have another night,' he says in my ear, and then he breaks away from me and runs up the gangplank to his ship.

I wait on the quayside until I see him at the rail, and I kiss my cold hand to him. 'Come back soon,' I call. 'Be safe. Come back soon.'

'I always come back to you,' he calls back. 'You know that. I will come back soon.'

The dark nights grow shorter, but the king does not recover. Some alchemists predict that the sunshine will bring him to life as if he were a seed in the darkness of the earth, and they wheel him to an eastern window every morning and make him face the grey disc of the wintry sun. But nothing wakes him.

Edmund Beaufort, Duke of Somerset, is not released from his rooms in the Tower of London; but neither is he accused. Richard, Duke of York, has enough power over the council of lords to make them arrest the duke, but not enough to persuade them to try him for treason.

'I am going to see him,' the queen announces.

'Your Grace, people will talk,' I warn her. 'They are already saying things about you that don't bear repeating.'

She raises an eyebrow.

'So I won't repeat them,' I say.

'I know what they are saying,' she declares boldly. 'They are saying that he is my lover and that the prince is his son, and this is why my husband the king has not acknowledged him.'

'Reason enough not to visit him,' I caution.

'I have to see him.'

'Your Grace . . .'

'Jacquetta, I have to.'

I go with her, and take two of her other ladies. They wait outside while the queen and I go into his rooms. He has a privy chamber with a bedroom beside it. The rooms, stone-walled with arrowslit windows, are pleasant enough, close to the royal apartments in the White Tower; he is not by any means in a dungeon. He has a table and a chair and some books, but he is pale from being kept indoors and he is looking thinner. His face lights up when he sees her and he drops to his knee. She hurries towards him and he passionately kisses her hands. The Constable of the Tower stands at the door, his back turned tactfully to the room. I wait at the window looking out over the grey tide of the cold river. Behind me, I can hear the duke rise to his feet and I can sense him mastering himself so that he does not reach for her.

'Will you sit, Your Grace?' he asks quietly and puts the chair near the little fire for her.

'You can sit beside me,' she says. I turn and see him pull up a small stool, so they are close enough to whisper.

They are hand-clasped, his mouth to her ear, her turning to murmur to him, for half an hour, but when I hear the clock strike three, I go forwards and curtsey before her. 'Your Grace, we have to go,' I say.

For a moment I am afraid that she is going to cling to him, but she tucks her hands inside her sweeping sleeves, strokes the border of ermine as if for comfort, and rises to her feet. 'I will come again,' she says to him. 'And I will do as you suggest. We have no choice.'

He nods. 'You know the names of the men who will serve you. It has to be done.'

She nods and looks at him once, longingly, as if she wants his touch more than anything in the world, as if she cannot bear to leave, then she ducks her head and goes quickly out of the room.

'What has to be done?' I ask as soon as we are outside, walking down the stone stairs towards the watergate. We came in a barge without flags and standards; I was anxious that as few people as possible knew that she was meeting the man accused of treason and named as her lover.

She is alight with excitement. 'I am going to tell the parliament to appoint me as regent,' she says. 'Edmund says the lords will support me.'

'Regent? Can a woman be a regent in England? Your Grace, this is not Anjou. I don't think a woman can be a regent here. I don't think a woman can reign in England.'

She hurries ahead of me, down the steps and onto the barge. 'There's no law against it,' she replies. 'Edmund says. It is nothing but tradition. If the lords will support me we will call a parliament and tell the parliament that I will serve as regent until the king is well again or – if he never wakes – until my son is old enough to be king.'

'Never wakes?' I repeat in horror. 'The duke is planning for the king to sleep forever?'

'How can we know?' she asks. 'We can't do nothing! You can be sure that Richard, Duke of York, is not doing nothing.'

'Never wakes?'

She sits herself at the rear of the barge, her hand impatiently on the curtain. 'Come on, Jacquetta. I want to get back and write to the lords and tell them my terms.'

I hurry to take a seat beside her and the oarsmen cast off and take the barge out into the river. All the way back to the palace I find I am squinting at the sun and trying to see three suns, and wondering what three suns might mean.

The queen's demand to be regent of England and rule the country with all the rights and wealth of the king during the illness of her husband does not resolve the whole problem as she and Edmund Beaufort confidently predicted. Instead there is uproar. The people now know that the king is sick, mysteriously sick and utterly disabled. The rumours of what ails him range from the black arts of his enemies, to poison given to him by his wife and her lover. Every great lord arms his men and when he comes to London marches them into his house, for his own protection, so the City is filled with private armies and the Lord Mayor himself imposes a curfew and tries to insist that weapons are left at the City gates. Every guild, almost every household, starts to plan their own defence in case fighting breaks out. There is an air of constant tension and anger; but no battle cries. As yet, nobody could name the sides, nobody knows the causes; but everybody knows that the Queen of England says that she will be king, that the Duke of York will save the people from this virago, that the Duke of Somerset has been locked up in the Tower of London to save the City from ruin, and that the King of England is sleeping, sleeping like Arthur under the lake, and perhaps he will only waken when ruin walks the land.

People ask me where my husband is, and what is his view. I say grimly that he is overseas, serving his king in Calais. I do not proffer his view which I don't know; nor my own – which is that the world has run mad and there will be three suns in the sky before all this is over. I write to him, and send messages by the trading ships that go between here and Calais, but I think the messages do not always get through. In early March I write shortly, '*I am with child again*,' but he does not reply, and then I know for sure that either they are not delivering my messages, or he is unable to write.

He was appointed as commander in Calais under the captaincy of the Duke of Somerset. Now the Duke of Somerset is in the Tower, charged with treason. What should a loyal commander do? What will the garrison do?

The lords and parliament go again to Windsor to see the king.

'Why do they keep going?' the queen demands, seeing the barges come back to the steps at the palace, and the great men in their furred robes helped ashore by their liveried servants. They trudge up the steps like men whose hopes have failed. 'They must know he won't wake. I went myself and shouted at him and he didn't wake. Why would he wake for them? Why don't they see that they have to make me regent and then I can hold down the Duke of York and his allies and restore peace to England?'

'They keep hoping,' I say. I stand beside her at the window and we watch the doleful procession of the lords wind their way to the great hall. 'Now they will have to nominate a regent. They can't go on without any king at all.'

'They will have to nominate me,' she says. She sets her jaw and stands a little taller. She is queenly, she believes she is called by God to rise into a yet greater role. 'I am ready to serve,' she says. 'I will keep this country safe, and hand it to my son when he is a man. I will do my duty as Queen of England. If they make me regent I will bring peace to England.'

They make the Duke of York regent and they call him 'Protector of the Realm'.

'What?' Margaret is beside herself, striding up and down the privy chamber. She kicks a footstool and sends it flying, a maid in waiting lets out a sob and cowers in the window, the rest of the ladies are frozen with terror. 'They called him what?'

The hapless knight who brought the message from the council of the lords trembles before her. 'They named him as Protector of the Realm.'

'And what am I to do?' she demands of him. She means the question to be rhetorical. 'What do they suggest that I do, while this duke, this mere kinsman, this paltry cousin of mine, thinks to rule my kingdom? What do they think that I, a princess of France, a queen of England, am going to do, when a jumped-up duke from nowhere thinks to pass laws in my land?'

'You are to go to Windsor Castle and care for your husband,' he says. The poor fool thinks he is answering her question. He realises swiftly that he would have done better to keep his mouth shut.

She goes from fire to ice. She freezes and turns to him, her eyes blazing with rage. 'I did not hear you exactly. What did you say? What did you dare to say to me?'

He gulps. 'Your Grace, I was trying to tell you that the lord protector ...'

'The what?'

'The lord protector commands ...'

'What?'

'Commands ...'

She crosses the floor in two swift paces and stands before him, her tall headdress overtopping him, her eyes boring into his face. 'Commands me?' she asks.

He shakes his head, he drops to his knees. 'Commands that your household go to Windsor Castle,' he says to the rushes beneath his knees. 'And that you stay there, with your husband and your baby, and play no part in the ruling of the country which will be done by him as lord protector, and the lords and the parliament.'

She goes to Windsor. There is a tantrum like a thunderstorm up and down the royal apartments, in and out of the chambers; but she goes. Really, she can do nothing but go. The Duke of York, whose own wife Cecily once came to the queen to eat humble pie and request a place on the council for him, rises high on the wheel of fortune. The council believes he is the only man who can restore order to the kingdom, who can prevent the dozens of small battles breaking out at every county quarrel, thinks that he is the only man who can save Calais, trusts that he will take the kingdom and hold it until our king, our sleeping king, comes back to us. It is as if they think the country is cursed and the Duke of York is the only man who can unsheathe his sword and stand in the doorway against an invisible enemy, and hold the post until the king awakes.

The queen – who had thought to be king herself – is cut down to wife, is pushed aside to be a mother. She goes as she is bidden, and they pay her the expenses of her household, reduce the numbers of horses in the stable, and ban her from returning to London without invitation. They treat her as if she is an ordinary woman, a woman of no importance, they reduce her to the care of her husband and the guardian of her son.

Edmund Beaufort is still in the Tower; he cannot help her. Indeed, she cannot defend him, her protection means nothing, who can doubt that he will be tried and beheaded? Those lords who have loved her as a queen dare not imagine her as a regent. Though their own wives may run their lands when they are away, their own wives are given no title and draw no fees. They don't like to think of women in power, women as leaders. The ability of women is not acknowledged; indeed, it is concealed. Wise women pretend that all they are doing is running a household when they command a great estate; they write for their husband's advice while he is away and they hand back the keys on his return. The queen's mistake is to claim the power and the title. The lords cannot bear the thought of a woman's rule, they cannot bear to even think that a woman can rule. It is as if they want to put her back into the confinement chamber. It is as if the king her husband, by falling asleep, has set her free, free to command the kingdom; and that the duty of all the other great men is to return her to him. If they could put her to sleep like him, I think they would.

The queen is confined to Windsor. Richard is trapped in Calais. I live as her lady in waiting, as an estranged wife; but in truth we all wait. Every day Margaret goes to see the king and every day he neither sees her nor hears her. She commands the doctors to be gentle with him, but sometimes her own temper snaps and she goes in and rails at him, cursing into his deaf ears.

I live with the queen and I long for Richard and I am aware all the time of the rise of trouble on the streets of London, the danger on the country roads, the rumours that the north is up against the Duke of York, or up for their own ambitions – who knows with these wild lands on the border? The queen is plotting, I am sure of it. She asks me one day if I write to Richard, and I tell her that I write often, and send my letters with the wool merchants taking the fleeces to Calais. She asks if the ships come back empty, if they were to carry men how many could be landed, if they could sail laden up the river to the Tower.

'You are thinking that they could come from Calais and rescue the Duke of Somerset from the Tower,' I say flatly. 'That would be to ask my husband to lead an invasion against the regent and protector of England.'

'But in defence of the king,' she says. 'How could anyone call that treason?'

'I don't know,' I say miserably. 'I don't know what treason is any more.'

The plan comes to nothing for we get news of an uprising in Calais. The soldiers have not been paid and they lock up their officers in the barracks and raid the town and seize the trade goods, and sell them and keep the money for their wages. There are reports of looting and rioting. The queen finds me, in the stable yard of Windsor Castle, ordering my horse to be saddled and a guard to come with me to London. 'I have to know what is happening,' I say to her. 'He could be in terrible danger, I have to know.'

'He won't be in danger,' she assures me. 'His men love him. They may have locked him in his quarters so that they can raid the wool stores but they won't hurt him. You know how beloved he is. Both he and Lord Welles. The men will release him when they have stolen their wages and drunk the town dry.'

They bring my horse to me and I climb up on the mounting block and into the saddle, awkward with my big belly. 'I am sorry, Your Grace, but I need to know that for myself. I'll come back to you as soon as I know he is safe.'

She raises a hand to me. 'Yes, come back without fail,' she says. 'It is a lonely, lonely place here. I wish I could sleep the days away like my husband. I wish I could close my eyes and sleep forever, too.'

I hardly know where to go in London to get news. My house has been closed down, there is no-one there but a few guards for safety, the parliament is not sitting, the Duke of York is no friend of mine. In the end I go to the wife of Lord Welles who is commanding in Calais with Richard. My manservant announces me and I walk into her solar chamber.

'I can guess why you have come,' she says, rising and kissing me formally on the cheek. 'How is Her Grace the queen?'

'She is well in her health, thank God.'

'And the king?'

'God bless him, he is no better.'

She nods and sits down and gestures me to take a stool near hers. Her two daughters come forwards with a glass of wine and biscuits, and then step back, as well-behaved girls should do, so that the adults can talk in private.

'Charming girls,' I remark.

She nods. She knows I have sons who will have to marry well.

'The oldest one is betrothed,' she says delicately.

I smile. 'I hope she will be happy. I have come to you for news of my husband. I have heard nothing. Have you any news of Calais?' I ask.

She shakes her head. 'I am sorry. There is no news to be had. The last ship to get out of the port said that there was an uprising, the soldiers insisting on their pay. They had captured the wool store and were selling the goods for their own profit. They were holding the ships in the harbour. Since then the merchants will not send their cargoes to Calais for fear that their own stocks are captured. So I don't know anything, and I can't get any news.'

'Did they say what your husband, or mine, was doing?' I ask. I have a great feeling of dread that Richard would not sit idly by while his men took the law into their own hands.

'I know they are both alive,' she says. 'Or at any rate they were three weeks ago. I know your husband cautioned the men and said that what they were doing was common theft, and they threw him into a cell.' She sees the terror on my face and puts her hand on mine. 'Really, they did not hurt him but locked him up. You will have to be brave, my dear.'

I swallow down the tears. 'It has been so long since we have been at home together,' I say. 'And he has had one hard service after another.'

'We are all lost under the rule of a sleeping king,' she says gently. 'The tenants on my lands say that nothing will grow, nothing will ever grow in a kingdom where the king himself lies like a fallow field. Will you go back to court?'

I give a little sigh. 'I have to,' I say simply. 'The queen commands it, and the king says nothing.'

In August I go to Grafton to see my children, and I try to explain to the older ones, Anne, Anthony, and Mary, that the king is well, but sleeping, that the queen has done nothing wrong but is confined with him, that their father's commander Edmund Beaufort, Duke of Somerset, is in the Tower, accused but not on trial, and that their father – and it is at this point that I have to grit my teeth and try to appear calm – their father is commanding the castle of Calais but is imprisoned by his own soldiers, the Captain of Calais is now Richard, Duke of York, and sooner or later their father will have to answer to him.

'Surely, the Duke of York will hold Calais, just as the Duke of Somerset would have done?' Anthony suggests. 'Father won't like a new commander being put over him, but nobody can doubt that the Duke of York will send money to pay the soldiers and arms for the castle, won't he?'

I don't know. I think of the terrible year when I saw Richard wear himself out trying to hold soldiers to a cause when they had neither weapons nor wages. 'He should do,' I say carefully. 'But we none of us can be sure what the duke will do, even what he can do. He has to govern as if he is king; but he is not king. He is only a lord among many lords, and some of them don't even like him. I just hope he does not blame your father for holding Calais for England, I just hope he lets him come home.'

I go into my confinement in Grafton, sending a message to

Richard when the baby is safely born. She is a girl, a beautiful girl, and I call her Margaret, for the queen who is beating against the times we live in, like a bird against a window. I come out of confinement and see my little girl in the arms of my wet nurse and then kiss my other children. 'I have to go back to court,' I say. 'The queen needs me.'

The autumn is long and quiet for us in Windsor. Slowly the trees start to grow yellow and then golden. The king gets no better, he does not change at all. The baby prince starts to pull himself to his feet, so that he can stand, and tries to take his first steps. This is the most interesting thing that happens in the whole year. Our world shrinks to the castle, and our lives to watching over a small baby and a sick man. The queen is a doting mother, she comes to the little prince's nursery morning and night, she visits her husband every afternoon. It is like living under a spell, and we watch the baby grow as if we feared he might do nothing but sleep. Half a dozen of us always go to the nursery in the morning as if we have to see for sure that the little prince has woken after another night. Apart from this we go through the motions of a court, attending on the king. But all we can do is sit with him as he sleeps. Every afternoon we sit with him and watch the slow rise and fall of his chest.

Richard sends me a letter as soon as he can get his reports into the hands of a ship's captain. He writes to the king's council – pointedly he does not address the lord protector – to say that the men cannot be commanded without wages. Without money from the treasury the merchants of Calais are forced to pay for their own defence: the garrison there regards itself almost independent of England. Richard asks the council for orders, though he points out that it is only he and Lord Welles who are waiting for orders. All the rest, the great garrison, the soldiers, the sailors in the port, the merchants and the citizens, are taking the law into their own hands. To me, he writes to say that no-one in the town accepts the lordship of the Duke of York, no-one knows what to believe about the king, and do I think Edmund Beaufort is likely to get out of the Tower and reclaim his power? At the very end of the letter he writes to me that he loves and misses me. 'I count the days,' he writes.

> *I am heart-sore without you, my beloved. As soon as I can hand over this garrison to a new commander I will come home to you, but I do believe that if I were not here now the town would fall to the French who know full well the straits we are in. I am doing my duty as best I can to the poor king and to our poor country as I know you are too. But when I come home this time I swear I will never be parted from you again.*

WINDSOR CASTLE, WINTER 1454

The Duke of York, determined to show his mastery over Calais, and to prevent a French attack, musters a small fleet and takes ship to the garrison saying he will enter it, pay the soldiers, make peace with the Calais merchants, hang any traitors and be recognised as the Constable of Calais.

Calais is formidably fortified. It has been England's outpost in Normandy for generations, and now the soldiers have control of the fort and when they see the sails of York's fleet they place the chain across the mouth of the harbour, they turn the guns of the castle to the seaward side, and York finds himself staring down the barrel of his own cannon, refused entry to his own city.

They bring the news to us as we are sitting with the king, one cold afternoon in November. Margaret is exultant. 'I will see your husband honoured for this!' she exclaims. 'How York must be humbled! How shamed he must be! Out at sea, with a great fleet, and the city of Calais refusing him entry! Surely now the lords will put him out of office? Surely they will fetch Edmund from the Tower?'

I say nothing. Of course, all I am wondering is whether my husband will have stood by while his men mutinied, disobeying his order to admit their new captain. Or whether – and far worse, far more dangerous for us – he himself led them to defy the Duke of York, commanding them from the high tower to turn the guns

337

on the lord regent, the legally appointed Protector of England. Either way he will be in danger, either way the duke is his enemy from this hour.

The king, strapped in his chair, makes a little noise in his sleep; the queen does not even glance at him.

'Think of York, bobbing about in his ship and the guns trained down on him,' she gloats. 'I wish to God they had shot him. Think how it would be for us if they had only sunk his ship and he had drowned. Think if your Richard had sunk him!'

I cannot stop myself from shuddering. Surely, Richard would never have allowed his garrison to open fire on a royal duke appointed by the king's council? I am sure of that, I have to be sure of that.

'It's treason,' I say simply. 'Whether we like York or not, he is appointed by Privy Council and parliament to rule in the king's place with his authority. It would be treason to attack him. And to have Calais open fire on English ships is a terrible thing to show to the French.'

She shrugs. 'Oh! Who cares? To be appointed by his own placemen is no appointment,' she says. '*I* did not appoint him, the king did not appoint him, as far as I am concerned he has just seized power. He is a usurper and your husband should have shot him as soon as he was in range. Your husband failed to shoot him. He should have killed him when he could.'

Again the king makes a little noise. I go to his side. 'Did you speak, Your Grace?' I ask him. 'Do you hear us talking? Can you hear me?'

The queen is at his side, she touches his hand. 'Wake up,' she says. It is all she ever says to him. 'Wake up.'

Amazingly, for a moment, he stirs. Truly he does. For the first time in more than a year, he turns his head, he opens his eyes, he sees, I know he does, he sees our absolutely amazed faces, and then he gives a little sigh, closes his eyes, and sleeps again.

'Physicians!' the queen screams and runs to the door, tears it open and shouts for the doctors who are dining and drinking and resting in the presence room outside. 'The king is awake! The king is awake!'

They come tumbling into the room, wiping their mouths on their sleeves, putting down their glasses of wine, leaving their games of chess, they surround him, they listen to his chest, they raise his eyelids and peer into his eyes, they tap his temples and prick his hands with pins. But he has slid away into sleep again.

One of them turns to me. 'Did he speak?'

'No, he just opened his eyes and gave a little sigh and then went back to sleep.'

He glances towards the queen and lowers his voice. 'And his face, was it the look of a madman, when he woke? Was there any understanding in his eyes or was he blank, like an idiot?'

I think for a moment. 'No. He looked just like himself, only coming from a deep sleep. Do you think he will wake now?'

The excitement in the room is dying down very fast as everyone realises that the king is quite inert, though they go on pulling him and patting him and speaking loudly in his ears.

'No,' the man says. 'He is gone again.'

The queen turns, her face dark with anger. 'Can't you wake him? Slap him!'

'No.'

The little court at Windsor has been settled for so long to a routine that revolves around the queen and her little boy who is now learning to speak, and can stagger from one waiting hand to another. But things are changing. In the king's rooms I think he is beginning to stir. They have been watching over him, and feeding him and washing him, but they had given up trying to cure him, as nothing that they did seemed to make any difference. Now we are starting to hope again that in his own time and without any physic, he is coming out of his sleep. I have taken to sitting with him for the morning, and another lady waits with him till evening. The queen visits briefly every afternoon. I have been watching him, and I think his sleep is lifting, I think it is getting lighter, and sometimes I am almost certain that he can hear what we say.

Of course, I start to wonder what he will know, when he comes out of his sleep. More than a year ago he saw a sight so shocking that he closed his eyes and went to sleep so that he should see it no more. The last words he heard were mine, when I said, 'Don't look. Don't see.' If he is opening his eyes again, ready to look, ready to see, I cannot help but wonder what he will remember, what he will think of me, and if he will think that I am to blame for his long vigil in darkness and silence.

I grow so concerned that I dare to ask the queen if she thinks the king will blame us for the shock of his illness.

She looks at me limpidly. 'You mean the terrible news from France?' she says.

'The way he learned it,' I reply. 'You were so distressed and the duke was there. I was there too. Do you think the king might feel that we should have told him the bad news with more care?'

'Yes,' she says. 'If he ever gets well enough to hear us, we will say that we were sorry that we did not prepare him for the shock. It was so terrible for us all. I myself cannot remember anything about that evening. I think I fainted and the duke tried to revive me. But I don't remember.'

'No,' I agree with her, understanding that this is the safest course for us all. 'Neither do I.'

We celebrate Christmas in the hall of Windsor Castle. It is a little feast for a sadly diminished household but we have gifts and fairings for each other and little toys for the baby prince, and then, just a few days later, the king wakes, and this time, he stays awake.

It is a miracle. He just opens his eyes, and yawns and looks around him, surprised to be seated in a chair in his privy chamber in Windsor, surrounded by strangers. The doctors rush for us, and the queen and I go in alone.

'Better not frighten him with a great crowd,' she says.

We go in quietly, almost as if we are approaching some wounded animal that might take fright. The king is rising to his feet, a doctor on either side to help him support himself. He is unsteady, but he lifts his head when he sees the queen and he says, uncertainly, 'Ah.' I can almost see him seeking her name in the confusion in his mind. 'Margaret,' he says at last. 'Margaret of Anjou.'

I find there are tears in my eyes and I am holding back sobs at the wreck of this man who was born to be King of England and who I first knew when he was a boy as handsome as little Edward March, the York son. Now this hollowed-out man takes one tottering step, and the queen makes a deep curtsey to him. She does not reach out to touch him, she does not go into his arms. It is like the young woman and the Fisher King in the legend: she lives with him but they never touch. 'Your Grace, I am glad to see you well again,' she says quietly.

'Have I been ill?'

One deeply secret glance passes between her and me.

'You fell asleep, into a deep sleep, and no-one could wake you.'

'Really?' He passes his hand over his head, and he sees for the first time the scar from a burning poultice on his arm. 'Gracious me. Did I bump myself? How long was I asleep?'

She hesitates.

'A long time,' I say. 'And though you were asleep for a long time, the country is safe.'

'That's good,' he says. 'Heigh ho.' He nods at the men who are holding him up. 'Help me to the window.'

He shuffles like an old man to the window and looks out at the water meadows and the river that still flows through the frosty white banks, just as it always did. He narrows his eyes against the glare. 'It's very bright,' he complains. He turns and goes back to his chair. 'I'm very tired.'

'Don't!' An involuntary cry escapes from the queen.

They ease him back into his chair, and I see him observe the straps on the arms and on the seat. I see him consider them, owlishly blinking, and then he looks around the stark bareness of the room. He looks at the table of physic. He looks at me. 'How long was it, Jacquetta?'

I press my lips together to hold back an outburst. 'It was a long time. But we are so pleased you are better now. If you sleep now, you will wake up again, won't you, Your Grace? You will try to wake up again?'

I really fear he is going back to sleep. His head is nodding and his eyes are closing.

'I am so tired,' he says like a little child, and in a moment he is asleep again.

We sit up through the night in case he wakes again; but he does not. In the morning the queen is pale and strained with anxiety. The doctors go in to him at seven in the morning and gently touch his shoulder, whisper in his ear that it is morning, and to their amazement he opens his eyes and sits up in his bed, and orders that the shutters be opened.

He lasts till dinnertime, just after midday, and then sleeps again, but he wakes for his supper and asks for the queen, and when she enters the privy chamber he orders a chair to be set for her, and asks her how she does.

I am standing behind her chair as she answers him that she is well, and then she asks, gently, if he remembers that she was with child when he fell asleep.

His surprise is unfeigned. 'No!' he exclaims. 'I remember nothing. With child, did you say? Gracious, no.'

She nods. 'Indeed, yes. We were very happy about it.' She shows him the jewel he had made for her, she had it in its case, ready to remind him. 'You gave me this to celebrate the news.'

'Did I?' He is quite delighted with it. He takes it in his hand and looks at it. 'Very good workmanship. I must have been pleased.'

She swallows. 'You were. We were. The whole country was pleased.'

We are waiting for him to ask after the baby; but clearly, he is not going to ask after the baby. His head nods as if he is drowsy. He gives a tiny little snore. Margaret glances at me.

'Do you not want to know about the child?' I prompt. 'You see the jewel that you gave the queen when she told you she was with child? That was nearly two years ago. The baby has been born.'

He blinks, and turns to me. His look is quite without understanding. 'What child?'

I go to the door and take Edward from his waiting nurse. Luckily, he is sleepy and quiet. I would not have dared to bring him lustily bawling into this hushed chamber. 'This is the queen's baby,' I say. 'Your baby. The Prince of Wales, God bless him.'

Edward stirs in his sleep, his sturdy little leg kicks out. He is a toddler, handsome and strong, so unlike a newborn baby, that my confidence wavers even as I carry him towards the king. He is so heavy in my arms, a healthy child of fifteen months. It seems nonsensical to be presenting him to his father like a newborn. The king looks at him with as much detachment as if I am bringing a fat little lamb into the royal rooms.

'I had no idea of it!' he says. 'And is it a girl or a boy?'

The queen rises up and takes Edward from me, and proffers the sleeping child to the king. He shrinks away. 'No, no. I don't want to hold it. Just tell me. Is this a girl or a boy?'

'A boy,' the queen says, her voice quavering with disappointment at his response. 'A boy, thank God. An heir to your throne, the son we prayed for.'

He inspects the rosy face. 'A child of the Holy Spirit,' he says wonderingly.

'No, your own true-born son,' the queen corrects him sharply. I look and see that the doctors and their servants and two or three ladies in waiting will have heard this damning pronouncement from the king. 'He is the prince, Your Grace. A son and heir for you, and a prince for England. The Prince of Wales; we christened him Edmund.'

'Edward,' I snap. 'Edward.'

She recovers herself. 'Edward. He is Prince Edward of Lancaster.'

The king smiles radiantly. 'Oh, a boy! That's a bit of luck.'

'You have a boy,' I say. 'A son and heir. *Your* son and heir, God bless him.'

'Amen,' he says. I take the little boy from the queen and she sinks down again into her chair. The boy stirs and I hold him against my shoulder and rock gently. He smells of soap and warm skin.

'And is he baptised?' the king asks conversationally.

I can see Margaret grit her teeth with irritation at this slow questioning of those terrible days. 'Yes,' she says pleasantly enough. 'Yes, he is baptised, of course.'

'And who are the godparents? Did I choose them?'

'No, you were asleep. We – I – chose Archbishop Kemp, Edmund Beaufort, Duke of Somerset, and Anne, Duchess of Buckingham.'

'Just who I would have chosen,' the king declares, smiling. 'My particular friends. Anne who?'

'Buckingham,' the queen enunciates carefully. 'The Duchess of Buckingham. But I am grieved to tell you that the archbishop is dead.'

The king throws up his hands in wonder. 'No! Why, how long have I been asleep?'

'Eighteen months, Your Grace,' I say quietly. 'A year and a half. It has been a long time, we were all of us very afraid for your health. It is very good to see you well again.'

He looks at me with his childlike trusting gaze. 'It is a long time, but I remember nothing of the sleep. Not even my dreams.'

'Do you remember falling asleep?' I ask him quietly, hating myself.

'Not at all!' he chuckles. 'Only last night. I can only remember falling asleep last night. I hope when I sleep tonight that I wake up again in the morning.'

'Amen,' I say. The queen has her face in her hands.

'I don't want to sleep another year away!' he jokes.

Margaret shudders, and then straightens up and folds her hands in her lap. Her face is like stone.

'It must have been very inconvenient for you all,' he says benevolently, looking round the privy chamber. He does not seem to understand that he has been abandoned by his court, that the only people here are his doctors and nurses and us, his fellow prisoners. 'I shall try not to do it again.'

'We will leave you now,' I say quietly. 'This has been a great day for us all.'

'I am very tired,' he says confidingly. 'But I do hope to wake tomorrow.'

'Amen,' I say again.

He beams like a child. 'It will be as God wills, we are all of us in His hands.'

THE PALACE OF PLACENTIA, GREENWICH, LONDON, SPRING 1455

With the king awake, it is not to be how God wills; but how the queen wills. She sends a message at once to the council of lords, so explosive in tone and so dangerous in temper that they release the Duke of Somerset at once from the Tower, laying on him the embargo that he may not go within twenty miles of the king, nor engage in any form of political life. The duke, setting his London house in order and speedily arming his retinue, sends at once to his friends and allies and tells them that no-one will keep him from the king and that the Duke of York will be the first to realise that he has seized power.

As if to celebrate their return to the centre of England, the queen and the king open the palace at Greenwich and summon the lords. The Duke of York obeys the summons and resigns his position as Protector of the Realm, and finds his other title, that of Constable of Calais, is to be lost too. It is given back once more to Edmund Beaufort, Duke of Somerset, out of jail and gloriously returned to greatness.

He walks into the queen's rooms in the palace as handsome and richly dressed as if he had been to the court of Burgundy for new clothes, not waiting for his trial for treason in the Tower. The wheel of fortune has thrown him high again, and there is no greater man at the court. All the ladies flutter as he comes into

346

the room, nobody can take their eyes off him. He kneels in the centre of the room to Margaret, who flies across the room, her hands outstretched, the moment she sees him. He bows his dark head and takes both of her hands to his lips, inhaling the perfume on her fingers. The maid in waiting beside me lets out a little envious sigh. Margaret stands completely still, quivering at his touch, then she very quietly says, 'Please rise, my lord, we are glad to see you at liberty again.'

He gets to his feet in one graceful movement, and offers her his arm. 'Shall we walk?' he suggests, and the two of them lead the way into the great gallery. I follow with a lady in waiting, and I nod to the rest of them to stay where they are. Carefully, I dawdle behind, so that my companion cannot overhear their whispered speech.

He bows and leaves her at the end of the gallery and Margaret turns to me, her face alight. 'He is going to advise the king that the Duke of York need not be admitted to the council,' she says delightedly. 'We are only going to have those of the House of Lancaster around us. Anything that York gained while he was protector will be taken away from him, and his brother-in-law, the Earl of Salisbury, and that overgrown cub, Richard Neville the Earl of Warwick, will not be invited either. Edmund says that he will turn the king against our enemies, and that they will be banned from all positions of power.' She laughs. 'Edmund says that they will be sorry for the day that they put him in the Tower and confined me to Windsor. He says they will go on their knees to me. He says the king hardly knows where he is, or what he is doing, and that between us, the two of us can command him. And we will throw down our enemies, perhaps into jail, perhaps to the gallows.'

I put out my hand to her. 'Your Grace ... ' But she is too delighted with the thought of revenge to hear a word of caution.

'Edmund says that we have everything to play for now. We have the king returned to health and willing to do whatever we say, we have a son and heir that nobody can deny, and we can teach

York a lesson that he will never forget. Edmund says that if we can prove York was planning to usurp the throne then he is a dead man.'

Now I do interrupt. 'Your Grace, surely this is going to send the Duke of York into outright rebellion? He is bound to defend himself against such charges. He will demand that the council renew the charges against the Duke of Somerset and then it will be the two of you and yours, against him and his.'

'No!' she replies. 'For the king himself has declared before the lords that Somerset is a true friend and loyal kinsman and nobody will dare say anything against him. We are going to hold a council at Westminster, and York is not to be invited, and then we are going to hold a hearing against him in Leicester where he will be accused in his absence. And the Midlands are loyal to us, though London is sometimes uncertain. This is the end of the duke in his pride; and the beginning of my revenge on him.'

I shake my head; there is nothing I can say to make her see that the Duke of York is too powerful to force into enmity.

'You, of all people, should be pleased!' she exclaims. 'Edmund promises me that he will bring your husband, Richard, home.'

Everyone has their price. Richard is mine. At once I forget to urge caution. I grasp her hands. 'He will?'

'He promised me. The king is going to give Edmund the keys to Calais, in front of everyone. Richard will be commended as a loyal commander and come home to you, York will be arrested, the kingdom will be ruled rightly by Edmund Beaufort and me, and we will all be happy again.'

I am happy, I am in his arms, my face crushed against his padded jacket, his arms around me as tight as a bear, so that I cannot breathe. When I look up into his beloved weary face he kisses me so hard that I close my eyes and think myself a besotted girl again. I catch a breath and he kisses me some more. Dockyard workers and sailors shout encouragement and bawdy comments, but Richard does not even hear them. Beneath my cloak his hands stray from my waist and clutch at my hips.

'Stop right there,' I whisper.

'Where can we go?' he asks, as if we were young again.

You would think we were youths again.

'Come to the palace,' I say. 'Come on. Are your things packed?'

'Damn my things,' he says cheerfully.

We walk handfast from the dockyard at Greenwich towards the palace, creep in by the back stairs like a lad and a slut from the stables, bolt my door and stay bolted in all day and all night.

At midnight I send for some food and we eat wrapped in sheets beside the warm fire.

'When shall we go to Grafton?'

'Tomorrow,' he says. 'I want to see my children, and my new daughter. Then I shall come straight back, and I shall have to take ship, Jacquetta.'

'Ship?' I ask.

He grimaces. 'I have to take Beaufort's orders myself,' he says. 'The fort has been torn apart from the inside out. I cannot leave them without a captain. I shall stay until the duke replaces me, and then I shall come straight home to you.'

'I thought you were home now!' I cry out.

'Forgive me,' he says. 'I would fear for the garrison if I did not go back. Truly, my love, these have been terrible days.'

'And then will you come home?'

'The queen has promised, the duke has promised, and I promise it,' he says. He leans forwards and pulls a lock of my hair. 'It is hard to serve a country such as ours, Jacquetta. But the king is well now and taking his power, our house is in the ascendancy again.'

I put my hand over his. 'My love, I wish it were so, but it is not as easy as this. When you see the court tomorrow, you will see.'

'Tomorrow,' he says, puts his jug of ale aside and takes me back to bed.

We snatch a few days together, long enough for Richard to understand that the queen and the duke plan to turn the tables entirely, and accuse Richard of York of treason and throw him and his allies down. We ride to Grafton in thoughtful silence, Richard greets his children, admires the new baby, and tells them he has to return to Calais to keep order at the garrison but that he will come home again.

'Do you think that they will persuade the Duke of York to beg pardon?' I ask him as he is saddling his horse in the stable yard. 'And if he confesses and obeys the king will you be able to come straight home?'

'He did so before,' my husband says steadily. 'And the king – sick or well – is still the king. The queen and the duke believe that they have to attack Richard of York to defend themselves, and if they defeat him then they will be proved right. I have to keep Calais for England and for my own honour, and then I will come home. I love you, my wife. I will be home soon.'

At first the plan goes beautifully. Richard returns to Calais, pays the soldiers, and tells the garrison the king is in his power again, advised by the Duke of Somerset, and the House of Lancaster is in the ascendancy. The Privy Council turn against the man they called on as their saviour and agree to meet without the Duke of York. They choose the safe haven of Leicester for this meeting, the heartlands of the queen's influence, her favourite county, and the traditional base for the House of Lancaster. Their choosing Leicester makes them feel safe; but it tells me, and anyone else who cares to consider, that they are afraid of what the citizens will think in London, of what they will say in the villages of Sussex, of what they will do in Jack Cade's home of Kent.

It is hard to get everyone to act: the lords and the gentry have to be summoned, the plan has to be explained, so that everyone understands the Duke of York is to be ill paid for loyal service to the country, his achievements traduced, and he and his allies are to be excluded from the council and the country turned against them.

The king is so slow to leave for Leicester that he comes to bid farewell to the queen, Edmund Beaufort on his right, Henry Stafford, the Duke of Buckingham, on his left, on the very day that he had said he would arrive in Leicester. His nobility behind him are dressed for the road, some wearing light armour, most of them dressed as if riding out for pleasure. I look from one familiar face to another. There is not a man here who is not either kin to the House of Lancaster, or paid by the House of Lancaster. This is no longer the court of England, drawing on the support of many families, of many houses, this is the court of the House of Lancaster, and anyone who is not part of it is an outsider. And anyone who is an outsider is an enemy. The king bows low to Margaret and she formally wishes him a safe journey and prosperous return.

'I am sure it will be easily done and peacefully concluded,' he says vaguely. 'My cousin, the Duke of York, cannot be allowed to defy my authority, my authority, you know. I have told the Yorkist lords that they are to disband their armies. They can keep two hundred men each. Two hundred should be enough, shouldn't it?' He looks at the Duke of Somerset. 'Two hundred is fair, isn't it?'

'More than fair,' replies Edmund, who has about five hundred men in livery, and another thousand tenants that he can call up at a moment's notice.

'So I shall bid you farewell, and see you at Windsor when this work is done,' the king says. He smiles at Beaufort and the Duke of Buckingham. 'My good kinsmen will take care of me, I know. You can be sure that they will be at my side.'

We go down to the great doorway to wave as they ride by. The king's standard goes in front, then the royal guard, and the king comes next. He is wearing riding clothes for the journey, he looks thin and pale compared to the two most favoured dukes on either side of him. As they go by, the Duke of Somerset pulls off his hat to Margaret, and holds it to his heart. Hidden by her veil, she puts her fingers to her lips. The lesser noblemen, then the gentry, then the men at arms follow. There must be about two thousand men riding out with the king and they rumble past us, the great war horses with their mighty hooves, the smaller horses carrying goods and gear, and then the booted tramp of the foot soldiers who march in disciplined ranks, and the stragglers who follow.

The queen is restless at the Palace of Placentia, though the household is confident and busy, waiting for news of the king's success with his hand-picked council. The gardens that run down to the river are beautiful with the white and pale pink of dancing cherry blossom, and when we walk to the river in a wind the petals whirl about us like snow and make the little prince laugh, and he chases after them, his nursemaid bowed over him as he wobbles on his fat little legs. In the fields at the riverside the late daffodils are still bobbing their butter-yellow heads and the hedges of the meadows are burnished white with flowers, the blackthorn thickly blooming on black spikes, the hawthorn a budding green of promise. At the riverside the willows rustle their boughs together and lean over the clear water, green water below reflecting the green leaves above.

In the chapel we are still saying prayers for the health of the king and giving thanks for his recovery. But nothing cheers the queen. She cannot forget that she was imprisoned by the lords of her own country, forced to wait on a sleeping husband, fearful that she would never be free again. She cannot forgive Richard, Duke of York, for the humiliation. She cannot be happy when the only man who stood by her in those hard months, enduring captivity as she did, has marched away again, to meet their enemy. She does not doubt that he will be victorious; but she cannot be happy without him.

Margaret shudders as she comes into her apartments, though there is a good fire in the grate, bright tapestries on the walls, and the last rays of the sun are warming the pretty rooms. 'I wish they had not gone,' she says. 'I wish they had summoned the Duke of York to London to answer us there.'

I don't remind her that York is a great favourite in London; the guilds and the merchants trust his calm common sense, and flourished when he established peace and good order in the city and country. While the duke was lord protector the tradesmen could send their goods out along the safe roads, and taxes were reduced with the profligate royal household under his control. 'They'll be back soon,' I say. 'Perhaps York will plead for forgiveness as he did before, and they will all come back soon.'

Her uneasiness affects everyone. We dine in the queen's rooms, not in the great hall, where the men at arms and the men of the household grumble that there is no cheer, even though the king has recovered. They say that the court is not how it should be. It is too silent, it is like an enchanted castle under a spell of quietness. The queen ignores the criticism. She summons musicians to play only to her, in her rooms, and the younger ladies dance but they only go through the paces without the handsome young men of the king's retinue to watch them. Finally, she commands one of the ladies in waiting to read to us from a romance, and we sit and sew and listen to a story about a queen who longed for a child in midwinter, and gave birth to a baby who was made entirely of snow. When the child grew to manhood, her husband took him on crusade, and he melted away into the hot sand, poor boy; and then they had no son, not even one made of ice.

This miserable story makes me ridiculously sentimental and I feel disposed to sit and weep and brood over my boys at Grafton, Lewis that I will never see again, and my oldest, Anthony, thirteen this year, who must soon have his own armour and go and serve as a squire to his father or another great man. He has grown up in no time, and I wish he were a baby again and I could carry him on my hip. It makes me long to be with Richard again, we have never been so long apart in our lives before. When the Duke of York is thrown down by the king, then Edmund Beaufort will take up his command in Calais and order Richard home, and our lives can get back to normal once more.

Margaret summons me to her bedroom and I go to sit with her as they lift the tight headdress which fits like a cap, low over her ears, uncoil the plaits and brush out her hair. 'When do you think they will come home?' she asks.

'Within the week?' I guess. 'If all goes well.'

'Why should it not all go well?'

I shake my head. I don't know why she should not be happy and excited, as she was when this plan was first explained to her by the Duke of Somerset. I don't know why the palace, which is always such a pretty home for the court, should seem so cold and lonely tonight. I don't know why the girl should have picked a story about a son and heir who melts away before he can inherit.

'I don't know,' I say. I shiver. 'I expect it will all be well.'

'I am going to bed,' she says crossly. 'And in the morning we can go hunting and be merry. You are poor company, Jacquetta. Go to bed yourself.'

I don't go to bed as she bids me, though I know I am poor company. I go to my window and I swing open the wooden shutter and I look down over the water meadows in the moonlight and the long silver curve of the river, and I wonder why I feel so very low in my spirits on a warm May night in England, the prettiest month of the year, when my husband is coming home to me after grave danger, and the King of England is riding out in his power and his enemy is to be brought down.

Then, the next day, in the late afternoon, we get news, terrible news, unbelievable news. Nothing is clear to us, as we order messengers to be brought before the queen, as we demand that men scrambling away from some sort of battle are captured and brought to the royal chambers to say what they saw, as we send men speeding out towards St Albans on the road going north, where it seems that the Duke of York, far from riding peaceably to his ordeal, and waiting patiently to be arraigned as a traitor, instead mustered an army and came to plead with the king that his enemies be set aside and that the king be a good lord for all England and not just for Lancaster.

One man tells us that there was some sort of riot in the narrow streets, but that he could not see who had the advantage as he was wounded and was left where he fell. Nobody helped him, a thing most discouraging for a common soldier, he said, one eye on the queen. 'Makes you wonder whether your lord cares for you at all,' he grumbles. 'It's not good lordship to leave a man down.'

Another man, riding back to us with news, says that it is a war: the king raised his standard, and the Duke of York attacked, and the Duke of York was cut down. The queen is out of her chair, her hand to her heart at this report; but later in the evening, the messenger that we sent to London comes back and says that from what he can gather in the streets, the greatest fighting was between the Duke of Somerset and the Earl of Warwick's men, and that the Earl of Warwick's men fought through the gardens and over the little walls, climbed over hen-houses and waded through pigsties to get to the heart of the town, avoiding the barricades and coming from a direction that no-one could have predicted, surprising the Duke of Somerset's men, and throwing them into confusion.

Margaret strides about her room, furious with waiting, mad with impatience. Her ladies shrink back against the walls and say nothing. I stop the nursemaid in the doorway with the little prince. There will be no playtime for him this afternoon. We have to know what is happening; but we cannot discover what is happening. The queen sends out more messengers to London and three men are commanded to ride on to St Albans with a private note from her to the Duke of Somerset, and then all we can do is wait. Wait and pray for the king.

Finally, as it grows dark and the servants come in with the lights and go quietly round lighting sconces and branches of candles, the guards swing open the doors and announce, 'King's messenger.'

The queen rises to her feet, I go to stand beside her. She is trembling slightly, but the face she shows to the world is calm and determined.

'You may come in and tell me your message,' she says.

He strides in and drops to his knee, his hat in his hand. 'From His Grace the king,' he says, and shows in his clasped fist a ring. Margaret nods to me and I go forwards and take it.

'What is your message?'

'His Grace the king wishes you well, and sends his blessing to the prince.'

Margaret nods.

'He says he is in good company with his fair kinsman the Duke of York this night, and will come in the company of His Grace to London tomorrow.'

Margaret's long-held breath comes out as a little hiss.

'The king bids you be of good cheer and says that God will arrange all things and all things will be well.'

'And what of the battle?'

The messenger looks up at her. 'He sent no message about the battle.'

She bites her lower lip. 'Anything else?'

'He asks you and the court to give thanks for his escape from danger this very day.'

'We will do so,' Margaret says. I am so proud of her restraint and dignity that I put my hand gently on her back, in a hidden caress. She turns her head and whispers, 'Get hold of him as he leaves and find out what in the name of God is happening,' and then she turns to her ladies and says, 'I will go straight away and give thanks for the safety of the king, and the court will come with me.'

She leads the way out of the rooms to the chapel and the court has no choice but to follow her. The messenger starts to fall into line at the back; but I touch his sleeve, take his arm, back him into a convenient corner as if he were a skittish horse, and fore-stall anyone else getting hold of him.

'What happened?' I demand tersely. 'The queen wants to know.'

'I delivered the message as I was told,' he says.

'Not the message, fool. What happened during the day? What did you see?'

He shakes his head. 'I saw only a little fighting, it was in and out of the streets and the yards and the ale-houses. More like a brawl than a battle.'

'You saw the king?'

He glances around, as if he fears that people might overhear his words. 'He was struck in the neck by an arrow,' he says.

I gasp.

The messenger nods, his eyes as round with shock as my own. 'I know.'

'How ever was he within range?' I demand furiously.

'Because the Earl of Warwick brought his archers through the streets, up the gardens and in and out of the alleys. He didn't come up the main street like everyone expected. Nobody was ready for him to advance like that. I don't think anyone has ever led an attack like that before.'

I put my hand to my heart and know with a pulse of pure joy that Richard was stationed in Calais and not in the king's guard when Warwick's men came like murderers in and out of the little alleys. 'Where was the royal guard?' I demand. 'Why did they not shield him?'

'Cut down around him, most ran off,' he says succinctly. 'Saw the way it was going. After the duke died . . .'

'The duke?'

'Cut down as he came out of a tavern.'

'Which duke?' I insist. I can feel my knees are shaking. 'Which duke died as he came out of the tavern?'

'Somerset,' he says.

I grit my teeth and straighten up, fighting a wave of sickness. 'The Duke of Somerset is dead?'

'Aye, and the Duke of Buckingham surrendered.'

I shake my head to clear it. 'The Duke of Somerset is dead? You are sure? You are certain sure?'

'Saw him go down myself, outside a tavern. He had been hiding in it, he wouldn't surrender. He broke out with his men, thought he would fight himself out; but they cut him down on the threshold.'

'Who? Who cut him down?'

'The Earl of Warwick,' he says shortly.

I nod, recognising a death-feud. 'And where is the king now?'

'Held by the Duke of York. They will rest tonight and pick up the wounded, they are looting St Albans, of course, the town will be all but destroyed. And then tomorrow they will all come to London.'

'The king is fit to travel?' I am so afraid for him, this is his first battle and it sounds like a massacre.

'He is going in state,' the messenger says mirthlessly. 'With his good friend the Duke of York on one side, the Earl of Salisbury, Richard Neville, on the other, and the earl's son, the young Earl of Warwick, hero of the battle, leading the way holding the king's sword.'

'A procession?'

'A triumphant procession, for some of them.'

'The House of York has the king, they are carrying his sword before them, and they are coming to London?'

'He is going to show himself wearing the crown so that everyone knows he is well, and in his right mind at the moment. In St Paul's. And the Duke of York is going to set the crown on his head.'

'A crown-wearing?' It is hard not to shiver. It is one of the sacred moments of a reign, when a king shows himself to his people in his coronation crown again. It is done to tell the world that the king has returned to them, that he is in his power. But this is going to be different. This will show the world that he has lost his power. He is going to show the world that the Duke of York holds the crown but lets him wear it. 'He is going to allow the duke to crown him?'

'And we are all to know that their differences have been resolved.'

I glance towards the door. I know that Margaret will be waiting for me, and I will have to tell her that the Duke of Somerset is dead, and her husband in the hands of her enemy.

'Nobody can think that this is a lasting peace,' I say quietly. 'Nobody can think that the differences are resolved. It is the start of bloodshed, not the end of it.'

'They had better think it, for it is going to be treason even to talk about the battle,' he says grimly. 'They say we must forget about it. As I came away, they passed a law that we were all to say nothing. It is to be as if it never was. What d'you think of that, eh? They passed a law to say we must be silent.'

'They expect people to behave as if it didn't happen!' I exclaim.

His smile is grim. 'Why not? It wasn't a very big battle, my lady. It wasn't very glorious. The greatest duke hid in a tavern and came out to his death. It was all over in half an hour, and the king never even drew his sword. They found him hiding in a tanner's shop amid the flayed hides and they chased his army through the pigsties and gardens. It isn't one that any of us are going to be proud to remember. Nobody will be telling this at the fireside ten years from now. No-one will tell his grandson about it. All of us who were there will be glad to forget it. It's not as if we were a happy few, a band of brothers.'

I wait in Margaret's rooms as she leads the court back from their thanksgiving for the king's safekeeping. When she sees my grave face, she announces that she is tired and will sit with me alone. When the door closes behind the last of the ladies in waiting, I start to take the pins out of her hair.

She grips my hand. 'Don't, Jacquetta. I can't bear to be touched. Just tell me. It's bad, isn't it?'

I know that in her place I would rather know the worst thing first. 'Margaret, it breaks my heart to tell you – His Grace the Duke of Somerset is dead.'

For a moment she does not hear me. 'His Grace?'

'The Duke of Somerset.'

'Did you say dead?'

'Dead.'

'Do you mean Edmund?'

'Edmund Beaufort, yes.'

Slowly, her grey-blue eyes fill with tears, her mouth trembles, and she puts her hands to her temples as if her head is ringing with pain. 'He can't be.'

'He is.'

'You're sure? The man was sure? Battles can be so confusing, it could be a false report?'

'It might be. But he was very sure.'

'How could it be?'

I shrug. I am not going to tell her the details now. 'Hand-to-hand fighting, in the streets . . .'

'And the king sent me a message ordering me to lead a service of thanksgiving? Is he completely insane now? He wants a service of thanksgiving when Edmund is dead? Does he care for nothing? Nothing?'

There is a silence, then she gives a shuddering sigh as she realises the extent of her loss.

'The king perhaps did not send the message for thanksgiving,' I say. 'It will have been ordered by the Duke of York.'

'What do I care for that? Jacquetta – how shall I ever manage without him?'

I take her hands to prevent her from pulling at her hair. 'Margaret, you will have to bear it. You will have to be brave.'

She shakes her head, a low moan starting in her throat. 'Jacquetta, how shall I manage without him? How shall I live without him?'

I put my arms around her and she rocks with me, the low cry

of pain going on and on. 'How shall I live without him? How am I going to survive here without him?'

I move her to the big bed, and press her gently down. When her head is on the pillow her tears run back from her face and wet the fine embroidered linen. She does not scream or sob, she just moans behind her gritted teeth, as if she is trying to muffle the sound, but it is unstoppable, like her grief.

I take her hand and sit beside her in silence. 'And my son,' she says. 'Dear God, my little son. Who will teach him what a man should be? Who will keep him safe?'

'Hush,' I say hopelessly. 'Hush.'

She closes her eyes but still the tears spill down her cheeks and still she makes the quiet low noise, like an animal in deathly pain.

She opens her eyes and sits up a little. 'And the king?' she asks as an afterthought. 'I suppose he is well as he said? Safe? I suppose he has escaped scot-free? As he always does, praise God?'

'He was slightly injured,' I say. 'But he is safe in the care of the Duke of York. He is bringing him to London with all honour.'

'How shall I manage without Edmund?' she whispers. 'Who is going to protect me now? Who is going to guard my son? Who is going to keep the king safe, and what if he goes to sleep again?'

I shake my head. There is nothing I can say to comfort her, she will have to suffer the pain of his loss and wake in the morning to know that she has to rule this kingdom, and face the Duke of York, without the support of the man she loved. She will be alone. She will have to be mother and father to her son. She will have to be king and queen to England. And nobody may ever know, nobody can even guess, that her heart is broken.

In the next few days she is not like Margaret of Anjou, she is like her ghost. She loses her voice, she is struck like a mute. I tell her ladies in waiting that the shock has given her a pain in the throat, like a cold, and that she must rest. But in her shadowy room, where she sits with her hand to her heart in silence, I see that in holding back the sobs, she is choking on her own grief. She dares make no sound, for if she spoke she would scream.

In London there is a terrible tableau enacted. The king, forgetful of himself, forgetful of his position, of his sacred trust from God, goes to the cathedral of St Paul's for a renewed coronation. No archbishop crowns him; in a mockery of the coronation itself it is Richard of York who puts the crown on the king's head. To the hundreds of people who crowd into the cathedral and the thousands who hear of the ceremony, one royal cousin gives the crown to another, as if they were equals, as if obedience was a matter of choice.

I take this news to the queen as she sits in darkness, and she stands up, unsteadily, as if she is remembering how to walk. 'I must go to the king,' she says, her voice weak and croaky. 'He is giving away everything we have. He must have lost his mind again and now he is losing the crown and his son's inheritance.'

'Wait,' I say. 'We can't undo this act. Let us wait and see what we can do. And while we wait you can come out of your rooms, and eat properly, and speak to your people.'

She nods, she knows she has to lead the royal party, and now she has to lead it alone. 'How will I do anything without him?' she whispers to me.

I take her hands, her fingers are icy. 'You will, Margaret. You will.'

I send an urgent note to Richard by a wool merchant that I have trusted before. I tell him that the Yorks are in command again, that he must prepare himself for them to try to take the garrison, that the king is in their keeping and that I love and miss him. I don't beg him to come home, for in these troubled times I don't know if he would be safe at home. I begin to realise the court, the country, and we ourselves are sliding from a squabble between cousins into a war between cousins.

Richard, Duke of York, acts quickly, as I thought he would. He suggests to the palace officials that the queen should meet her husband at Hertford Castle, a day's ride north of London. When her steward tells her, she rounds on him. 'He's going to arrest me.'

The man steps back from her fury. 'No, Your Grace. Just to give you and the king somewhere to rest until parliament opens in London.'

'Why can't we stay here?'

The man shoots a despairing look at me. I raise my eyebrows, I'm not disposed to help him, for I don't know why they want to send us to Henry's childhood home either, and the castle is completely walled, moated, and gated, like a prison. If the Duke of York wants to lock away the king, queen and the young prince he could hardly choose a better place.

'The king is not well, Your Grace,' the steward finally admits. 'They think he should not be seen by the people of London.'

This is the news we have been dreading. She takes it calmly. 'Not well?' she asks. 'What do you mean by "not well"? Is he sleeping?'

'He certainly seems very weary. He is not asleep as he was before; but he took a wound to his neck, and was very frightened. The duke believes he should not be exposed to the noise and bustle of London. The duke believes he should be quiet at the castle, it was his nursery, he will be comforted there.'

She looks at me, as if for advice. I know she is wondering what Edmund Beaufort would have told her to do. 'You may tell His Grace, the duke, that we will journey to Hertford tomorrow,' I say to the messenger, and as he turns away I whisper to the queen, 'What else can we do? If the king is sick we had better get him out of London. If the duke commands us to go to

Hertford we cannot refuse. When we have the king in our keeping we can decide what to do. We have to get him away from the duke and his men. If we hold the king in our keeping at least we know he is safe. We have to have possession of the king.'

He does not look like the king who rode out to reprimand the great lord with his two friends at his side, dressed for a day of pleasure. He looks as if he has collapsed in on himself, a pillow king with the stuffing gone, a bubble king deflated. His head is down, an ill-tied bandage round his throat shows where the Warwick archers nearly ended the reign altogether, his robe is trailing from his shoulders because he has not tightened his belt, and he stumbles over it, like an idiot, as he walks into the poky presence chamber of Hertford Castle.

The queen is waiting for him, surrounded by a few of her household and his, but the great lords of the land and their men have stayed in London, preparing for the parliament which is going to do the bidding of the Duke of York. She rises up when she sees him and goes forwards to greet him, stately and digni-fied, but I can see her hands shaking until she tucks them inside the shelter of her long sleeves. She can see, as I can see, that we have lost him again. At this crucial moment, when we so badly need a king to command us: he has slipped away.

He smiles at her. 'Ah,' he says, and again there is that betray-ing pause as he searches for her name. 'Ah, Margaret.'

She curtseys and rises up and kisses him. He puckers his lips like a child.

'Your Grace,' she says. 'I thank God that you are safe.'

365

His eyes widen. 'It was a terrible thing,' he says, his voice thin and slight. 'It was a terrible thing, Margaret. You have never seen such a terrible thing in your life. I was lucky that the Duke of York was there to take me safely away. The way that men behave! It was a terrible thing, Margaret. I was glad the duke was there. He was the only one who was kind to me, he is the only one who understands how I feel . . .'

Moving as one, Margaret and I go towards him. She takes his arm and leads him into the private rooms, and I stand blocking the way after them, so that no-one can follow them. The door closes behind them, and her chief maid looks at me. 'And what happens now?' she asks wryly. 'Do we all fall asleep again?'

'We serve the queen,' I say with more certainty than I feel. 'And you in particular, mind your tongue.'

I have no letter from Richard, but a stonemason who went over to supervise some building work takes the trouble to ride out to Hertford Castle with news for me. 'He is alive,' is the first thing he says. 'God bless him, alive and well and drilling the men and maintaining the guard and doing all that he can to keep Calais for England . . .' He drops his voice. 'And for Lancaster.'

'You have seen him?'

'Before I came away. I couldn't speak to him, I had to take ship, but I knew you would want news of him and if you have a letter for him, Your Grace, I will carry it back for you. I go back next month unless there are new orders.'

'I will write at once, I will write before you leave,' I promise. 'And the garrison?'

'Loyal to Edmund Beaufort,' he says. 'They had your husband locked up while they broke into the warehouses and sold the wool, but once they had taken their wages they let him out again and released the ships from port. That's how I left on the day of his release. Of course, nobody knew then that the duke was dead. They will know now.'

'What d'you think they will do?'

He shrugs. 'Your husband will wait for his orders from the king. He is the king's man through and through. Will the king command him to hold Calais against the new captain – the Earl of Warwick?'

I shake my head.

'Drifted off again?' the merchant asks with cruel accuracy.

'I am afraid so.'

The king sleeps during the day, he eats lightly and without appetite, he prays at every service, sometimes he rises in the night and wanders in his nightgown around the castle and the guards have to call the groom of his bedchamber to take him back to his bed. He is not melancholy, for when there is music he will tap his hand to the beat and sometimes nod his head; once he lifts up his chin and sings a song in a wavering piping voice, a pretty song about nymphs and shepherds, and I see a pageboy cram his knuckles in his mouth to stop the laughter. But most of the time, he is once again a lost king, a watery king, a moon king. He has lost his print upon the earth, he has lost any fire, his words are written on the water, and I think of the little crown charm which I lost in the river and which told me so clearly that there was no season when the king would come back to us: the gleam of his gold would be drowned in the deep water.

GROBY HALL, LEICESTERSHIRE, AUTUMN 1455

I take permission from the queen to leave court and go to my daughter's home at Groby Hall. The queen laughingly remarks that she could stop a cavalry charge more easily than she could deny me permission to go. My Elizabeth is with child, her first baby, and it is due in November. I too am expecting a baby, a child made from our day and night of lovemaking when Richard came home and went again. I expect to see Elizabeth safely out of childbed and then I will go to my own home and confinement.

Richard will not be here to see this, his first grandchild, of course. He won't be at my side at Groby Hall, while I wait for Elizabeth's firstborn, nor at our home at Grafton when I go into my birthing chamber, nor when I return to Hertford Castle, nor in London. His lord the Duke of Somerset is dead and his command, that Richard should return to me, will not be obeyed. Richard cannot keep his promise to come home to me while the future of Calais is so uncertain. The Earl of Warwick is the new Constable of Calais and Richard will have to decide whether or not to admit the new commander, or defy him. Once again Richard is far from me, having to decide which side to join, his loyalty on one side, his greater safety on another, and we cannot even write to each other, as Calais has barricaded itself in again.

Elizabeth's mother-in-law, Lady Grey, greets me at the door, resplendent in a gown of deep blue velvet, her hair arranged in two great plaits on either side of her head, which makes her round face look like a baker's stall with three great buns. She sweeps me a dignified curtsey. 'I am so glad you have come to keep your daughter company during her confinement,' she says. 'The birth of my grandchild is a most important event for me.'

'And mine for me,' I say, staking my claim with relish, there being no doubt in my mind that this will be my daughter's son, my grandson, and Melusina's descendant. All that he will have of the Grey family will be the name, and I have paid for that already with Elizabeth's dowry.

'I will show you to her room,' she says. 'I have given her the best bedroom for her confinement. I have spared neither trouble nor expense for the birth of my first grandchild.'

The house is large and beautiful, I grant them that. Elizabeth's three rooms look east towards Tower Hill, and south to the old chapel. The shutters are all closed but there is a gleam of autumn sunshine through the slats. The room is warm with a good fire of thick logs, and furnished well with a big bed for sleeping, a smaller day bed, a stool for visitors and a bench along the wall for her companions. As I enter, my daughter rises up from the day bed, and I see in her the little girl that I loved first of all my children, and the beautiful woman she has become.

She is broad as a beam, laughing at my expression as I take in her size. 'I know! I know!' she says and comes into my arms. I hold her gently, her big belly between us. 'Tell me it's not twins.'

'I tell her it's a girl if she carries her so low and broad,' Lady Grey says, coming in behind me.

I don't correct her; we will have time enough to see what this baby is, and what it will do. I hold Elizabeth's broad body in my arms, and then I cup her beautiful face in my hands. 'You are more lovely than ever.'

It is true. Her face is rounded and her golden hair has

darkened a little, after a summer spent indoors, but the exquisite beauty of her features, the fine-drawn nose and eyebrows, the perfect curve of her mouth, are as lovely as when she was a girl.

She makes a little pout. 'Only you would think so, Lady Mother. I cannot get through doorways, and John left my bed three months ago because the baby kicks me so much when I lie down that I move about all night and he cannot sleep.'

'That will soon be over,' I say. 'And it's good that he has strong legs.' I draw her back to the day bed and lift up her feet. 'Rest,' I say. 'You will have enough to do within a few days.'

'Do you think days?' Lady Grey asks.

I look at Elizabeth. 'I can't tell yet,' I say. 'And a first child often takes his time.'

Lady Grey leaves us, promising to send up a good dinner as soon as it grows dark. Elizabeth waits for the door to close behind her, and says, 'You said "his"; you said "his" time.'

'Did I?' I smile at her. 'What d'you think?'

'I did the wedding ring spell,' she says eagerly. 'Shall I tell you what it said?'

'Let me try,' I say, as excited as a girl. 'Let me try with my ring.'

I slip my wedding ring from my finger and take a thin gold chain from my neck. I put the ring on the chain, wondering a little that I should be so blessed as to be dowsing for my daughter, to see what her baby will be. I hold the chain over her belly and wait for it to hang still. 'Clockwise for a boy, widdershins for a girl,' I say. Without my moving it, the ring begins to stir, slowly at first as if in a breeze, and then more positively, round and round in a circle. Clockwise. 'A boy,' I say, catching it up and restoring the ring to my finger and the chain to my neck. 'What did you think?'

'I thought a boy,' she confirms. 'And what are you going to have?'

'A boy too, I think,' I say proudly. 'What a family we are making, I swear they should all be dukes. What will you name him?'

'I am going to call him Thomas.'

'Thomas the survivor,' I say.

She is instantly curious. 'Why d'you call him that? What is he going to survive?'

I look at her beautiful face and for a moment it is as if I am seeing her in a stained-glass window, in a shadowy hall, and she is years away from me. 'I don't know,' I say. 'I just think he will have a long journey and survive many dangers.'

'So when do you think he will come?' she asks impatiently.

I smile. 'On a Thursday, of course,' I reply, and quote the old saying: 'Thursday's child has far to go.'

She is diverted at once. 'What was I?'

'Monday. Monday's child is fair of face.'

She laughs. 'Oh, Lady Mother, I look like a pumpkin!'

'You do,' I say. 'But only till Thursday.'

It turns out that I am right on both counts, though I don't crow over Lady Grey, who would make a bad enemy. The baby is a boy, he is born on a Thursday, and my Elizabeth insists he shall be called Thomas. I wait until she is up and about, I take her to be churched myself, and when she is well and the baby feeding, and her husband has stopped coming to me ten times each day to ask if I am sure that everything is well, I go to Grafton to see my other children, and promise them that their father is bravely serving his king, as he always does, and he will come home to us, as soon as he can, as he always does, that their father has sworn to be faithful to us over and over, that he will always come home to me.

I go into my confinement in December, and the night before the baby is born I dream of a knight as brave and as bold as my husband, Sir Richard, and a country dry and hot and brown, a flickering standard against a blazing sun, and a man who is afraid of nothing. When he is born he is just a tiny crying baby and I hold him in my arms and wonder what he will be. I call him Edward, thinking of the little prince, and I feel certain that he will be lucky.

HERTFORD CASTLE, SPRING 1456

Richard does not come home, though I write to him from the hushed and fearful court to tell him he is a father again and now a grandfather too. I remind him that Anthony must be sent to serve some great lord; but how am I to judge which one, in this new world that is ruled by York once again? I don't even know if he gets the letter; certainly I don't get a reply.

The garrison and town of Calais are at war with themselves, and are no more welcoming to the newly nominated commander, the victorious young Earl of Warwick, than they were to the former constable, his ally, the Duke of York. I imagine, and I fear, that Richard is keeping the York allies out of the castle and holding the town for Lancaster. A forlorn hope, and a lonely posting. I imagine that he is keeping faith with Lancaster and thinks that to hold Calais for the silent king is the best service he can offer. But through the Christmas feast and the winter months, I cannot get any news of him, except to know that he is alive, and that the garrison has sent word that they will never admit the Earl of Warwick to the castle which is loyal to the man he killed: the dead Lord Somerset.

It is not until spring that things start to improve. 'The king is better,' Margaret announces to me.

I look at her doubtfully. 'He speaks better than he did,' I agree. 'But he is not himself yet.'

She grits her teeth. 'Jacquetta – perhaps he will never be as he was. His wound has healed, he can speak clearly, he can walk without stumbling. He can pass as a king. From a distance he can look commanding. That has to be enough for me.'

'For you to do what?'

'For me to take him back to London, show him to the council, and take the power from the Duke of York once more.'

'He is the shell of a king,' I warn her. 'A puppet king.'

'Then it will be me who pulls the strings,' she promises. 'And not the Duke of York. While we are here and allow the protectorate to reign, the Duke of York takes all the posts, all the fees, all the taxes and all the favours. He will strip the country bare and we will end up with nothing. I have to put the king back on his throne and York back in his place. I have to save my son's inheritance for when he can come of age and fight his own battles.'

I hesitate, thinking of the king's nervous tremor of the head, of the way he flinches at sudden noise. He will be unhappy in London, he will be frightened in Westminster. The lords will appeal to his judgement and demand that he rules. He cannot do it. 'There will be continual quarrels in the council and shouting. He will break down, Margaret.'

'I will order your husband home,' she tempts me. 'I will tell the king to pardon the garrison and allow the guard home. Richard can come home and see his grandson, and meet his son. He has not even seen your new baby.'

'A bribe,' I remark.

'A brilliant bribe,' she replies. 'Because it's irresistible, isn't it? So do you agree? Shall we set the king to claim his throne again?'

'Would you stop on this course if I disagree with you?'

She shakes her head. 'I am determined. Whether you are with me or not, Jacquetta, I will take command through my husband, I will save England for my son.'

'Then bring Richard home and we will support you. I want him in my life again, in my sight, and in my bed.'

WESTMINSTER PALACE, LONDON, SPRING 1456

Richard's recall from Calais is one of the first acts of the restored king. We go in state to Westminster and announce the king's recovery to the council. It goes better than I had dared to hope. The king is gracious and the council openly relieved at his return; the king is now to govern with the advice of the Duke of York. The king pardons the garrison of Calais for refusing to admit both York and Warwick, and he signs a pardon especially for Richard, to forgive him for his part in the rebellion against the lord protector.

'Your husband is a loyal servant to me and my house,' he remarks to me, when he comes to the queen's rooms before dinner. 'I will not forget it, Lady Rivers.'

'And may he come home?' I ask. 'He has been away such a long time, Your Grace.'

'Soon,' he promises me. 'I have written to him and to Lord Welles that I myself appoint the Earl of Warwick as Captain of Calais and so they can take it as my command that they are to admit him. When they admit the earl, and he takes up his post, your husband can come home.' He sighs. 'If only they would live together in loving kindness,' he says. 'If only they would be as birds in the trees, as little birds in the nest.'

I curtsey. The king is drifting into one of his dreams. He has a vision of a kinder world, a better world, which nobody could deny. But it is no help for those of us who have to live in this one.

The king's pain at his unexpected wound, his shock at the brutality of battle and the cruelty of death in the streets of St Albans seems to have gone very deep. He says that he is well now, we have given thanks in a special Mass, and everyone has seen him walk without stumbling, talk to petitioners, and sit on his throne; but neither the queen nor I can feel confident that he won't drift away again. He especially dislikes noise or disagreement, and the court, the parliament and the king's council is riven with faction; there are daily quarrels between the followers of the York lords and our people. Any trouble, any discord, any unhappiness, and his gaze drifts away, he looks out of the window and he falls silent, slipping away in a daydream. The queen has learned never to disagree with him, and the little prince is whisked from the room whenever he raises his voice or runs about. The whole court tiptoes about its business so as not to disturb the king, and so far we have managed to keep him in at least the appearance of kingship.

The queen has learned to control her temper, and it has been very sweet to see her discipline herself so that she never startles or alarms her husband. Margaret has a quick temper and a powerful desire to rule, and to see her bite her tongue and hear her lower her voice so as not to confront the king with the usurpation of his powers is to see a young woman growing into wisdom. She is kind to him in a way that I thought she could never be. She sees him as a wounded animal, and when his eyes grow vague or he looks about him, trying to remember a word or a name, she puts her hand gently on his and prompts him, as sweetly as a daughter with a father in his dotage. It is a sorry end for the marriage that started in such hopes, and the king's hidden weakness is her hidden grief. She is a woman sobered by loss: she has lost the man she loved, she has lost her husband; but she does not complain of her life to anyone but me.

To me, her temper is not muted, and often she blazes out when we are alone. 'He does whatever the Duke of York tells him,' she spits. 'He is his puppet, his dog.'

'He is obliged to govern with the agreement of the duke, and with the earls of Salisbury and Warwick,' I say. 'He has to answer the objection that the Privy Council made against him: that he was only for Lancaster. Now there is a parliament which is influenced by all the great men, York as well as Lancaster. In England, this is how they like it, Your Grace. They like to share power. They like many advisors.'

'And what about what I like?' she demands. 'And what about the Duke of Somerset who lies dead, thanks to them? The dearest, truest ... ' She breaks off and turns away so that I cannot see the grief in her face. 'And what about the interest of the prince, my son? Who will serve me and the prince? Who will satisfy our likes – never mind those of the council?'

I say nothing. There is no arguing with her when she rages against the Duke of York. 'I won't stand for it,' she says. 'I am taking the prince and going to Tutbury Castle for the summer, and then on to Kenilworth. I won't stay in London, I won't be imprisoned in Windsor again.'

'Nobody is going to imprison you ... '

'You can go and see your children,' she rules. 'And then you can meet me. I won't stay in London to be ordered about by the duke and insulted by the citizens. I know what they say about me. They think I am a virago married to a fool. I won't be so abused. I shall go and I shall take the court with me, far from London and far from the duke, and he can give what orders he likes; but I won't have to see them. And the people of London can see how they like their city when there is no court here, and no council and no parliament. I will see them go bankrupt, they will be sorry when I take the court away and give our presence and our wealth to the people of the Midlands.'

'What about the king?' I ask carefully. 'You can't just leave him in London on his own. It is to throw him into the keeping of the Duke of York.'

'He will join me when I order it,' she says. 'No-one will dare to tell me that my husband shall not be with me, when I command it. The duke will not dare to keep us apart, and I am damned if he will have me locked up in Windsor again.'

GRAFTON, NORTHAMPTONSHIRE, SUMMER 1456

I wait for Richard to come home to us at Grafton, enjoying my summer with our children. Elizabeth is at Groby with her new baby and her sister Anne is visiting her. I have placed Anthony with Lord Scales, serving as his squire, learning the ways of a noble house, and Lord Scales as it happens has a daughter, an only daughter, his heiress, Elizabeth. My Mary is thirteen now, and I must look around for a husband for her; she and her sister Jacquetta are staying with the Duchess of Buckingham, learning the ways of that house. My boy John is at home; he and Richard are set to their studies with a new tutor, Martha will join them in the schoolroom this year. Eleanor and Lionel are still in the nursery, with their two-year-old sister Margaret, and their little brother Edward.

I don't have to wait long for my husband's return. First I get a message that Richard has been released from his duty at Calais, and then – hard on the heels of the messenger – I see the dust on the road from Grafton coming up the drive to the house and I pick up Edward out of the cradle and hold him to me, shading my eyes with my hand and looking down the road. I plan that Richard shall ride up and see me here, my newest baby in my arms, our house behind me, our lands safe around us, and he will know that I have kept faith with him, raised his children, guarded his lands, as he has kept faith with me.

I can see, I think I can see, the colours of his standard, and then I am certain it is his flag, and then I know for sure that the man on the big horse at the head of the company is him, and I forget all about how I want him to see me, thrust Edward into the arms of his wet nurse, pick up my skirts and start to run down the terrace of the house, down the steps to the road. And I hear Richard shout, 'Holloa! My duchess! My little duchess!' and see him pull his horse to a standstill and fling himself down, and in a moment I am in his arms and he is kissing me so hard that I have to push him away, and then I pull him close again to hold him to me, my face to his warm neck, his kisses on my hair, as if we were sweethearts that have been parted for a lifetime.

'Beloved,' he says to me, breathless himself. 'It has been forever. I was afraid you would forget all about me.'

'I have missed you so,' I whisper.

My tears are wet on my cheeks and he kisses them, murmuring, 'I missed you too. Dear God, there were times when I thought I would never get home.'

'And you are released? You don't have to go back again?'

'I am released. Warwick will put in his own men, I hope to God I never see the town again. It was a misery, Jacquetta. It was like being in a cage for all that long time. The countryside outside is unsafe, the Duke of Burgundy raids and the King of France threatens, we were constantly alert for an invasion from England and the York lords, and the town was on the brink of bankruptcy. The men were mutinous, and nobody could blame them, and worst of all I was never sure what I should do for the best. I could not tell what was happening in England. And then, I could get no news of you. I didn't even know if you were safely up from childbirth ...'

'I kept writing,' I say. 'I kept writing but I guessed you didn't get the letters. And sometimes I couldn't find anyone to take a message. But I sent you fruits and a barrel of salted pork?'

He shakes his head. 'I never got a thing. And I was desperate for a kind word from you. And you had to manage all alone – and with a new baby!'

'This is Edward,' I say proudly and beckon to the wet nurse to come up and hand our son to his father. Edward opens his dark blue eyes and regards his father gravely.

'He is thriving?'

'Oh yes, and all the others too.'

Richard looks around at his other children, tumbling out of the front door, the boys pulling off their caps, the girls running towards him, and he goes down on his knees to them, spreading his arms wide so they can all run at him and hug him. 'Thank God I am home,' he says with tears in his eyes. 'Thank God for bringing me, safe, to this my home, and my wife and my children.'

That night in bed, I find I am shy, fearing that he will see a difference in me – another year gone by, and another birth to broaden my hips and thicken my waist – but he is gentle and tender with me, loving as if he was still my squire and I was the young duchess. 'Like playing a lute,' he says with a roll of laughter under the whisper. 'You always remember the way, when it is in your hand again. The mind can play tricks; but the body remembers.'

'And is there many a good tune played on an old fiddle?' I demand with pretend offence.

'If you find a perfect match then you keep it,' he says gently. 'And I knew when I first saw you that you were the woman I would want for all my life.' Then he gathers me into his warm shoulder and falls asleep, holding me tightly.

I fall asleep in his arms like a mermaid diving into dark water but in the night something wakes me. At first I think it may be one of the children, so I struggle awake and slide from under the covers to sit on the side of the bed to listen. But there is no sound in our quiet house, just the creak of a floorboard and the sigh of wind through an open window. The house is at peace, the master is safely home at last. I go into the chamber outside our bedroom and open the window and swing wide the wooden shutter. The summer sky is dark, dark blue, as dark as a silk ribbon, and the moon is on the wax, like a round silver seal, low on the horizon, sinking down. But in the sky, towards the east, is a great light – low over the earth, a blaze of light, shaped like a sabre, pointing to the heart of England, pointing to the Midlands, where I know Margaret is arming her castle and preparing her attack on the Yorks. I gaze up at the comet, yellow in colour, not white and pale like the moon, but golden, a gilt sabre pointed at the heart of my country. There is no doubt in my mind that it foretells war and fighting and that Richard will be in the forefront as ever, and that now I have new men to worry about as well: Elizabeth's husband, John, and Anthony, my own son, and all the other sons who will be raised in a country at war. For a moment I even think of the young son of the Duke of York that I saw with his mother that day at Westminster: young Edward, a handsome boy; no doubt his father will take him to war and his life will be at risk too. The sabre hangs in the sky above us all, like a sword waiting to fall. I look at it for a long time, and think that this star should be called the widow-maker; and then I close the shutter and go back to my bed to sleep.

KENILWORTH CASTLE, WARWICKSHIRE, SUMMER 1457

Richard and I join the court at the very heart of Margaret's lands, in the castle she loves best in England: Kenilworth. As my guard and I ride up, I see to my horror that she has prepared it for a siege, just as the night sky foretold. The guns are mounted and looking over the newly repaired walls. The drawbridge is down for now, bridging the moat, but the chains are oiled and taut, ready to raise it in a moment. The portcullis is glinting at the top of the arch, ready to fall at the moment the command is given, and the number and the smartness of the household show that she has manned a castle here, not staffed a home.

'She is ready for a war,' my husband says grimly. 'Does she think Richard of York would dare to attack the king?'

We come into her presence as soon as we have washed off the dust from the road and find her sitting with the king. I can see at once that he is worse again; his hands are trembling slightly and he is shaking his head, as if denying his thoughts, as if wanting to look away. He shivers a little, like a frightened leveret that only wants to lie down in the springing corn and be ignored. I cannot look at him without wanting to hold him still.

Margaret looks up as I come in and beams her happiness to see me. She declares, 'See, my lord, we have many friends: here is Jacquetta, Lady Rivers, the Dowager Duchess of Bedford. You remember what a good friend she is to us? You remember her first husband who was your uncle John, Duke of Bedford? And here is her second husband, the good Lord Rivers who held Calais for us, when the bad Duke of York wanted to take it away.'

He looks at me but there is no recognition in his face, just the blank gaze of a lost boy. He seems younger than ever, all his knowledge of the world has been forgotten, his innocence shines out of him. I hear Richard behind me make a small muffled exclamation. He is shocked at the sight of his king. I had warned him several times; but he had not realised that the king had become a prince, a boy, a babe.

'Your Grace,' I say, curtseying to him.

'Jacquetta will tell you that the Duke of York is our enemy, and we must prepare to fight him,' the queen says. 'Jacquetta will tell you that I have everything prepared, we are certain to win. Jacquetta will tell you that when I say the word our troubles are over and he is destroyed. He has to be destroyed, he is our enemy.'

'Oh, is he French?' the king asks in his little-boy voice.

'Dear God,' Richard mutters quietly.

I see her bite her lip to curb her irritation. 'No,' she says. 'He is a traitor.'

This satisfies the king for only a moment. 'What is his name?'

'The Duke of York, Richard. Richard, Duke of York.'

'Because I am sure someone told me that it was the Duke of Somerset who was a traitor, and he is in the Tower.'

This sudden reference to Edmund Beaufort, and from the king himself, is shockingly painful to her, and I see her suddenly go pale and look away. She takes a moment and when she turns back to us she has herself utterly under control. I see that she has grown in determination and courage this summer, she is forging herself into a powerful woman. She has always been strong-willed; but now she has a sick husband and a rebellious country, and she is turning herself into a woman who can protect her husband and dominate her country.

'No, not at all. Edmund Beaufort, the Duke of Somerset, was never a traitor and anyway, now he is dead,' she says very quietly and steadily. 'He was killed at the battle of St Albans by the Duke of York's ally, the wicked Earl of Warwick. He died a hero, fighting for us. We will never forgive them for his death. D'you remember we said that? We said that we would never forgive him.'

'Oh no ... er ... Margaret.' He shakes his head. 'We must forgive our enemies. We forgive our enemies as we hope to be forgiven. Is he French?'

She glances at me and I know my horror is plain on my face. She pats his hand gently and rises up from her throne and falls into my arms, as easily as if she were my little sister, weeping for some hurt. We turn together to the window, leaving Richard to approach the throne and speak quietly to the king. My arm is around her waist as she leans against me; together we look, unseeing, over the beautiful sunny gardens inside the thick castle walls, laid out below us like a piece of embroidery in a frame. 'I have to command everything now,' she says quietly. 'Edmund is dead, and the king is lost to himself. I am so alone, Jacquetta, I am like a widow with no friends.'

'The council?' I ask. I am guessing that they would put York back in as lord protector if they knew how frail the king truly is.

'I appoint the council,' she says. 'They do as I say.'

'But they will talk ...'

'What they say in London doesn't matter to us here, at Kenilworth.'

'But when you have to call a parliament?'

'I will summon them to Coventry where they love me and honour the king. We won't go back to London. And I will only summon the men who honour me. No-one who follows York.'

I look at her, quite appalled. 'You will have to go to London, Your Grace. Summer is all very well; but you cannot move the court and the parliament from the city forever. And you cannot exclude the men of York from government.'

She shakes her head. 'I hate the people there and they hate me. London is diseased and rebellious. They take the side of parliament and York against me. They call me a foreign queen. I shall rule them from a distance. I am Queen of London but they shall never see me, nor have a penny of my money, nor a glimpse of my patronage nor a word of my blessing. Kent, Essex, Sussex, Hampshire, London – they are all my enemies. They are all traitors, and I will never forgive them.'

'But the king . . . '

'He will get better,' she says determinedly. 'This is a bad day for him. Today is a bad day. Just today. Some days he is quite well. And I will find a way of curing him, I have doctors working on new cures all the time, I have licensed alchemists to distil waters for him.'

'The king doesn't like alchemy, or anything like that.'

'We have to find a cure. I am issuing licences to alchemists to pursue their studies. I have to consult them. It is allowed now.'

'And what do they say?' I ask her. 'The alchemists?'

'They say that he has to be weak as the kingdom is weak; but that they will see him reborn, he will be as new again, and the kingdom will be as new again. They say he will go through fire and be made as pure as a white rose.'

'A white rose?' I am shocked.

She shakes her head. 'They don't mean York. They mean as pure as a white moon, as pure as white water, driven snow, it doesn't matter.'

I bow my head, but I think it probably does matter. I glance back at Richard. He is kneeling beside the throne and the king is leaning forwards to speak earnestly to him. Richard is nodding, gentle as when he is talking to one of our little boys. I see the king, his head shaking, stammering over a sentence, and I see my husband take his hand and say the words slowly, carefully, as a kind man will speak slowly to an idiot.

'Oh, Margaret, oh my Margaret, I am so sorry for you,' I blurt out.

Her grey-blue eyes are filled with tears. 'I am all alone now,' she says. 'I have never been so alone in all my life before. But I will not be turned on the wheel of fortune, I will not fall down. I will rule this country, and make the king well, and see my son inherit.'

Richard thought that she could not rule the country from the Midlands; but summer comes and goes, the swallows swirl every evening around the roofs of Kenilworth, and every evening there are fewer and fewer as they are flying south, slipping away from us, and still the queen refuses to go back to London. She rules by command, there is no pretence of discussion. She simply orders a royal council who are picked to do her bidding and never argue with her. She does not call a parliament of the commons who would have demanded to see the king in his capital city. Londoners are quick to complain that the foreigners who steal their trade and overcharge decent Englishmen are the result of a foreign queen who hates London and will not defend honest merchants. Then a French fleet raids the coast and goes further than any has dared to go before. They enter right into the port of Sandwich, and loot the town, tearing the place apart, taking away everything of value and firing the marketplace. Everyone blames the queen.

'Are they really saying that I ordered them to come?' she exclaims to Richard. 'Are they mad? Why would I order the French to attack Sandwich?'

'The attack was led by a friend of yours, Pierre de Brézé,' my husband points out drily. 'And he had maps of the shoals and the river bed: English maps. People ask how did he get them if not from you? They are saying that you helped him because you may need him to help you. And you swore that you would see Kent punished for their support of Warwick. You know, de Brézé played a merry jest on us. He brought balls and racquets and played a game of tennis in the town square. It was an insult. The people of Sandwich think that you set him on to insult them. That this is French humour. We don't find it funny.'

She narrows her eyes at him. 'I hope you are not turning Yorkist,' she says quietly. 'I should be sorry to think that you turned against me, and it would break Jacquetta's heart. I should be sorry to see you executed. You have avoided death a hundred times, Richard Woodville. I should be sorry to be the one who ordered it.'

Richard faces her, without flinching. 'You asked me why people blame you. I am telling you, Your Grace. It does not mean that I think such things, except I am puzzled by de Brézé holding the charts. I am only making a fair report. And I will tell you more: if you do not control the pirates and the French ships in the narrow seas then the Earl of Warwick will sail out of Calais and do it for you, and everyone will hail him as a hero. You do not damage his reputation by letting pirates rule the narrow seas, by letting de Brézé raid Sandwich: you damage your own. The southern towns have to be protected. The king has to be seen to respond to this challenge. You have to make the narrow seas safe for English ships. Even if you don't like Kent it is the beach-head of your kingdom, you have to defend it.'

She nods, her anger dissipated at once. 'Yes, I see. I do see, Richard. I just hadn't thought of the south coast. Would you draw up a plan for me? How we should protect the south coast?'

He bows, steady as always. 'It would be my honour, Your Grace.'

ROCHESTER CASTLE, KENT,
NOVEMBER 1457

'Well, I for one don't think much of your plan,' I say to him sarcastically. We are in an old damp castle on the wide wet estuary of the Medway in November: one of the greyest coldest darkest months of the English year. The castle was built by the Normans for defence, not for comfort; and it is so cold and so miserable here that I have commanded the children to stay at home at Grafton rather than join us. Richard's piecemeal map of the southern coast of England is spread before us on his work table, the towns that he knows are vulnerable ringed in red, as he considers how to fortify and defend them with no armaments, and no men. 'I would have hoped that your plan would have had you posted to garrison the Tower and we could have been in London for Christmas,' I say. 'For sure, that would have suited me better.'

He smiles, he is too absorbed to reply properly. 'I know. I am sorry for it, beloved.'

I look a little closer at his work. He does not even have a complete map of the coastline, no-one has ever drawn such a thing. This is pieced together from his own knowledge and from the reports of sailors and pilots. Even fishermen have sent him little sketches of their own bay, their own dock, the reefs and shoals outside their harbour. 'Is the queen sending you enough weapons?'

He shakes his head. 'She has a huge grant from parliament to raise archers and buy cannon, to use against the French; but there is nothing issued to me. And how can I fortify the towns with no men to serve and no cannon to fire?'

'How can you?' I ask.

'I shall have to train the townsmen,' he says. 'And these are all towns on the coast, so at least I have ships' captains and sailors if I can persuade them to enlist. I shall have to get them trained up into some kind of defence.'

'So what is she doing with the money?' I ask.

Now I have his full attention, he looks up at me, his face grave. 'She is not protecting us against France, she is arming her men in London,' he says. 'I think she plans to charge the Earl of Warwick, the Earl of Salisbury and the Duke of York with treason, and bring them to London to stand trial.'

I gasp. 'They will never come?'

'She is certainly preparing for them to come. If they come at all, they will bring their own forces and their own retinue and she will need her thirteen hundred archers,' my husband says grimly. 'I think she is preparing for war with them.'

We are summoned, along with the rest of the lords, in the cold days after Christmas, to a London more dark and suspicious than ever before, to find that far from accusation and punishment, the king has overruled the queen and plans a reconciliation. He has risen up, fired by a vision. He is suddenly well again and strong and burning with an idea to resolve the conflict between the two great houses by demanding that the York lords shall pay for their cruelties at St Albans by being fined, building a chantry for the honoured dead, and then swearing to end the blood feud with the heirs of their enemies. The queen is calling for the Earl of Warwick to be impeached for treason; but the king wants him forgiven as a repentant sinner. The whole of London is like a keg of dynamite with a dozen boys striking sparks around it, and the king quietly saying the Pater Noster, uplifted by his new idea. The vengeful heirs of Somerset and Northumberland go everywhere with their swords at the ready and the promise of a feud which will last for ten generations; the York lords are impenitent – the Earl of Warwick's men richly turned out in their liveries, Warwick a by-word for generosity and gifts to Londoners, boasting that already they hold Calais and the narrow seas and who dare gainsay them? And the Lord Mayor has armed every good man in London and commanded him to patrol to keep the peace, which just introduces another army for everyone to fear.

The queen summons me in the twilight of a winter afternoon. 'I want you to come out with me,' she says. 'There is a man I want you to meet.'

Together we don our capes, pull up our hoods to shield our faces. 'Who is it?'

'I want you to come with me to an alchemist.'

I freeze, like a deer scenting danger. 'Your Grace, Eleanor Cobham consulted alchemists, and Eleanor Cobham was imprisoned for eleven years and died in Peel Castle.'

She looks at me blankly. 'And so?'

'One of the fixed plans of my life is not to end as Eleanor Cobham.'

I wait. For a moment her heart lifts, her face smiles, she dissolves into laughter. 'Ah Jacquetta, are you telling me you are not some mad ugly bad old witch?'

'Your Grace, every woman is a mad ugly bad old witch, somewhere in her heart. The task of my life is to conceal this. The task of every woman is to deny this.'

'What do you mean?'

'The world does not allow women like Eleanor, women like me, to thrive. The world cannot tolerate women who think and feel. Women like me. When we weaken, or when we get old, the world falls on us with the weight of a waterfall. We cannot bring our gifts to the world. The world we live in will not tolerate things that cannot be understood, things that cannot be easily explained. In this world, a wise woman hides her gifts. Eleanor Cobham was an enquiring woman. She met with others who sought the truth. She educated herself and she sought masters with whom to study. She paid a terrible price for this. She was an ambitious woman. She paid the price for this too.' I wait to see if she has understood; but her round pretty face is puzzled. 'Your Grace, you will put me in danger if you ask me to use my gifts.'

She faces me, she knows what she is doing. 'Jacquetta, I have to ask you to do this, even if it is dangerous for you.'

'It is a great demand, Your Grace.'

'Your husband, the Duke of Bedford, asked for nothing less. He married you so that you would serve England in this way.'

'I had to obey him: he was my husband. And he could protect me.'

'He was right to ask you to use your gifts to save England. And now I ask it too, and I will protect you.'

I shake my head. I have a very real sense that there will come a time when she will not be there and I will face a court like Joan of Arc, like Eleanor Cobham, a court of men, and there will be documents written against me and evidence produced against me and witnesses who will swear against me, and no-one will protect me.

'Why now?'

'Because I think the king is under a spell, and has been for years. The Duke of York, or Duchess Cecily, or the French king or somebody – how should I know who? – but someone has put him under a spell that makes him like a sleeping baby, or makes him like a trusting child. I have to make sure he never slips away from us again. Only alchemy or magic can protect him.'

'He is awake now.'

'He's like a wakeful child now. He has a dream of harmony and peace and then he will fall asleep again, smiling at his lovely dream.'

I pause. I know she is right. The king has slipped through to another world and we need him in this one. 'I will come with you. But if I think your alchemist is a charlatan, I will have no truck with him.'

'That's the very reason I want you to come,' she says. 'To see what you think of him. But come now.'

We go on foot, through the darkened streets of Westminster, hand in hand. We have no ladies in waiting, not even a guard. For one moment only, I close my eyes in horror at what Richard my husband would say if he knew that I was taking such a risk and with the queen herself. But she knows where she is going. Sure-footed on the muck of the streets, imperious to the crossing-sweepers, with a little lad going ahead of us with a flaming torch, she guides us down the narrow lanes, and turns into an alley. At the end of it is a great door set in the wall.

I take the iron ring set beside it, and pull. A great carillon answers us, and the sound of dogs barking somewhere at the back. The porter opens the grille. 'Who calls?' he asks.

Margaret steps up. 'Tell your master that she of Anjou has come,' she says.

At once the door swings open. She beckons to me, and we go inside. We step into a forest, not a garden. It is like a plantation of fir trees inside the tall walls, in the very heart of London, a secret woodland like a London garden under an enchantment to grow wild. I glance at Margaret and she smiles at me as if she knows how this place will strike me: as a hidden world within the real one; perhaps it is even the doorway to another world inside this.

We walk down a twisting path which takes us through the green shadow of towering trees and then to a small house, over-burdened with dark trees around it, sweet-scented boughs leaning on every roof, chimneys poking through foliage and singeing the needles of the pine trees. I sniff the air, there is the smell of a forge, thin smoke from hot coals, and the familiar, never-forgotten scent of sulphur. 'He lives here,' I say.

She nods. 'You will see him. You can judge for yourself.'

We wait, beside a stone bench before the house, and then a little door swings open and the alchemist comes out, a dark cloak around him, wiping his hands on his sleeves. He bows to the queen and directs a piercing look at me.

'You are of the House of Melusina?' he asks me.

'I am Lady Rivers now,' I say.

'I have long wanted to meet you. I knew Master Forte, who worked for your husband the duke. He told me that you had the gift of scrying.'

'I never saw anything that made much sense to me,' I say.

He nods. 'Will you scry for me?'

I hesitate. 'What if I see something which is against the law?'

He looks at the queen.

'I say it is allowed,' she rules. 'Anything.'

His smile is gentle. 'Only you and I will see the looking glass, and I will keep it secret. It shall be as a confessional. I am an ordained priest; I am Father Jefferies. No-one will know what you see, but you and I. I will tell Her Grace only the interpretation.'

'Is it to find the spell which will heal the king? It is to do good for him?'

'That is my intention. I am already preparing some waters for him, I think that your presence at the moment of distilling will make the difference. He is well now, he can stay awake now, but I think he has some deep wound inside. He has never grown away from his mother, he has never truly become a man. He needs to transform. He needs that change from a child to a man, it is an alchemy of the person.' He looks at me. 'You have lived at his court, you have known him for many years. Do you think this?'

I nod. 'He is of the moon,' I tell him unwillingly. 'And cold, and damp. My lord Bedford used to say he needed fire.' I nod towards Margaret. 'He thought Her Grace would bring fire and power to him.'

The queen's face works as if she is about to cry. 'No,' she says sadly. 'He has all but put me out. He is too much for me. I am chilled, I have all but lost my spirit. I have no-one who can make me warm any more.'

'If the king is cold and wet the kingdom will sink beneath floods of tears,' the alchemist says.

'Please do it, Jacquetta,' the queen whispers. 'We will all three swear never to tell anyone about this.'

I sigh. 'I will.'

Father Jefferies bows to the queen. 'Will you wait here, Your Grace?'

She glances to the half-open door of his house. I know she is longing to see inside. But she submits to his rules. 'Very well.' She wraps her cloak around herself and sits on the stone bench.

He gestures to me to go inside and I step over the threshold. In the room on the right there is a great fireplace in the centre with a fire of charcoal warming a big-bellied cauldron. In the cauldron, in warm water, is a great vessel with a silver tube which passes through a cold bath; at the end of the tube is the steady drip of an elixir made from the steam. The heat in the room is stifling, and he guides me to the room on the left where there is a table and a great book and beyond it: the scrying mirror. It is all so familiar, from the sweet smell of the elixir to the scent of the forge outside, that I pause for a moment and am back in the Hôtel de Bourbon at Paris, a maid and yet a bride, the new wife of the Duke of Bedford.

'Do you see something?' he asks eagerly.

'Only the past.'

He puts a chair before me and takes the curtain from the mirror. I see myself reflected back, so much older than the girl who was commanded to look in the mirror at Paris.

'I have some salts for you to sniff,' he says. 'I think it will help you to see.'

He takes a little purse from the drawer in the table and opens the drawstring. 'Here,' he says.

I take the purse in my hand; inside is some white powder. I hold it to my face and cautiously breathe in. There is a moment when my head seems to swim and then I look up, and there is the scrying mirror, but I cannot see my own reflection. My image has disappeared, and in my place there is a swirl of snow, and white flakes falling like the petals of white roses. It is the battle I saw once before, the men fighting uphill, a swaying bridge which falls, throwing them into the water, the snow on the ground turning red with blood, and always the swirling petals of the white snow. I see the iron grey of wide, wide skies; it is the north of England, bitterly cold, and out of the snow comes a young man like a lion.

'Look again.' I can hear his voice, but I cannot see him. 'What is going to become of the king? What would heal his wound?'

I see a small room, a dark room, a hidden room. It is hot and stuffy, and there is a sense of terrible menace in the warm silent darkness. There is only one arrowslit of a window in the thick stone walls. The only light comes from the window, the only brightness in the darkness of the room is that single thread of light. I look towards it, drawn by the only sign of life in the black. Then it is blocked as if by a man standing before it, and there is nothing but darkness.

I hear the alchemist sigh behind me as if I have whispered my vision to him, and he has seen it all. 'God bless,' he says quietly. 'God bless him and keep him.' Then he speaks a little more clearly. 'Anything else?'

I see the charm that I threw into the deep water of the Thames tied to the ribbons, a different ribbon for each season, the charm shaped like a crown that washed away and told me that the king would never come back to us. I see it deep in the water, dangling on a thread, then I see it being pulled to the surface, up and up, and then it breaks from the water like a little fish popping on the surface of a summer stream, and it is my daughter Elizabeth who smilingly pulls it from the water, and laughs with joy, and puts it on her finger like a ring.

'Elizabeth?' I say wonderingly. 'My girl?'

He steps forwards and gives me a glass of small ale. 'Who is Elizabeth?' he asks.

'My daughter. I don't know why I was thinking of her.'

'She has a ring shaped like a crown?'

'In my vision she had the ring that signified the king. She put it on her own finger.'

He smiles gently. 'These are mysteries.'

'There is no mystery about the vision: she had the ring that was the crown of England, and she smiled and put it on her finger.'

He drops the curtain across the mirror. 'Do you know what this means?' he asks.

'My daughter is to be close to the crown,' I say. I am puzzling through the scrying. 'How could such a thing be? She is married to Sir John Grey, they have a son, and another baby on the way. How can she put the crown of England on her finger?'

'It is not clear to me,' he says. 'I will think on it, and perhaps I will ask you to come again.'

'How could Elizabeth have a ring like a crown on her finger?'

'Sometimes our visions come darkly. We don't know what we see. This one is very unclear. It is a mystery. I will pray on it.'

I nod. When a man wants a mystery it is generally better to leave him mystified. Nobody loves a clever woman.

'Will you come here and pour this liquid into a mould?' he asks me.

I follow him into the first room and he takes a flask from the wall, shakes it gently and then hands it to me. 'Hold it.' I cup the bowl in my hands and at once I feel it grow warm under the heat of my fingers.

'Now pour it,' he says, and gestures to the moulds that are on his table.

Carefully, I fill each one with the silvery liquid and then pass the flask back to him.

'Some processes call for the touch of a woman,' he says quietly. 'Some of the greatest alchemy has been done by a husband and wife, working together.' He gestures to the bowl of warm water that is over the charcoal stove. 'This method was invented by a woman and named for her.'

'I have no skills,' I say, denying my own abilities. 'And when I have visions they are sent by God and are unclear to me.'

He takes my hand and tucks it under his arm as he leads the way to the door. 'I understand. I will send for you only if I cannot manage to work for the queen without you. And you are right to hide your light. This is a world that does not understand a skilled woman, it is a world that fears the craft. We all have to do our work in secret, even now, when the kingdom needs our guidance so much.'

'The king will not get better,' I say suddenly, as if the truth is forced out of me.

'No,' he agrees sadly. 'We must do what we can.'

'And the vision I had of him in the Tower . . .'

'Yes?'

'I saw him, and then someone stood before the window and it was all dark . . .'

'You think he will meet his death in the Tower?'

'Not just him.' I am filled with a sudden urgency. 'I feel, I don't know why, it is as if one of my own children were in there. A boy of mine, perhaps two of my boys. I see it, but I'm not there, I can't prevent it. I can't save the king, and I can't save them either. They will go into the Tower and not come out.'

Gently, he takes my hand. 'We can make our own destiny,' he says. 'You can protect your children, we can perhaps help the king. Take your visions to church and pray, and I will hope for understanding too. Will you tell the queen what you have seen?'

'No,' I say. 'She has enough sorrows for a young woman already. And besides, I know nothing for certain.'

'What did you see?' Margaret demands of me as we walk home, anonymous in our cloaks through the crowded dark streets. We link arms in case we are jostled, and Margaret's bright hair is covered by her hood. 'He would tell me nothing.'

'I had three visions: none of them very helpful,' I say.

'What were they?'

'One of a battle, uphill in snow, and a bridge which gave way and threw the soldiers into the stream.'

'You think it will come to a battle?' she demands.

'You think it won't?' I say drily.

She nods at my common-sense appraisal. 'I want a battle,' she declares. 'I'm not afraid of it. I am not afraid of anything. And the other vision?'

'Of a small room in the Tower, and the light going out.'

She hesitates for a moment. 'There are many small rooms in the Tower, and the light gets blocked for many young men.'

A cold finger is laid on the nape of my neck. I wonder if a child of mine will ever be housed in the Tower and one dawn see the light blocked as a big man moves across the arrowslit. 'That's all I saw,' I say.

'And your last vision, you said there were three?'

'A ring shaped like a crown, which signified the crown of England, and it was in deep water and it was drawn out of the water.'

'By who?' she demands. 'Was it me?'

It is very rare that I lie to Margaret of Anjou. I love her and, besides, I am sworn to follow her and her house. But I would not name my beautiful daughter to her as the girl who holds the ring of England in her hand.

'A swan,' I say at random. 'A swan took the ring of the crown of England in its beak.'

'A swan?' she asks me breathlessly. 'Are you sure?' She pauses in the middle of the street and a carter shouts at us and we step aside.

'Just so.'

'What can it mean? Do you see what it means?'

I shake my head. I had only conjured the swan because I didn't want to mention my daughter's name in this vision. Now, as so often, I find that the lie needs another lie.

'A swan is the badge of heir to the House of Lancaster,' she reminds me. 'Your vision means that my son Edward will take the throne.'

'Visions are never certain . . .'

Her smile is radiant. 'Don't you see? This is the solution for us? The king can step aside for his son,' she says. 'This is my way forwards. The swan is my boy. I will put Prince Edward on the throne of England.'

Although he has launched one of the most controversial and dangerous meetings that parliament has ever had to endure, although he has summoned three magnates who have brought their own armies, the king is joyously at peace with himself and with the world. He has every faith that these great matters will best be agreed in loving kindness without him; he plans to arrive after everything has been decided, to give it all his blessing. He absents himself from London to pray for peace, while they argue and calculate the price of agreement, threaten each other, come near to blows, and finally forge a settlement.

It drives Margaret beside herself to see her husband step back from his work of ruling his lords to become the king who will intercede only with heaven for his country's safety – but leaves it to others to make it safe. 'How can he summon them to London and just abandon us?' she demands of me. 'How can he be such a fool to make half a peace?'

It is indeed only half a peace. Everyone agrees that the York lords should pay for attacking the king's own standard and they promise to pay great fines to the Lancaster heirs, to compensate them for the deaths of their fathers. But they pay in tally sticks which were given to them from the king's exchequer – worthless promises of royal wealth which the king will never honour, but which Lancaster can never refuse, because to do so would be to admit that the kingdom is penniless. It is a brilliant joke and a powerful insult to the king. They promise to build a chantry at St Albans for Masses for the souls of the fallen, and they all vow to keep a future peace. Only the king thinks that a blood feud that is set to go down the generations can be thus halted with sweet words, a bouquet of sticks, and a promise. The rest of us see lies laid upon deaths; dishonour on murder.

Then the king returns to London from his retreat and declares a loveday – a day when we shall all walk together, hand-in-hand, and all will be forgiven. 'The lion shall lie down with the lamb,' he says to me. 'Do you see?'

I do see – I see a city riven with faction, and ready to make war. I see Edmund Beaufort's son, who lost his father at St Albans, is ordered to walk hand-in-hand with the Earl of Salisbury, and they stand at arm's length, fingers touching, as if they could feel wet blood on their fingertips. Behind them comes his father's killer, the Earl of Warwick, and he walks handfast with the Duke of Exeter, who has sworn secretly that there shall be no forgiveness. Next comes the king, looking well, glowing with happiness at this procession that he thinks shows to the people that the peers are united under his rule once more, and behind him comes the queen.

She should have walked alone. As soon as I saw her, I knew that she should have walked alone, like a queen. Instead the king has placed her hand-in-hand with the Duke of York. He thinks it shows their friendship. It does not. It says to the whole world that they were enemies once, and that they could be enemies again. It says nothing of goodwill and forgiveness but it exposes Margaret as a player in this deadly game – not a queen above faction, but a queen militant, and York as her enemy. Of all the follies on this day when we all went hand-in-hand – Richard and I among the others – this is the worst of them.

The loveday peace lasts only for eight months. I leave court in the summer for my confinement and give birth to another baby, a daughter whom we call Katherine, and when she is well and strong and thriving at the breast of the wet nurse, we leave home and stay with my daughter Elizabeth at Groby Hall. She is brought to bed with a child and she has another boy.

'What a blessing you are to the Greys,' I say to her as I am leaning over the cradle. 'Another baby: and a boy.'

'You would think they would thank me for it,' she says. 'John is as dear to me as ever but his mother does nothing but complain.'

I shrug. 'Perhaps it is time for the two of you to move to one of the other Grey houses,' I suggest. 'Perhaps there is not room for two mistresses in Groby Hall.'

'Perhaps I should come to court,' Elizabeth says. 'I could serve Queen Margaret and stay with you.'

I shake my head. 'It is no pleasant place at the moment,' I say. 'Not even for the lady in waiting that you would be. Your father and I have to go back and I dread what I will find.'

I return to a court busy with rumour. The queen requires that the Earl of Warwick takes the almost impossible task of keeping the narrow seas safe for English shipping; but at the same time hands over the fortress of Calais to Edmund Beaufort's son, the new young Duke of Somerset, an inveterate enemy of all the York lords.

This is to ask a man to do difficult and dangerous work and to give the reward to his rival. Warwick of course refuses. And just as Richard predicted, the queen hopes to entrap him with an accusation of treason. In November she publicly blames him for piracy – using his ships out of Calais – and a parliament packed with her supporters commands him to come to London and stand trial. Proudly he arrives to defend himself and confronts them all, a courageous young man alone before his enemies. Richard comes out of the royal council room to find me waiting outside, and tells me that Warwick shouted down the accusations and claimed in turn that the loveday agreement had been betrayed by the queen herself. 'He is raging,' he says. 'And it's so heated it could come to blows.'

Just at that moment there is a crash against the council chamber door and at once Richard jumps forwards, drawing his sword, his other arm outstretched to shield me. 'Jacquetta, go to the queen!' he shouts.

I am about to turn and run when my way is barred by men in the livery of the Duke of Buckingham, storming down the hall with their swords drawn. 'Behind you!' I say quickly to Richard and step back against the wall as the men come towards us. Richard is on guard, sword drawn to defend us, but the men run past us without a glance and I see from the other direction Somerset's guard are ready, blocking the hall. It is an ambush. The council doors are flung open and Warwick and his men, in tight formation, come out fighting. They have been attacked in the very council chamber and outside the men are waiting to finish them off. Richard steps abruptly back and crushes me against the wall. 'Stay quiet!' he commands me.

Warwick, sword like a flail, goes straight at his enemies, stabbing and striking, his men tight behind him. One loses his sword and I see him punch out in rage. One falls and they step over him to hold the defensive box around their commander: clearly they would die for him. The hall is too narrow for a fight, the soldiers jostle one another and then Warwick puts down his bare head, shouts 'À Warwick!', his battle-cry, and makes a run for it. Moving as one, his men charge at their attackers, they break out and are free, the men of Somerset and Buckingham running after them like hounds after deer, and they are gone. We hear a bellow of rage as the royal guard catches the Buckingham men and holds them, and then the noise of running feet as Warwick gets away.

Richard steps back and pulls me to his side, sheathing his sword. 'Did I hurt you, love? I am sorry.'

'No, no . . .' I am breathless with shock. 'What was that? What is happening?'

'That, I think, was the queen sending the two dukes to finish what their fathers started. The end of the truce. And that, I think, was Warwick drawing his sword in the demesne of a royal palace and getting away to Calais. Betrayal and treason. We'd better go to the queen and see what she knows about this.'

By the time we get to her rooms the privy chamber door is closed and her women are outside in her presence chamber, gossiping furiously. They rush towards us as we come in, but I brush them aside and tap on the door and she calls me and Richard in together. The young Duke of Somerset is there already, whispering to her.

She glances at my shocked face and hurries to me. 'Jacquetta, were you there? Not hurt?'

'Your Grace, the Earl of Warwick was attacked in the council chamber itself,' I say bluntly. 'By men in the livery of Buckingham and Somerset.'

'But not by me,' the twenty-two-year-old duke says, as pert as a child.

'Your men,' my husband observes, his tone level. 'And it is illegal to draw a sword in the royal court.' He turns to the queen. 'Your Grace, everyone will think this is ordered by you, and it is most treacherous. It was in the council chamber, in the demesne of the court. You are supposed to be reconciled. You gave your royal word. It is dishonourable. Warwick will complain and he will be right to do so.'

She flushes at that and glances at the duke, who shrugs his shoulders. 'Warwick doesn't deserve an honourable death,' he says pettishly. 'He did not give my father an honourable death.'

'Your father died in battle,' Richard points out. 'A fair fight. And Warwick has begged and been given your forgiveness, and paid for a chantry in your father's name. That grievance is over and you have been paid for the loss of your father. This was an attack inside the safety of the court. How will the council do its business if a man risks his life attending? How will any of the York lords dare to come again? How can men of goodwill come to a council which attacks its own members? How can a man of honour serve such a rule?'

'He got away?' the queen ignores Richard to ask me, as if this is all that matters.

'He got away,' I say.

'I should think he will get away all the way to Calais and you will have a powerful enemy in a fortified castle off your shores,' Richard says bitterly. 'And I can tell you that not one town in a hundred can be defended against attack on the south coast. He could sail up the Thames and bombard the Tower, and now he will think himself free to do so. You have broken his alliance for nothing and put us all in danger.'

'He was our enemy at any time,' young Somerset remarks. 'He was our enemy before this.'

'He was bound by a truce,' Richard insists. 'And by his oath of allegiance to the king. He honoured it. Attacking him in the council chamber releases him from both.'

'We shall leave London,' the queen rules.

'That's not the solution!' Richard explodes. 'You can't make an enemy like this and think that all you need do is flee. Where will be safe? Tutbury? Kenilworth? Coventry? Do you think to abandon the southern counties of England altogether? Shall Warwick just march in? Is it your plan to give him Sandwich, as you have given him Calais? Shall you give him London?'

'I shall take my son and go.' She rounds on him. 'And I shall raise troops, loyal men, and arm. When Warwick lands he will find my army waiting for him. And this time we will beat him and he will pay for his crime.'

ON CAMPAIGN, SUMMER–AUTUMN 1459

The queen is like a woman possessed by a vision. She takes the court with her to Coventry, the king in her train. He has no say in what happens now, he is startled by the failure of his truce and the sudden rush into war. She defies advice to be careful, she can smell victory and she is eager for it. She enters Coventry with all the ceremony of a reigning king, and they bow to her as if she were the acknowledged ruler of the country.

No-one has seen a Queen of England like this before. She is served on one knee, like a king. She sits under the royal canopy. She musters men, she demands a levy of every man from every county in England, ignoring the traditional way of raising an army which is that each lord calls out his own men. From Cheshire she recruits her own army, she calls it the prince's army, and she distributes his own badge, the new livery of the swan. She calls his captains the Knights of the Swan and promises them a special place in the battle that is certain to come.

'The swan children wore collars of gold and were hidden by their mother to appear like swans, and they all came back but one,' I say, uneasy at her sudden love of this badge, at her invoking this old myth. 'This is nothing to do with Prince Edward.'

The prince looks up at me and beams one of his sudden radiant smiles. 'Swan,' he repeats. She has taught him the word. She has sewn two swan badges of silver on his collar.

'You said you had seen the crown of England taken by a swan,' she reminds me.

I flush, thinking of the lie I told to hide the real vision, of my daughter Elizabeth laughing with a ring shaped like a crown on her finger. 'It came to me like a daydream, Your Grace, and I warned you that it might mean nothing.'

'I will take England, if I have to turn into a swan myself to do it.'

We move to Eccleshall Castle fifty miles north of Coventry in September, and we are less and less like a court, more like an army. Many of the ladies in waiting have gone back to their homes as their husbands have been summoned to march with the queen militant. Some of them stay away. The few ladies who travel with me and the queen all have husbands in her rapidly growing army; we are like a baggage train on the march, not a court. The king is with us, and the prince; both of them go out daily to attend the musters of men as Margaret brings in more and more recruits that she houses in the buildings inside the castle walls and in tents in the fields around. She calls on the loyal lords to come to her support, she parades the young prince before them. He is only six years old, he rides his little white pony around the ranks of the men, straight-backed and obedient to his mother's commands. His father comes to the castle gate, and holds up his hand as if blessing the thousands of men who are under his standard.

'Is it the French?' he asks me wonderingly. 'Are we going to take Bordeaux?'

'There is no war yet,' I reassure him. 'Perhaps we can avoid war.'

Old James Touchet, Lord Audley, is to command the army, and Lord Thomas Stanley is to support him. Lord Audley comes to the queen with the news that the York lords are assembling their forces in England and mustering their men.

They are planning to meet at York's castle at Ludlow; and so
the Earl of Salisbury will have to march south from his castle
of Middleham, in the North of England, to Ludlow, on the
borders of Wales. Lord Audley swears that we will catch him
as he marches nearby, and take him by surprise as he hurries
to join the other treasonous lords. Our forces will be about ten
thousand men; thousands more will come with Lord Stanley.
Salisbury has a force of less than half that number – he is marching to his death, hopelessly undermanned, and he does not
know it.

I find it a grim process, watching the men arm, check their
weapons and their equipment, and form up in ranks. Elizabeth's
husband, Sir John Grey, on his beautiful horse, leads an armed
band of his tenants on the two-day march from his home. He
tells me that Elizabeth cried unstoppably as he left and seemed
filled with foreboding. She asked him not to go, and his mother
ordered her to her room, like a naughty child.

'Should I have stayed with her?' he asks me. 'I thought it my
duty to come.'

'You are right to do your duty.' I repeat the worn phrase which
allows wives to release their husbands, and women to send their
sons to war. 'I am sure you are right to do your duty, John.'

The queen appoints him as head of cavalry. Anthony, my
heir and most precious son, comes from our home at Grafton
and will fight alongside his father. They will ride to the battle
and then dismount and fight on foot. The thought of my son in
battle makes me so sick that I cannot eat for fear.

'I am lucky,' Richard says stoutly to me. 'You know I am
lucky, you have seen me ride out to a dozen battles and I always
come safe home to you. I will keep him at my side, he will be
lucky too.'

'Don't say it! Don't say it!' I put my hand over his mouth. 'It's
to tempt fate. Dear God, do you have to go out this time?'

'This time, and every time, until the country is at peace,' my
husband says simply.

'But the king himself has not commanded it!'

'Jacquetta, are you asking me to turn traitor? Do you want me to wear a white rose for York?'

'Of course not! Of course not. It's just . . .'

Gently, he takes me in his arms. 'It's just what? Just that you cannot bear to see Anthony in danger?'

Ashamed, I nod. 'My son . . .' I whisper, anguished.

'He is a man now, danger comes to him like snow in winter, like flowers in springtime. He is a brave young man, I have taught him courage. Don't you teach him to be a coward.'

My head comes up at that, and my husband chuckles. 'So you don't want him to go to war; but you don't want him to be a coward? Where's the sense in it? Now you be brave, and come and see us march out, and wave your hand and smile and give us your blessing.'

We go to the door together, his hand warm on my waist. The queen has ordered the army to troop before the drawbridge of the castle and the little prince is there on his white pony. Anthony comes from the ranks and kneels swiftly before me, and I put my hand down on the warm soft hair of his precious head.

'God bless you, my son.' I can hardly speak for the tightness in my throat. I can feel the tears hot in my eyes. He rises up and stands before me, excited and ready to go. I want to add, 'And do what your father tells you, and keep your horse near you so that you can get away, and stay out of danger, and there is no need to get too close to the fighting . . .' but Richard draws me close and kisses me quickly on the mouth to silence me.

'God bless you, my husband,' I say. 'Come home safely to me, both of you.'

'I always do,' Richard replies. 'And I will bring Anthony safe home too.'

The queen and I, her ladies in waiting, and the prince and his household stand and wave as they march past us, the standards flapping in the breeze and the men looking eager and confident. They are well equipped, the queen has used the money granted her by parliament which was supposed to improve defence against the French to pay for weapons and boots for this army. When they are gone and the dust has settled on the lane, the queen orders the prince to go with his nurse and turns to me.

'And now we wait,' she says. 'But when they find Salisbury and join battle I want to see it. I'm going out to watch it.'

I almost think she is joking, but the next day we get a message sent from James Touchet to say that his scouts have found the Earl of Salisbury's men and he is lying in wait for them near a little village called Blore Heath. At once the queen orders her horse as if we are going out on a ride for pleasure. 'Are you coming with me?' she asks.

'The king would not like you to put yourself in danger,' I say, already knowing that the king's opinions mean nothing to her.

'He won't even know that I have gone and come back again,' she says. 'And I have told my ladies we are going out hawking.'

'Just you and me?' I ask sceptically.

'Why not?'

'No hawks?'

'Oh, come on!' she says, as impatient as a girl. 'Don't you want to watch over Richard? And your son Anthony?'

'We'll never be able to see them,' I say.

'We'll climb a tree,' she replies, and then steps up on the mounting block, swings her leg over her horse and nods to the groom to pull down her gown over her boots. 'Are you coming? For I will go without you if I have to.'

'I'm coming,' I say, and I mount and ride beside her as we go towards Blore Heath.

We are greeted with a messenger from James Touchet who suggests that we might like to go to the church at nearby Muckle-stone, where we will be able to see the battlefield from the belfry.

The noble lord is arranging a viewing tower as if for a day's jousting. We clatter into the little village, sending chickens fluttering away from our horses' hooves, and leave the horses at the village forge.

'You can shoe my horse while he is waiting here,' the queen says to the blacksmith, throwing him a penny, then she turns and leads the way to the church.

Inside it is quiet and dim, and we take the winding stone stair upwards and upwards to where the bell is hung in the tower. It is like a great watchtower, the bell behind us, a stone parapet before us, and clearly across the fields we can see the road from the north, and in the distance the trail of dust that is the marching army of the Earl of Salisbury.

The queen touches my arm, her face alight with excitement, and points ahead. We can see a great hedge and behind it the standards of our army. I put my hand over my eyes and scowl, trying to identify the Rivers flag in case I can make out Anthony or my husband nearby, but it is too far to see. Our forces are perfectly positioned, Salisbury will not know they are there, nor in what numbers, until he comes out of the little wood either side of his road, and then they will face him. There is something very dreadful about looking down on the battlefield, as if we were stone gargoyles on the tower, watching the deaths of mortals for sport. I look at the queen. She does not feel this, she is alight with excitement, her hands clasped tight together as the outriders at the front of the York army come briskly out from the wood, and fall back when they see the mighty force before them arranged in battle order on the little hill with a small river between them.

'What are they doing?' the queen demands irritably, as we see a herald ride out from each side and meet in the middle ground between the two armies.

'Parleying?' I ask.

'There is nothing to talk about,' she says. 'He is named a traitor. Lord Audley's instructions are to take him, or kill him, not to talk to him.'

As if to confirm the instructions, the heralds break off and ride back to their own ranks and almost at once there is a storm of arrows from the Lancaster side, shooting downhill and finding targets. A sigh, a defeated sigh, comes from the York side and we can see the men going down on their knees in a swift prayer, before rising to their feet and pulling on their helmets.

'What are they doing?' the queen asks avidly.

'They are kissing the ground,' I say. There is something terrible about the doomed men putting their lips to the earth that they think will be their deathbed. 'They are kissing the ground where they will be buried. They know they will be defeated and yet they are not running away.'

'Too late to run,' the queen says harshly. 'We would chase them and kill them.'

From our vantage point we can see that the Yorks are outnumbered by almost two to one, perhaps even more. This is not going to be a battle, it is going to be a massacre.

'Where is Lord Stanley?' the queen demands. 'He wanted to lead the attack but I ordered him to be in support. Where is he?'

I look around. 'Could he be hiding in ambush?'

'Look!' she says.

The very centre of the York army, where they should be at their strongest, is giving way before the arrows. 'They're retreating!' the queen cries. 'We're winning! So quickly!'

They are. The men at the very centre of the line are turning, dropping their weapons, and running away. At once I see our cavalry come forwards and start the charge downhill, towards the stream. I clasp my hands together as I see Elizabeth's husband, out in front, thundering into the shallow water and riding across, struggling up the steep banks of the far side, just as the York forces inexplicably swing round and run back into the very heart of the battle, picking up their weapons and returning to the fight.

'What's happening?' Margaret is as bewildered as I am. 'What are they doing?'

'They've come back,' I say. 'They've turned. It was a trick, and now our cavalry is bogged down in the river and the Yorks are able to fight them from the bank. They have tricked us off our good position, into the river, and our men can't get out.'

It is a terrible sight. Our men in battle armour on their metal-plated horses go plunging into the water, and then struggle to get up the other side of the stream where they are battered by the York men at arms, wielding great swords, war axes and pikes. The knights fall from their horses, but cannot get to their feet to defend themselves, the horses' hooves crash down through the water to crush them as they struggle to rise, or weighed down by their flooded breastplates they drown, scrambling in the churning waters of the stream. Those who can grab a stirrup leather try to pull themselves up but the Yorks are dancing up and down the dry banks, quick to thrust a knife in an unguarded armpit or lean towards the stream to slash at a throat, or one of the strong soldiers steps into the stream, swinging a great battle axe, and down goes the Lancaster knight into the water, which blooms red. It is a savage muddle of men and horses. There is nothing beautiful about it, or noble, or even orderly, nothing like the battles that are made into ballads or celebrated in the romances. It is a savage mess of brutish men killing each other for blood lust. A few of the Lancaster lords scramble up the bank on their great war horses and tear through the York lines and disappear – they simply run away. Worse, even more of them, hundreds of them, drop their swords point down to indicate they are not fighting, pull up their horses into a walk, and go slowly, humbly, towards the enemy lines.

'What are they doing?' Margaret is aghast. 'What is my cavalry doing? Is it a trick?'

'They are changing sides,' I say. My hand is on the base of my throat as if to hold my thudding heart. I am so afraid that John Grey may be turning traitor as the queen and I watch. Hundreds of cavalrymen have turned from our side to the Yorks': surely, he must be among them.

'My cavalry?' she asks disbelievingly.

Her hand creeps into mine and we stand in silence, watching the slow progress of the horsemen across the battlefield, towards the Yorks, with their standards drooped down low in surrender. Stray horses plunge and kick and pull themselves out of the stream and trot away. But many, many men are left struggling in the stream until they do not struggle any more.

'John,' I say quietly, thinking of my son-in-law at the head of the cavalry charge. For all I know he is drowned in his armour, and not turned traitor at all. From this distance I can see neither his standard nor his horse. He will leave my daughter a widow and two little boys fatherless, if he is choking in that red water this afternoon.

The armies break off from engagement, retreating to their own lines. From the banks of the river, even in the water, the wounded men stir and call for help.

'Why don't they attack?' Margaret demands, her teeth bared, her hands gripped tight together. 'Why don't they attack again?'

'They're regrouping,' I say. 'God spare them, they are regrouping to charge again.'

As we watch, the horsemen who are left of the Lancaster force charge once more, down the hill at a brave pace; but still they have to get through the stream. This time, knowing the danger, they force the horses into the water and then in a great bound, up the steep banks, spurring them on to the York lines, and battle is joined. They are followed by the men who are fighting on foot, I know that my son and my husband will be among them. I cannot see them, but I can see the movement of the Lancaster forces as they come forwards like a wave, struggle through the stream, and break on the rock of the York line which holds, and fights, and they slug at each other, until we can see our line fall back, and the men on the wings start to slip away.

'What are they doing?' the queen demands incredulously. 'What are they doing?'

'We are losing,' I say. I hear the words in my own voice but I cannot believe it, not for a moment. I cannot believe that I am here, high as an eagle, remote as a soaring gull, watching my husband's defeat, perhaps watching my son's death. 'We are losing. Our men are running away, it is a rout. We thought we were unbeatable; but we are losing.'

It is getting darker, we can see less and less. Suddenly, I realise that we are in terrible danger, and we have put ourselves here by our own folly. When the battle is lost and the York soldiers chase the Lancaster lords to their deaths, hunting them down through the lanes, they will come to this village and they will scale this tower and they will find the greatest prize of the battle: the queen. Our cause will be lost forever if they can take the queen and win control of the prince and the king. Our cause will be lost and I will have lost it, letting her persuade me to come to this church and climb up to watch a life-or-death battle as if it was a pretty day of jousting.

'We have to go,' I say suddenly.

She does not move, staring into the greyness of the twilight. 'I think we're winning,' she says. 'I think that was another charge and we broke through their line.'

'We're not winning, and we didn't break through, we are running away and they are chasing us,' I say harshly. 'Margaret, come on.'

She turns to me, surprised by my use of her name, and I grab her by the hand and pull her towards the stone stairs. 'What d'you think they'll do with you if they catch you?' I demand. 'They'll hold you in the Tower forever. Or worse, they'll break your neck and say you fell from your horse. Come on!'

Suddenly she realises her danger, and she races down the stone steps of the tower, her feet pattering on the stone treads. 'I'll go alone,' she says tersely. 'I'll go back to Eccleshall. You must stop them coming after me.'

She is ahead of me as we run to the forge where the blacksmith is just about to put the shoes on her horse.

'Put them on backwards,' she snaps.

'Eh?' he says.

She gives him a silver coin from her pocket. 'Backwards,' she says. 'Put them on backwards. Hurry. A couple of nails to each shoe.' To me she says, 'If they want to follow me they will have no tracks. They will see only the horses coming here, they won't realise I was going away.'

I realise I am staring at her, the queen of my vision, who had her horseshoes on backwards. 'Where are we going?'

'I'm going,' she says. 'Back to Eccleshall to fetch the prince and the king and to raise the main army to chase the Earl of Salisbury all the way to Ludlow if we have to.'

'And what am I to do?'

She looks at the blacksmith. 'Hurry. Hurry.'

'What am I to do?'

'Will you stay here? And if they come through, you are to tell them that I was going to meet my army at Nottingham.'

'You're leaving me here?'

'They won't hurt you, Jacquetta. They like you. Everyone likes you.'

'They are an army hot from the battlefield, they have probably just killed my son-in-law, my husband and my son.'

'Yes, but they won't hurt you. They won't make war on women. But I have to get away, and get the prince and the king safe. You will save me if you tell them I have gone to Nottingham.'

I hesitate for a moment. 'I am afraid.'

She holds out her hand to me and she makes the gesture that I taught her myself. The pointing-finger gesture that draws the circle in the air, which shows the wheel of fortune. 'I am afraid too,' she says.

'Go on then.' I release her.

The smith hammers in the last nail, the horse walks a little awkwardly but he is sound enough. The smith drops to his hands and knees in the dirt and Margaret steps on his back to get into the saddle. She raises her hand to me. 'À tout à l' heure,' she says as if she is just going out for a little ride for pleasure, and then she digs her heels in her horse's sides and she goes flying off. I look down at the ground; the marks in the soft earth clearly show a horse coming into the forge, but there is no sign of one leaving.

Slowly, I walk to where the track goes through the little village of Mucklestone, and wait for the first York lords to ride in.

It grows dark. In the distance at Blore Heath I hear a cannon shot, and then another, slowly through the night. I wonder that they can see anything to fire upon. Groups of men come by, some of them supporting their wounded companions, some of them with their heads down, running as if from fear itself. I shrink back inside the forge and they don't see me as they go by. They don't even stop to ask for drink or food, all the windows and doors in the village are barred to all soldiers – whatever badge they wear. When I see a Lancaster badge I step out into the lane. 'Lord Rivers? Sir Anthony Woodville? Sir John Grey?' I ask.

The man shakes his head. 'Were they on horses? They'll be dead, missus.'

I make myself stand, though my knees are weak beneath me. I lean against the door of the forge and wonder what I should do, alone at a battlefield, and if Richard is dead out there, and my son, and my son-in-law. I wonder if I should go out to the heath and look for Richard's body. I cannot believe I would not know of his death. I would surely sense it, when I was so close to the battle that I could even see the churning of the stream where he might have drowned?

'Here,' the blacksmith says kindly, coming out of his little cottage to put a dirty mug in my hand. 'What are you going to do, lady?'

I shake my head. There is no pursuing force to misdirect, the York men are not coming through this way, just the broken remnants of our army. I fear that my husband is dead but I don't know where to look for him. I am weak with fear and with a sense of my own lack of heroism. 'I don't know,' I say. I feel utterly lost. The last time I was lost and alone was in the forest when I was a girl in France, and Richard came for me then. I cannot believe that Richard will not come for me now.

'Better come in with us,' the blacksmith says. 'Can't stay out here all night. And you can't go to the battlefield, my lady, there are thieves working the place, and they'd stab you as soon as look at you. You'd better come in with us.'

I shrug, I don't know what I should do. There is no point standing in the street if no-one is going to come past me to ask where the queen has gone. I have done my duty by hurrying her away, I don't need to stand out till dawn. I duck my head under the narrow doorway of the cottage and step into the small dark earth-floored room and the stench of five people sleeping, cooking, eating and pissing in the same space.

They are kind to me. What they have, they share. They have a corner of black bread made with rye; they have never tasted white bread. They have a thin gruel made with vegetables and a rind of cheese. They have small ale to drink which the goodwife brews herself and they give me the first gulp from an earthenware cup which tastes of mud. I think that these are the people we should be fighting for, these are the people who live in a rich country, where land is fertile and water is clean, where there are more acres to grow than farmers to harvest. This is a country where wages should be high and markets should be rich and busy. And yet it is not. It is a land where no-one can sleep safely in their bed at night for fear of raids or brigands or thieves, where the king's justice is bought and paid for by the king's friends, where an honest working man is tried for treason and hanged if he asks for his rights, and where we cannot seem to stop a French courtier landing in our own ports and laying them waste.

We say that we are the rulers of this country but we do not make a rule of law. We say that we command these people but we do not lead them to peace or prosperity. We, their own lords, quarrel among ourselves, and bring death to their door as if our opinions and thoughts and dreams are worth far more than their safety and health and children.

I think of the queen, riding through the night with her horse-shoes on backwards so that no-one can know where she has gone, and her army lying face down in Hempmill Brook, perhaps my husband and my son among them. The blacksmith's wife, Goody Skelhorn, sees me grow pale and asks me if the gruel has turned my stomach.

'No,' I say. 'But my husband was fighting today, and I am afraid for him.' I can't even bear to tell her of my fears for my boy.

She shakes her head, and says something about terrible times. Her accent is so broad that I can hardly make out what she says. Then she spreads a flea-filled rug on a straw mattress that is their best bed, beside the dying fire, and shows me that I can lie down. I thank her, I lie down, she joins me on one side and her daughter on the other. The men sleep on the other side of the fire. I lie on my back and wait for the long sleepless night to wear away.

Through the night we hear the clatter of hooves down the village street, and occasional shouts. The girl, the woman, and I cower like frightened children together: this is what it is like to live in a country at war. There is nothing of the grace of the joust or even the inspiration of great principles – it is about being a poor woman hearing a detachment of horse thunder down your street and praying that they do not stop to hammer on your frail door.

When dawn comes the goodwife gets up and cautiously opens the door and peers outside. When it seems safe she goes out and I hear her clucking to her hens and releasing the pig to roam around the village and eat the rubbish. I get up from the bed and scratch the swelling insect bites on my arms and neck and face. My hair is falling down from the careful coiled plait on the top of my head, I feel filthy, I am afraid that I smell; but I am alive. I did not stand and misdirect the invading lords as the queen asked me to do, I hid like a serf in a peasant's cottage and was glad of their kindness. I ducked out of sight when I heard the horses in the night and I lay down on dirty straw. In truth, I would have given anything to stay alive last night, and I would give anything to know my husband and sons are alive this dawn. I am fearful and low. I don't feel much of a duchess this morning.

The girl gets up, shakes out her petticoat which serves as both underwear and nightgown, pulls on a dress of coarse fustian over the top, rubs her face on the corner of a dirty apron and she is ready for the day. I look at her and think of the scented bath that is waiting for me at Eccleshall Castle and the clean linen that I will put on. Then, before I grow too confident of my own future comforts, I remember that I can't be sure that the court will be at Eccleshall Castle, nor that my son and husband will come home to me.

'I must leave,' I say abruptly.

I go outside and the smith is tacking up my horse. His wife has a mug of small ale for me, and a heel of stale bread. I drink the ale and dip the bread in it to make it soft enough to eat, then I give them my purse. There is silver in it, and some copper coins, a fortune for them, though it was next to nothing for me. 'Thank you,' I say, and I wish I could say more: that I am sorry for the ruin that this king and queen have brought upon them, I am sorry that they work hard and yet cannot rise from the poverty of their home, I am sorry that I have slept on linen all my life and seldom thought of those who sleep on straw.

They smile. The girl is missing a rotting tooth at the front of her face and it gives her a gap-toothed grin like a little child. 'D'ye know the way?' the woman worries. It is all of nine miles, she has never been so far from her home.

'You go to Loggerheads and they will set you on the road there,' the smith volunteers. 'But take care, the soldiers will be making their way home too. Shall I send the lad with you?'

'No,' I say. 'You will be busy in the forge today, I should think.'

He hefts my purse and grins up at me. 'It's a good day already,' he says. 'The best we've had in all our lives. God bless you, my lady.'

'God bless you,' I say, and turn my horse to the south.

I have been riding for about half an hour when I hear a blast of trumpets and see the dust of a great army on the move. I look around me for somewhere to hide but this is wide empty country, the fields are broad and bare and the hedges are low. I pull my horse over to an open gateway by a field and think that if they are the York army or York reinforcements then I can rein in, sit tight, look like a duchess, and let them go by. Perhaps they will have news of my husband and my boy.

When they are half a mile from me, I can make out the king's standard, and I know that I am safe for the moment, as the army comes up, the queen and the king himself at the head.

'Jacquetta!' she cries out with genuine joy. 'God bless you! Well met!'

She pulls her horse over to the side of the road to let the army keep on marching past us. Thousands of men are following her. 'You are safe!' she says. 'And well! And the king here is so angry at the death of Lord Audley that he is marching himself to bring the York lords to account.' She lowers her voice. 'He has suddenly come to his senses and said he will lead the army himself. I'm so happy. He says he will never again forgive them, and he is going to avenge the death of our true friend.'

'Lord Audley is dead?' I ask. I can feel myself starting to tremble at the thought of what her next words might be. 'And do you have news ...'

A man from the centre of the knights thrusts his horse forwards and pushes up his visor to show his face. 'It's me!' my husband yells. 'Jacquetta! Beloved! It's me!'

I gasp, he is unrecognisable, as they all are, weighed down in their armour and with helmets on. But he comes forwards, jumps down from his horse with a clatter, throws his helmet aside and pulls me into his arms. His breastplate is hard against me, the greaves on his arms cut into my back but I cling to him and kiss him and swear to him that I love him.

'And Anthony is safe,' he says. 'And Elizabeth's husband. We all came through scot-free. I told you I was lucky.'

'Don't look at me, I must smell,' I say, suddenly remembering my clothes and my hair and the raised welts of flea bites on my skin. 'I am ashamed of myself.'

'You should never have stayed there,' he says, glancing at the queen. 'You should never have been there. You should never have been left there.'

Margaret gives me a merry smile. 'He has been most angry with me,' she says. 'He is not speaking to me for rage. But see, here you are, safe now.'

'I am safe now,' I agree.

'Now come! Come!' she urges. 'We are on the trail of the traitor Salisbury. And we are not far behind him.'

We have a wild couple of days, riding at the head of the royal army. The king is restored to health by action, he is once again the young man that we thought might rule the kingdom. He rides at the head of his army and Margaret rides beside him, as if they were true husband and wife: friends and comrades in deed as well as by contract. The weather is warm, a golden end of summer, and the harvest is in from the fields leaving golden stubble, criss-crossed by hundreds of loping hare. There is a big harvest moon in the evenings so bright that we can march late into the night. One night we set up tents and camp, just as if we were on an evening hunting party. We have news of the York lords; they have met together at Worcester and swore a solemn oath of loyalty in the cathedral, and sent a message to the king.

'Send it back to them,' the queen snaps. 'We have seen what their loyalty is worth. They killed Lord Audley and Lord Dudley, they killed Edmund Beaufort. We won't parley with them.'

'I think I might send a public pardon,' the king says mildly. He beckons the Bishop of Salisbury to his side. 'A public pardon so that they know they can be forgiven,' he says.

The queen compresses her lips and shakes her head. 'No message,' she says to the bishop. 'No pardon,' she says to the king.

Like a rat outside its hole, Richard, Duke of York, takes his stand outside his own town of Ludlow. He and the two lords, Warwick and Salisbury, take up position, on the far side of the Ludford Bridge. On our side of the river the king flies the royal standard, and sends one last offer of pardon to any soldier who abandons his loyalty to the Duke of York, and comes over to us.

That night, my husband comes into the royal chambers where the queen and I and a couple of ladies are sitting with the king. 'I have a comrade who served with me in Calais who wants to leave the Earl of Salisbury and come to our side,' Richard says. 'I have promised him full pardon and a welcome. I have to know that he can trust this.'

We all look to the king who smiles mildly. 'Of course,' he says. 'Everyone can be forgiven if they truly repent.'

'I have your word, Your Grace?' Richard asks.

'Oh yes. Everyone can be forgiven.'

Richard turns to the queen. 'And I have yours?'

The queen rises from her chair. 'Who is it?' she asks eagerly.

'I cannot advise my friend to come to you unless you, yourself, guarantee his safety,' Richard says tightly. 'Do you promise him your pardon for serving against you, Your Grace? Can I trust to your word of pardon?'

'Yes! Yes!' the queen exclaims. 'Who will join us?'

'Andrew Trollope, and the six hundred trained and loyal men under his command,' Richard announces, and steps aside to allow the slim hard-faced man into the royal presence. 'And that,' Richard says to me, as he comes to stand beside me, 'has just decided the battle.'

Richard is right. As soon as they know that Trollope has turned his coat and come over to us with his men, the three York lords disappear, like mist in the morning. They slip away, overnight, abandoning their men, abandoning their town, even abandoning Cecily Neville the Duchess of York, the wife of Richard the duke. When our army pours into the town of Ludlow, and starts to strip away everything they can carry, she is standing there, with the keys of the castle in her hand, waiting for the queen. She, who has always been a proud woman, married to a royal lord, is most terribly afraid, I can see it on her white face; and I, who had to wait in Mucklestone for their victorious army to sweep by, take no pleasure in seeing such a proud woman brought down so low.

'You have the keys of the castle for me,' the queen sings out, looking down on the duchess from high on her great horse.

'Yes, Your Grace,' Cecily says steadily. 'And I plead for my own safety, and for the safety of these my children.'

'Of course,' the king says at once. 'Sir Richard – take the keys and escort the duchess to a safe place, her children with her. She is under my protection.'

'Hold a minute,' Margaret says. 'What children are these?'

'This is my daughter Margaret,' Duchess Cecily says. A tall girl of thirteen blushes painfully red and curtseys low to the queen, recovers from her mistake and curtseys again to the king. 'This is my son George, and my youngest boy Richard.'

I would judge George to be about eleven years of age and Richard about seven. They both look stunned with shock, as well they might; for they are boys who yesterday thought their father was heir to the throne of England, likely to fight his way through to the throne, and today find themselves facing the king's army and their father run away. A crash from a house behind us and a piercing scream from a woman, begging for help as she is pulled down and raped, reminds us all that we are in the middle of a war, talking in a battlefield.

'Take them away,' the king says quickly.

'And your husband has left you here?' the queen torments the defeated duchess. 'Do you remember how you insisted that you be admitted to my chamber when I had just given birth to my baby, and you told me that your husband must visit my husband when he was ill, in the time of our travail? He forced his way into the Privy Council once, but now we see he just ups and goes. He is present where he is not wanted; but when he is needed, he just abandons you. He declares war and then disappears from the battlefield!'

The duchess sways on her feet, her face as white as skimmed milk. Smoke drifts across the market square, someone somewhere has fired a thatch. The woman who screamed for help is sobbing in rhythmic pain. I see the little boy Richard look around at the sound of someone smashing an axe into a locked door and the babble of an old voice praying to be spared, calling for mercy to someone who is not listening.

'Your Grace,' I say to the queen. 'This is no place for any of us. Let us leave the lords to regain control of the men and get out of this town.'

To my surprise she smiles at me, a gleam of malice that shows clearly before she drops her eyes to her horse's mane and hides her expression. 'It's a very blunt weapon: an army of uncontrolled men,' she says. 'When York raised an army against me, he cannot have imagined that I would bring my army against him and that it would be like this. He has taught me a lesson that I have learned well. An army of poor men is a terror indeed. He nearly frightened me. He must be sorry now, now that there is an army of poor men tearing apart his home town.'

The little dark-haired boy Richard flushes in temper, looks up,

opens his mouth as if to shout his defiance. 'Let's go,' I say
swiftly, and my husband calls a couple of horses forwards, lifts
the duchess into the saddle without ceremony, settles her children in the saddle before three cavalrymen, and we leave the
town. As we clatter over the bridge I can hear another woman
scream and the noise of running feet. Ludlow is paying the price
for the flight of their lord, the Duke of York.

'Yes, but not his death,' my son Anthony observes. The three of
us are riding home to Grafton together, our men straggling down
the road behind us. I observe, but try to make it clear that I have
not seen, that they are weighed down with loot; every one of
them has some cloth bound tight in his pack, or a piece of plate,
or a cup of pewter. They were our tenants but we put them in the
queen's army and they fought by her rules. They were told that
they might loot Ludlow to punish the treasonous York lords and
we will never muster them to ride out for us again if we spoil their
sport and demand that they hand back the goods they have
thieved. 'While York lives, while Warwick lives, while Salisbury
lives, the wars are not over; they are only put off for a little while
longer.'

Richard nods. 'Warwick is back in Calais, Richard Duke of
York back in Ireland. The kingdom's greatest enemies have
returned to refuge, safe in their castles overseas. We will have to
prepare for an invasion again.'

'The queen is confident,' I say.

The queen is tremendously confident. November comes and
still she does not return to London, hating London and blaming
the London ballad-makers and chap-book sellers for her unpop-
ularity in the kingdom. Their tales and songs describe her as a
wolf, a she-wolf who commands a Fisher King – a man reduced
to a shell of what he should be. The most bawdy rhymes say she
cuckolded him with a bold duke and popped their bastard in the

royal cradle. There is a drawing of a swan with the face of Edmund Beaufort, waddling towards the throne. There are songs and ale-house jokes about her. She hates London and the apprentices who laugh at her.

Instead she orders the parliament to come to Coventry – as if parliaments can be ordered by a woman like outriders – and they obediently come as if they were her messengers, bound to do her bidding when she orders new oaths of loyalty to the king but also to her by name, and to the prince. Nobody has ever sworn loyalty to a queen before – but they do now. She cites the three York lords for treason, takes their lands and fortunes, and hands them out as if it were all the twelve days of Christmas come early. She orders the Duchess Cecily to attend so that she can hear her husband named as a traitor, and listen to the death sentence passed on him. Everything the York lords owned, every rood of land, every banner, every honour and title, every purse of gold, is stripped from them. The poor Duchess of York, now a royal pensioner and a pauper, goes to live with her sister, the queen's loyal lady, Anne the Duchess of Buckingham, in something between house arrest and torment; a half-life for a woman who was once called 'Proud Cis' and now finds herself a married woman with a husband in exile, a mother missing her oldest son, Edward, the daughter of a great house who has lost all her lands and her inheritance.

SANDWICH, KENT, AND CALAIS, WINTER 1460

Richard is ill paid for warning the queen that the Warwick ownership of Calais has put an enemy on our shoreline, for as soon as the fighting is done and the peace won, she asks him to go to Sandwich and reinforce the town against attack.

'I'll come too,' I say at once. 'I can't bear you to be in danger and me far away. I can't bear for us to be parted again.'

'I'm not going to be in danger,' he lies to reassure me, and then, catching my sceptical expression, he giggles like a boy caught out in a blatant falsehood. 'All right, Jacquetta, don't look at me like that. But if there is any danger of an invasion from Calais you will have to go home to Grafton. I'll take Anthony with me.'

I nod. It's useless to suggest that Anthony is too precious to be exposed to danger. He is a young man born into a country constantly at war with itself. Another young man, of just his age, is Edward March, the Duke of York's son, across the narrow seas, serving his apprenticeship in soldiering with the Earls of Warwick and Salisbury. His mother, the Duchess of York, held in England, will not be able to get a word to him. She will have to wait and worry, as I wait and worry. This is not a time when mothers can hope to keep their sons safe at home.

Richard and I take a house in the port of Sandwich, while

Anthony commands the men at Richborough Fort nearby. The town has still not recovered from the French raid of only a few years ago, and the burned-out shells of houses are a vivid statement of the danger from our enemies, and the narrowness of the seas between us. The town defences were destroyed in the raid, the French fired cannon at the sea walls and captured the town's own armament. They mocked the citizens, playing tennis in the market square as if to say that they cared nothing for Englishmen, that they thought us powerless. Richard sets builders to work, begs the armourer at the Tower of London to cast new cannon for the town, and starts to train the townsmen to form a guard. Meanwhile, just a mile away, Anthony drills our men and rebuilds the defences of the old Roman castle that guard the river entrance.

We have been in the town little more than a week when I am suddenly frightened from sleep by the loud clanging of the tocsin bell. For a moment I think it is the goose bell which rings in the darkness of five o' clock every morning, to wake the goose girls, but then I realise that the loud constant clanging of the bell means a raid.

Richard is out of bed already, pulling on his leather jerkin and snatching up his helmet and his sword.

'What is it? What is happening?' I shout at him.

'God knows,' he says. 'You stay safe in here. Go to the kitchen and wait for news. If Warwick has landed from Calais, get down into the cellar and bolt yourself in.'

He is out of the door before he can say more and then I hear the front door bang and a yelling from the street, and the clash of sword on sword. 'Richard!' I shout and swing open the little window to look down into the cobbled street below.

My husband is unconscious, a man has hold of him and is in the act of dropping his body to the cobblestones. He looks up and sees me. 'Come down, Lady Rivers,' he says. 'You cannot hide or run.'

I close the casement window. My maid appears in the doorway, shaking with fear. 'They have the master, he looks as if he is dead. I think they have killed him.'

'I know,' I say. 'I saw. Get my gown.'

She holds the gown for me and I step into it, let her tie the laces and then put on my slippers and go downstairs, my hair in its night-time plait. I pull up the hood of my cape as I step out into the icy-cold January street. I look around but all I can see, as if engraved on my eyelids, is the man lowering Richard to the ground, and the fall of Richard's limp hand. At the end of the street I can make out half a dozen guardsmen struggling with a man. A glimpse of his face, as he looks desperately towards me, shows me Anthony. They are taking him on board ship.

'What are you doing with my son? That is my son, release him.'

The man does not even bother to answer me, and I run across the slippery cobbles to where they have left Richard on the ground, like a dead man. As I reach him he stirs and opens his eyes, he looks dazed. 'Jacquetta,' he says.

'My love. Are you hurt?' I am dreading him saying that he has been stabbed.

'A cracked head. I'll live.'

A man roughly takes him under the shoulders. 'Carry him into our house,' I order.

'I'm taking him on board,' the man says simply. 'You're to come too.'

'Where d'you think you are taking us? On whose authority? This is not an act of war, it is a crime!'

He ignores me. One man takes Richard's boots, he holds his shoulders, they lug him like a carcase. 'You may not take him,' I insist. 'He is a lord of the realm, under the command of the king. This is rebellion.'

I put my hand on the man's arm but he simply ignores me and lugs Richard down to the quayside. Behind me, all around me, I can hear men shouting and women screaming as the soldiers go through the town, taking what they want, throwing open doors and banging the precious glass out of windows.

'Where do you think you are taking my husband?'

'Calais,' he says shortly.

It's a quick voyage. Richard recovers his senses, they give us clean water and something to eat, Anthony is unhurt. We are locked in a little cabin at first and then, once the ship is at sea and the great sail unfurled and creaking, they let us out on deck. For a little while we cannot see any land, England is lost behind us, but then we see a dark line ahead of us on the horizon, and as we watch we can see the squat mound of the city and, on its crest, the round walls of the castle. I realise I am returning to Calais under guard, as a hostage, to the town that I once entered as a duchess.

I glance at Richard and see that he remembers this too. This is an outpost which was under his command. Now he is a prisoner. This is the turn of fortune's wheel indeed.

'Take care,' he says quietly to me and to our son. 'They shouldn't harm you, Jacquetta, they know you, and they like you. And they don't make war on women. But the queen's treatment of the Duchess of York will have angered them and we are quite in their power. No-one is going to rescue us. We will have to get out of this alive, by our own wits. We are quite alone.'

'The Duke of Somerset holds Guisnes Castle, he might come for us,' Anthony suggests.

'Won't get within half a mile,' my husband says. 'I have fortified this town, son, I know its strengths. Nobody will take it by force this century. So we are hostages in enemy hands. They have every reason to spare you, Jacquetta, and many a good reason to kill me.'

'They can't kill you,' I say. 'You have done nothing wrong but be loyal to the king from the day you were born.'

'That's why I'm the very man they should kill,' he says. 'It will fill the others with fear. So I am going to mind my manners and speak gently, and if I have to swear to give up my sword to save my life, I will do that. And –' he addresses Anthony, who flings himself aside with an impatient word, 'and so will you. If they ask for our parole and for our promise that we never take arms against them, we will give that too. We have no choice. We are defeated. And I don't plan to be beheaded on the gallows that I built here. I don't plan to be buried in the cemetery that I tidied and cleared. Do you understand?'

'I do,' Anthony says shortly. 'But how could we have let ourselves be taken!'

'What's done is done,' Richard says sternly. 'These are the fortunes of war. All we have to think about now is how to get out of this alive. And we are going to do this by speaking sweetly, biding our time, and keeping out of a rage. More than anything, my son, I want you to be polite, surrender if you have to, and come out of this alive.'

They keep us on the ship till nightfall, they do not want Richard paraded through the town and seen by the people. The influential merchants of Calais love him for defending them when the castle was claimed by York. The men of the town remember him as a loyal and brave captain of the castle whose word was law and could be trusted like gold. The troop of Calais love him as a firm and just commander. It was the experience of serving under Richard that persuaded the six hundred men to change sides at Ludlow, and support the king. Any troop that has been commanded by him will follow him to hell and back. Warwick does not want this most popular captain to appeal to the people as he goes through the town.

So they wait till late at night and bring us like secret captives into the great hall of the castle under cover of darkness, and the sudden blaze of torches is blindingly bright after the black streets outside. They bring us through the gateway, under the stone arch and then into the great hall with blazing fires at either end and the men of the garrison at the trestle tables, uneasy at the sight of us.

The three of us stand, like penniless runaways from a war, and look around the great hall, the vaulted ceiling with the smoke-blackened beams, the torches ablaze in the sconces all round, some men standing, drinking ale, some seated at dining trestle tables, and some rising to their feet at the sight of my husband and pulling off their caps. At the top of the hall, the Earl of Salisbury, his son the Earl of Warwick, and the young Edward, Earl of March, son of Richard, Duke of York, sit at the head table, raised on the dais, the white rose of York on a banner behind them.

'We have taken you as prisoners of war and will consider your parole,' the Earl of Warwick starts, solemn as a judge from his seat at the head table.

'It was not an act of war, since I am under the command of the King of England; an act against me is an act of rebellion and treason against my king,' Richard says, his deep voice very strong and loud in the hall. The men stiffen at the note of absolute defiance. 'And I warn you that anyone who lays a hand on me, on my son, or on my wife, is guilty of rebellion and treason and illegal assault. Anyone who harms my wife is, of course, not worthy of his spurs nor of his name. If you make war on a woman you are no better than a savage and should be thrown down like one. Your name will be defamed forever. I would pity a man who insulted my wife, a royal duchess and an heiress of the House of Luxembourg. Her name and her reputation must protect her wherever she goes. My son is under my protection and under hers, a loyal subject of an ordained king. We three are all loyal subjects of the king and should be free to go our own ways. I demand safe passage to England for the three of us. In the name of the King of England, I demand it.'

'So much for the soft answer that turneth away wrath,'

Anthony says quietly to me. 'So much for surrender and parole. My God, look at Salisbury's face!'

The old earl looks likely to explode. 'You!' he bellows. 'You dare to speak to me like this?'

The York lords are seated high on the dais and Richard has to look up at them. They rise from their chairs and glower down at him. He is utterly unrepentant. He walks towards the stage, and stands, his hands on his hips. 'Aye. Of course. Why not?'

'You don't even deserve to be in our company! You have no right even to speak without being spoken to. We are of the blood royal and you are a nobody.'

'I am a peer of England and I have served under my king in France and Calais and England, and never disobeyed him or betrayed him,' Richard says very loudly and clearly.

'Unlike them,' Anthony supplements gleefully to me.

'You are an upstart nobody, the son of a groom of the household,' Warwick shouts. 'A nothing. You wouldn't even be here if it was not for your marriage.'

'The duchess demeaned herself,' young Edward of March says. I see Anthony stiffen at the insult from a youth of his own age. 'She lowered herself to you, and you raised yourself only by her. They say she is a witch who inspired you to the sin of lust.'

'Before God, this is unbearable,' Anthony swears. He plunges forwards and I snatch at his arm.

'Don't you dare move, or I will stab you myself!' I say furiously. 'Don't you dare say a thing or do a thing. Stand still, boy!'

'What?'

'You are not fit to come among us,' Salisbury says. 'You are not fit to keep company.'

'I see what they are doing, they're hoping you will lose your temper,' I tell him. 'They are hoping you will attack them and then they can cut you down. Remember what your father said. Stay calm.'

'They insult you!' Anthony is sweating with rage.

'Look at me!' I demand.

He darts a fierce glance at me and then hesitates. Despite my hasty words to him, my face is utterly calm, I am smiling. 'I was not the woman left in Ludlow marketplace when my husband ran away,' I say to him in a rapid whisper. 'I was the daughter of the Count of Luxembourg when Cecily Neville was nothing more than a pretty girl in a northern castle. I am the descendant of the goddess Melusina. You are my son. We come from a line of nobles who trace their line back to a goddess. They can say what they like behind my back, they can say it to my face. I know who I am. I know what you were born to be. And it is more, far more, than they.'

Anthony hesitates. 'Smile,' I command him.

'What?'

'Smile at them.'

He raises his head, he can hardly twist his face into a smile but he does it.

'You have no pride!' Edward of March spits at him. 'There is nothing here to smile at!'

Anthony inclines his head slightly, as if accepting a great compliment.

'You let me speak like this of your own mother? Before her very face?' Edward demands, his voice cracking with rage. 'Do you have no pride?'

'My mother does not need your good opinion,' Anthony says icily. 'None of us care what you think.'

'*Your* own mother is well,' I say to Edward gently. 'She was very distressed at Ludlow, to be left on her own in such danger, but my husband, Lord Rivers, took her and your sister Margaret and your brothers George and Richard to safety. My husband, Lord Rivers, protected them when the army was running through the town. He made sure that no-one insulted them. The king is paying her a pension, and she is in no hardship. I saw her myself a little while ago and she told me she prays for you and for your father.'

It shocks him into silence. 'You have my husband to thank for her safety,' I repeat.

'He is base-born,' Edward says, as someone repeating a lesson by rote.

I shrug my shoulders as if it is nothing to me. Indeed, it is nothing to me. 'We are in your keeping,' I say simply. 'Base or noble. And you have no cause to complain of us. Will you give us safe passage to England?'

'Take them away,' the Earl of Salisbury snaps.

'I would like my usual rooms,' Richard says. 'I was captain of this castle for more than four years, and I kept it safe for England. I usually have the rooms that look over the harbour.'

The Earl of Warwick curses like a tavern owner.

'Take them away,' Salisbury repeats.

We don't have the rooms of the captain of the castle, of course, but we have good ones looking over the inner courtyard. They keep us only for a couple of nights and then a guard comes to the door and says that I am to be taken by ship to London.

'What about us?' my husband demands.

'You're hostages,' the soldier says. 'You're to wait here.'

'They are to be held with honour? They are safe?' I insist.

He nods to Richard. 'I served under you, sir, I'm Abel Stride.'

'I remember you, Stride,' my husband says. 'What's the plan?

'My orders are to hold you here until we move out, and then to release you, unhurt,' he says. 'And I'll obey them, and no others.' He hesitates. 'There's not a man in the garrison would harm you, sir, nor your son. My word on it.'

'Thank you,' my husband says. To me he whispers, 'Go to the queen, tell her they are preparing to invade. Try and see how many ships you can count in the pool. Tell her I don't think they have many men, perhaps only two thousand or so.'

'And you?'

'You heard him. I'll get home when I can. God bless you, beloved.'

I kiss him. I turn to my son, who goes down on his knee for my blessing and then comes up to hug me. I know he is broad and strong and a good fighter, but to leave him in danger is almost unbearable.

'Your Grace, you have to come now,' the guard says.

I have to leave them both. I don't know how I get up the gangplank of the merchant ship or into the little cabin. But I have to leave them both.

COVENTRY, SPRING 1460

The court is in Coventry, readying for war, when I arrive in England and take the queen the news that our enemies in Calais are holding my husband and son, and that they are certain to invade this year.

'Jacquetta, I am so sorry,' Margaret says to me. 'I had no idea. I would never have put you in danger like that . . . when they told me that you had been captured I was beside myself.' She glances around and whispers to me, 'I wrote to Pierre de Brézé, the Seneschal of Normandy, and asked him to take Calais and rescue you. You know what would happen to me if anyone found out I am writing to him. But you are this important to me.'

'I was never in any great danger,' I say. 'But the rebel lords taunted Richard and Anthony and I think if they could have killed them in a brawl they would have done so.'

'I hate them,' she says simply. 'Warwick and his father, York and his son. They are my enemies till death. You know the rumours they are spreading now?'

I nod. They have spoken slander against this queen from the moment she arrived in England.

'They are openly saying that my son is a bastard, that the king knew nothing about his birth and christening and also – nothing about his conception. They think to disinherit him with slander, since they cannot hurt him by war.'

'Do you have news of the Yorkist lords?'

'They have met,' she says shortly. 'I have spies at York's little court in Ireland and they tell me. Warwick went to meet the Duke of York in his castle in Ireland. We know that they met, we can guess they plan to invade. We cannot know when for sure.'

'And are you ready for an invasion?'

She nods grimly. 'The king has been ill again – oh, not very ill – but he has lost interest in everything but praying. He has been at prayer for all of this week and sleeping, sometimes as much as sixteen hours a day . . .' She breaks off. 'I never know if he is here or if he has gone. But, at any rate, I am ready, I am ready for anything. I have the troops, I have the lords, I have the country on my side – all but the perfidious people of Kent and the guttersnipes of London.'

'When, do you think?' I do not really need to ask. All campaigns start in the summer season. It cannot be long before they bring the news that York is on the march from Ireland, and Warwick has set sail from Calais.

'I'll go and see my children,' I say. 'They will be anxious about their father and their brother.'

'And then come back,' she says. 'I need you with me, Jacquetta.'

NORTHAMPTON, SUMMER 1460

In June, in the richest greenest easiest month of the year, the York lords make their move from Calais, and Richard, Duke of York, bides his time in Ireland, letting them do his dirty work for him. They land, as my husband predicted, with only a small force of about two thousand, but as they march their ranks are swelled with men who run out of the fields and from the stable yards to join them. Kent has not forgotten Jack Cade or the harvest of heads, and there are many who march out for Warwick now, who remember the queen swearing that she would make a deer park of their home. London throws the City gates open to Warwick and poor Lord Scales finds himself once again alone in the Tower, with orders to hold it for the king, whatever the cost. The York lords do not even trouble themselves to starve him out, they leave Lord Cobham in charge of the City and march north, to Kenilworth, looking for their enemy: us.

Every day they add recruits, everywhere they go men flock to join them. Their army swells, they grow stronger, they pay wages with money voted to them by the towns that they march by. The mood of the country has swung against the queen and her puppet king. The people want a leader they can trust to hold the country to peace and justice. They have come to think that Richard, Duke of York, will be their protector and they fear the queen for the danger and uncertainty that comes in her train.

The queen makes the Duke of Buckingham the commander of the king's armies and the king is taken out of his monastic retreat to fly the royal standard, which flaps miserably in the wet weather. But this time, nobody deserts before a blow is struck because they cannot bear to attack the king's personal flag. No powerful troop abandons the cause of the York lords. Everyone is becoming hardened. The king sits quietly in his tent below his standard and the peacemakers – among them the Bishop of Salisbury – go to and fro all morning, hoping to broker a settlement. It cannot be done. The York lords send personal messages to the king but the Duke of Buckingham intercepts them. They will settle for nothing less than the queen and her advisors banned from their influential place beside the king, they will trust nothing else. And the queen will not compromise. She wants to see them dead: it is as simple as that. There are really no grounds for parley at all.

The royal army is before Delapre Abbey at Northampton, dug in before the River Nene with sharp staves set in the ground in front of them. No cavalry charge can take them here, no head-on attack can possibly succeed. The queen, the prince and I are waiting at Eccleshall Castle again.

'I almost want to ride out and watch,' she says to me.

I try to laugh. 'Not again.'

It is raining now, and it has been raining for the last two days. We stand together at the window looking out at the lowering grey skies with the dark clouds on the horizon. Below us, in the courtyard, we can see the bustle of messengers arriving from the battlefield. 'Let's go down,' says Margaret, suddenly nervous.

We meet them in the great hall as they are coming in, dripping wet.

'It's over,' the man says to the queen. 'You told me to come the moment that I could see which way it was going and so I waited for a while and then I came.'

'Have we won?' she asks urgently.

He makes a grimace. 'We are destroyed,' he says bluntly. 'Betrayed.'

She hisses like a cat. 'Who betrayed us? Who was it? Stanley?'

'Grey of Ruthin.'

She rounds on me. 'Your daughter's kinsman! Your daughter's family are unfaithful?'

'A distant relation,' I say at once. 'What did he do?'

'He waited till York's son, the young Edward of March, charged him. Our line was well protected, we had the river behind us and a ditch before us fortified with sharp staves, but when the York boy came up at the head of his men, Lord Grey put down his sword and just helped him over the barricades with all his troop, and then they fought their way down our own lines. They were inside our lines, our men couldn't get away from them. We were perfectly placed when we started, then we found we were perfectly trapped.'

She goes white and staggers. I hold her by the waist and she leans against me. 'The king?'

'I went as they were fighting their way towards his tent. His lords were outside, covering his retreat, they were shouting to him to get away.'

'Did he go?'

The darkness of his face tells us that he did not, and perhaps the lords gave their lives for nothing. 'I didn't see. I came to warn you. The battle is lost. You had better get yourself away. I think they may have the king.'

She turns to me. 'Get the prince,' she says.

Without a word I hurry to the royal nurseries and find the boy in his travelling cape and riding breeches, his toys and books packed. His governor stands beside him. 'Her Grace the queen commands that her son shall come at once,' I say.

The man turns gravely to the six-year-old boy. 'You are ready, Your Grace?'

'I am ready, I am ready now,' the little prince says bravely.

I hold out my hand but he does not take it. Instead he walks ahead of me and stands before the door, waiting for me to open it for him. At another time this would be amusing. Not today.

'Oh, go on!' I say impatiently, and open the door and bustle him through.

In the great hall the queen's jewel boxes and chests of clothes are being rushed through the door to the stables. The queen is outside, her guard is mounting up. She pulls her hood over her head and nods at her son as he comes out with me.

'Get on your horse, we have to hurry,' she says. 'The bad York lords have won and perhaps captured your father. We have to get you to safety. You are our only hope.'

'I know,' he says gravely, and steps up on the mounting block as they bring his horse to him.

To me she says, 'Jacquetta, I will send for you as soon as I am safe.'

My head is whirling at the speed of this rout. 'Where are you going?'

'To Jasper Tudor in Wales to start with. If we can invade from there I will, if not France, or Scotland. I will win back my son's inheritance, this is just a setback.'

She leans down from her saddle and I kiss her, and smooth her hair under the hood. 'God speed,' I say. I try to blink the tears from my eyes but I can hardly bear to see her fleeing, with her baggage and her guard and her little son, from the country that I brought her to with such hopes. 'God speed.'

I stand in the courtyard as the small train walks to the road and then sets off, at a steady canter, due west. She will be safe if she can get to Jasper Tudor; he is a faithful man and he has been fighting for his lands in Wales ever since she gave them to him. But if they catch her on the way? I shudder. If they catch her on the way then she and the House of Lancaster are lost.

I turn to the stable yard. The grooms are carrying away everything they can take, the looting of the royal goods is beginning. I shout for one of my men and tell him to pack up everything that is mine and guard it. We are leaving at once. We will go home to Grafton and all I can do is hope that Richard and Anthony come there.

GRAFTON, NORTHAMPTONSHIRE, SUMMER 1460

It is a weary ride to Grafton, a long journey of nearly a hundred miles, through countryside which is loyal to Warwick the invader. At every stop there is a panic-stricken exchange of news: what do we know? What have we seen? And always – is the queen bringing her army this way? I order my men to give out that I am a widow travelling privately on a pilgrimage, and we stay at an abbey for one night, and a church house the second, and on the third we bed down in a barn, always avoiding the inns. Even so, the gossip that is swirling around the country comes to me every evening. They say that the king has been taken to London and that Richard Duke of York has landed from Ireland, and is proceeding in royal state to the capital city. Some say that when he gets there he will become protector and regent once more, some say that he will rule the king from behind the throne, the king will be his little doll, his poppet. I say nothing. I wonder if the queen has got safely to Wales, and I wonder if I will ever see my husband or my son again.

It takes us four days to get home and as we turn up the familiar track to the house I feel my heart lift. At least I shall see my children and stay with them safely and quietly here while the great changes in the country take place without me. At least I can find a refuge here. As we ride up, I hear someone start tolling the bell in the stable yard, to warn the household of the arrival of an armed troop, ourselves, and the front door opens and the men at arms spill out of the house. At their head – I could not mistake him, I would know him anywhere – is my husband Richard.

He sees me in the same moment and comes bounding down the steps at the front of the house, so fast that my horse shies and I have to hold her still as he pulls me from the saddle and into his arms. He kisses my face and I cling to him. 'You're alive!' I say. 'You're alive!'

'They let us go as soon as they had made landfall themselves,' he says. 'Didn't even take a ransom. They just released us from the castle at Calais and then I had to find a ship to bring us home. Took us into Greenwich.'

'Anthony is with you?'

'Of course. Safe and sound.'

I twist in his arms to see my son, smiling at me from the doorway. Richard releases me and I run to Anthony as he kneels for my blessing. To feel his warm head under my hand is to know that the greatest joy of my life is restored to me. I turn back to my husband and wrap my arms around Richard once more.

'Have you news?'

'The York lords win all,' Richard says shortly. 'London greeted them like heroes, Lord Scales tried to get away from the Tower and was killed, and the Duke of York is making his way to London. I think they'll appoint him Protector. The king is safe in the Palace of Westminster, completely under the rule of Warwick. They say his wits are gone again. What of the queen?'

I glance around; even on the terrace of my own manor house I am afraid that someone will hear where she is, and betray her. 'Gone to Jasper Tudor,' I whisper. 'And from there to France or Scotland, I should think.'

Richard nods. 'Come in,' he says gently to me. 'You must be weary. You weren't near the battle, were you? You had no danger on the roads?'

I lean against him and feel the familiar sense of relief that he is by my side. 'I feel safe now, at any rate,' I say.

GRAFTON, NORTHAMPTONSHIRE, WINTER 1460–61

We live as we did when we were first married, as if we had no work to do but to keep the lands around Grafton, as if we were nothing but a squire and his wife. We don't want the attention of the York lords as they make the country their own, impose massive fines on the lords they now call traitors, take posts and fees from the men they have defeated. There is a greed here, and a thirst for revenge, and all I want is for it to pass us by. We live quietly and hope to escape notice. We hear, in snatches of gossip from travellers who ask for a bed for the night, and occasional visitors, that the king is living quietly at Westminster Palace in the queen's rooms while his conquering cousin, Richard, Duke of York, has taken up residence in the king's own apartments. I think of my king in the rooms that I knew so well and I pray that he does not slide into sleep again to escape a waking world which is so hard on him.

The duke forges an extraordinary agreement with the Privy Council and the parliament: he will be regent and Protector of the Realm until the death of the king and then he will become king himself. A peddler, who comes by with York ribbons of white and white roses of silk in his pack, says that the king has agreed to this and is going to take vows and become a monk.

'He's not in the Tower?' I ask urgently. I have a horror of the king being sent to the Tower.

'No, he is living freely as a fool at the court,' he says. 'And York will be the next king.'

'The queen will never consent to it,' I say incautiously.

'She's in Scotland, so they say,' he replies, spreading his goods before me. 'Good riddance. Let her stay there, I say. D'you want some pepper? I have some pepper and a nutmeg so fresh that you could eat it whole.'

'In Scotland?'

'They say she is meeting with the Scottish queen and they are going to bring an army of harpies down on us,' he says cheerfully. 'An army of women – think of that as a horror! A nice little polished mirror here? Or look, some hairnets of gold thread. That's real gold, that is.'

We celebrate Christmas at Grafton. Elizabeth comes to stay with her husband, Sir John, and their two boys: Thomas is five years old now and Richard just two. All my children come home for the twelve days of the feast, and the house is alive with their singing and dancing and chasing each other up and down the wooden staircase. For the six youngest children, from Katherine, who at two can only toddle after her bigger siblings, imploring them not to leave her behind, through Edward, Margaret, Lionel, Eleanor, and Martha, the oldest of the nursery at ten years, the return of their older brothers and sisters is like an explosion of noise and excitement. Richard and John are inseparable, young men of fourteen and fifteen years, Jacquetta and Mary are thoughtful young women, placed in the houses of neighbours in these difficult times. Anthony and Anne are the oldest of course. Anne should be married by now, but what can I do when the whole country is turned upside down and there is not even a court for her to join as a maid in waiting? And how am I to find Anthony the bride he should have when I cannot tell who will be wealthy and in the favour of the king next month – let alone ten years from now? There is a promise between him and the daughter of Lord Scales, but Lord Scales is dead and his family disgraced like us. And finally, and most puzzling for me, who should be planning matches for my children and looking around for the great houses where they should be placed to learn the skills they need: how can I know which will stay loyal to Lancaster, when the House of Lancaster is a king living in the queen's rooms, an absent queen, and a boy of seven? And I cannot yet bring myself to consider an alliance with anyone who serves the traitorous House of York.

I think I will keep all the children at home with us at Grafton till the spring, perhaps longer. There can be no positions for us at the new royal household which will be the York court – since there are now York placemen and lords and members of parliament I assume that soon there will be York courtiers and ladies in waiting. Cecily Neville, the Duchess of York, riding high on fortune's wheel, is sleeping in the king's apartments under a canopy of cloth of gold like a queen herself; she must think that every day is Christmas. Clearly, we can never attend a York court: I doubt that any of us will ever forgive or forget the humiliation in the great hall at Calais Castle. Perhaps we will learn to be exiles in our own lands. Perhaps I shall now, at the age of forty-five, with my last child learning to talk, live in a country that is like that of my childhood: with one king in the north of the kingdom and one in the south, and everyone forced to choose which they think is the true one, and everyone knowing their enemy, and everyone waiting for revenge.

I really despair of organising the future of our family in such a world, at such a time, and instead I take comfort in the future of our lands. I start to plan to enlarge our orchard and go to a farm near Northampton where I can buy some whips of trees. Richard tells me that the seas are safe for shipping and he will get better prices for the wool from his sheep this year in the market at Calais. The roads are safe to and from London, the Duke of York is restoring the powers of the sheriffs and commanding them to see that justice is done in every county. Slowly, the counties are starting to rid themselves of bandits and thieves on the highway. We never admit it, not even to each other; but these are great improvements. We start to think, never saying it out loud, that perhaps we can live like this, as country landowners in a country at peace. Perhaps we can grow an orchard, farm our sheep, watch our children come to adulthood without the fear of treachery and war. Perhaps Richard Duke of York has thrown us down from the court, but given us peace in the country.

Then, at the end of January, I see three riders come splashing down the lane, their horses' hooves cracking the ice in the puddles. I see them from the nursery window where I am watching Katherine as she sleeps, and I know at once that they are bringing us bad news, and that these cold winter months of stillness are over. It was not a peace at all, it was just the usual winter break in a war that goes on and on forever. A war that will go on and on forever until everyone is dead. For a brief moment I even think that I will close the shutters on the windows and sit in the nursery and pretend that I am not here. I will not have to respond to a call that I don't hear. But it is only a moment. I know that if I am summoned I have to go. I have served Lancaster for all my life, I cannot fail now.

I bend over the little crib and kiss Katherine on her warm smooth baby forehead and then I leave the nursery and close the door quietly behind me. I walk slowly down the stairs, looking over the wooden banister as down below Richard throws a cape around his shoulders and picks up his sword, and goes out to see the visitors. I wait inside the great hall, listening.

'Sir Richard Woodville, Lord Rivers?' says the first man.

'Who wants him?'

The man lowers his voice. 'The Queen of England. Do you answer to her? Are you faithful still?'

'Aye,' Richard says shortly.

'I have this for you,' the man says and proffers a letter.

Through the crack in the doorway I see Richard take it. 'Go round the back to the stables,' he says. 'They'll see you have food and ale. It's a cold day. Go into the hall and warm yourselves.

This is a loyal house; but there is no need to tell anyone where you come from.'

The men salute in thanks, and Richard comes into the entrance hall, breaking the seal.

'"*Greetings, well-beloved . . .*"' he starts to read, and then breaks off. 'It's a standard letter, she has probably sent out hundreds. It's a summons.'

'To arms?' I can taste my own fear.

'Me and Anthony. We're to go to York, she's mustering there.'

'Will you go?' Almost, I want to ask him to refuse.

'I have to. This may be the last chance for her.' He is reading down the letter and he gives a long low whistle. 'Good God! Her men have taken Richard Duke of York and killed him.' He looks up at me, clenches the letter in his fist. 'My God! Who would have thought it? The protector dead! She has won!'

'How?' I cannot believe this sudden leap to victory. 'What are you saying?'

'She just writes he rode out from his castle, that must be Sandal – why would he ever do that? You could hold that place for a month! And that they cut him down. Good God, I can't believe it. Jacquetta, this is the end of the York campaign. This is the end of the Yorks. Richard of York dead! And his son alongside him.'

I gasp as if his death is a loss to me. 'Not young Edward! Not Edward of March!'

'No, his other son, Edmund. Edward of March is in Wales somewhere, but he can do nothing now his father is dead. They are finished. The Yorks are defeated.' He turns the letter over. 'Oh, look, she's written a note at the end of the letter. She says, "Dear Sir Richard, come at once, the tide is turning for me. We have crowned Richard of York with a paper crown and set his head on a spike at the Micklegate. Soon we will put Warwick's face up beside him, and everything will be as it should be again."' He puts the letter into my hand. 'This changes everything. Would you believe it? Our queen has won, our king is restored.'

'Richard of York is dead?' I read the letter for myself.

'Now she can beat Warwick,' he says. 'Without the alliance with York he's a dead man. He's lost the regent and lord protector, it's all over for them. They have no-one who can pretend to be heir to the throne. Nobody would ever have Warwick as lord protector, he has no claim to the throne at all. The king is the only man who can be king, once more. The House of York is finished, we have only the House of Lancaster. They have made a mistake which has cost them everything.' He gives a whistle and takes the letter back. 'Talk about fortune's wheel: they are thrown down to nothing.'

I go to his side and look over his shoulder at the queen's familiar scrawl on the clerk's letter. In one corner she has written, *Jacquetta, come to me at once.*

'When do we leave?' I ask. I am ashamed at my own reluctance to hear this call to arms.

'We'll have to go now,' he says.

We take the great north road to York, certain that the queen's army will be marching down to London, and we will meet them on the way. At every stop during the cold days, at every night in inns or abbeys, or the great houses, people are talking about the queen's army as if it were an invading force of foreigners, as if it were a source of terror. They say that she has soldiers from Scotland and that they march barefoot over stones, their chests naked even in the worst of weather. They are afraid of nothing and they eat their meat raw, they will run down the cattle in the fields and gouge flesh from their flanks with their bare hands. She has no money to pay them and she has promised them that they can have anything they can carry if they will take her to London and rip out the heart of the Earl of Warwick.

They say that she has given the country to the King of France in return for his support. He will sail his fleet up the Thames and lay waste to London, he will claim every port on the south coast. She has already signed over Calais to him, she has sold Berwick and Carlisle to the Scots queen. Newcastle will be the new line of the frontier, the north is lost to us forever and Cecily Neville, the York widow, will be a Scots peasant.

There is no point trying to argue with this mixture of terror and truth. The queen, a woman in armour, leading her own army, with a son conceived by a sleeping husband, a woman who uses alchemy and possibly the dark arts, a French princess in alliance with our enemies, has become an object of utter horror to the people of her country. With the Scots behind her, she has become a winter queen, one who comes out of the darkness of the north like a wolf.

We stop for two nights at Groby Hall to see Elizabeth and meet with her husband, Sir John Grey, who has mustered his men and will march north with us. Elizabeth is strained and unhappy.

'I can't bear waiting for news,' she says. 'Send to me as soon as you can. I can't bear the waiting. I wish you didn't have to go out again.'

'I wish it too,' I say softly to her. 'I've never ridden out with such a heavy heart. I am tired of war.'

'Can't you refuse to go?'

I shake my head. 'She is my queen, and she is my friend. If I did not go for duty I would go for love of her. But what about you, Elizabeth? Do you want to go and stay with the children at Grafton while we are away?'

She makes a little grimace. 'My place is here,' she says. 'And Lady Grey would not like me to be away. I am just so fearful for John.'

I put my hand on her restless fingers. 'You have to be calm. I know it is difficult, but you have to be calm and hope for the best. Your father has been out to battle a dozen times and each time it is as bad as the first – but each time he has come home to me.'

She catches my hand. 'What do you see?' she asks me very

quietly. 'What do you see for John? It is him I fear for, much more even than Anthony or Father.'

I shake my head. 'I can't foretell,' I say. 'I feel as if I am waiting for a sign, as if we all are. Who would have thought that we brought Margaret of Anjou, that pretty girl, to England for this?'

ON THE MARCH, SPRING 1461

We ride as a small troop, my son-in-law John, Richard, Anthony and me at the head of our tenants and household men. We can go no faster than their marching pace and the road is flooded in some parts and as we get further and further north it starts to snow. I think of the signs that my lord John Duke of Bedford asked me to see; I remember a vision of a battle in snow, that ended in blood, and I wonder if we are riding towards it.

Finally, on the third day, the scout that Richard has sent ahead comes cantering back and says that all the country people have bolted their doors and shutters because they believe that the queen's army is a day's march away. Richard calls a halt and we go to a manor farm to ask for a bed for the night and a barn where our men can sleep. The place is deserted, they have locked the door and abandoned the house. They would rather take to the hills than welcome the true Queen of England. We break in, and forage for food, light the fire, and order the men to stay in the barn and the yard and to steal nothing. But everything valuable has been taken away and hidden already. Whoever lived here feared the queen as a thief in the night. They left nothing for the queen and her army, they would certainly never fight for her. She has become an enemy to her own people.

At dawn the next day, we understand why. There is a great hammering on the front door and as I get out of bed there is a wild face glowering at the window, and in a moment the little pane of glass is smashed and a man is in the room, another coming through the window behind him, a knife in his teeth. I scream 'Richard!' and snatch up my knife and face them. 'I am the Duchess of Bedford, friend to the queen,' I shout.

The man says something in reply, I cannot understand a word of it. 'I am of the House of Lancaster!' I say again. I try in French: '*Je suis la duchesse de Bedford.*'

'Get ready to stand aside,' Richard says quietly behind me. 'Jump to your right when I say . . . Now.'

I fling myself to the right as he lunges forwards and the man folds over Richard's sword with a terrible gurgle. Blood gushes from his mouth, he staggers, hands out towards me, as he falls to the floor, groaning terribly. Richard puts his booted foot on the man's belly and pulls out his sword; there is a flood of scarlet blood and the man screams in pain. His comrade disappears out through the window as Richard bends down with his dagger and quickly cuts the man's throat as he would slaughter a pig.

There is a silence.

'Are you all right?' Richard asks, wiping his sword and dagger on the curtains of the bed.

I feel the vomit rising in my throat. I gag, and I put my hand over my mouth and run to the door.

'Do it there,' Richard says, pointing to the fireplace. 'I don't know if the house is safe.'

I retch into the fireplace, the smell of my vomit mingling with the smell of hot blood, and Richard pats my back. 'I've got to see what's happening outside. Lock yourself in here, and bolt the shutters. I'll send a man to guard the door.'

He is gone before I can protest. I go to the window to swing the shutter closed. Outside in the winter darkness I can see a couple of torches around the barn but I cannot tell if they are our men or the Scots. I bolt the shutters. The room is pitch black now but I can smell the dead man's blood oozing slowly from his wounds, and I feel for the bed and step around him. I am so afraid that he will reach out from hell and grasp my ankle that I can hardly get to the door and then I bolt it as Richard ordered, and, horribly, the fresh corpse and I are locked in together.

There is shouting outside and the sudden terrifying blast of a trumpet, and then I hear Richard outside the door. 'You can come out now, the queen is arriving, and they have the men back in ranks. Those were her scouts, apparently. They were on our side.'

My hands are shaking as I unbolt the door and throw it open. Richard has a torch and in its flickering light his face is grim. 'Get your cape and your gloves,' he says. 'We're falling in.'

I have to go back into the room past the dead man to get my cape, which was spread over the bed for warmth. I don't look at him, and we leave him there, unshriven, dead in his own blood with his throat cut.

'Jacquetta!' she says.

'Margaret.' We hold each other, arms wrapped around each other, cheeks warm one to the other. I feel the energy of her joy and optimism coursing through her slight body. I smell the perfume in her hair and her fur collar tickles my chin.

'I have had such adventures! You will never believe the journeys I have made. Are you safe?'

I can feel myself still trembling with shock from the violence in the bedroom. 'Richard had to kill one of your men,' I say. 'He came in my bedroom window.'

She shakes her head disapprovingly, as at a minor foible. 'Oh! They are hopeless! Good for nothing but killing people. But you must see our prince,' she says. 'He is a young man born to be king. He has been so brave. We had to ride to Wales and then take ship to Scotland. We were robbed and wrecked! You'll never believe it.'

'Margaret, the people are terrified of your army.'

'Yes, I know. They are tremendous. You will see, we have such plans!'

She is radiant, she is a woman in her power, free at last to take her power. 'I have the lords of Somerset, Exeter and Northumberland,' she says. 'The north of England is ours. We will march south and when Warwick comes out to defend London we will crush him.'

'He will be able to raise London against you,' I warn her. 'And the country is terrified of your army, not welcoming at all.'

She laughs aloud. 'I have raised the Scots and the north against him,' she says. 'They will be too afraid even to lift a weapon. I am coming like a wolf into England, Jacquetta, with an army of wolves. I am at the very height of the wheel of fortune, this is an unbeatable army because nobody will dare to take the field against them. People run from us before we even arrive, I have become a bad queen to my people, a scourge in the land, and they will be sorry that they ever raised a sword or a pitchfork against me.'

We ride south with the queen's army, the royal party at the head of the marching men, the pillaging, looting and terror going on behind us in a broad swathe that we know about, but ignore. Some of the men ride off from the main column to forage for food, breaking into barns, raiding shops and isolated little farms, demanding a levy from villages; but others are madmen, men from the north like Vikings going berserk, killing for the sake of it, stealing from churches, raping women. We bring terror to England, we are like a plague on our own people. Richard and some of the lords are deeply shamed and do what they can to impose some order on the army, controlling their own levies, demanding that the Scots fall in and march. But some of the other lords, the queen herself, and even her little boy, seem to revel in punishing the country that rejected them. Margaret is like a woman released from the bonds of honour, she is free to be anything she likes for the first time in her life, she is free of her husband, she is free of the constraints of the court, she is free of the careful manners of a French princess, she is free, at last, to be wicked.

On the second day of our march, the four of us riding at the head of the army see a lone horseman, standing by the roadside, waiting for us to come up. Richard nods to Anthony and John. 'Go and see who that is,' he says. 'Take care. I don't want to find that he's a scout and Warwick is the other side of the hill.'

My two boys canter slowly towards the man, holding the reins in their left hands, their right hands held down, outspread, to show they are holding no weapon. The man trots towards them, making the same gesture. They halt to speak briefly then all three turn and ride towards us.

The stranger is filthy from the mud of the road and his horse's coat is matted with sweat. He is unarmed, he has a scabbard at his side but he has lost his sword.

'A messenger,' Anthony says with a nod to the queen who has pulled up her horse and is waiting. 'Bad news, I am afraid, Your Grace.'

She waits, impassively, as a queen should wait for bad news.

'Edward of March has come out of Wales like a sun in winter,' the man says. 'I was there. Jasper Tudor sent me to tell you to beware the sun in splendour.'

'He never did,' my husband interrupts. 'Jasper Tudor never sent such a message in his life. Tell us what you were ordered to say, fool, and don't embroider.'

Corrected, the man straightens in his saddle. 'Tudor told me to say this: that his army is defeated and that he is in hiding. We met the York force and we lost. Sir William Herbert led the Yorks against us; Edward of March was at his side. They broke the Welsh line and rode right through us, Jasper sent me to you to warn you. He was on his way to join you when Edward blocked our path.'

The queen nods. 'Will Jasper Tudor come on to join us?'

'Half his army is dead. The Yorks are everywhere. I doubt he'll get through. He might be dead now.'

She takes a breath but says nothing.

'There was a vision,' the man offers, one eye on Richard.

'Who else saw it?' he demands irritably. 'Anyone? Or just you? Or you just think you did?'

'Everyone saw it. That's why we lost. Everyone saw it.'

'No matter,' my husband says.

'What was it?' the queen asks.

My husband sighs and rolls his eyes.

'In the sky, over Edward Earl of March, when he raised his standard, the morning sun came up, and then there were three suns. Three suns in the sky above him, the middle one shining down on him. It was like a miracle. We didn't know what it meant; but we could see he was blessed. We didn't know why.'

'Three suns,' the queen repeats. She turns to me. 'What does it mean?'

I turn away as if she might see, reflected in my eyes, the three suns I saw, dazzling on the water of the Thames. These are three suns I know, these three suns I have seen. But I did not know then what they meant, and I still don't know now.

'Some said it was the blessed Trinity honouring Edward March. But why would Father, Son and Holy Ghost bless a rebel? Some said it was him and his two living brothers, born to rise high.'

The queen looks at me. I shake my head and stay silent. I was hoping that I would see the season when the king would recover when I went out in that cold dawn and looked at the shine on the waters of the river. I was looking for the rising of my king but instead I saw three suns rising out of the mist and burning brightly.

'What does it mean?' The man asks the question in my direction, as if he expects me to know.

'Nothing,' my husband says stoutly. 'It means that there was a bright dawn and you were all dazzled by fear.' He turns back to the man. 'I don't want to know about visions, I want to know about a day's march. If Edward brings his troop due west and marches as quick as he can, when d'you think they will get to London?'

The man thinks, he is so weary he cannot calculate the days. 'A week? Three, four days?' he asks. 'He's fast. He's the fastest commander in battle I have ever seen. Could he be here tomorrow?'

That night my husband disappears from our camp, and comes back late, as the queen is about to retire. 'Your Grace, I ask permission to bring a friend to join us.'

She rises. 'Ah, Richard, you are a good man in my service. You brought me a great commander in Sir Andrew Trollope who won Ludford for us without raising his sword. Who do you have now?'

'I have to have your oath that you will forgive him for former error,' he says.

'I forgive him,' she says easily.

'He is pardoned?' Richard confirms.

'He has a royal pardon. You have my word.'

'Then, may I present Sir Henry Lovelace, who is proud to come to serve you,' he says.

She extends her hand and Richard's friend steps forwards, bows and kisses it. 'You have not always been my friend, Sir Henry,' she observes coolly.

'I didn't know then that York would try to take the crown,' he says. 'I joined him only to see the council well run. And now York is dead. I have joined you late: before your last battle and your final victory, I know. But I am proud to join you now.'

She smiles on him, she can still invoke that irresistible charm. 'I am glad to have you in my service,' she says. 'And you will be well rewarded.'

'Sir Henry says that Warwick is dug in around St Albans,' my husband tells her. 'We must defeat him before Edward March can come up and reinforce him.'

'We're not afraid of a boy of nineteen, are we? Andrew

Trollope will command my army, with you, Lord Rivers. And we will attack at once, as you suggest.'

'We'll draw up a plan,' Richard says. 'And Sir Henry will go back to Warwick and serve alongside him until we join in battle. We'll march tonight, in darkness. With good luck we will come upon them when they think we are still a day away.'

The queen smiles on him. 'I'll get ready,' she says.

We wait. The royal army with the Scots forces goes almost silently down the lane in the darkness. The Scots are barefoot, they have no horses, they can disappear into the night with no sound. They like coming unexpectedly out of the darkness to kill. Richard is at the head, our son Anthony commanding a troop, and John is leading the cavalry. The queen and I doze in our chairs, either side of a banked-in fire in the hall of the Dominican friary at Dunstable, dressed in riding clothes, ready to get to our horses and ride forwards or away, depending on the luck of the battle. She keeps the prince beside her, though he is restless, playing with his badge of the swan. He says he wants to ride with the men, he may only be seven years but he is old enough to kill his enemies. She laughs at him but never checks him.

ST ALBANS, SPRING 1461

We have to wait all day. As darkness falls, one of the queen's household comes riding back to us and says that the town is taken, St Albans is ours, and the terrible shame of our earlier defeat there is wiped out. The prince drops his livery badge and runs for his sword and the queen gives the order to her household that we can proceed. As we ride south, filled with excitement at our triumph, the guards around us, their swords drawn, we can hear the noise of battle, the erratic firing of guns with damp powder. It starts to snow, cold wet flakes which melt on our shoulders and heads. Occasionally we see men, running from the battle, coming up the road towards us, but when they catch sight of our troop, swords out at the ready, they vault over a gate and get into a field, or melt through the hedge and disappear. We can't tell if they are Warwick's men or our own.

We halt outside the town and the queen orders two scouts to go forwards. They are jubilant when they return.

'Warwick grouped his men on Nomansland Common, and was firing on our men. But then Sir Henry Lovelace led his men out of Warwick's army leaving a gap in his line, and our cavalry charged straight at it.'

The queen makes a fist of her hand and holds it to her throat. 'And?'

'We broke the line!' the man shouts.

'Huzzah!' the prince calls. 'Huzzah!'

'We broke Warwick?'

'He's sounded the retreat, he's off like a scalded cat. His men are running away or surrendering. We've won, Your Grace. We've won!'

The queen is laughing and crying at once, the prince is beside himself. He draws his little sword and whirls it round his head.

'And the king?' she says. 'My husband the king?'

'Lord Warwick brought him to the battle; but left him and all the baggage as he fled. He's here, Your Grace.'

She looks suddenly stunned. They have been apart for seven months, and she has been on the road, in hiding, or marching, for every day of their separation, living like a brigand, living like a thief; while he has been in the queen's rooms in Westminster Palace or praying in a monastery, weak as a girl. Of course she is afraid that he has lost his wits again. Of course she fears that she will be a stranger to him. 'Take me to him.' She glances back at me. 'Come with me, Jacquetta. Ride with me.'

As we ride along the road the wounded and defeated soldiers clear out of our way, heads down, their hands outspread, fearing a blow. As we get closer to the town we see the dead lying in the fields. In the High Street Warwick's crack archers are fallen among their bows, their heads cleaved open by battle axes, their bellies ripped with swords. The queen rides through it all, blind to the misery of it, and the prince rides beside her, beaming at our victory, his little sword held up before him.

They have made a camp for the queen away from the horrors of the town. The royal standard is flying over her tent, a brazier is burning inside, there are carpets down against the mud. We go into the big tent that serves as her presence chamber, a little tent behind will be her bedroom. She seats herself on her chair, I stand beside her, the prince between the two of us. For the first time in days she looks uncertain. She glances at me. 'I don't know how he will be,' is all she says. She puts her hand on the prince's shoulder. 'Take him out if his father is unwell,' she says quietly to me. 'I don't want him to see . . .'

The flap of the door opens and they bring the king inside. He is warmly dressed in a long gown and riding boots and a thick cape around his shoulders, the hood pulled up over his head. Behind him, standing in the doorway, I recognise Lord Bonville and Sir Thomas Kyriell, men who served with my first husband in France, loyal men, good men, who joined the cause of York in the early days, and stayed with the king throughout the battle to keep him safe.

'Oh,' the king says vaguely, taking in the queen and his son. 'Ah . . . Margaret.'

A shiver goes through her as she sees, we all see, that he is not well again. He can barely remember her name, he smiles distantly at the prince, who kneels to his father for his blessing. Henry puts an absent-minded hand on the young boy's head. 'Ah . . .' he says. This time he cannot find the name in his muddled mind at all. 'Ah . . . yes.'

The prince rises. He looks up at his father.

'This is Sir Thomas, and Lord Bonville,' the king says to his wife. 'They have been very good . . . very good.'

'How?' she spits.

'They kept me amused,' he says, smiling. 'While it was all going on, you know. While the noise was going on. We played marbles. I won. I liked playing when the noise was going on.'

The queen looks past him at Lord Bonville. He goes down on one knee. 'Your Grace, he is very weak,' he says quietly. 'Sometimes he doesn't know himself. We stayed with him to stop him wandering off and getting hurt. He gets lost if he's not watched. And then he gets distressed.'

She leaps to her feet. 'How dare you? This is the King of England,' she says. 'He is perfectly well.'

Bonville is silenced by the look on her face but Sir Thomas Kyriell hardly hears her, he is watching the king. He steps forwards to steady Henry who is swaying and looks as if he might fall. He guides the king into the queen's vacated chair. 'No, I am afraid he is not well,' he says gently, helping Henry to sit. 'He can't tell a hawk from a handsaw, Your Grace. He is far from us all, God bless him.'

The queen whirls around to her son in a white-faced fury. 'These lords have held your father the king prisoner,' she says flatly. 'What death would you have them die?'

'Death?' Bonville looks up, shocked.

Sir Thomas, still holding the king's hand in a comforting grip, says, 'Your Grace! We have kept him safe. We were promised safe conduct. He gave us his own word!'

'What death would you have these rebels die?' she repeats, staring at her son. 'These men, who kept your father prisoner, and now dare tell me that he is ill?'

The little boy puts his hand on the hilt of his sword as if he would like to kill them himself. 'If they were common men I would put them on the gallows,' he says in his little-boy piping voice, each word beautifully spoken as his tutor has taught him. 'But since they are lords and peers of the realm, I say they should be beheaded.'

The queen nods at her guards. 'Do as the prince says.'

'Your Grace!' Sir Thomas does not raise his voice so as not to frighten the king who is clinging to his hand.

'Don't go, Sir Thomas,' the king says. 'Don't leave me here with . . .' He glances at the queen but he cannot find her name again in his addled brain. 'We can play again,' he says as if to tempt his friend to stay with him. 'You like to play.'

'Your Grace.' Sir Thomas holds his hand and gently closes his other one over it in a warm clasp. 'I need you to tell Her Grace the queen that I have cared for you. You said that we should stay with you and we would be safe. You gave us your word! Do you remember? Don't let the queen behead us.'

The king looks confused. 'I did?' he asks. 'Oh yes, I did. I promised them they would be safe. Er – Margaret, you won't hurt these men, will you?'

She has a face of ice. 'Not at all,' she says to him. 'You have nothing to worry about.' And to the guard she says, 'Take them out.'

I whisper urgently. 'Margaret – they have his word.'

'Three fools together,' she hisses. To the guards she nods again. 'Take them out.'

We have lodgings in the dorter house of the abbey of St Albans, overlooking the frozen orchard. The fighting was in the streets around the abbey and many of the wounded are coming in to the chapter house and the barns, where the nuns are caring for them, and the monks carrying them out for burial when they die. I have managed to get a tub for Richard and he is washing himself with jugs of water. He has taken a wound to his sword arm and I have sponged it with thyme water from home, and bandaged it tightly. Anthony, thank God, is unhurt.

'Where's John?' I ask. 'Is he with the cavalry?'

Richard has his back to me as he gets out of the tub, dripping water all over the floor. I cannot see his face. 'No.'

'Where is he?'

His silence alerts me. 'Richard, is he hurt? Richard? Is he here in the abbey?'

'No.'

I'm afraid now. 'Where is he? He's not hurt? I must go to him. I should send to Elizabeth, I promised her I would.'

Richard ties a sheet around his waist, wincing slightly. He sits down by the little fire. 'I am sorry, Jacquetta. He's dead.'

'Dead?' I say stupidly.

'Yes.'

'John?' I repeat.

He nods.

'But the cavalry broke Warwick's line, they won the battle for us. The cavalry won this battle.'

'John was in the lead. He took a spear in the belly. He's dead.'

I sink down onto the stool. 'This will break Elizabeth's heart,' I say. 'Dear God. He is nothing but a boy. And you have come through unscathed so many times!'

'It's luck,' he says. 'He wasn't lucky, that's all. He was unlucky, God save him. Did you foresee it at all?'

'I never foresaw a future for them,' I say bitterly. 'But I said nothing and I let her marry him though I could see nothing ahead for the two of them. But it was a good match and I wanted her well married and rich. I should have warned her, I should have warned him. I have the Sight sometimes; but I might as well be blind.'

He leans forwards and takes my hand. 'It's just fortune,' he says. 'A cruel goddess. Will you write to Elizabeth? I can send a man with a message.'

'I'll go to her,' I say. 'I can't bear that she should hear this from anyone but me. I'll go and tell her myself.'

I leave St Albans at dawn and ride through the fields. I sleep one night in an abbey and one in an inn. It is a weary journey but the grey skies and the muddy lanes match my mood. I am part of a victorious army on a winning campaign but I have never before felt so defeated. I think of the two lords on their knees before Margaret and the enmity in her face. I think of her son, our little prince, and his boyish treble when he ordered two good men to be killed. I ride blindly, hardly seeing the way. I know myself to be losing my faith.

It takes me two days to get to the little village of Groby and as I ride in through the great gates of the Hall, I wish I was not there. Elizabeth herself opens the door, and as soon as she sees me, she knows why I have come.

'Is he wounded?' she asks; but I see that she knows he is dead. 'Have you come to fetch me?'

'No, I am sorry, Elizabeth.'

'Not wounded?'

'He is dead.'

I had thought she would collapse but she takes the blow and then straightens herself and stands very tall. 'And have we lost again?' she asks impatiently, as if it means nothing either way.

I get down from my horse and throw the reins at a groom. 'Feed him and water him and rub him down,' I say. 'I have to leave the day after tomorrow.' To Elizabeth I say, 'No, dearest. We won. Your husband led the charge that broke Warwick's line. He was very brave.'

She looks at me, her grey eyes blank with misery. 'Brave? D'you think it was worth it? This victory in this little battle, another battle, another little victory in exchange for him?'

'No,' I say honestly. 'For there will be another battle and your father and Anthony will have to fight in it again. It goes on and on.'

She nods. 'Will you come and tell his mother?'

I step over the threshold into the warm shadows of Groby Hall and know that I will have to do the worst, the very worst thing that one woman can do to another: tell her that her son is dead.

When I get back to St Albans I find most of the town empty, the shops gutted and the houses barred. The townspeople are terrified of the queen's army, which has looted all the valuables and foraged all the food for an area of ten miles all around the town. 'Thank God you're back,' Richard says to me, helping me from my horse in the front yard of the abbey. 'It is like trying to command the enemy. The monks have left the abbey, the townspeople have fled from the town. And the Lord Mayor of London has sent for you.'

'For me?'

'He wants you and the Duchess of Buckingham to meet him and agree whether the king and the queen can enter London.'

I look at him blankly. 'Richard, London has to admit the King and Queen of England.'

'They won't,' he says flatly. 'They have heard what it is like here. The merchants won't have this army anywhere near their warehouses, shops and daughters, if they can possibly prevent it. It's as simple as that. What you have to do is to see if you can get an agreement that they let the king and queen into Westminster Palace with their household, and feed and quarter the army outside.'

'Why me? Why not the master of the queen's household? Or the king's confessor?'

His smile is bitter. 'It is an honour for you, actually. The Londoners don't trust anyone. Not anyone of her army or of the king's advisors. They trust you because they remember you coming into London as the pretty duchess, all that long time ago. They remember you in the Tower when Jack Cade came in. They remember you at Sandwich when Warwick took you. They think they can trust you. And you can meet the Duchess of Buckingham there.'

He puts his arm around my waist and his mouth to my ear. 'Can you do this, Jacquetta? If you can't, say the word and we go back to Grafton.'

I lean against him for a moment. 'I am sick of it,' I say quietly. 'I am sick of the fighting and I am sick of the death and I don't think she can be trusted with the throne of England. I don't know what to do. I thought of it all the way to Groby and all the way back again, and I don't know what I think or where my duty lies. I can't foresee the future and I can't even say what we should do tomorrow.'

His face is grim. 'This is my house,' he says simply. 'My father served the House of Lancaster and I have too. My son follows me. But this is hard on you, my love. If you want to go home you should go. The queen will have to release you. If London bars the gates on her, it is her own doing.'

'Would they really lock her out of her own city?'

He nods. 'She's not loved, and her army is a terror.'

'Did they ask for no-one else to speak for her?'

He smiles wryly. 'Only the pretty duchess will do.'

'Then I must do it,' I decide reluctantly. 'London has to admit the King and Queen of England. What will become of the country if they close the gates to their own king? We have won the battle, she is Queen of England, we have to be able to enter London.'

'Can you go now?' he asks. 'For I imagine that Warwick has met up with his friend Edward March and they will be coming towards us. We should get the king and queen into the Tower of London and in possession of the City at once. Then they can parley or they can fight. But we have to hold the kingdom.'

I look at the stable yard where the cavalry horses nod their heads over the stalls. One of them will be John Grey's horse, without his rider, now and for ever.

'I can go now,' I say.

He nods. They bring me out a fresh horse, Richard helps me into the saddle. The door behind us opens from the abbey and the queen comes out.

'I knew you'd go for me,' she says to me with her sweetest smile. 'Agree to anything for me. We have to get into London before Edward gets here.'

'I'll do what I can,' I say. 'How is His Grace today?'

She nods to the abbey. 'Praying,' she says. 'If wars were won by prayers we would have won a hundred times over. And see if you can get them to send us some food. I can't keep my army from raiding.' She looks at Richard. 'I've issued orders but the officers cannot command them.'

'The devil from hell couldn't command them,' Richard says grimly. He puts his hand on my knee and looks up at me. 'I'll be waiting for you,' he promises. 'Anthony will lead your guard. You'll be safe.'

I glance over to where Anthony is mounting into his saddle.

He throws me a smiling salute. 'Come on then,' I say. Anthony shouts a command to our guard and we ride out of the abbey courtyard, south down the road to London.

We meet Anne the Duchess of Buckingham and her little train a few miles from the City. I smile at the duchess and she nods at me, a little toss of her head that shows me that she can hardly believe we are suing for the royal family to enter their capital. She has lost a son in this war, her lined face is weary. She leads the way to Bishopsgate where the Lord Mayor and the aldermen come out to meet us. They don't want to admit us, not even over the threshold. The duchess sits up high on her horse with a face like thunder, but I get down and the Lord Mayor kisses my hand and the aldermen pull off their bonnets and bow their heads as I smile around at them. Behind them I see the London merchants and the great men of the City; these are the men I have to persuade.

I tell them that the king and queen, the royal family of England with their son the prince, require entry to their own house, in their own city. Are these men going to deny their own anointed king the right to sit on his own throne or sleep in his own bed?

I see them mutter among themselves. The sense of ownership of property is a powerful argument to these men, who have worked so hard to earn their beautiful houses. Is the prince to be denied the right to walk in his father's garden?

'His own father denied him!' someone calls out from the back. 'King Henry hasn't slept in his own bed or sat on his own chair since he handed it all over to the Duke of York! And the queen took to her heels. They gave away their palace, not us. It's their own fault they are not at home.'

I start again, addressing the Lord Mayor but speaking clearly enough so that they can hear me beyond the stone arch of the gate, in the streets beyond. I say that the women of the City know the queen should be admitted to raise the prince in her own palace; a woman has a right to her own home. That the king should be master in his own house.

Someone laughs at the mention of the king, and shouts a bawdy joke that he has never been master in his own house and probably not master in his own bed. I see that the months of York's rule have left them certain that the king has no powers, that he is unfit to rule as the York lords said.

'I would send the queen's army the food they need,' the Lord Mayor says to me in an undertone. 'Please assure Her Grace of that. I had the wagons ready to leave but the citizens stopped me. They're very afraid of the Scots in her army. What we hear is terrifying. In short, they won't let them in, and they won't allow me to send supplies.'

'People are leaving the City,' an alderman steps forwards to tell me. 'Closing up their houses and going to France, and she's only at St Albans. Nobody will stay in London if she comes any closer. The Duchess of York has sent her boys George and Richard to Flanders for their safe-keeping, and this is the duchess who surrendered to her once before! Now she swears that she won't again. Nobody trusts her, everyone fears her army.'

'There is nothing to fear,' I insist. 'Let me make you an offer: how would this be? How would it be if the queen agrees to leave the army outside? Then you could let the royal family in, and their household with them. The king and queen have to be safe in the Tower of London. You cannot deny them that.'

He turns to the senior aldermen and they mutter together. 'I am asking this in the name of the King of England,' I say. 'You all swore to be loyal to him. Now he asks that you admit him into your city.'

'If the king will guarantee our safety' – the Lord Mayor turns to me – 'we will admit the king and the royal family and their household. But not the Scots. And the king and the queen have to promise that the Scots will be kept outside the walls, and that the City will not be sacked. Four of us will come with you, to tell the queen this.'

Anthony, who has been standing behind me, rigid as any commander, silent while I do my work, cups his hands for my foot and helps me into the saddle. He holds my horse as the Lord Mayor comes close for a quiet word. I lean down to hear him.

'Has the poor king stopped weeping?' he asks. 'When he was living here under the command of the Duke of York, he wept all the time. He went to Westminster Abbey and measured out the space for his own tomb. They say he never smiled but cried all the time like a sorrowful child.'

'He is happy with the queen and with his son,' I say steadily, hiding my embarrassment at this report. 'And he is strong, and issuing orders.' I do not say that the order was to end the looting of the abbey and town of St Albans, and that it had no effect at all.

'Thank you for coming here today, Your Grace,' he says, stepping back.

'God bless the pretty duchess!' someone shouts from the crowd. I laugh and raise my hand.

'I remember when you were the most beautiful woman in England,' a woman says from the shadow of the gate.

I shrug. 'Truly, I think my daughter is now,' I say.

'Well, God bless her pretty face, bring her to London so we can all see her,' somebody jokes.

Anthony swings into his saddle and gives the command, the four aldermen fall in behind me and the duchess, and together we head north to tell the queen that the City will let them in, but will never admit her army.

We find the queen with the royal household, now advanced to Barnet – just eleven miles north of London, dangerously close, as the aldermen riding with us remark. She has hand-picked the troops who are advancing with her; the worst of the northern raiders are kept at some distance, at Dunstable, where they are amusing themselves by tearing the town apart.

'Half of them have simply deserted,' Richard says to me gloomily as we go to the queen's presence chamber. 'You can't blame them. We couldn't feed them and she had said outright that she would never pay them. They got sick of waiting to get into London and have gone home. God help the villages that lie in their path.'

The queen commands that the aldermen and the duchess and I go back to London and demand entrance for the royal family and a household of four hundred men. 'That's all!' she says irritably to me. 'Surely you can make them admit me with an entourage which Richard, Duke of York, would have considered a nothing!'

We ride at the head of the household troops and we get to Aldgate where the Lord Mayor meets us again.

'Your Grace, I cannot let you in,' he says, nervously eyeing the troops who are standing in ranks behind me, Richard at their head. 'I would do so if it were left to me, but the citizens of London won't have the queen's men in their streets.'

'These are not the northern men,' I say reasonably. 'Look, they wear the livery of the Lancaster lords, men who have come and gone through the city for all time. See, they are commanded by my husband, a lord you know well. You can trust them, you can trust the queen when she has given her word. And there are only four hundred.'

He looks down at the cobbles below his feet, up at the sky above us, at the men behind me, he looks anywhere but into my eyes. 'Truth is,' he says finally, 'the city doesn't want the queen here, or the king, or the prince. They don't want any of them. Sworn to peace or not.'

For a moment I can hardly argue. I too have thought that I wanted neither queen nor king nor prince in my life. But who is there, if not them? 'She is the Queen of England,' I say flatly.

'She is our ruin,' he replies bitterly. 'And he is a holy fool. And the prince is none of his begetting. I am sorry, Lady Rivers, I am sorry indeed. But I cannot open the gates to the queen nor to any of her court.'

There is a shout and a noise of running feet coming to the

gate. The troops behind me grasp their weapons and I hear Richard order 'Steady!' as Anthony takes one swift step to stand beside me, his hand on the hilt of his sword.

A man runs to the Lord Mayor and whispers urgently in his ear. He rounds on me, his face suddenly flushed red with rage. 'Did you know of this?'

I shake my head. 'No. Whatever it is. I know of nothing. What's happening?'

'While we are standing here, talking to you, the queen has sent a party to raid Westminster.'

There's a roar of anger from the crowd. 'Hold ranks, steady,' Richard shouts at our guard. 'Close up.'

'I did not know,' I say quickly to the Lord Mayor. 'I swear on my honour I did not know. I would not so have betrayed you.'

He shakes his head at me. 'She is faithless and a danger, and we want no more of her,' he says. 'She used you to divert us and try to take us by force. She is faithless. Tell her to go away and take her soldiers with her. We will never admit her. Make her go away, Duchess, help us. Get rid of her. Save London. You take the queen from our door.' He bows to me and turns on his heel. 'Duchess, we are counting on you to deliver us from that she-wolf,' he shouts as he runs under the great gateway. We stand in our ranks as the big doors of Aldgate are pushed shut, slammed tight in our faces, and then we hear the bolts shooting home.

We march north. It seems that though we won the last battle we are losing England. Behind us, the City of London throws open the gates to the young Edward, the Duke of York's oldest son and heir, and they take him to the throne and proclaim him King of England.

'It means nothing,' the queen says as I ride beside her up the north road. 'I am not troubled by it.'

'He's crowned king,' Richard says quietly to me that night. 'It means that London closed its doors to us but admitted him and crowned him king. It means something.'

'I feel that I failed her. I should have been able to persuade them to let her in.'

'When she had sent her soldiers around to Westminster? You were lucky to get us out without a riot. You failed her, perhaps, but you saved London, Jacquetta. No other woman could have done it.'

YORK, SPRING 1461

The king, the queen, the prince and the members of their household are housed in York, the royal family at the abbey, the rest of us wherever in the city that we can find rooms. Richard and Anthony ride out almost straight away with the army commanded by the Duke of Somerset, to block the road north and prepare the stand against Warwick and the boy who now calls himself king: Cecily Neville's handsome son, Edward.

The king rises to the danger he is in, his wits sharpened on the ride, and writes a letter to Edward's army reproaching them for rebellion, and commanding them to come over to our side. The queen rides out every day with the prince, calling on men to leave their villages and their occupations and join the army and defend the country against the rebels and their rebel leader, the false king.

Andrew Trollope, the royals' best general, advises that the army should make its stand on a ridge, some fourteen miles south of York. He puts Lord Clifford as an advance guard to prevent the Yorks crossing the River Aire, and Clifford tears the bridge down, so that when the young Edward marches up the road from London there is no way across. Boldly, Edward orders his men into the water, and as the snow falls on them in the swirling current in the evening light, they work on the bridge, up to their waists in freezing water with the winter floods running strong. It is easy work for Lord Clifford to ride down on them, kill Lord Fitzwalter and wipe out the troop. Richard sends me a note:

Edward's inexperience has cost him dear. We have sprung the first trap, he can come on to Towton and see what we have for him here.

Then I wait for more news. The queen comes to York Castle and we both put on our capes and go up Clifford's Tower. The armies are too far away for us to see anything, and the light is failing, but we both look south.

'Can't you wish him dead?' she asks. 'Can't you strike him down?'

'Warwick?' I ask.

She shakes her head. 'Warwick would change his coat, I know it. No, curse that boy Edward, who dares to call himself king.'

'I don't know how to do such things, and I never wanted to know. I'm not a witch, Margaret, I'm not even much of a wise woman. If I could do anything right now I would make my son and husband invulnerable.'

'I would curse Edward,' she says. 'I would throw him down.'

I think of the boy the same age as my son, the handsome golden-haired boy, the pride of Duchess Cecily's heart. I think of him losing his temper in Calais, but his quick flush of shame when I told him that we had guarded his mother. I think of him bowing over my hand outside the queen's rooms in Westminster. 'I have a liking for him,' I say. 'I wouldn't ill-wish him. Besides, someone else will kill him for you, before the day is out. There has been enough killing, God knows.'

She shivers and pulls up her hood. 'It's going to snow,' she says. 'It's late in the year for snow.'

We go to the abbey for dinner and the king leads her in through the great hall filled with his household. 'I have written to Edward Earl of March,' he says in his fluting voice. 'I have asked for a truce for tomorrow. It is Palm Sunday, he cannot think of fighting a battle on Palm Sunday. It is the day of Our Lord's entry into Jerusalem. He must want to be at prayer. We will all be at prayer on such a holy day, it is God's will.'

The queen exchanges a quick look with me.

'Has he replied?' I ask.

He casts his eyes down. 'I am sorry to say that he refused a truce,' he says. 'He will risk the fortunes of war, on the very day that Our Lord went into Jerusalem. Edward thinks to ride out on the very morning that Our Lord rode to His holy city. He must be a very hardened young man.'

'He's very bad,' Margaret says, biting down on her irritation. 'But it must be to our advantage.'

'I shall order the Duke of Somerset not to give battle,' the king tells us. 'Our men should not make war on a Sunday, not on Palm Sunday. They must just stand in their ranks to show our faith in God. If Edward charges they must turn the other cheek.'

'We have to defend ourselves,' the queen says quickly. 'And God will bless us all the more for defending ourselves against such a faithless act.'

The king considers. 'Perhaps Somerset should withdraw until Monday?'

'He has a good position, Your Grace,' I say gently. 'Perhaps we should wait and see what is the outcome. You have offered a holy truce – that must be enough.'

'I shall ask the bishop for his view,' the king says. 'And I shall pray tonight for guidance. I shall pray all night.'

The king performs his vigil in the minster, the monks from the abbey coming and going in the great church as he prays. I go to bed but I am wakeful too; I cannot sleep for thinking of Richard and Anthony, out all night in the cold, a north wind blowing snow, with a battle coming tomorrow on a holy day.

In the morning the sky is heavy and white as if the clouds are pressing down on the very walls of the city. At about nine o'clock it starts to snow, great white flakes swirling round in dizzy circles and lying on the frozen ground. The city seems to huddle down under the snowflakes, which come thicker and thicker.

I go to the queen's rooms and find her prowling around, her hands tucked in her sleeves for warmth. The king is praying at the abbey, she is giving orders for their goods to be packed up again. 'If we win we will advance on London and this time they will open the gates to me. Otherwise . . . ' She does not finish the sentence, and both of us cross ourselves.

I go to the window. I can hardly see the city walls, the snow is blinding, it is a blizzard blowing around and around. I put my hand over my eyes, I have a memory of a vision of a battle uphill in snow, but I cannot see the standards and I do not know, when the snow turns red, whose blood is staining the slush.

We wait, all day we wait for news. One or two men come limping into York with wounds to be dressed and they say that we had a good position on the hillside but the snow made it hard for the archers, and impossible for the cannon. 'He always has bad weather,' the queen remarks. 'The boy Edward always fights in bad weather. He always has a storm behind him. You would think he was born of bad weather.'

They serve dinner in the hall but there is almost no-one there to eat – just the household staff who are too old or too frail to be pressed into service or are maimed from earlier battles in the queen's service. I look at a serving man who is deft with his one remaining arm and I shudder as I think of my whole-limbed son, somewhere out in the snow, facing a cavalry charge.

The queen sits proudly at the centre of the high table, her son at her side, and makes a tableau of eating. I am at the head of the table of her ladies and I push some ragout around my plate for the entire meal. Anyone who does not have a husband or a son or a brother in the field called North Acres eats with a good appetite. The rest of us are sick to our bellies with fear.

In the afternoon a steady stream of men start to come in from the battle, the ones who can still walk. They tell of hundreds dying on the road to York, thousands dead on the battlefield. The abbey hospital, the poor men's hospital, the leper hospital, all the sanctuaries and hostels throw open their doors and start to strap on rough bandages, pack wounds, and amputate. Mostly they start to stack dead bodies for burial. It is like a charnel house in York, the south gate sees a constant flow of men staggering like drunkards, bleeding like stuck calves. I want to go down to look in every face, for fear that I will see Richard or Anthony glaring sightlessly back, his face blown away by one of the new handguns or smashed to a pulp by an axe; but I make myself sit by the window in the queen's apartments, some sewing in my hands, always listening for the roar and rumble of an approaching army.

It gets dark; surely the day is over? Nobody can fight in the dark, but the bells toll for compline and still nobody comes to tell us that we have won. The king is on his knees in the abbey, he has been there since nine this morning and it is now nine o'clock at night. The queen sends his grooms of the bedchamber to fetch him from his prayers, feed him, and put him to bed. She and I wait up, by a dying fire, her feet up on her travelling box of jewels, her travelling cape laid over the chair beside her.

We sit up all night, and at dawn, in the cold light of the earliest spring morning, there is a bang on the door of the abbey and Margaret starts up. We hear the porter slowly opening the door and a voice asking for the queen. Margaret snatches up her cloak and goes down. 'Wake the king,' she says to me as she goes.

I run to the king's apartments and shake his grooms of the bedchamber awake. 'News from the battle, get His Grace ready to leave,' I say shortly. 'Now.'

Then I hurry down to the great entrance hall and there is a man in Clifford livery on his knees before the queen.

She turns her white face to me and for a moment I see the frightened girl that would not marry on her wedding day unless someone told her future. I did not foresee this, then. I wish I had been able to warn her. 'We have lost,' she says bleakly.

I step forwards. 'My husband?' I ask. 'My son?'

The man shakes his head. 'I don't know, Your Grace. There were too many to see. The field was covered in dead, it was as if everyone in England was dead. I have never seen ...' He puts his hands over his eyes. 'Some of them were getting away over a little bridge,' he said. 'The Yorks came after them and there was fighting on the bridge and then it broke and they all went into the waters, Lancaster, Yorks, all in together, and they drowned in their heavy armour. The meadow is covered in corpses, the river, filled with men, is running red. The snow is falling on everything like tears.'

'Your lord,' Margaret whispers. 'Lord Clifford.'

'Dead.'

'My commander, Sir Andrew Trollope.'

'Dead. And Lord Welles, and Lord Scrope. Hundreds of lords, thousands of soldiers. It looks like the final day when the dead come from the ground but they are not moving. They are not rising up. Every man in England is down. The wars must be over now, for every man in England is dead.'

I go to her and take her icy hand. The king comes down the stairs and looks at the two of us, hand-clasped, horrified.

'We have to go,' Margaret says. 'We have lost a battle.'

He nods. 'I did warn him,' he says irritably. 'I did not want fighting on a holy day; but he would not be warned.'

Behind him, down the stairs, come the grooms of the household carrying his Bible and his crucifix, his prayer stool and his altar. Margaret's clothes and her crate of furs follow.

We go out into the yard. 'Come with me?' she asks, like a girl again. 'I don't want to go alone.'

Not for a moment do I think I will go with her. I will leave her now, even if I never see her again in all my life. 'I have to look for Richard, and Anthony,' I say. I can hardly speak. 'I will have to go out and find their bodies. I may have to see them buried. Then I will go to my children.'

She nods. The horses are saddled and ready, they put the goods into a wagon, her jewels are strapped behind her on her horse. The prince is in the saddle already, dressed warmly in his riding cape with his bonnet on his head, his swan badge pinned at the front. 'We will be avenged for this,' he says cheerfully to me. 'I will see the traitors dead. I swear it.'

I shake my head. I am sick of vengeance.

They lift Margaret into the saddle and I go to stand near her. 'Where will you go?'

'We'll regroup,' she says. 'They can't all be dead. We'll raise more men. I'll get more money from Scotland, from France. I have the king, I have the prince, we will come back and I will put Edward March's head on the spike at Micklegate Bar beside his father's rotting face. I'll never stop,' she says. 'Not while I have my son. He was conceived to be king, he was born to be king, I have raised him to be king.'

'I know,' I say. I step back and she holds up her hand to give the signal for them to ride out. She waves them out, and then she tightens her grip on the reins and looks down at me, her face warm with love. She holds out her hand, she extends her finger, in the air she makes the sign for the wheel of fortune, then she clicks to her horse and digs in her heels, and she is gone.

All day more and more men come hobbling into the city, looking for food, looking for someone to strap their wounds. I wrap myself in my cape and get my horse from the stables and ride, in the opposite direction to all the others of the royal court: I ride south down the road to Towton, looking in the faces of all the hundreds and hundreds of men that I pass, for someone I recognise. I am hoping to see Richard or Anthony, I am afraid when I see a man hopping with a makeshift crutch, I freeze when I see a brown curly head face down in a ditch, a congealing patch of blood in the hair. I ride down the road with one man to go before me, and every time we meet a man on horseback, head down, slumped in the saddle, I ask him if he has seen Lord Rivers, or if he knows what happened to his company. Nobody knows.

I start to see that it was a long, long battle, fought in snow so thick that nobody could see further than the end of their sword. Enemies loomed up out of a white blindness and thrust blindly and were blindly cut down. The Lancastrian archers were firing against the wind into driving snow and missed their mark. The Yorks, with the wind behind them, fired uphill and scythed down the Lancaster men, waiting to charge. When the lines met they barged and stabbed and hacked at each other, not knowing what they were doing nor who was winning. One man tells me that, when night fell, half of the survivors dropped down on the bat- tlefield and slept among the dead, covered with snow as if they were all to be buried together.

The road is crowded with men, so many men, so bedraggled in their livery or working clothes that I cannot tell one from another and their sheer numbers and misery force me off the road so I stand in a gateway and gaze at them as they go by. It seems as if it will never end, this procession of men who have escaped death but are still bloodstained, and bruised, and wet with snow.

'Lady Mother? Lady Mother?'

I can hear his voice, and for a moment I think I am imagining it. 'Anthony?' I say disbelievingly. I slide down from my horse and stumble forwards until I am almost submerged in the sea of wounded men who barge towards me and jostle me. I pull at their arms and look into their shocked grey faces. 'Anthony? Anthony!'

From a group of men he steps out. My gaze rakes him from head to foot in an instant, taking in his weary eyes, his grim smile, his unharmed body. He is holding his arms out to me and his hands, his precious hands, are whole, he is not missing a finger, his arms are not slashed to the bone. He is standing upright. His helmet is off and his face, though grey with weari- ness, is unmarked. 'Are you all right?' I ask incredulously. 'My son? Are you all right? Have you got through this unhurt?'

His smile has lost its joyous light. 'I'm safe,' he says. 'I thank

God who guarded me the whole long night and day. What are you doing here? It's like hell, here.'

'Looking for you,' I say. 'And ... Anthony, where is your father?'

'Oh!' he exclaims, realising what I am thinking. 'Oh no, don't, Mother. He is fine. He's not injured. He's just ...' He looks around. 'Here he is.'

I turn and there is Richard. I would hardly have recognised him. His breastplate is dented across his heart, his face blackened with smoke and blood, but he walks towards me, as he always walks towards me, as if nothing could ever separate us.

'Richard,' I whisper.

'Beloved,' he says hoarsely.

'You're safe?'

'I always come home to you.'

We go west, to get away from the road to York which is choked with men falling to their knees and crying for water, and lined with those who have fallen out to die. We ride cross-country across the broad plain of York until we find a farmhouse where they allow us to sleep in the barn, wash in the stream, and sell us food. We eat farmer's broth: a speck of overstewed mutton with gruel and carrots, and we drink their small ale.

When he has eaten and is looking less drained I ask, tentatively for I fear his reply, 'Richard, the queen is going north to regroup, and then on to Scotland to raise more recruits, and then she says she will come back. What are we going to do?'

There is a silence. Anthony and my husband exchange a long look as if they have been dreading what they are about to say.

'What is it?' I look from one to the other. 'What has happened?'

'We're finished,' Anthony volunteers. 'I am sorry, Lady Mother. I have handed in my sword. I have sworn loyalty to York.'

I am stunned. I turn to Richard.

'I too,' he says. 'I would not serve the queen again, not in such an army, not under such a command. But anyway, we lost on the battlefield, we handed in our swords and surrendered. I thought

Edward would have us executed but –' He has a ghost of a smile. 'He was merciful to us. He took our swords from us, I am dishonoured. I am no longer a knight, I am sorry. We swore fealty to him, and it is over for us. I cannot take arms against him. I was defeated, I surrendered my sword. I am sworn to the House of York. I cannot serve Henry or Margaret: they are outlaws now to me.'

It is his use of their names that shakes me as much as anything, that tells me that everything is over, and everything is changed. 'Henry,' I repeat as if saying the name for the very first time. 'You call the king Henry.'

'The king's name is Edward,' my husband says as if repeating a lesson. 'King Edward.'

I shake my head. Even though I had ridden all day against the tide of wounded men, I had not thought of our cause as lost. I have been with Margaret for so long that I can think only in terms of battles. I thought that we had lost another battle, but that there would be yet another battle after this. Now, as I look at my husband's weary face and the hollow eyes of my son, I say, 'You think that Henry and Margaret will never win back the throne?'

He shows me his empty scabbard, where his beautifully embossed sword used to be. 'I cannot help them to it, at any rate,' he says. 'I have surrendered my sword to the new king. I am sworn.'

'We are no longer of the House of Lancaster?' I am still incredulous.

Anthony nods. 'It's over,' he says. 'And we are lucky to have escaped with our heads on our necks.'

'That's all that matters,' I say, grasping at a truth. 'That must be all that matters, at the very end. You are alive, and your father. At any rate, that's what matters most to me.'

We lie, that night, like a poor family, in the straw together under our heaped capes for warmth, our small troop of men in the stable with our horses. Richard's arm is around me, all the night long. 'We'll go to Grafton,' I whisper as I fall asleep. 'And we will be squires again, and we will think of all of this as a romance, a story that someone might write one day.'

GRAFTON, NORTHAMPTONSHIRE, SPRING 1464

I gather my children about me and Elizabeth comes home with her two boys from Groby Hall. She is all but penniless; her mother-in-law will not pay her dower and in these troubled times we have neither power nor influence to make her keep her side of the marriage contract which gave me such pride and pleasure only a few years ago, and now means nothing.

Richard and Anthony are given official pardons and appointed to the Privy Council. The new king turns out to be an astute commander of men, a king for all parties. He rules with the advice of the Earl of Warwick who put him on the throne, but he calls as many of the lords into government as will come. He does not favour York lords, he truly seems to want to be a king for all the people of the country. A few lords go into exile, a few are with the queen, sometimes in Scotland, sometimes in France, forever raising forces, threatening England, planning a return. I think I will never see her again, the pretty French girl who would not marry until I had told her what her destiny would be. It has been the wheel of fortune indeed. She was the greatest woman in England and now she cannot have so much as a roof over her head in her own country; but she is hunted down like the last wolf.

I hardly ever hear of her, my news is all of the parish and the gossip is all from the neighbouring town. I see my son Anthony married to Elizabeth, Lady Scales, I start to consider suitable partners for my other children; but we do not command the wealth and the power that we had when Margaret of Anjou was on the throne and I was her dearest friend and lady in waiting, and my husband one of the great men of court. Now we are only squires of Grafton and though I find I am interested in my growing orchard, and even more in my children and grandsons, it is hard for me to look at other small country squires and think that my children should be married among them. I expect more for them. I want more for them.

Especially for my Elizabeth.

One day in spring, I go to the great chest in my bedroom, and I take out the purse that my great-aunt Jehanne gave me, all those years ago. I look at the charms, and at all the choices that there might be in the world for Elizabeth: a young woman – but not in the first blush of her youth; a beauty – but not a maiden; a clever scholarly girl – but not with the faith to make an abbess. I choose the charm of a ship to signify that she might travel, I choose the charm of a little house to signify that she might win her dower lands and get a house for herself, and I am about to choose a third charm, when one of them breaks from the bracelet and falls into my lap. It is a ring for a small finger curiously wrought in the shape of a crown. I hold it up to the light and look at it. I start to try it on my own finger and then I hesitate. I don't want it on my finger, I don't know what it means. I tie it on a long black thread, and tie the other two on their own long black threads and I go out of the house as the early silver moon starts to rise in the pale sky.

'Can we come with you, Lady Grandmother?' Her boys appear from nowhere, mud on their faces as usual. 'Where are you going with that basket?'

'You can't come with me,' I say. 'I am looking for plover eggs. But I will take you tomorrow if I find a nest.'

'Can't we come now?' asks Thomas, Elizabeth's oldest boy.

I put my hand on his head, his warm silky curls remind me of Anthony when he was a loving little boy like this one. 'No. You must find your mother and eat your supper and go to bed when she orders you. But I will take you with me tomorrow.'

I leave them and go across the gravel garden at the front of the house, through the wicket gate and down to the river. There is a little bridge across the river, a couple of small wooden planks where the children like to come to fish, and I go across, ducking my head under the upturned branches of the ash tree, and scramble down the little bank to the trunk of the tree.

I put my arms around the tree to tie the three strings around it, and my cheek lies against the rippled grey bark. For a moment I listen. Almost I can hear the heart of the tree beating. 'What will become of Elizabeth?' I whisper, and it is almost as if the leaves can whisper back to me. 'What will become of my Elizabeth?'

I have never been able to foresee her future, even though of all my children she has always been the one that promised so much. I have always thought she might be especially blessed. I wait; the leaves rustle. 'Well, I don't know,' I say to myself. 'Perhaps the stream will tell us.'

Each charm is now tied to the tree by its own long dark string and when I throw them out into the water, as far as they can go, I hear three splashes like a salmon snapping a fly, and they are gone, and the threads are invisible.

I stand for a moment and look into the moving water. 'Elizabeth,' I say quietly to the stream. 'Tell me what will become of Elizabeth, my daughter.'

At dinner that night my husband says that the king is recruiting soldiers for a new battle. He will be marching north. 'You won't have to go?' I say in sudden alarm. 'Nor Anthony?'

'We'll have to send men, but to be honest, my dear, I don't think they would especially want us in the line.'

Anthony gives a rueful chuckle. 'Like Lovelace,' he says, and his father laughs.

'Like Trollope.'

'I should ask King Edward to enquire into my dower,' Elizabeth remarks. 'For sure my boys will have nothing unless I can find someone who will make Lady Grey keep her promise to me.'

'Kidnap him as he rides by,' Anthony suggests. 'Fall on your knees to him.'

'My daughter will do no such thing,' my husband rules. 'And we can provide for you here, until you reach agreement with Lady Grey.'

Elizabeth sensibly holds her tongue, but the next day, I see her wash her boys' hair and dress them in their Sunday suits and I say nothing. I splash a little perfume of my own brewing on the veil of her headdress, but I give her neither apple blossom nor apple. I believe there is not a man in the world who could ride past my daughter and not stop and ask her name. She puts on her plain grey gown and sets off from the house holding her boys firmly by their hands, walking down the track to the road from London, where the king is certain to ride by with his troop.

I watch her go, a pretty young woman on a warm spring day, and it is like a dream to see her, stepping lightly down the lane between the hedges where the white roses are coming into flower. She is walking out to her future, to claim her own, though I still don't know what her future will be.

I go to the still room, and take down a small jar, sealed tight with a waxed cork. It is a love philtre I made for Anthony's wedding night. I take it to the brew house and put three drops in a jug of our best ale, and take it to the great hall, with our best glasses, and then I wait, quietly with the spring sunshine coming through the mullioned windows and a blackbird singing in the tree outside.

I don't have to wait very long. I look down the road and there is Elizabeth, smiling and laughing, and walking beside her is the handsome boy that I first saw outside the queen's rooms when he bowed over my hand so politely. Now he is a grown man and the King of England. He is leading his great war horse and high up on its back, clinging to the saddle, their faces bright with joy, are my two grandsons.

I leave the window and open the great hall door to them myself. I see Elizabeth's flush and the young king's bright smile, and I think to myself this is fortune's wheel indeed – can it be? Can such a thing be?

AUTHOR'S NOTE

I discovered the character of Jacquetta when I was working on the history of her daughter, Elizabeth Woodville, who made her extraordinary secret marriage to Edward IV under her mother's supervision. Jacquetta was one of the named witnesses at the wedding, along with the priest, perhaps two others, and a boy to sing the psalms. She then arranged the secret honeymoon nights for the young couple.

Indeed, she may have done more. She was later accused of enchanting the young king into marriage with her daughter; and figures of lead said to represent Edward and Elizabeth, bound together with gold wire, were produced at her trial for witchcraft.

Enough here to intrigue me! I have spent my life as an historian of women, their place in society and their struggle for power. The more I read about Jacquetta, the more she seemed to me to be the sort of character I particularly love: one who is overlooked or denied by the traditional histories, but who can be discovered by piecing together the evidence.

She lived an extraordinary life, and one that is nowhere coherently recorded. In the absence of any biography of Jacquetta, I wrote my own essay and published it with two other historians, David Baldwin writing on Elizabeth Woodville, and Mike Jones writing on Margaret Beaufort in *The Women of the Cousins' War: The Duchess, the Queen, and the King's Mother* (Simon &

Schuster, 2011). Readers who want to trace the history behind my novels may be interested in this collection.

Jacquetta married the Duke of Bedford and lived as the first woman of English-ruled France. Her second marriage was for love: she married Sir Richard Woodville, experienced disapproval and had to pay a fine for stepping outside the rules of marriage for royal kinswomen. She served Margaret of Anjou as one of her most favoured ladies in waiting, and was at her side through most of the troubled years of the Wars of the Roses – then known as the Cousins' War. On the defeat of the Lancastrians at the terrible battle of Towton, her son Anthony and her husband Richard surrendered to the victorious Edward IV. The family would probably have lived quietly at peace under the new York regime, if it had not been for the beauty of their widowed daughter, the passionate nature of the young king, and who knows – the magic of Jacquetta.

The family became kin to the king and Jacquetta took full advantage of her rise, becoming once again the leading lady at the royal court. She lived long enough to endure the murder of her beloved husband and son, to support her daughter through defeat and flight into sanctuary, and to witness her son-in-law's triumphant return to the throne. For most of her life Jacquetta was at the very centre of the great events. Often she was a player.

Why she has not been studied is a mystery to me. But she belongs to that large population of women whose lives have been ignored by historians in favour of the lives of prominent men. Also this period is relatively neglected compared to – say – more recent times, or even the Tudor period. I expect more historians will work on the fifteenth century, and I hope there will be more research into its women, including Jacquetta.

I suggest that she was inspired by her family legend of Melusina, the water goddess, whose story is beautifully described in Luxembourg Museum as part of the history of the county. To this day the city guides point out the rocks through which Melusina's bath sank, when her husband broke his promise and spied on her. Certainly, the legend of Melusina was used in the art and alchemy of the period, and Jacquetta owned a book that told the story of her goddess ancestor. I think it very important that we as modern readers understand that religion, spiritualism and magic played a central part in the imaginative life of medieval people.

There is a thread running through the historical record associating Jacquetta and even Elizabeth with witchcraft, and I have based some fictional scenes on this. The use of playing cards to predict the future was a medieval practice; we would call the cards 'tarot'. Alchemy was regarded as a spiritual and scientific practice, and Margaret of Anjou licensed alchemists when she was looking for a cure for her husband's illness, which was indeed blamed by some on witchcraft. The practice of herbalism and planting by the phases of the moon was well known in most households, and the rise of anxiety about witchcraft occurs throughout Europe around 1450 onwards. The trial and punishment of Eleanor Cobham is based on the historical records and she was one of the witch-hunt victims.

There follows a bibliography listing the books that I have read for this novel, and readers may also like to visit my website www.PhilippaGregory.com for new essays, historical debates, and responses to questions about this and other novels in the series. The next novel will be about the daughters of Richard Neville, the Earl of Warwick, and I am already enjoying the research and excited about writing the story.

BIBLIOGRAPHY

Amt, Emilie, *Women's Lives in Medieval Europe* (New York, Routledge, 1993)

Baldwin, David, *Elizabeth Woodville: Mother of the Princes in the Tower* (Stroud, Sutton Publishing, 2002)

Barnhouse, Rebecca, *The Book of the Knight of the Tower: Manners for Young Medieval Women* (Basingstoke, Palgrave Macmillan, 2006)

Bramley, Peter, *The Wars of the Roses: A Field Guide & Companion* (Stroud, Sutton Publishing, 2007)

Castor, Helen, *Blood & Roses: The Paston Family and the Wars of the Roses* (London, Faber and Faber, 2004)

Cheetham, Anthony, *The Life and Times of Richard III* (London, Weidenfeld & Nicolson, 1972)

Chrimes, S. B., *Lancastrians, Yorkists, and Henry VI* (London, Macmillan, 1964)

Cooper, Charles Henry, *Memoir of Margaret: Countess of Richmond and Derby* (Cambridge, Cambridge University Press, 1874)

Duggan, Anne J., *Queens and Queenship in Medieval Europe* (Woodbridge, Boydell Press, 1997)

Field, P.J.C., *The Life and Times of Sir Thomas Malory* (Cambridge, D.S. Brewer, 1993)

Freeman, J., 'Sorcery at Court and Manor: Margery Jourdemayne the witch of Eye next Westminster', *Journal of Medieval History*, 30 (2004), 343–357

Godwin, William, *Lives of the necromancers: or, An account of the most eminent persons in successive ages, who have claimed for themselves, or to whom has been imputed by others, the exercise of magical power* (London, F. J. Mason, 1834)

Goodman, Anthony, *The Wars of the Roses: Military Activity and English Society 1452–97* (London, Routledge & Kegan Paul, 1981)

Goodman, Anthony, *The Wars of the Roses: The Soldiers' Experience* (Stroud, Tempus, 2006)

Griffiths, Ralph A., *The Reign of King Henry VI* (Stroud, Sutton Publishing, 1998)

Grummitt, David, *The Calais Garrison, War and Military Service in England, 1436–1558* (Woodbridge, Boydell & Brewer, 2008)

Haswell, Jock, *The Ardent Queen: Margaret of Anjou and the Lancastrian Heritage* (London, Peter Davies, 1976)

Hicks, Michael, *Warwick the Kingmaker* (London, Blackwell Publishing, 1998)

Hipshon, David, *Richard III and the Death of Chivalry* (Stroud, The History Press, 2009)

Hughes, Jonathan, *Arthurian Myths and Alchemy: The Kingship of Edward IV* (Stroud, Sutton Publishing, 2002)

Jones, Michael. K., and Underwood, Malcolm G., *The King's Mother: Lady Margaret Beaufort, Countess of Richmond and Derby* (Cambridge, Cambridge University Press, 1992)

Karras, Ruth Mazo, *Sexuality in Medieval Europe: Doing unto Others* (New York, Routledge, 2005)

Laynesmith, J. L., *The Last Medieval Queens: English Queenship 1445–1503* (Oxford, Oxford University Press, 2004)

Levine, Nina, 'The Case of Eleanor Cobham: Authorizing History in 2 Henry VI', *Shakespeare Studies*, 22 (1994), 104–121

Lewis, Katherine J., Menuge, Noel James, Phillips, Kim M. (eds), *Young Medieval Women* (Basingstoke, Palgrave Macmillan, 1999)

MacGibbon, David, *Elizabeth Woodville (1437-1492): Her Life and Times* (London, Arthur Barker, 1938)

Martin, Sean, *Alchemy & Alchemists* (London, Pocket Essentials, 2006)

Maurer, Helen E., *Margaret of Anjou: Queenship and Power in Late Medieval England* (Woodbridge: The Boydell Press, 2003)

Neillands, Robin, *The Wars of the Roses* (London, Cassell, 1992)

Newcomer, James, *The Grand Duchy of Luxembourg: The Evolution of Nationhood* (Luxembourg, Editions Emile Borschette, 1995)

Péporté, Pit, *Constructing the Middle Ages: Historiography, Collective Memory and Nation Building in Luxembourg* (Leiden and Boston, Brill, 2011)

Phillips, Kim M., *Medieval Maidens: Young women and gender in England, 1270–1540* (Manchester, Manchester University Press, 2003)

Prestwich, Michael, *Plantagenet England 1225–1360* (Oxford, Clarendon Press, 2005)

Ross, Charles Derek, *Edward IV* (London, Eyre Methuen, 1974)

Rubin, Miri, *The Hollow Crown: A History of Britain in the Late Middle Ages* (London, Allen Lane, 2005)

Seward, Desmond, *A Brief History of The Hundred Years War* (London, Constable, 1973)

Simon, Linda, *Of Virtue Rare: Margaret Beaufort: Matriarch of the House of Tudor* (Boston, Houghton Mifflin Company, 1982)

Storey, R. L., *The End of the House of Lancaster* (Stroud, Sutton Publishing, 1999)

Thomas, Keith, *Religion and the Decline of Magic* (New York, Weidenfeld & Nicolson, 1971)

Vergil, Polydore and Ellis, Henry, *Three Books of Polydore Vergil's English History: Comprising the Reigns of Henry VI, Edward IV and Richard III* (Kessinger Publishing Legacy Reprint, 1971)

Ward, Jennifer, *Women in Medieval Europe 1200–1500* (Essex, Pearson Education, 2002)

Warner, Marina, *Joan of Arc: the image of female heroism* (London, Weidenfeld & Nicolson, 1981)

Weinberg, S. Carole, 'Caxton, Anthony Woodville and the Pro-
logue to the "Morte D'Arthur"', *Studies in Philology*, 102: no
1 (2005), 45–65

Weir, Alison, *Lancaster and York: The Wars of the Roses* (London,
Cape, 1995)

Williams, E. Carleton, *My Lord of Bedford, 1389–1435: being a life
of John of Lancaster, first Duke of Bedford, brother of Henry V
and Regent of France* (London, Longmans, 1963)

Wilson-Smith, Timothy, *Joan of Arc: Maid, Myth and History*
(Stroud, Sutton Publishing, 2006)

Wolffe, Bertram, *Henry VI* (London, Eyre Methuen, 1981)

GARDENS
FOR THE GAMBIA

Philippa Gregory visited The Gambia, one of the
driest and poorest countries of sub-Saharan Africa,
in 1993 and paid for a well to be hand-dug in a
village primary school at Sika. Now – nearly 200
wells later, she continues to raise money and
commission wells in village schools, community
gardens and in The Gambia's only agricultural
college. She works with her representative in
The Gambia, headmaster Ismaila Sisay, and their
charity now funds pottery and batik classes,
bee-keeping and adult literacy programmes.
A recent deep well paid for by the Rotary Club of
Temecula provides clean water to a clinic.

GARDENS FOR THE GAMBIA is a registered charity in
the UK and the US, and a registered NGO in
The Gambia. Every donation, however small, goes to
The Gambia without any deductions. If you would
like to learn more about the work that Philippa calls
'the best thing that I do', visit her website
www.PhilippaGregory.com and click on GARDENS FOR
THE GAMBIA where you can make a donation and
join with Philippa in this project.

*'Every well we dig provides drinking water for a
school of about 600 children, and waters the
gardens where they grow vegetables for the school dinners.
I don't know of a more direct way to feed hungry
children and teach them to farm for their future.'*
Philippa Gregory

X

LA·ROUE·DE·FORTUNE